ALARM CALL

ALARM CALL

Quintin Jardine

headline

First published in Great Britain in 2004
by HEADLINE BOOK PUBLISHING

10 9 8 7 6 5 4 3 2 1

Cataloguing in Publication Data is available from the British Library

ISBN 0 7553 2102 2 (hardback)
ISBN 0 7553 2103 0 (trade paperback)

Typeset in Times by Avon DataSet Ltd,
Bidford-on-Avon, Warwickshire

Printed and bound in Great Britain by
Mackays of Chatham plc, Chatham, Kent

HEADLINE BOOK PUBLISHING
A division of Hodder Headline
338 Euston Road
London NW1 3BH

www.headline.co.uk
www.hodderheadline.com

This is dedicated to the lovely Wendy,
now and as we'll always remember her.

Acknowledgements

The author's thanks go to:

Jeff Hatfield, of Uncle Edgar's Mystery Bookstore, Minneapolis, for having a certain fictional lady on his mailing list, and giving Oz her address.

Steve Horwitz, for preventing Oz from committing several traffic violations.

Ken Howey, for coming up with a great, if entirely unwitting, line one night in the Mallard, which I was too slow to hit on when it happened, but up with which I've caught here.

Alma Lee, the tireless director of the Vancouver International Writers' (and Readers') Festival, for her local knowledge.

The profusely illustrated Sheldon McArthur, of the Mystery Bookstore, Westwood Village, Los Angeles, for letting Oz and Prim hide out there for a while.

The Palmer Family, entrepreneurs extraordinary.

San Francisco Police Department, with the reminder that this is a work of fiction, and complete acceptance that the scene on page 180 is in no way representative of the behaviour of any actual member of that fine force.

Eileen, for the duck . . .

Well, hello again; I've been expecting you.

It's been a while, a year and more, since you made me let you in on my last dark secret.

Thinking back, I probably left you wondering whether I was kidding myself in believing that I had put it all behind me, and that nothing would bubble up to the surface and spoil my party.

If I did, you can relax, or curse, depending on how you really feel about me. There has been no fall-out from that business, and having come this far down the road, there ain't going to be any.

I suppose that, once I'd told you all about it, you might have made some pretty damning moral judgements about me. If you did . . . well, all I can say is that it's your call. I'm not sorry about what I did; my only regret is that I was left with no other choice.

Has it given me nightmares? No, not a single one; not a new one, at any rate. Do I feel remorseful? No, not in the slightest.

Actually, since all that stuff happened, I've been too busy even to think about it. As always, what I've been doing hasn't been exactly conventional . . .

1

Nobody's luck holds good for ever . . . or so they say. Personally, I have no evidence to prove that assertion, but plenty to disprove it. Every morning I waken . . . yes, okay, I concede that occasionally I don't waken till the afternoon, but only if I have an extra big lump of jet-lag, an occupational hazard in my business, to work off; some movie actors may make a virtue of boogieing all night, but not this happy family man. Anyhow, as I was saying . . .

Christ, that brings something back, and a tear to my eye in the process. In my callow(-er) years, after I'd flown the family nest and embarked upon that determined shagathon known as university education, I made a point of phoning my mother every couple of days. (If I'd known how long she had left to live I'd have gone home to see her every other day, but there's no point in dwelling on that.)

I didn't call her about anything in particular, not to beg extra funds or anything like that . . . she and my dad spoiled me in that respect . . . but simply because I missed her more than I'd ever imagined I would when I set off from Anstruther into the real world outside, the Happy Wanderer with my metaphorical knapsack on my back. (Actually, in those days I really didn't know what missing her was like; I found out after she died.)

We didn't talk about anything in particular; she'd ask me if I was feeding myself properly, and I'd ask her if she was feeding my dad properly, just joking around, that sort of stuff. My mum was a great listener; she humoured my homesickness (I'd never have admitted it then, but that's what it was) but she had a wonderful way of bringing my ramblings to an end, and . . . she thought . . . of sending me back to work.

We all have our habits and foibles in speech, those little things we say as conversation shifters, pauses for thought. The most common among mine was that great nonsense word of the Scottish language, 'anyhow'. She was always chiding me about it when I was a kid; she was afraid that my sister Ellie and I would grow up with impenetrable East Neuk accents, and took great pains to ensure that we didn't. Shoddy language was not allowed, period. However, that's not to say it didn't happen.

In those long conversations with her, sooner or later, I would fall from grace. It usually happened when I'd run out of things to say, but wasn't ready for 'Cheerio'; there would be a silence, which, once I'd worked out what to say next, I would break with a deep breath, and an 'Anyhow'. When I did, she would give that incredibly warm chuckle of hers and say, 'Oz, if we're down to the "anyhow"s, it's time you got on with your life,' and that would be that, for another couple of days.

For all the crazy stuff that's happened to me over the last five years, since I stumbled into acting, I like to think I've kept my feet on the ground, and that my boots . . . or shoes more often these days . . . still fit me. It would be easy to believe my press cuttings . . . the favourable ones, that is; I never have any trouble accepting the bad . . . and getting altogether too pleased with myself.

While I might get a bit showbiz from time to time, it never gets out of hand, for one simple reason: my mum's always around when it happens. She's my safety valve; she comes into my mind with a gentle smile and a shake of her head to bring me back to being the boy she brought up and to make sure that I'm not getting too big for my footwear.

Okay, after some of the things I've told you, you may say that if she's been good for my ego, there's another side of me she's ignored. That's not true, because not even she knew all of me, and everything of which I've shown myself capable from time to time.

But mothers are love, and love is blind.

Anyhow, as I was saying: every morning I waken, look at Susie lying there beside me . . . I always surface before she does when

4

I'm not jet-lagged, now that wee Jonathan no longer requires to be plugged into the mains at some ungodly hour . . . and I pinch myself . . . no kidding, I really do give myself a nip . . . just to make sure that I'm still alive, and not observing all this through a celestial telescope.

In the last few years I've come to think of myself as the luckiest man on the planet, and now I reckon I must be one of the happiest as well. Sure, there are dark memories: for a start, there was my mother's death, and then the loss of Jan, my soulmate from childhood and my first wife. There was all that bad stuff with Primavera Phillips, who beguiled me for a while, and with whom I shared one of the shortest marriages on record, before she pissed off with a B-list actor. And then, as you know, about eighteen months back there was another local difficulty when someone took it into his head to attack Susie's construction business, the Gantry Group.

Those things all happened, there's no hiding from them, but they're all in their wee mental boxes . . . some with extra heavy padlocks so they don't break out and they don't stop me enjoying the incredibly good . . . and incredibly large . . . fortune that's come my way.

It was after we got back from Australia that the small cloud edged its way over the horizon.

I had been out there working on another project for Miles Grayson, my friend and former brother-in-law, and I had taken Susie, wee Janet and wee Jonathan with me. We were there making a movie called *Red Leather*, about England's Aussie cricket tour in 1932 and 1933, the bodyline series in which the English captain, Douglas R. Jardine (me), came up with an innovative if homicidal way of beating the Aussies, who were inspired at that time by the legendary Don Bradman (Miles). If you don't know anything about cricket, take some time to look at Bradman's record and then compare him with anyone else who ever picked up a bat. All of the rest, even the greatest of them, pale into insignificance alongside him; that's how good he was.

When the project was announced, Hollywood's collective

eyebrows rose and its media exclaimed, 'What?' They were convinced that for all Miles's record of box-office success as a film-maker, a picture about cricket would be doomed. They argued that very few Americans knew anything about the game, and that most of those who did profess to knowing the rules didn't understand them . . . a bit like Brits and baseball, I suppose.

It was one of their more spectacular mistakes.

In fact, the movie isn't about cricket, it's about the incredible confrontation that exploded between the two nations, England and Australia, over Jardine's tactic of bowling not at the wicket (those three bits of wood with two smaller bits of wood on top that the bowlers are supposed to try to hit with the ball) but at the batsmen (batters, if you're American) themselves. They didn't wear helmets in those days, so inevitably the row came to a literal head when an unfortunate Aussie named Oldfield had his skull fractured by Harold Larwood, the English speed demon. Larwood actually apologised to his victim as he was being carted off to hospital, but since Oldfield was unconscious at the time, he did not respond.

All hell broke loose. Jardine came under pressure to change his tactics, but refused; all the arguments were about the spirit of the game, since what he was doing wasn't against the rules. He even sacked one of his best players, and until then one of his best friends, the Nawab of Pataudi . . . all this took place in the great days of Empire, remember . . . when he sided with the victims.

The Australian Cricket Board was forced to act. They sent a cable to London asking for the game's ruling authority, the MCC, to instruct Jardine to change his 'unsporting' tactic. But the grandees in London, who hadn't seen what was happening . . . there was no telly in 1932, was there, never mind satellites . . . took exception to the use of the adjective and a stalemate ensued. The situation became so tense that at one stage an emissary from Buckingham Palace intervened to calm things down.

Then, when peace looked like breaking out, the dour and inflexible Jardine refused to continue the tour unless the hosts apologised for their accusation of lack of sportsmanship, and withdrew it. The affair ended with the cowed Australians continuing

6

to act as live bait for Larwood for the rest of the series, and going down to abject defeat. Only it didn't end there: bad feeling persisted between the two countries for years afterwards, Jardine was put aside as an embarrassment to the London Establishment, and even in Australia there were feuds and grudges over some of the things that had been said and done.

Forget the game; that was secondary to the plot . . . it had to be, because sports movies, as such, never really work. But take a look at the contemporary accounts of the drama as it played out, and you'll realise that Miles's so-called folly was a certain winner, anywhere.

It was the best script I'd ever worked on, and the best role I'd ever played in my growing career. When the movie was released, timed for the start of a cricket Test series in London, and at the height of the summer sports season in the US, it was a huge hit, and so was I. My reviews were the best I'd ever had, even in the American media. Until then they'd treated me politely, but rarely with anything approaching enthusiasm.

To be honest, their praise didn't come as a surprise. I'd found Jardine an easy character to play. Maybe that was because his inflexibility and lack of humour suited my limited range, but none of the critics suggested that. I'd missed out on award nominations for my previous project, *Mathew's Tale*, but quite a few suggested that I'd pick up some this time. I was quite happy to bask in their optimism.

So was Susie. When we got together, she took a pretty sanguine view of my acting career. She never said as much, but I'm pretty sure that she regarded it as lightweight, something not to be taken seriously. The money didn't impress her either: the family construction business, which she ran, had a massive turnover and its annual profits put my film income in the shade.

But as time went on, things changed. Our move to the estate overlooking Loch Lomond, and our acquisition of a small staff . . . children's nurse, housekeeper, gardener and personal assistant (actually, he's a minder, but we don't like to call him that) . . . brought her to realise that our lifestyle was changing and that it

7

was my doing as much as hers. It was really brought home to us in April, when we made the *Sunday Times* Rich List for the first time, and not just the Scottish section either. As the limelight began to shine more brightly on me, Susie even started to enjoy stepping out to the odd showbiz bash . . . 'if only to keep an eye on you,' was how she put it, but I knew that wasn't the whole truth.

The biggest change in her was her attitude to her own business. When we went to Australia *en famille*, she left Phil Culshaw, a director, in temporary charge of the Gantry Group, with the understanding that when we got back from Australia, she would pick up the reins and resume her role as CEO, with Phil replacing me as chairman, a job I'd only taken on out of necessity, as a short-term measure. To my surprise, she changed her mind: rather than return full-time, she opted to take the chair herself, with Culshaw continuing as managing director on a permanent basis. Contrary to what was written in one of the Scottish broadsheets, I had no influence on her decision. She didn't discuss it with me at all, or tell me about it until the deed was done.

'It makes sense,' she said, when she broke the news. 'The bankers like Phil, so it's a good move from their viewpoint. On top of that, Oz, the group needs to expand or it'll stagnate. That means raising capital by floating the business on the stock exchange, and I don't fancy driving that through. I'm only just into my thirties: I want to devote more time to the kids, and to you. You need a proper manager, not just an agent, and I'm not letting anyone else do that job.'

That wasn't an offer, it was an order. I obeyed.

From that point on, Susie became as committed to me as she was to the Gantry Group. She ran my life, literally, and I loved it, and her for it.

So what about that small cloud I mentioned earlier? Actually, it turned out to be more like a monsoon.

2

You know you've made the A list when . . .

- The money on offer from the glam mags for exclusive family lifestyle photographs reaches seven figures.
- The producer of *Parkinson* phones you at home and invites you to do the show . . . with no other guest stars.
- Your latest movie is made into a video game, and you're on a percentage of the gross.
- You're asked to front a multi-media advertising campaign for the world's leading men's fragrance.
- Your sister starts to treat you like she did when you were in primary school, just to make sure you don't get too big for your boots.
- Your insurance company forbids you to take part in a charity five-a-side football tournament, in case you break something and bugger up a movie schedule.
- Your agent flies from Hollywood to see you, instead of the other way around.

That was where I found myself after the release of *Red Leather*: if not on top of the tree, then pretty near it.

Roscoe Brown, my smart guy in LA, didn't even have to be asked to get on the plane: he proposed it himself. (I hadn't gone totally showbiz myself, you understand.) We had told the glam mag where to stick their money, and if Roscoe had asked, I'd have gone to the States. But in truth I was more than happy to be picking him up from the airport, rather than the other way around, because it gets seriously hot in southern California in the summer, and because I'd developed a serious antipathy to being away from Susie and the kids.

I'd gone from the Australian project straight into shooting the few scenes I had in the third Bob Skinner movie, *Skinner's Trail*, produced as before by Miles's company, but directed this time by Ewan Capperauld. Since much of the story takes place in Spain, my character, Andy Martin, had less action than usual and that suited me fine, especially since the money had gone up regardless. Nevertheless it involved a month's work in Edinburgh and another couple of weeks on the sound-stage in Surrey; I made it home as often as I could, but I still spent too many miserable nights in hotel rooms.

Not that I wasn't offered alternatives, mind you . . . that comes with A-list status too. Randy Rhona Waitrose, who plays Skinner's daughter in the series, offered me the chance to 'compare parts', as she put it, but I knew that she was only trying to live up to her image, and she wasn't offended when I turned her down . . . again.

When I said that I picked up Roscoe from Glasgow Airport, I was exaggerating a little. What I actually did was send our personal assistant to collect him. Conrad Kent had joined us in succession to Jay Yuille, who had followed his dick to Washington, after meeting an American girl in St Andrews. The last task he had performed for me was to recruit his replacement, and I have to say that the boy Jay done good. Conrad's background was similar to Jay's, something military, but no details offered or asked for.

At first glance he's a slightly built guy, but he dresses to give that effect. There's steel beneath the double-breasted blazer, be in no doubt of that. He has a Jamaican father and a Welsh mother, a degree in geology from Leeds University, he likes Van Morrison, Mary Chapin Carpenter and Bryn Terfel, three of my in-car favourites, and best of all he's a four-handicap golfer, a status to which I've aspired all my life, but never yet attained. When Jay put him forward on a list of three, that was the deciding factor in his favour.

10

An added bonus lay in the fact that he came as a matched pair. He's married to a lady called Audrey: she was an army clerk . . . that's where they met . . . so she has good typing and IT skills. She didn't ask for a job, but as soon as we'd had a chance to size her up, Susie and I knew that there was one there for her: thus, she became our secretary.

If I'd expected Roscoe to be a red-eyed mess when he got in from LA, I'd have been disappointed. He looked as if he'd been picked up off the Edinburgh train, not a connecting flight from Heathrow. I've never been able to sleep on any part of an aircraft, not even on the long haul to Australia. My agent has that gift: he'd flown across America and then the Atlantic, stretched out flat in first class.

'Hi, Oz,' he greeted me, snappily, as he stepped into the conservatory that serves as our office, his shiny skin so black that he made Conrad look pale. 'You ready to get down to business?'

I'd just come out of a hard work-out in the gym, plus wee Jonathan was cutting teeth and had kept us up for half the night: the guy was fresher than me. We must have made some contrast, me in tracksuit bottoms, a sweaty T-shirt and trainers, Roscoe in a sharp Italian suit. We must have, because Susie laughed out loud.

'You wouldn't thank him if he did,' she said. 'Oz, go and shower, before the ventilation system breaks down.'

So I did as I was told. When I returned, my agent was sitting in one of our big guest chairs. He had wee Jonathan perched on his knee, and he was looking as awkward as anyone I've ever seen, and terrified too, in case the kid drooled on the Armani cashmere. I picked him up and returned him to his mum.

Our latest office toy at the time was a big Gaggia coffee machine. I fixed Roscoe a nice *latte* (isn't it funny how coffee with milk sounds more inviting in Italian?) and sat down behind my side of the huge partner desk set-up that Susie and I share. I nodded towards Roscoe's hand-tooled Zero Halliburton briefcase. 'So what's in there?' I asked him.

'Some very interesting propositions, my friend,' he replied, opening his seriously expensive executive's accessory, and taking out a folder of papers.

I held up a hand. 'Before we get into them, make me understand one thing. Why are we doing this face to face and not by e-mail or even over a video-conference link? I don't want to project a classic Scots stereotype here, but I don't reckon for a minute that you'll be picking up the tab for your travel expenses.'

He gave me one of those big Denzel ivory grins. 'If I'd thought that would worry you, I'd have travelled coach. Oz, we're discussing multi-million-dollar business here, stuff that's highly sensitive commercially. New-age communications may be slick, but they are way too easy to spy on. If one studio gets wind of another's project, it's not unknown for them to try to beat them to the punch with something similar. Remember a few years back when we had a spate of volcano movies?'

'Could I ever forget? They were bloody awful.'

'That's what happens when you rush things. They made money, though. Top-class marketing covers up a multitude of stuff. Look at *The Blair Witch Project*.'

'I'd rather not,' I told him. 'Once was enough. I sat through it waiting for the scary stuff that never happened. The hype had me believing I was going to piss my pants, but all I did was yawn.'

Roscoe laid his folder on the desk. 'None of these will make anyone do that,' he said.

'Let's hear about them, then.'

'I've got five here,' he said. 'Two are no-goes . . .'

'Why?'

'They're not worthy of a star of your importance.'

'Aw, come on!' I heard myself laugh, but it sounded strained. Actually, what he had said had unnerved me. No, it was more than that: the whole situation, me on top of the pile, red carpets everywhere I went, Roscoe and everyone else coming to me, it was all beginning to get to me.

I never set out to become an actor. I was a guy enjoying an easy life, until someone thought that 'Private Enquiry Agent', which I was, meant 'Private Detective', which I wasn't, and I found myself involved in a piece of work that led to me role-playing on camera. It turned out that I was good at it, and the whole thing just took off after that. I hadn't started out with stars in my eyes, and while I had enjoyed the ride, I hadn't prepared myself mentally for the level I had reached. I wasn't sure I could handle it. I wasn't sure I wanted to handle it.

Roscoe made it worse. 'I'm serious, Oz,' he insisted. 'Some of the projects that have been put to us might have borne consideration a couple of years back, but not any more.'

I looked across the desk. Susie and Audrey were sitting on the other side. 'What if I'd rather be back where I was two years ago?'

His eyes tightened, just a little, but I caught it. 'That's not an option, Oz,' he said quietly. 'You're not being offered second or third billing any more.'

'What if I turn them all down?'

He frowned. 'Why would you want to do that?'

'Maybe I'd like a break.'

'Give it another two years: till then, build on what you've achieved. Hollywood has been looking for a new Sean Connery for years. That's why they're so excited about you.'

I felt my eyebrows shoot up. 'Sherioushly?' I exclaimed: that drew a laugh. 'Listen, Roscoe,' I went on, 'that's hugely flattering, but it's not me. I'm an accidental hero.'

'So was Sir Sean. He was a promising young actor, then Bond happened. The rest is legend. *Red Leather* is your *Doctor No*.'

'And what if I say just that, "No"? Look around you, man. I'm filthy rich already, I have an amazing wife I'm crazy about, I have two kids I'm crazy about. I don't have to do any more of this. I can walk away now and devote the rest of my life to them, and frankly, even after you've told me what's in that pile of papers, however much money it means, that's the most attractive option open to me.'

Roscoe sagged a little in his chair: for a moment I thought that the jet-lag had finally hit him. And then he drew a breath. 'You think so?' he asked coolly. 'Mr Blackstone, let me explain some stuff. You seem to think that this business is some sort of a game

13

that you can play for a while and then give up. Well, sorry, sir, but it isn't. It is a very serious enterprise, one that employs tens and hundreds of thousands of people around the globe. Rightly or wrongly, it is built around people like you. Stars, each one of them, are industries in themselves, providing livelihoods for a hell of a lot of people, from the directors at the top of the off-camera creative team, through the writers, cameramen, focus pullers, grips, dolly drivers, the makeup people. Did you take time to watch the end credits of *Red Leather*? Did you count the number of names there? All those people . . . including you . . . were employed because of one man, Miles Grayson. His presence secured the money that underwrote the project.'

'A lot of it was his own,' I pointed out.

'Not all of it, but so what? Where did he acquire the personal finance to invest in his own project? From other projects funded by other people, cinematic icebergs of which he was just the tip. That's where you are now, sir: you're up there, clear of the water, with a hell of a lot of other people below the surface who are depending on you. You get self-indulgent and walk away, they will suffer.'

'There will be other projects for them.'

'Not that simple. The business revolves around the A list. It rises and it falls depending on the number of seriously marketable stars there are around; that is why they are all, every one of them, so important. And then we get to the really vital people.'

'Who?'

'The people who gave you the money you're enjoying. Those ordinary men and women who've made you wealthy simply by going to your movies and buying your videotapes and DVDs. Those people have formed personal relationships with you: to them you're family too, whether you like it or not. You gonna disown them? You gonna say, "Thanks but I've got enough now"?'

'I don't own them,' I snapped. 'They don't own me.'

He stared back at me as if I was a stranger, and maybe I was: he hadn't seen that side of me before. 'No,' he said quietly, 'but you owe them.'

'And do I owe you too, Roscoe?'

'Maybe, but I'm not including myself in this argument. I don't need you, if that's what you mean. I have other clients, all of whom feel loyalty towards me. They're all right there on a list on my agency website, alphabetically, from Adams to Zederbaum. Go on, take a look, why don't you? When you came to me, most of them were bigger than you were. They've seen you shoot up the pecking order, but none of them object too much, because they understand the nature of the industry, and believe it or not, a few are hoping that I'll be able to place them in supporting parts in your productions. But don't you worry, boss: my son will go to Harvard, when he's old enough, without your help, if that's the way it has to be.'

That brought me up short: I'd never thought of Roscoe Brown as a family man. An unfamiliar feeling swept over me as I realised that I'd never thought of him as anything other than someone who could do me a lot of good. Unfamiliar or not, I recognised it as shame.

He picked up the folder. 'You have the power, Oz: the power to walk away, the power to disappoint them, the film-makers who are looking for work through you and the fans who are looking forward to watching your career develop. Say the word, I'll put these papers away and I'll be on the first plane back to Hollywood. In fact, I reckon that's what I'm going to do with or without . . .'

'Enough!' Susie's shout jolted us both. When I turned back towards her, I saw that her hands were clenched into fists and that the knuckles were showing white. 'Roscoe,' she growled, 'you try that and you won't make it through that door.' Then she looked at me with the same expression she uses when she's giving Janet a rollicking. 'Oz, stop this nonsense right now. And don't think you can map out my future without consulting me about it. If you think I've backed out of a business I love just to watch you sit about the house all day drinking beer and getting fat, then think again. I've done it to support you in your career. The kids and I don't want your undivided attention. You're a great dad as it is: being around all the time won't make you any better. The fact is we want to bask

15

in your movie-star glory. So whatever it is you've got up your arse right now, get rid of it and look at what's on the table.'

'But, love,' I protested, 'you heard that: the new Sean Connery, for Christ's sake.'

'That's crap, I agree: there's only one Sean and only ever will be. But you don't have to believe it just because a few silly journalists are saying it. You concentrate on being the first Oz Blackstone and let them get on with it.'

There's no arguing with my wife when she's in full flow . . . well, there might be, but I've never been brave enough to try it.

'Okay, Roscoe,' I said, a chastened man, 'the moody's over. Let's talk business.'

'Yes, sir.' He put the folder back on the table.

I tried a funny, to lighten the atmosphere. 'With all this Sean stuff, they don't want me to play James Bond, do they?'

My agent frowned: I'd forgotten that he's a very literal man. 'Not yet,' he replied. 'The guy in the part at the moment is under contract for at least one more. But after him, you're high on the list. What we have on offer now, though, is the lead role in an action drama about the second Gulf War, shooting in Morocco next spring, followed by a killer part in a huge version of *Don Quixote*.'

'Where will that be filmed? Mexico?'

'Spain. Where else?'

See? Nice guy, but he's had a total sense of humour bypass. 'Indeed. Who are the directors?'

'Spielberg's doing the war movie and *Quixote* is Minghella's.' Now *there* were two compliments.

'What's the money?'

'The war movie's offering five, the other, four: our price is seven for each.'

'Excuse me,' Audrey interrupted. I had asked her to take a record of the meeting. 'Is that million?'

He looked at her, patiently. 'Of course.'

'US dollars?' I queried.

'They tried that: I told them that everything's euros these days.'

16

'Thank God for President Bush.'

'Let's not go that far,' Roscoe murmured, his voice low as if he was afraid the room was bugged. 'Oz,' he asked, 'have you given any more thought to going offshore, as I suggested?'

'You mean setting up an official residence in Monaco, or Jersey?'

'Yes.'

'Susie and I have discussed it, but we're not keen.'

'There would be big tax benefits. And where's the down-side? You already spend a lot of the year outside Britain. When you went to Australia you took your family.'

'Too much time: I thought I'd made my feelings clear on that. No, Roscoe, we have family reasons for staying here. Our kids have to know where home is. Plus, my sister's a lone parent, and I'm a sort of surrogate dad to her boys.'

'Tell your kids that home is where you are. Tell your sister to remarry.'

I laughed at that one. 'You've got a funny side after all. You tell her.'

Actually, he was on safer ground than he might have been. My sister had a steady relationship and it was getting more serious by the minute. She had moved on from her occasional flings with her big German sex toy, and had taken up with an advocate she'd happened upon at a party.

I'd met the guy once: I'd found him a bit of a dry stick, and I hadn't taken to him. Neither had Jonny, my older nephew, but Ellie certainly seemed to. I'd had Ricky Ross, my security consultant, check him out at an early stage, but he'd come up clean. His name was Harvey January, and Ricky had described him as a man on his way to a judge's red robes.

'No,' I said, 'it's not off the agenda for good, but Susie and I don't fancy being nomads. For now, we'll live with the alternative, and that's paying the tax. We'll still be left with a bit more than sixty per cent of a hell of a lot.'

'Okay, but I'll bring it up again, trust me on that.'

'If you must. So, these two projects: do you have the scripts with you?'

'Yeah, and I've read 'em. You should agree, once I've nailed down the money side.'

'If you recommend it, I do. But they're both next year. You said there was a third serious proposition.'

'There is, and it'll fill up fall for you. It's a movie about a rock singer, who tries to break a recording contract, only he finds out that the label his manager signed him to has Mafia connections. They fix him so he'll never sing again. But he wins out in the end: he makes it bigger as a stand-up comedian than he ever was before. It's an updated remake of an old Sinatra movie.'

'I think I've seen it: as I remember, it was too long.'

'It was: this version will be shorter.'

'Did you think to ask if I can sing?'

'It's rock and roll, for Christ's sake!' He paused, looking a trifle anxious. 'You can sing, can't you?'

I threw back my head and gave him the first four lines of 'Bonnie Mary of Argyll'. 'Where do we shoot?' I asked him.

'Location in Chicago and New York, beginning October: sound-stage work in Toronto. Wrap by year-end.'

I nodded approval. I'd never been to Chicago, but New York and Toronto are two of my favourite cities. 'How much are we getting?'

'The same: seven million euros, and that's settled. They came in offering six, but they rolled over quick when I told them what you cost now. Plus they'll find you an apartment in Toronto for the duration of the project. It's an easy commute to NYC and across the lakes to Chicago.'

I looked at Susie. 'Autumn in Canada?' She smiled; she really was getting to like being a movie star's wife. 'Not an apartment,' I told Roscoe. 'Make it a family house, and big enough for Ethel the nanny, plus Conrad and Audrey. Conrad goes everywhere we do.'

'Okay, I'll tell the producers. I've got the script for that too: you should start on it right away.'

'I'll look at it. Who's directing?'

'A guy called Weir Dobbs. It's his first big project.'

18

Nothing he had told me, not even the fact that he had jacked my fee up to a level I thought was stratospheric, surprised me more than that. 'Who cast me?' I asked.

'He did. He called me himself: told me that after *Red Leather* he wasn't doing the movie without you.'

I whistled softly. Weir Dobbs and I had a history: he had been Miles Grayson's assistant director on the first movie I ever made and for a time we had not got on. We had so not got on that in the midst of one difficult session I had bounced him several times off a studio wall. Now he just had to have me in his picture . . .

Looking back, I realise that was the moment when I finally accepted what I was, and what I'd become, and understood that my career had attained a momentum that was indeed out of my control, for that time at least.

I put away the thought. 'You'll give me a schedule?'

'Of course.'

'Have a separate session with Audrey on that, please: she manages my diary completely these days.'

Roscoe nodded. 'Will do, Oz. Now, the other two projects I mentioned, those I'm going to recommend you turn down: let's discuss them.'

I held up a hand. 'No, let's not. You've steered me straight on the three positives. I'll trust your judgement on the others.'

'You sure?'

I stood up and stretched out my hand. As he shook it I told him, 'You have our complete confidence, mine and Susie's. I hear what you've said to me and I appreciate your coming all this way to say it. But that's enough shop for now: we're going to take you to lunch, and you're going to tell us all about your family.'

3

We took him to the Buchanan Arms, an old-established eatery not far from our place. It turned out that he has one son from a marriage that ended in divorce around the time I became his client.

He talked happily about Roscoe junior all through lunch, until his voice began to slur and his eyes became heavy. He put it down to the jet-lag catching up with him (and passing him at high speed in the outside lane), but I reckoned at the time that I should have talked him out of that pint of cask-conditioned ale. In my experience, some Americans just can't handle our beer at all.

A couple of hours' sleep in the afternoon sorted him out, though. In the evening he and Audrey mapped out my schedule for the three projects I'd agreed to do. It looked good: I wasn't due in Toronto for three months. I had a couple of promotional things coming up for the latest Skinner movie, but for now mostly it would be quality time I could spend at home with Susie and the kids.

My wife and I saw Roscoe on his way next morning. This time I did the driving to the airport, just to let him see that I knew I owed him. I promised that I would look at the scripts and sign all the contracts the minute I received them. As we waved him goodbye, heading off for the departure lounge, I looked around. 'You know,' I said to Susie, 'I always hate being here without my passport in my pocket. It gives me wanderlust. D'you fancy going somewhere?'

'Just like that?'

'More or less.'

'Yes, but we're not going to. Janet's a bit young to be a jet-setter and wee Jonathan's teeth would make life fractious for everyone around him.'

'That's true,' I conceded. 'The wee sod bit me the other day. They're like bloody razors when they've just come through.'

She gave me a funny sideways look. 'Would you really have turned down all that money for the kids and me?'

'No . . .'

'Aah,' she said, 'so you were just acting Mr Big.'

'. . . I'd have turned it down for me as well,' I added. 'I'm not comfortable being public property, Sooz. I never planned for any of this to happen. It just did, and now it's acquired a momentum of its own. But I can't stop it; I see that now. What Roscoe said was true, too many people are involved with me right now.'

'It won't be for ever, love. In the meantime . . .' She paused in mid-sentence.

A fat middle-aged man in a business suit stepped up to me, right into my face, ignoring her completely. 'I hope you don't mind,' he began. I did, but he didn't give me a chance to tell him that. 'I don't normally do this sort of thing, Mr Blackstone, but my wife is a huge fan of yours. Could I have your autograph for her?'

His accent was posh Greater London: since I've been an actor I've become quite good at spotting them. He put down his briefcase and produced a Mont Blanc fountain pen and a diary from an inside pocket of his jacket, giving me a flash of its red lining. This was not clothing that had come off the peg at a discount store.

'Are there Brownie points in this for you?' I asked him.

'Thousands.'

'Do you need them?'

He blinked, taken aback. 'Well, you know,' he chuckled, tamely, 'it never does any harm.'

'What's your secretary's . . . sorry, your wife's name?' The speed with which he flushed up told me that I'd hit the mark.

'Lou-Lou,' he replied, and spelled it out for me.

I took the pen and the diary, opened it at a blank page for notes, and scribbled, 'To the lovely Lou-Lou, from your devoted fan, Oz Blackstone.' I closed it and returned it to him. I made to put the Mont Blanc in my pocket. He flinched but said nothing: I think he'd have let me keep it, if I hadn't grinned and handed it back to him. 'Hope it does you some good,' I told him. 'Have a nice trip, Mr . . .'

'Potter,' he said.

'Accountant?'

He looked sheepish. 'Well, yes, actually. It's that obvious?'

'It's the suit, mate; that, and the fact that your firm's name's embossed in gold on the cover of your diary. I used to be a sort of detective: as I was saying to my wife, sometimes I wish I still was.'

'Sometimes I wish I was one too. Thank you for your patience, and good luck with your career.'

I was hit by a spur-of-the-moment impulse. 'Do you have a card, Mr Potter?'

He looked surprised for a second, but then good business instincts kicked in. He produced one from his wallet and handed it over. I saw that his forename was Henry, but I decided not to go there. Instead I asked if I could use his pen again. I noted my private phone number on it, then handed both back.

'I need to do some very serious financial planning,' I told him, 'and I'd rather use London-based advisers than Scots, for a different perspective. I've heard good things about your firm, so if you want to tender for the project . . . in competition, of course . . . have someone give me a call.'

His chest seemed to puff out: I could tell that I'd made his morning for the second time in as many minutes.

'I will,' he exclaimed. 'Thank you very much.'

Susie watched him as he headed for the exit. 'Why did you do that?' she asked. 'Did you feel sorry for taking the piss out of him about his secretary?'

'Hey, I was entitled to do that. The guy is clearly trying to use me to get his leg over . . . or keep it over. No, I meant it: we need to take professional advice on how we should manage our money, and probably inheritance tax advice as well. His firm's called Clark Gow: they're a multinational, and I happen to know that they have a very big reputation in the entertainment business.'

'So have the Mafia.'

We left the airport, with a wave to Mr Potter in the taxi queue, and headed back home.

The three months of family bonding that stretched out before me was a pleasing prospect. Actually, I had more to do in that department than fuss over my kids. There was the matter of my father, as well.

For all of my adult life I had thought of Macintosh Blackstone as best friend as well as parent. And then he had done something extremely stupid, something that had led those who loved him most into serious, life-threatening trouble. I had seen it off, but the rift between us had been immediate and, on my part, long-lasting.

I had barely seen him since then: when wee Jonathan was born Susie and I had taken him across to Anstruther to show him off to Mary, my stepmother, rather than to his grandfather. I can be a ruthless, unforgiving bastard when I have to be, but also, I had begun to concede to myself, when I don't. For some time, my dad had been on my mind. I was still angry whenever I thought of him and of what he had done, but gradually, I began to wonder whether some of that anger had been directed at myself, for the way in which I had reacted, for the harshness of my judgement of him, and for the sentence of isolation that I had passed.

There was something else too: I missed him. He has always been my sounding-board, and I was honest enough with myself to recognise that a lot of my evolving discontent with fame could have been rationalised by some of his shrewd advice. Susie knew all this, of course, but she also knows me well enough to let me work it out for myself. She didn't know what had caused the breach, and she never asked. Just as well, for I couldn't have brought myself to tell her the truth.

Anyway . . . there I go again . . . the day after Roscoe's visit, I loaded my golf clubs into one of our executive toys, Susie's new Porsche Cayenne (she calls it our 'family mover') and told her I would be away for a while. There's a telepathy between us now: she knew what I was up to.

It was a Friday, so I knew that he'd finish work at lunchtime. For years it's been his custom to hold a Saturday-morning surgery, to encourage as many people as possible to come for routine dental check-ups. The waiting room was empty when I got there, but I could hear the drill, so I took a seat. Daisy, the nurse-receptionist, heard the doorbell and came through to see who the late and unbooked patient was. Her jaw dropped slightly when she saw me sitting there, picking up a nine-month-old copy of *Golf World*, but I put a finger to my lips and she got the message.

I waited until the sufferer in the chair had gone, and until I could hear the sounds of clearing up. Then the surgery door opened again, and I caught a glimpse of Daisy's white coat heading somewhere, anywhere, to leave us alone. I stood up and walked through. Mac the Dentist was facing me, unbuttoning his tunic, as I stepped into the big room. He looked at me, and I looked at him. Then I stepped forward and gave him a quick, strong hug. He nodded as I released him, and that was it.

'So how are you doing?' he asked me quietly.

'Don't you read the tabloids? Haven't you heard? I'm doing great; I'm the next big thing. Five years in the business and I'm an overnight success.'

'Yeah, but how the fuck are you?'

'I'm okay, Dad.'

'No bad dreams?'

I wondered what made him ask that. 'Just the one,' I told him, 'when wee Jonathan lets me sleep long enough: Jan's in it, but she isn't dead, just away visiting her mother.'

'What's the bad part?'

'When I wake up, and she's still dead. Don't get me wrong, though. I love Susie like crazy, and the kids too. But it's still there.'

'It always will be; I have the same dream about your mother. I don't think of it as bad, though, and I don't feel guilty about it, if that's worrying you. In fact I look forward to it: it's only the thought of it stopping that worries me.'

See? I'd been with him for less than a minute and he'd put my mind at rest already. 'So how the fuck are you?' I shot back at him.

'How do I look?'

'Slightly crumpled, a bit of a curmudgeon, reasonably benign for a dentist, could do with a haircut.'

'Ah, that's good. I haven't changed, then?'

'Not a bit.'

'I have on the inside.' He shot me a strange, apprehensive look. 'Oz, there's something I have to ask you, straight out. Those people: what happened to them had nothing to do with you, did it?'

'Not at all, I promise,' I replied, then saw the relief surge through him.

'Thank God for that. I've been afraid that was the real reason why you've been avoiding me.'

'No, Dad. I just thought we needed some space, that's all.' I'd told him the truth, but not the whole truth. He couldn't imagine that: I'm pretty sure it would kill him. 'You up for some golf?' I went on quickly. 'Or have you got something lined up already?'

'Nothing involving anyone else. I was planning to hit a few balls, that's all.'

'Okay, hit them with me.'

I had booked an afternoon time at the reasonably new Kingsbarns course. I'd thought about taking my nephews too, but I couldn't be sure in advance how my dad and I would get along. Besides, while he's a very tidy golfer, and could turn out to be the best of all of us, Colin's still only eleven, and the starter might have been a bit dubious about letting him on the course.

We had lunch in the clubhouse before we played. For all that he lived only three or four miles away, my father had never been there before. On the other hand, I'd taken part in a celebrity pro-am there about nine months past.

Until I was thirty, most of my golf was played with my dad. It wasn't until I started to mix it more that I realised how competitive I really am. My handicap's come down too, thanks to the practice holes I've laid out in the grounds of the Loch Lomond place, but if I'd expected Mac the Dentist to be a pushover I was in for a shock. His game looked better than it had in years, and he took care of me by a tidy three and two.

He was still grinning when we walked out of the changing room and into the bar. 'Okay,' I asked at last, as the waiter brought his Belhaven and my diet vanilla Coke, 'what have you been up to?'

'I've been playing with my grandsons. Jonny's down to a nine handicap now, and wee Colin's improving by a shot every couple of months, I'd say. They've helped me sharpen up my game. I can't have them taking the piss out of me, can I?'

'Mmm. I must get back to taking them out more often myself.'

'You might find it difficult to get into their diaries. Their mother's new flame's been showing an interest in them too.'

'Mr January, QC,' I murmured. 'What do you think of him?'

'Between you and me, and not to go back to your sister?'

'Of course.'

'I'm not sure about him yet. It's nothing I can put my finger on, just . . . ach, I don't know. I preferred that big pal of yours, Darius, whom she saw occasionally, although I knew it wasn't going anywhere. Maybe I'm being hard on this new guy. It's just that after Alan Sinclair, I don't want her to make another mistake. He's so fucking strait-laced, that's what worries me: he even calls me Macintosh.'

That was rich: half of Anstruther thought that my dad's first name was just plain Mac.

I laughed. 'When I met him he asked me straight out what Oz stood for.'

It was his turn to chuckle. 'Did you tell him?'

'I told him that I didn't stand for being called anything but Oz, except by my father, my sister and my wife. What do you call him? Son?'

'Never! I've only got one of them. Actually, I call him Mr January. Your sister doesn't appreciate that much, but I won't put on a false front for her. Is he good at what he does, do you know?'

'I'm told that he is. He specialises in taxation and reparations, but he's done some time in the Crown Office, so he knows the criminal side as well. That's the sort of profile an ambitious lawyer should have if he wants to go to the Supreme Court bench. If our Ellie marries the guy, there's a good chance she'll end up being Lady January.'

'So there isn't a Mrs January anywhere in the background? With a man that age, you wonder.'

'You are a cynical old bastard, aren't you?' I glanced at him. 'And I take after you, because I asked the same question myself. There was a wife, but she left him ten years ago: ran off with an actor, believe it or not.'

'Too dull for her, was he?'

'Thanks, Dad. Primavera ran off with an actor too, remember.'

'Christ, so she did! Sorry, son.'

'And a policeman, and a car salesman, and my best friend.'

'Oh dear; you never told me about those.'

'Why should I have? You liked her, remember?'

'So did you. You didn't treat her very well, though.'

'It's the first time you've said that to me as well.'

'Let's just say that love blinded me to your faults too: over the last year or so, I've been able to look at them more objectively.'

'*Touché*. The truth is that I didn't treat anyone too well in those days: Jan most of all.'

'Maybe not, but she understood. She told Mary that she thought, with you two having been together since you were kids, it was probably a good thing for you to go off and sow some wild oats. She knew you'd come back to her when you were ready.'

'Hey, it wasn't just me sowing oats!'

He grinned. 'She had to make you think that, didn't she? To keep you a wee bit jealous, like. She was a smart girl, was Jan.' He seemed to drift away for a second.

I brought him back, sharpish. 'Are you saying she used Prim, and Alison Goodchild before her?'

'No, I'm saying that you did. She accepted them, that was all.'

'Maybe.'

'Do you know what Prim's doing now?'

'She went back to nursing for a while, I believe: to get her head back together, so I understand. But to be honest, Dad, I don't want to know. I don't want her in my life any more, in any way.'

'That's a bit hard: you were married to her too, remember, even if it was a disaster.' He frowned. 'You're not still bearing a torch, are you?'

27

'Secretly lusting after her, you mean? Dad, there's no way that I want, or that I need, anything that Primavera Phillips has got.' I paused. 'How did we get into this, anyway? Why did you ask about her?'

'Because she called in to see me.'

'She did? When did she do that?'

'About a week ago, as it happens. She said she was just passing by, and looked in on the off-chance.'

'And you believed her?'

'Why not?'

'Prim never does anything on the off-chance. What did you talk about?'

A great hand scratched his chin. I'm a pretty strong guy, but I work at it: so is he and he doesn't . . . apart from yanking teeth, that is. 'As I remember, she asked how I was doing, and how Mary was, and Ellie and the boys.'

'Nothing about me?'

'Not specifically. I did tell her that I had a new grandson, and that your career was coming on in leaps and bounds. That got us into talking about you.'

'So what did she have to say?'

'She told me she was sorry that it hadn't worked out between you, but that, honestly, it was as much her fault as yours.'

'Big of her.'

'I thought so at the time, I must say.'

'If she's been to see you, why did you ask me what she's doing now?'

'Because she'd gone before it occurred to me to ask her. It was just a flying visit, as she said.'

'How did she look?'

'A bit plumper in places than when I saw her last, and her hair was different, but much the same otherwise.'

'How was her hair different?'

'It was longer and not so blonde. Now that I think of it, she was dressed differently too. I used to think of her as a shirt-and-jeans person, but when she called in she was wearing, well, designer

28

clothes, I suppose you'd call them. And she had more makeup on than I remember.'

'Was she alone?'

'I take it that you mean was she with a bloke? No, she was on her own. She said that she was driving her father's car: she'd been bored and so she'd decided to go for a run.'

'You'd buy anything off anyone, wouldn't you?' I said. 'She came to see you, and for no other reason. And with respect, Dad, she didn't come to find out how you were doing. God, and I called you a cynic earlier on.'

'Oz,' he protested, 'if she was that interested in you, why didn't she just call you? You've had the same mobile number for the last five or six years, and so has she.'

'How do you know that?'

'Because she told me. She said that if I ever wanted to contact her for anything, I could always get her on it.'

'Are you sure she was telling you that?'

'There you go again.'

He had a fair point about the mobile number, I suppose, but my suspicions were roused. Experience had taught me that with my ex-wife that was always the safest way to proceed. She had turned up, pumped my dad for information, and given nothing away except a phone number that she must have known would be mentioned to me. But she hadn't been as smart as she'd thought. She'd told me that whatever she was doing now, it wasn't nursing.

When she'd got into the habit of wearing her hair short, it was to make it fit easily and quickly under her cap, for she hated pinning it up on top of her head. The makeup style had come from the same era, and for similar reasons. When Susie and I are going out on the razzle, it takes her half an hour to do her face . . . not that she needs it. Primavera did the same job in five minutes.

I know my dad hadn't meant to unsettle me, but he had all the same. Long after I had dropped him off back in Anstruther, said, 'Hello and cheerio,' to my stepmother, and set off on the road back to the west, I was still thinking about Primavera Phillips Blackstone.

4

The kids were in bed when I got home, although Janet was still awake, waiting for Daddy to read her a story, as I tried to do every night when I wasn't away on a project. We were well into *The Hobbit*, at the part where Gandalf, Bilbo and the dwarfs had escaped from the goblins and found Beorn the skin-changer. My daughter loved it. A bit advanced for a three-and-three-quarter-year-old? Maybe, but I had started her on *The House at Pooh Corner*, only to have to abandon it because I couldn't read much of it before cracking up with laughter. Whatever: for a bright kid, a story's a story.

We moved further down the road that goes on for ever, until her eyes grew heavy, and she showed the first signs of nodding off. (It's the way you tell them, Oz.) I kissed her goodnight, changed my shirt, and went down to the drawing room, where Susie was waiting, dressed for dinner. (It's not a house rule: it's just something she likes to do, and I go along with it.)

She handed me a glass of something white and slightly acidic. (No, not Anne Robinson: it was Gran Vina Sol, I think.) 'How is he, then?' she asked.

I played the game. 'Who?'

'Mac, who else?'

'Maybe I've got a mistress.'

'In that case, after last night you've got more stamina than I gave you credit for. But I don't think that even you would be crass enough to take my car when you visit her. You left your mobile, and you didn't say where you were going, but you took your clubs. They're your tools for mending fences.'

'I'd better never try to fool you,' I told her. 'Yes, I went to see my dad.'

'How did it go?'

'Fine. We're pals again.'

'Did he tell you why he wasn't speaking to you?'

Christ! She'd got it completely wrong. That was a first for Susie . . . well, maybe not, if you count Mike Dylan, but he'd fooled everyone, so I'll let her off with that one. I chose not to correct her. 'We didn't talk about the past.'

'So what did you?'

'The excellent shape of his golf game at first, then families and people.'

'Let me guess, you took Ellen's new boyfriend apart between you.'

'Shrewd as ever, my darling. My dad thinks he's a wanker too.'

She grinned, mischievously. 'Then you're both off the mark, according to what Ellie told me last time we had a girlie talk. Seriously, though, I'd advise you both to try to like him, because she does.'

'You'd better include Jonny in that warning too.'

'Jonny liked Darius: any new boyfriend was going to find him a tough nut to crack.'

'I like Darius too, but I never thought for a minute that he would last. Ellie needs attention, not just an occasional shag when the pair of them can fit it in. That's why her marriage broke up: it died because of her isolation and boredom. That's the thing that worries me most about this guy: when I met him he struck me as self-obsessed.'

'Your whole bloody profession's self-obsessed, Oz, my love.'

'Not completely. I, for one, find time to be completely obsessed by my wife and children.'

'You've learned from past mistakes, have you?'

I whistled. 'Ouch! Which mistakes are you talking about?'

'I meant your second try at marriage.'

'I hope so. Speaking of which, or whom, whatever it should be, my dad had a visit from Primavera.'

31

I could see her bridle. 'Did he now? What did she want?'

'Nothing, he said. It was purely a just-passing, drop-in, "How're you doing?" sort of thing, or so she assured him.'

'But you're not assured?'

'Not for a second. Prim doesn't do casual.'

Susie snorted. 'Neither do you: everything has to have a purpose, like this morning, for an example. When you swanned off, I knew you were up to something.'

'But you let me go without a word?'

'Sure, because I knew you'd come back and tell me. So, did she ask Mac about you?'

'Apparently not. She probably subscribes to *Empire*, the movie magazine. But she wants to talk to me, though.'

'Did she tell him that?'

'Not directly.' I described the way that Prim had let him know that she still had the same mobile number. 'Like I said, that wasn't innocent. There was a purpose to it.'

'Maybe she fancies him.'

I frowned at her as she topped up my glass. 'Don't say that, even in jest.'

'Hey, don't get so serious,' she exclaimed. 'Call her.'

'You're joking again.'

'No, I am not. If you're right and she really does want to contact you, she'll work out a way, or eventually she'll pluck up the courage to come here. I don't fancy that, so I'd rather you just phoned her and got it over with.'

'That's pretty magnanimous of you.'

'Like hell it is. I don't want anything to do with the woman, and I don't like the idea of ex-daughters-in-law calling on my father-in-law. But I don't want her hanging over us like a black cloud, so bloody well call her, and if you have to, bloody well see her.'

'That's pretty generous, then, or is it brave?'

'Brave?' she said, almost incredulously. 'Why should courage come into it? My love, do you think I've achieved what I have in business without being just a wee bit self-confident? I'm sure of myself and I'm sure of you. I can see off Prim any day of the week.'

32

She could too. 'All right, I'll give her a ring, but not tonight.'

She winked at me. 'You've still got her number, then?'

'Good question. I don't think I do. I'll get it from my dad.'

'No need. I'll have it in the database on my computer. I never throw away anything like that.'

We moved through to the dining room: Susie had cooked an all-in-one meal in our three-tier steamer and the housekeeper had left us a salad starter. She and Willie the gardener are the only members of our small staff who don't live in. Ethel, the nanny, has a suite in the big house, while Audrey and Conrad have the gatehouse.

We ate without much conversation; when Susie cooks she likes her efforts to be appreciated. We had reached the cheeseboard when we heard wee Jonathan bawling upstairs. I went to check on him, but by the time I got to the nursery, Ethel had things in hand, rubbing Bonjela gently on to his angry gums.

When I went back to the table there was a piece of paper beside my cheese plate with a mobile number written on it in my wife's clear hand. 'There you are,' she said.

'Tomorrow,' I told her.

'You'll be busy: you have a few other calls to make. You've been in demand today.'

'By whom?'

'A man from a television company rang about something he'd like you to be in.'

'No detail?'

'No, and at that point I didn't have time to interrogate him, because your friend Mr Potter came up on the other line . . . Remember? The accountant at the airport? He said if you still want his firm to pitch for the business you mentioned, he'd like a brief so he can put a proposal together.'

'We'll put something together tomorrow.'

'We?'

'Sure, your financial situation's interlinked with mine. This is a joint venture and we don't do anything you're not happy with.'

Susie grinned. 'I'm glad you said that: you saved me the trouble. After him,' she continued, 'Roscoe rang: he's talked to people since he got back to LA. Everything's fine and all the numbers are agreed.'

'Great. It makes Potter's pitch all the more important. I'll talk to him face to face tomorrow, over an Internet link. Was that all?'

'Hell, no! Your future brother-in-law called.'

'Harvey January?'

She nodded.

'He didn't call himself that, did he?'

'No, that was just me winding you up. He said that he's appearing in the High Court in Glasgow next week, and he wants to invite you to lunch.'

'What did you tell him?'

'I told him Rogano, on Tuesday, upstairs, and you're paying.'

'You what?'

'You heard.'

'I'm sure I'm doing something else on Tuesday.'

'What?'

'Anything. I'll think of something.'

'You have to get to know the man, Oz. He's not going to go away.'

'Maybe I could persuade him.'

'Don't even try. This man's a lawyer: you can't intimidate him.'

'I suppose you've booked a table too.'

'Twelve thirty, in your name.'

'Bitch from hell!'

She smiled sweetly. 'When I have to be.'

'Fine. I'm going to call Ellie, though, to see if she knows about this.'

'Don't you dare!'

'Why not? You scared she'll savage him if she doesn't?'

'Maybe. I know you and your sister: you're a bloody coven, the pair of you.'

I beamed back at her. 'No. She's the witch: I'm a mere imp.'

'Don't sell yourself short. You'll meet him, though?'

'Okay, if you're asking nicely.'

'I am, really.'

'Fine. Want to watch some telly?'

'If you can find anything worth watching, okay.' She paused. 'Oh, shit, I nearly forgot. There was one other thing. You had a call from Everett Davis.'

That was another one I hadn't been expecting, but it was welcome nonetheless. Everett, also known as Daze, is the president of the Global Wrestling Alliance, which he founded and built, from its original European base in Glasgow, into one of the world's top sports entertainment companies. He's a great friend, and I owe him a lot, because he, along with Miles Grayson, was responsible for getting me into the movie business.

'That's magic,' I said. 'Is he in town?'

'No, he's in the US, but he didn't tell me which part. All he said was that he's upset with you, and he wants to talk to you about it.'

I felt a cold shiver run through me. Everett Davis is seven feet two inches tall and is, when he wants to be, just about the most dangerous man on the planet.

And he was upset: with me.

5

I shouldn't have slept on it: I should have called him there and then. But I didn't. Instead, I spent a good part of the night tossing and turning and wondering what the hell I had done to rattle the big man's enormous cage. Hard as I tried, I couldn't come up with any answers.

The last time I'd seen him had been in London during the studio work on the third Skinner movie. He'd called to say that his wrestling circus was in town, and he, Liam Matthews, Jerry 'The Behemoth' Gradi and I all had dinner in Passione, a seriously good restaurant off Euston Road. He'd been in good form that night: his business was booming and his stock-market listing was making him (and me too) even richer by the day. I hadn't heard from him since.

I couldn't call him next morning either. As Susie had said, all he'd told her was that he was in the States, without naming one of the fifty. That meant a time difference of between five and nine hours . . . more if he happened to be in Hawaii . . . and I didn't fancy making him even grumpier by waking him in the middle of the night.

So instead, after my morning work-out, swim and breakfast, and after I'd spent some time playing with Janet in her tree-house for gardens without trees, I sat down behind my desk and called Primavera's mobile number. It took her a while to answer; when she did, she sounded as if she'd just woken up.

'Yes,' she grumbled.

'Where the hell are you?' I asked her.

'Oz? Is that you?'

'No, this is an Internet service which wakes people using the voices of famous movie stars. Your meter is running, and you have three minutes and seventeen seconds left.'

'You're crazy. What do you want?'

'Why did you go to see my old man?'

'I was in Anstruther. I decided that I couldn't possibly leave without calling in on him, so I did.'

'Are the Enster fish suppers really so good that you drove all the way from Perthshire for one?'

'Don't be daft.'

'Are you having problems with your teeth?'

'No.'

'What other reason did you have to be in my home town, other than to call in on my father?'

'I told him. I was bored, so I got into Dad's car and went for a run.'

'Shite. When you get bored you go out and pick up a guy. I'll credit you with not trying to pull him, so what was it about?'

She sighed. 'Okay, I admit it. I wanted to get in touch with you, or rather, I wanted you to get in touch with me. But you knew that all along, didn't you?'

'Of course I did, but you can thank Susie for my taking the bait.' I glanced at my wife across the huge desk.

'Susie?'

'She insisted that I call you, otherwise, girlie, you'd still be sound asleep. Look, why the charade? Why didn't you just ring me?'

'I don't have your number any more.'

'You've got my mobile number. I never changed it.'

'I thought you'd have been bound to by now. But even if I'd known that, I wouldn't have done it. I'd have expected you to hang up on me.'

'Do you think I hate you? Last time we saw each other, going on for four years ago, did we or did we not part as friends?'

'I suppose we did, although you thumping my boyfriend wasn't very friendly.'

37

'I didn't thump him!' I protested. 'Miles did.'

'He beat you to the punch, that was all. He didn't want you breaking your hand on poor Nicky's head and ruining his precious filming schedule.'

'Poor Nicky, is it? He's not still around, is he?'

'No, not since just after Miles thumped him.'

'So who is?'

'Nobody at the moment.' Her voice seemed to change as she said it.

'But there was?'

'Yes.'

'Did you get hurt again?'

'Worse than that: oh, my dear Oz, much worse than just plain hurt.'

I had known Primavera happy, sad, angry, triumphant, hurt, indignant, sober and on occasion drunk. We had shared some very traumatic times, and a few pretty decent moments too. But in the seven or eight years since we had first met, I had never heard such desolation in her voice.

'When did all this happen?'

'It's a long story.'

'Prim, why the hell didn't you just call me and tell me you were in trouble?'

'Because it's got nothing to do with you! And because I feel so stupid and betrayed, and damned ashamed.'

'So you staged that charade with my dad to smoke me out?'

'Yes, I suppose, although I wasn't thinking very clearly at the time. Not that I am now.'

'Where are you?' I asked her.

'At home.'

'Auchterarder? Are you still at your parents' place?'

'No, my home. I have a riverside flat in London.'

'Are you alone?'

'Am I ever.'

I looked at Susie. I raised my eyebrows, that was all, but she understood, and she nodded.

38

'I'll book you a flight to Glasgow, this afternoon. Pack some kit, and I'll call you back and give you the time.'

'I can't.' She sighed.

'Why not?'

'What would Susie say?'

'Susie's here and she says it's okay.'

'I'm hung over, Oz.'

'Take a couple of paracetamol tablets and drink plenty of orange juice: that always used to work for you. Go on, get your arse out of bed and get ready. What name are you using these days?'

'It still says Mrs Blackstone on my passport: I got a new one as soon as we got married, remember.'

'Sure. You were an optimist back then.'

She hadn't actually answered my question, but I let that pass. I hung up on her, then looked at Susie. 'Are you all right with that?' I asked her. She and Prim have a back story as well.

'If you think it's necessary.'

'I do. I've never heard her like that before. She's been hurt in some way and she can't handle it, hence the gauche cry for help.'

'But why cry to you? What about her sister and brother-in-law, Dawn and Miles?'

'Dunno.' I told Audrey, who was sitting at her desk, near ours, to book Prim's flight. Then I glanced at my watch; it was just short of ten. I knew that the Graysons were in Sydney. I did a quick calculation and worked out that it would be evening there. I retrieved Miles's mobile number from my computer and called it.

'Hiya, sport,' he boomed, as he picked up; I could hear party sounds in the background. He always slips into Aussie mode when he's home, whereas in California he can sound as American as the next guy. 'How did you know I was going to call you? I've had a couple of television stations asking me if I can get you out here. Any chance?'

'Nary a one, mate. I'm anchored to home for a while.'

'What's up, then?'

'Do you know what Prim's been up to lately?'

39

'Not a clue, mate. I haven't spoken to her since she did her thing with Nicky Johnson. You'd better talk to Dawn. Hold on, she's here.'

I waited for a few seconds, then heard my former sister-in-law's soft Perthshire tones. 'Oz. Good to hear from you. How are Susie and the kids?'

'Fine. How about yours?'

'Couldn't be better. What's this about my sister?'

'I've just been speaking to her. I get the impression that all's not well. Anything you can tell me?'

'Just that, and no more. She vanished off the radar for over three years, do you know that? She said that she was going back to nursing, to find herself again . . . our Prim can be even more dramatic than me . . . and she just disappeared. She didn't tell any of us where she was going. We couldn't contact her; we got Christmas cards as usual but that was all. Her mobile was always switched off and any messages Mum or I left were never returned, until a couple of years ago she called and said she was coming to Auchterarder for a visit. She did, stayed for a couple of weeks, told them nothing at all about what she'd been up to, then vanished again, with barely any warning that she was off.' Dawn paused. 'That was it, until a couple of weeks ago, when she landed on them again. She wouldn't say anything about what she'd been doing, not to Mum, not to Dad, not to me, other than that she'd decided to take a break from everyone. She stayed for a while, then, as before, pissed off again. You said you've spoken to her. D'you mean she got in touch with you?'

'In a manner of speaking.' I told her about the supposedly casual visit to my dad, and about our telephone conversation.

'She said, "Much worse than hurt"? God help whoever did it, then, for there's only one thing that my sister takes lying down. Take some advice, my dear Oz: don't get involved.'

'I'll hear what the story is, Dawn, and then I'll take a view.'

'Let me know what's happening.'

'Promise. Thanks; take care of that big koala of yours.'

When I put the phone down, Audrey was standing beside me.

40

'That's done. She's on the two o'clock shuttle from Heathrow, ticket to be collected. I didn't know you had two sisters, Oz.' She turned slightly pink when I explained who Prim was.

I turned to the business that had been lined up for me the day before. I called the man from the television company. He wanted me to play on one of those 'guess the celebrity' panel games. It would have meant letting cameras into our home, so I declined, politely but irrevocably, without a second thought.

Next, Susie, Audrey and I spent an hour drafting a brief for Mr Potter, and Clark Gow, his firm, setting out our financial position, as of that moment, and as it would be in two years, once I had completed my latest contracts and the partial flotation of the Gantry Group had gone through. When it was ready for transmission, Audrey called him and asked for his e-mail address so that she could send it.

'You know what he's going to tell us, don't you?' said Susie, when it was done. 'He's going to say the same as Roscoe did, that we should go and live in some tax haven or other.'

'Probably,' I conceded. 'So let's the two of us and our kids go for a walk round our bloody great garden to remind ourselves why we should stay here.'

6

It was a beautiful summer morning, the kind you wish you could bottle. I did the next best thing: I filmed it on my camcorder, Susie playing on the grass with wee Jonathan, Janet on the electric quad bike that I'd found for her, and all the time, the sun glistening and sparkling on Loch Lomond below us. We had no trouble convincing ourselves that we were going to live there happily for the rest of our days.

Actually we'd made the place even bigger: for added privacy and security we'd acquired some commercially useless woodland and fields from the neighbouring estate. The extension included some virtually bottomless bogs, which I'd had capped with concrete, for safety's sake. It all meant that we had so much land we'd bought a Mini to run around in . . . and because it's a lovely piece of design. Susie and I do like our toys.

The morning was so idyllic that I had almost forgotten the call I was going to have to make. It took Susie to remind me of it.

'Will Everett's office be open yet?' she asked, as we finished lunch, just after one o'clock. I knew that it would. As its name implies, his is a global business, so the switchboard in the New York headquarters is manned from seven a.m. on. I nodded and went back to the office.

I didn't expect him to be there: the GWA wrestlers are on the road a lot, and Everett, although he controls and runs the business, is still on the active list, so, after I had told her who I was, I simply asked his receptionist where he could be found. 'Right here, Mr Blackstone,' she replied. 'I'll put you through.'

I braced myself. A few seconds later, the big drawly voice was on the line. 'Oz, my man! This is an honour and a surprise. You found the time to call me.'

'What have I done?' I asked him, my voice all innocence. 'What's upset you?'

'You have to ask me? You blew me out, man. You turned me down flat and you didn't even have the stones to do it yourself: got your Mr Smooth from LA to do it instead.'

'What the hell are you talking about?'

'My proposition. You turned me down, Oz. I can't believe it.'

Oh, shit.

'What proposition?'

'You mean Mr Roscoe Goddamn Brown didn't even tell you about it? Well, I'll tell you something now, I am going to pay a call on that mother when I'm on the west coast next week and he will not enjoy it.'

'Now hold on there. Before you go off and commit homicide, or agenticide at least, this wasn't Roscoe's fault. Blame me, if you're going to blame anyone. Yes, he recommended that I decline whatever it is, but it was at the end of a very positive session on other things and I wanted to demonstrate my complete trust in him. So I told him that he didn't have to go through the details with me. I'm sorry, it was my mistake. Do you want to tell me about it now, or are you so deep in the huff that it's off the table?'

'If I do will you listen to me politely then turn me down again?'

'That depends on what it is and on the time frame. In three months' time, I'm pretty much committed through to next summer.'

'This would work, in that case.'

'Go on then.'

'Oz, I'm diversifying.'

'You're starting a dance troupe?'

'Hey, wouldn't that be something? Imagine Jerry Gradi in a tutu.'

'It worked for J. Edgar Hoover.'

He chuckled. 'Maybe, but not for the GWA. No, I'm going into the movie business. I have a project all set up as a vehicle for Liam Matthews, Jerry and a new girl we've got on board. It's written, the

43

director's in place and we're all ready to start shooting. There's only one thing left to do. I have a cameo role that I need to fill, the bad guy. It's perfect for you and I want you to do it. I'd only need you for a couple of weeks.'

'That's what you put to Roscoe?'

'Yup.'

'How much did you offer him?'

'A million dollars.'

'Everett, my next three movies will earn me over twenty million euros.'

If I'd had wax in my ear, the big man's whistle would have blown it right out. 'Jeez,' he exclaimed, 'I didn't realise you were in that bracket. No wonder your guy turned me down.'

'There might be more to it than that. You're a newcomer to the business, and he doesn't know you like I do.'

'I've got someone else in place for the part,' he said, perking up again, 'but nothing's signed yet. It's still yours if you want it. Maybe I could squeeze some more money out of the pot.'

'Friend, I'd do it for free,' I told him, meaning every word, 'but I've got Roscoe to consider. He earns his cut, and twenty per cent of nothing doesn't amount to much more than that. I'll tell you what. E-mail me the script today, and I'll take a quick look at it. What is it, anyway? I assume that with Liam and Jerry in the lead, it's not a remake of *Pride and Prejudice*.'

'Hell, no! It's an action thriller called *Serious Impact*, based on a novel by a hot young writer. It's set mostly in Las Vegas. I'll have someone send it to you right away.'

'Do that. I'll be speaking to Roscoe later today: I'll talk it through with him, I promise.' I paused, turning a thought over in my mind. 'Two weeks in Vegas, eh? When?'

'We'd need you the week after next. I'll book you the best suite in the Mandalay Bay, or the Bellagio, if you'd prefer to be in the heart of the Strip.'

'Okay, okay, you can ease off the arm lock now: I'll get back to you.' I put the phone back in the cradle.

'What was that about Las Vegas?' Susie asked.

44

'Everett fancies himself as a movie producer.'

'Are you going to do it?'

'That depends. Do you fancy it?'

'Not one bit. I've been to Vegas, at a convention with my dad when he was Lord Provost of Glasgow. It's not a place for kids, especially not in the summer: it's in the middle of a desert and it's ferociously hot.'

'We could leave the kids with Ethel,' I suggested tentatively.

The look she shot me was eloquent. It said, 'You're a self-indulgent bastard and a bad parent.'

'Okay, I'll turn it down.'

'No, I didn't mean that. It's your career, and Everett's your friend.'

'And you're my family and I promised you three months. That's more important.'

'How much money is he offering?'

When I told her, I thought she would explode. 'Are we so bloody wealthy that you can afford to turn down a million dollars for two weeks' not very hard work?'

'As a matter of fact, we are.'

'Like hell we are! Nobody is.'

'Okay, once I've seen the script . . . Audrey, when an e-mail arrives from someone in the GWA, print out the attachment, please . . . I'll talk to Roscoe about it. But I'm not inclined to go without you and the kids.'

Susie glanced at her watch. 'We can continue this later, Sir Galahad,' she said, 'but first you've got a plane to meet.'

7

I'm not saying I wouldn't have known her, but if I hadn't been expecting a different Primavera after my chat with my dad, I'd have been in for a shock.

The woman who came out of the arrivals doorway at Glasgow airport, wheeling a cabin bag behind her, was not she with whom I'd fallen in lust during the death-rattle of my dissolute and free-wheeling twenties. Not that she should have been, since eight years or so had elapsed (I've always been vague about dates), but the changes were pretty radical.

She was still attractive, no question about that, but she was thinner about the face. Much of its former roundness had gone, and the cheekbones, which I didn't remember noticing before, were now quite prominent. There were new creases about her eyes, in addition to the familiar laugh-lines, and the hairstyle was indeed new: it brushed her shoulders and it was tinted, a sort of strawberry colour.

The clothes were familiar, though. She might have got herself dolled up for her visit to Anstruther, but she had travelled in well-washed blue jeans, a pale blue sleeveless shirt and tan moccasins.

She didn't see me at first. I was standing behind a line of men, some in grey chauffeur uniforms, holding up boards with punters' names on them. She scanned them, as if she assumed that one of them was for her, and only then did her eye catch mine. She started slightly, then smiled, awkwardly. I gave her a wave then moved towards her.

There was something else different about her: she had been comfortably endowed in the chest department, a thirty-six C cup, as I remembered. She'd certainly not been in need of implants, and yet she looked as if she'd had some.

She stepped past the line of waiting drivers and we came face to face, for the first time in almost four years. For a moment I almost offered a handshake, until instinct and good manners made me lean forward and kiss her cheek, like someone greeting an old friend, rather than an ex-wife . . . although the two states are not mutually exclusive.

'Hello,' she said, and then something very strange happened. Her eyes moistened, and two big tears rolled down her cheeks.

I took her in my arms and hugged her to me for a few moments. Maybe I should have been more careful: being famous, I was aware that a few people were looking at us, but tears from Prim are about as rare as orange juice from a potato. 'Hey,' I murmured, 'I'm a professional kisser now. I've been coached and everything. I'm not supposed to get that kind of reaction.'

A laugh spluttered its way on to her crumpled face: I was relieved for I'd feared we were in for flood conditions. She fished in her shoulder-bag until she found a tissue, and dried her eyes. 'I'm sorry,' she whispered. 'You never used to have that effect on me.'

'Of course I did,' I protested. 'The way I behaved?'

As I looked at her, it all came back to me. Whatever it was that had bound us together, some vestiges of it had burned themselves into my brain, and would never go away. 'It's good to see you,' I heard myself say.

'And it's good to see you. In fact, you don't know how good it is. Oz, I have never felt so alone, or so much in need of you.'

'Why me?' I asked her, automatically. 'What about Miles? He's your brother-in-law, and he's one hell of an influential guy. He's on first-name terms with the Prime Minister . . .' I paused to consider the banality of that remark. '. . . okay, so is everyone, but I know for a fact that the Australian version phones him up for advice on a regular basis.'

'Maybe, but he won't give me any. Miles doesn't like me, ever since that Nicky business, and he's turned my sister against me too. Anyway, he's not you. He doesn't get the business done like you do.'

It was my turn for a sudden spluttering laugh. 'Hold on for a reality check, woman. I'm an actor: none of that stuff's for real.'

'You've done plenty of things for real in the time I've known you. There is nobody I could or would turn to before you.'

I felt a surge of pride as strong as any I've known when I've seen my name in lights. 'That's nice to know. But let's not talk about whatever it is here. Come back to the house and say hello to Susie and the kids.'

She gave a small 'Hmph!'

'Hey now,' I cautioned. 'You might think of her as the woman who stole your husband, but she knows about you having it off with her fiancé, so maybe it's best to call it quits and let the past lie undisturbed.'

She was taken considerably aback. 'She does? But how . . .'

'Shagging him was one thing. Writing to him was another.'

'God,' she gasped. 'Would you believe I'd forgotten about it?' Then she gave an old-style Prim chuckle. 'That might tell you how memorable the late Mike Dylan was.'

Not as late as you believe, I thought to myself, but that was our secret, Mike's and mine.

'Since you were my fiancée at the time,' I said, casually, 'I don't wish to know that.' I'd often wondered why I wasn't more upset when I found out about that incident. I dunno, maybe I saw the poetic justice in it.

Suddenly I wanted to get out of there: I put an arm around her shoulders and steered her towards the door, picking up her bag by the handle and carrying it rather than wheeling it behind me like a prat. As we walked towards the exit, she pressed herself against me for a second. 'I forgot to say "thanks", Oz,' I heard her say.

'Thank Susie, not me. If she'd said "no", you wouldn't be here.'

Prim said nothing at all on the way back to the house. That was just as well, for I don't really like to talk when I'm driving. Instead she listened to the music: I'd put some Brian Kennedy in the CD changer before I left. He'd been a favourite of hers from the moment I'd introduced them, but I hadn't chosen him for that reason.

He'd sung himself hoarse by the time we got there, and had been replaced by Ry Cooder and Manuel Galban playing mambo music: my recently acquired taste, but she seemed to like that too. She whistled as she stepped out of the car and saw my home. 'Very grand for a boy from Enster,' she exclaimed.

There was a squeal from the playground, followed by a yell of 'Daddy!' as a red-haired bundle came rushing towards us. I scooped her up in my arms. 'But not for this one,' I replied. 'Hey, kid, say hello to your auntie Prim, by name if not nature.' My daughter's response was a frown, rather than her usual bold grin; it was funny, but looking back at that moment, it was as if she recognised her as someone who had come to set ripples in the calm ocean of her existence.

'Hello, Janet,' said Primavera. 'Don't you look like your mother? You won't remember me, but I came to see you when you were a baby.'

'And that went down like a lead balloon,' I told her, 'so don't let's mention it inside.'

At that moment, the door opened. I hadn't expected Susie to come to greet us, but she did. I marked that down as a big gesture on her part, and so did Prim, for her face changed again. Uncertainty was something else I'd never known her to show before. Then my wife said, 'Come here,' and the two of them hugged. For all the nonsense, they'd been on decent terms in the past. Of course, Prim started crying again, didn't she? This time I left her to Susie to sort out.

'Hey,' I heard her say, as she swept her inside, 'there's no need for that. Come on; I'll show you your room and you can lie down for a bit.' Take me back five years and tell me that I'd wind up watching that scene and I'd have called you crazy.

I felt unsettled as I led Janet back to her tree-house, and for the first time, a little annoyed. I knew, I just knew, that something I did not want or need was about to erupt into my life. And it was my own bloody fault for being soft enough to invite it in.

8

When I was back indoors, after handing Janet back to Ethel, I went through to the office conservatory. Audrey was there on her own, so I guessed either that Prim was still 'lying down' or that Susie had reached the same conclusion as I had, namely that a drink would be more therapeutic.

There was a new document on my side of the desk. 'Everett's movie?' I asked. Our secretary nodded. I picked it up: it had a project number on the first page, that was all. Industrial espionage is a big part of movie life: clearly the big man knew that much about the business already. For all my wife's leaning on me, I still wasn't that keen on the idea, but I picked it up and began to glance through it.

I looked at the plot outline, then the shooting schedule, and saw right away that my potential part was a wee bit more than a cameo, as it had been described: I was only in around ten per cent of the scenes, but they were all quite lengthy and half of them were at the end.

I started to read through the script, or at least the sections that were of direct interest to me. It wasn't exactly Ingmar Bergman, but Everett's audience were more the action-before-intellect type, and by those standards it read okay. Well, no, that's not true: it read terribly, but with a bit of imagination, a bit of inflection here and there, backed up by good direction and editing, I reckoned that it would be okay. Whether I was in it or not, I didn't want my friend's first venture to be an embarrassment.

I was into the second scene when the door opened and the former and current Mrs Blackstones came in. They were both carrying tall glasses . . . Susie's looked like orange juice, but I took a guess that Prim's was Bacardi and tonic, unless she'd changed her tastes as well as her appearance.

My wife motioned me to follow, turning on her heel and leading the way from the office across to the conservatory wing on the west side of the house, where the pool is. Afternoon had given way to evening, but it was still warm in there: all the doors to the garden were open and the roof vents too, yet the automatic air-conditioning was still blowing.

'Where's my drink?' I grumbled, as the women settled into the wicker seats, set round the glass-topped table.

'In the fridge,' said Susie, pointing to the big cooler that we keep out there. I opened it, chose a bottle of a Belgian beer known colloquially as 'wife-beater', and joined them.

I looked at Prim. She had changed out of her travel clothes into a light top-and-trousers outfit, city gear rather than country: once again, this was someone I felt I knew only slightly.

'Okay,' I said, quietly. 'Let's hear it.'

She glanced at the floor, then at the shimmering surface of the pool. Finally she looked across at me. 'Two years ago,' she began, 'well, no, it'll be a bit more than that now, I met a man.'

In spite of myself, I grinned. 'When do we get to the surprise?' Susie fetched me a look that was the equivalent of a clout round the ear. 'Sorry, go on.'

'You know that I went back to nursing, after the last time I saw you, that is?'

I nodded. 'Dawn told me. She said it was to let you get your head back together, and to recover some of the old family values.'

A corner of her mouth flickered. 'Did you believe that?'

'I believed that Dawn believed it, and I even gave you the credit for believing it at the time yourself.'

'But you couldn't see it lasting?'

'To be honest, no: I reckoned you'd get bored before long and be off on your travels again.'

'Since you're that bloody clever, it's a pity you didn't tell me!'

'We were each other's keepers for long enough. Plus, we were in

51

the process of getting divorced, remember. So, how long did it take you to get bored out of your scone?'

She smiled wistfully and scratched her chin. 'It took a couple of months for me to realise why I'd left the profession in the first place, and another couple before I was going bats. I couldn't go back home, though. My mum had made a good physical recovery from her cancer, but she was still preoccupied with it emotionally, and she didn't need to be lumbered with my mid-thirties crisis. As for my father . . . Oz, you know him, you know what he's like.'

Yes, I know David Phillips: he's a very nice, kind man who's been content to let his wife and daughters rule most of his adult life. He is also from the Planet Zog.

'So you packed a bag, quit your job and disappeared into the night?' I prompted.

She scrunched up her eyebrows, as if she was pinching back more tears. 'I should have, months before I actually did, that is. I should have gone off to Africa or the US or wherever . . . And yet even now when I say that I don't mean it.'

I decided to push things along a bit, before she unravelled again. 'Where did you meet him?'

'You reckon you know me that well?' she shot back, bitterly. 'You just assume it was a man. Primavera's in trouble, so the cause has to be some bloke's pants hanging on the bedroom door. Is it that easy to diagnose?'

'You said that you met a man. Where did that happen?'

'Gleneagles Hotel,' she answered, her short-lived feistiness going out of her with a great sigh. 'After a couple of years, I decided that I had to see my parents again. So I quit my job, and headed north. It was good for a while, but all they did was hang about the house all day, so in the evenings I'd go along to Gleneagles for a drink. I went on my own, but the staff knew who I was, so they didn't worry that I was a high-class hooker or anything.'

'Did anyone else think that?'

'Gleneagles isn't that sort of place, Oz. Most of the time I just sat, read the magazines in the lounge and people-watched. Occasionally there would be a man there on his own, and we'd say hello to each other, but it was always very proper. Even when I met him, it was all above board.'

'Name of?'

'Wallinger; Paul Wallinger, bastard that he is.'

There was so much pure hatred in her tone that even Susie was startled. I try to listen to both sides of an argument before taking sides, but I knew right then that I didn't like Mr Wallinger.

'What was his story?'

'We met in the cocktail bar, my usual hang-out: I was on my third Bacardi, and just getting nicely relaxed, when he came in from the dining room, tall, dark-haired, tanned, clean-cut.'

My wife glanced at me. 'I know someone else who answers that description.'

Prim went slightly pink. 'To tell you the truth, that's what made me give him more than just one glance; he does have a passing resemblance to Oz. He didn't as much as look my way, though. He sat down at another table and ordered a Macallan, then he picked up one of the posh magazines and started to read it. Still he never even looked in my direction. That must have stirred my vanity, for when he glanced around to catch the waiter's eye, I made damn sure that mine got in the way too.'

I knew that scene. 'So you pulled him,' I suggested, 'not the other way around.'

'Oz,' said Susie, from the side, 'just shut up, will you?'

Prim shook her head. 'No, it has to be admitted, I pulled him, or at least I started the pulling. I brought it all down on my own empty bloody head.' She drained her glass.

My wife glanced at it, and at her own, by way of instruction: so I went off and refilled them. 'Thanks,' said Prim, as she took her fairly heavily iced-up Bacardi and tonic. (I didn't want her getting too drunk and maudlin.) 'I never thought I'd see you house-trained.'

'And I never thought I'd see you crying into your cocktails, so tell me how it happened.'

'Okay. That was how we met, casually, two respectable, lonely strangers in a very respectable place. He moved over to my table and we started to talk. He told me that he was American, a stockbroker working in London, and that he was in Scotland playing some classic golf courses. I told him that I was a nurse, and that I was visiting my parents, who lived locally.'

'No more than that?'

'Not at first; that night we just talked about Gleneagles, about Scotland, about the courses he was playing.'

'All about him?'

'Yeah, I suppose. I might have said a few things about my job, but that was all.'

'So you didn't tell him you were a millionaire divorcee, just to get his interest.'

'No! I told you.' She turned on me. 'Listen, if you're going to interrogate me like this I'll stop right now.'

'No, you won't: it's why you're here. But I'll shut up, if it makes it easier for you.'

'It will. I've been bottling this up for a while: you're the first people I've told about it, so just let it come out, please.'

'Okay, I promise.'

'Thanks. Right, where were we? Yes, talking that first night. As I said, it was all very bland, and after a while, I said I had to go. He thanked me for my company, as a gentleman would, then he asked if I came to Gleneagles often. When I told him that I did, he asked if I'd like to have dinner with him the next night, and I told him that would be nice.'

She took a sip of her weak Bacardi and made a face. 'As it happened it was nice. We had a very pleasant evening, and I'm sure that he never asked me a single thing about myself, until right at the end when, out of the blue, he said, "Why do you stay here?" I asked him what he meant, and he replied, "Don't think me presumptuous, but obviously you're bored here, just filling in time." That took me completely by surprise. I suppose I protested a bit, but in the end I had to admit that he was right. It was then that I told him that I'd just been divorced, and that I'd come home to reassess, as I put it. I still didn't mention your name, though, and he didn't ask me anything about you. Instead he told me that he'd just gone through the same experience, and was having difficulty coming out the other side. Next thing I knew, I was sympathising with him, telling him that there was a life afterwards and that it would all work out okay.'

'Did you . . . ?' I began, in spite of myself.

She cut me off short. 'I didn't prove it to him there and then, if that's what you were going to ask, but the next evening we had dinner again. I stayed for a bit after that, and all the next night. He was due to leave that morning: I suppose I would have said, "Thanks and goodbye," and given him a page in my scrap-book, but it didn't work out that way. Instead he asked me if I'd like to do something impulsive, and go with him to London, there and then, for a couple of weeks, to see how it worked out. He caught me at just the right moment. I thought about Auchterarder with him gone, that big barn of a house and my preoccupied parents, and I said, "Why the hell not?" So I went home, packed, said my farewells to Mum and Dad, without telling them where I was going, then went back to Gleneagles and to Paul. He had a hire car to take back to Edinburgh: I got a seat on his flight and by that evening we were in his place in Kensington.'

She paused for breath and Bacardi. 'Only it wasn't his place: it was a serviced apartment in a block that catered for business clients, the sort of accommodation you might take if you were coming into town for a few weeks' work. None of the people I met there were British; they were a mixture of Americans, Germans, Japanese and Chinese. He told me that his wife had taken him to the cleaners in the settlement, and he'd taken it on as a short-term measure till he got back on his feet. But it didn't really matter as far as I was concerned. I was in London, it was exciting, Paul was considerate and charming and I had my life back.'

'Doing what?' I asked.

'That's a good question,' Prim admitted. 'Now that I look back on it, I was doing nothing. Paul would go to work every day, Monday to Friday, and I'd shop. Either I'd walk down to Harrods, or I'd take a taxi up to the West End. Occasionally I'd do something cultural for the sake of it, maybe the National Gallery, or the British Museum, but mostly I hung out in Selfridges, or I'd take the Tube

55

up to Liverpool Street and meet Paul for lunch in a wine bar. The couple of weeks grew into a month, and it all sort of went on from there.'

She smiled, wryly. 'We stayed in the flat for three months, enough time for me to realise how poky it was and to want something better. When I said this to Paul, he made a face, and said he couldn't afford it. I remember laughing, and telling him not to worry, that I could. That was when I told him who I'd been married to and how much I'd got in the settlement. So we went house-hunting and found a nice two-bedroom flat in Battersea, a riverside development near Chelsea Bridge that looks up towards Westminster. All my money was invested at that stage, but I bought it on a mortgage till I could free some up. We moved in straight away, and it was wonderful. I was back on track, I had a nice, kind, loving man, a great lifestyle in an exciting city. What more could I want?'

'More of everything?'

'Once upon a time that might have been true.'

'So what changed you?'

'Your daughter did.' She looked at Susie. 'Remember that day I came to visit you, just after she was born?'

'Will I ever forget?' my wife murmured.

'I don't suppose you will, given that I was still married to Oz, and you'd just had his kid. I'm sorry, if it annoyed you, me doing that, but my head really was messed up then, nearly as badly as it is now. I arrived at your place full of bitterness and resentment against you,' she jerked a thumb in my direction, 'and him. Then I saw Janet, and something happened; she just melted me, she was so beautiful. And so did you in a way, because you were so happy. It came home to me, how badly I'd messed up and how generally stupid and selfish I'd been in my attitude to life, marriage and everything else.'

Out of the blue, a lump seemed to form in my throat: as I saw my daughter being born I'd felt exactly the same way. For the first time that day, I began to empathise with Prim, and to feel more sorry for her than angry with her.

'As my relationship with Paul developed, and we settled into the new house, I knew what I wanted to happen next. And it did. I got pregnant.' I should have guessed: that's where the enhanced bust must have come from.

'Was it planned?' asked Susie. Sure as hell, Janet wasn't.

'It was by me; I suppose I should have discussed it with Paul, but I didn't. I just stopped taking the pill.'

'Was that when he turned into a bastard? When he found out?'

'No, not at all. I was a bit apprehensive when I told him, but he couldn't have been more delighted. All through my pregnancy he fussed over me. He wouldn't let me do anything, or get stressed out in any way. He insisted that he take over my financial management, and, him being an expert and everything, I let him.'

I'd guessed from the start that something like this was coming, and I could see from her frown that Susie had too, but neither of us said anything.

'When Tom was born . . . that's what we called him, Tom . . . Paul was the perfect new father. He was as delighted as I was, just too chuffed to have been faking it. We did all the new mum and dad things, like putting him in his buggy and walking across the bridge for Sunday brunch, taking him to the park . . .'

I had to interrupt. 'Showing him off to his grandparents?'

'No. I kept putting that off. I hadn't spoken to Mum and Dad, or to Dawn, since I left with Paul. When I went back with my new baby I wanted it to be a real surprise. I'd planned to do it last Christmas, to drive up there and just turn up on the doorstep, but Paul came down with something, so we decided not to expose Tom to his bugs all the way up there in a car. We decided that we'd wait till Easter, but a couple of weeks before that, he told me he'd have to go to the US on business, so that got shelved. After all, there was plenty of time. Oh, yes,' she said, in a tone that was suddenly hard and bitter, 'all the time in the fucking world.'

She faltered, staring up at the drapes that shaded the glass roof, blinking hard and biting her lip.

'Or so I thought,' she went on quietly. 'So the stupid, doe-eyed, earth mother Primavera thought.'

'What happened?' I asked.

'It was just another Saturday, Oz, a couple of months ago. We had a routine on Saturdays: we'd go food shopping, all three of us. If the weather was bad we'd take a taxi to Putney, but if it was nice we'd walk across the bridge to Waitrose on the King's Road, get what we needed, have a coffee, then cab it back with the bags. I was all ready to go, but Paul said that he thought Tom was still a bit sleepy and to be honest so was he, so why didn't I just leave the guys together and go on my own? I took him at his word: I suppose if I'm being totally honest, I was quite pleased. Tom had been getting to be quite a handful. It was a nice warm spring day, and the sun was shining, so I walked. I took my time over it, got quite a lot of stuff, locked it in one of those safe deposit things in the supermarket, had a coffee, walked down the King's Road and bought a nice outfit, then picked up my shopping and took a taxi back home. And when I got there he was gone.'

She paused for another slug of Bacardi. 'I walked in, as usual, expecting the happy smile and the hug, as usual, but all I got was silence. I thought nothing of it at first: I just supposed that he'd decided to take Tom to the park. So I put the food away, and went to try on my new trouser suit again. When I went into the bedroom, I saw that Paul's wardrobe was open and empty. I didn't know what to do. I just sat down on the bed and started shaking. And then the quietness got to me, and I realised what had happened.'

'What do you mean?'

'The quietness, Oz, the absence of noise: when there's a baby in a house there's always something going on, or he's asleep. Tom never sleeps at midday any more. I ran through to the nursery . . . I still remember my heart hammering in my chest as I did . . . but it was empty too. The cot was there, and some of his toys, but all the rest, and his clothes, they were all gone.'

'You're saying that he'd taken Tom?'

'Of course,' she shouted, suddenly. 'Do you think I'd be this torn up about the fucking money? He stole my son, Oz. That bastard Paul Wallinger stole my son!' The crying began again, in earnest.

I left Susie to deal with that and went back through to the kitchen to mix Prim another drink, a real one this time. When I got back, she was sitting in her wicker chair, her shoulders hunched, rocking very slightly, backwards and forwards, as if that gave her comfort. 'Here,' I murmured, handing her the fresh Bacardi. She took it from me without even looking up, and drank half of it in a single swallow.

'What did you do about it?' I asked her.

'For a couple of hours I just sat there, trying to comprehend what had happened. I used my imagination as best I could, to see if I could come up with a logical explanation. But I couldn't and it just left me all the more scared. Finally, I called the police and told them that I wanted to report a child abduction. They responded quickly enough, two uniforms, then a couple of CID, but when I told them what had happened I could see them glaze over. They told me that since Paul's Tom's father, there had been no crime, and that, well, basically, ma'am, you're just wasting our bleedin' time. So I asked them if I could report them missing, and they said no, because, ma'am, he isn't bloody missing. He's packed and he's gone: Mr Wallinger knows where he is all right, and where his son is. His son, remember. He just doesn't want you to bloody know, does he? So then I said what about my baby, and they asked me if I had any reason to believe that Paul would harm Tom, and I had to say no, and they said, well, there you bloody are, then. They told me to sit tight, be patient and wait for the phone to ring and then they buggered off.'

'And did you? Sit tight, I mean?'

'What else could I do? I was terrified, I'd had a couple of drinks by that time, no, more than a couple, and even if I'd wanted to get out I couldn't, could I, in case Paul phoned to tell me where he was? I sat tight, all right . . . tight as a tick most of the time. I sat there for three days, Saturday, Sunday, Monday and into Tuesday, drinking a lot, eating very little and barely sleeping a wink. Finally, I made myself believe what had happened and believe that there wasn't going to be a phone call. So I got myself sober, had a bath, and made myself take a few hours' kip. When I woke up, on the Wednesday morning, I made some calls. The first was to a lawyer I'd used when I bought the flat. I told him what had happened and

59

asked what I could do. He told me to sit tight again . . . advice that I did not thank him for . . . while he hired a detective to make some preliminary enquiries.'

'I thought that would have been your first call,' I said, 'given that you and I were in that business together.'

'I told you, my mind was fucked up, or I would have. No matter, a man came to see me within two hours: his name was Gary Anderson, and he said that he was an ex-cop. He interviewed me, I gave him all the detail I could, and he said that he'd get on with it. He was very good, better than you and I ever were, or much quicker, anyway. He came back to see me at four o'clock next day, Thursday. He told me that Mr Paul Wallinger had flown from London Gatwick to Minneapolis on the previous Saturday afternoon, on a North-west flight. His infant son Tom was with him and they had travelled club class.'

'Minneapolis is a hub airport,' I told her. 'Did he have an onward booking?'

'No, he didn't: Anderson checked that. I asked him how he'd been able to get Tom on the plane without a passport. He told me that he'd been to the US Embassy and put him on his own, as an American citizen, which he is, just as much as he's British.'

'He was well prepared,' said Susie.

'He'd had two fucking years to prepare,' Prim shot back bitterly. 'Anderson checked his business background, at least the details I'd given him. Everything was phoney: the company he said he worked for didn't-exist. You probably think that makes me an idiot, living with someone for that long and knowing so little about what he did during the day. But honestly, it isn't so daft. I'd never visited Paul at his office, or had any reason to: he told me that his wasn't always a desk job, and that he spent most of his time out looking at the businesses he was interested in. That figured, for he'd often be away for a couple of days at a time, even when I was nearly due, and even when Tom was just an infant. As for a business phone number, he said that he didn't have a direct line and that he always used a mobile. "So what's he been living on?" I asked Anderson, but I didn't have to: I knew. He'd been living on me. When I

60

checked, all the household costs had come either out of my Visa account . . . I'd given him a card of his own, hadn't I? . . . or out of a joint account he'd set up for us, but never put anything into himself. Do you know, I even paid for his fucking flight to America, the one he left me on?'

'I hope you cancelled the card,' said Susie indignantly.

'Too right I did.'

'Did you keep the last statements?' I asked.

'Probably. Why?'

'They could come in handy,' I said, casually, but noting how off the ball she was, in that she didn't follow me. Task number one, Blackstone: get her off the drink so that her brain can work properly again. 'So, what about the money?' I knew that this was going to be bad: the guy was a con-man, and she'd let him take over her financial management. 'What have you got left?'

'I've got half a million, invested in an annuity that doesn't mature till I'm fifty-five and that I can't touch before then. I've got two hundred and fifty thousand in a Swiss account that, fortunately, I forgot to tell him about, and I've got the flat. Everything else is gone, sold or cashed up in the month before he left.'

It was my turn for the heavy frown. While Prim and I were together we'd amassed a right few quid, some jointly, some from the generous points arrangement on my first movie, and a hell of a lot from my shareholding in the GWA, after it went public. When we split up, so did the money, more or less straight down the middle: on the figures she'd quoted me, allowing for even modest capital growth, the guy had fleeced her, and how.

'He took around two and a half million?'

She nodded. 'Yes, but that's not the point: he's got Tom, Oz, he's got Tom.'

I got up, fetched myself another beer from the fridge, and walked towards the open doorway to the garden. I stood there thinking, letting the evening breeze cool me. After a while, I turned back to face the girls. 'Okay,' I said: that was all.

'What are you going to do, Oz?' asked Susie.

I looked at her, smiled, then shrugged my shoulders, just like

Nicolas Cage in one of my favourite movies, and stole his best line. 'What am I going to do?' I replied. 'I'm going to save the fucking day, that's what I'm going to do.'

9

The trouble with the grand statement was that I had no idea how I was going to make it happen. I knew one thing for sure, though: I wanted to meet Paul Wallinger. Arguably, the guy had a right to his own kid, but the money that he'd stolen from Prim had once been mine too, and I took a seriously dim view of that.

Actually, the financial side of it begged a lot of questions, but I decided to put them on hold for a while. Prim was strung out, no doubt about that, but she was also drinking way too much. When we were a couple, we'd been what I'd call normal thirty-something users of alcohol. We took it socially, and while often enough it would end the day, it never, ever began it; it worried me that my former wife had turned into someone who looked as if she put Bacardi on her corn flakes.

When I glanced at my watch and said that I'd fix dinner, Susie read my mind. She took Prim off to her room and talked her into sleeping off her latest cargo for a couple of hours.

I was in *Ready, Steady, Cook* mode, so I didn't spend too much time in the kitchen. I chopped some Chinese leaves into strips and mixed them with feta cheese, olives and red chillies, seeded, as a salad starter, then blended tomatoes and some coconut cream, and added a few mushrooms, baby corn, and whatever spices my hand fell upon, to create Oz Blackstone's celebrated impromptu pasta sauce. I set it simmering, cut some monkfish and salmon fillets into cubes, to be added later, and went back to the office. No, I did one other thing before that. I checked that we had plenty of bottled water, still and sparkling, in the fridge: there was going to be no more booze on offer that evening.

Back at my desk, I switched on my computer. Right at the top of my box was an e-mail from Roscoe, reporting progress on my three deals. I sent him an instant message asking if he was available for a face to face; a few seconds later a box popped up on my screen inviting me to switch on my web-cam.

It's my favourite means of communicating with my agent, other than across the desk: with both of us on high-speed broadband, the quality of both sound and vision is pretty good. I could see from the view through the window behind Roscoe that the LA weather was as usual. He was wearing a short-sleeved white shirt, and in the background I could hear the sound of air-conditioning at full hum.

'One of the offers we turned down,' I began, 'was from the Global Wrestling Alliance. Right?'

'Yes, it was, but the money was insufficient and there was no guarantee of distribution. They need you more than you need them, I'd say. It wouldn't have advanced your career, Oz.'

'Would it do it any harm, though?'

'The script itself read pretty well, and I rate Santiago Temple, the director. Liam Matthews has done well in the Skinner movies he's made with you. It would be okay if all other things were equal, but to be honest, they're offering way below your market value, and they don't have the financial flexibility to meet it.'

'I'm not worried about the money, Roscoe; Everett Davis is a very good friend; you must know that.'

'I do, but sometimes part of my job is to protect you from your friends.'

'I appreciate that, but I owe him, and this time I feel I have to do it. He wants me in Vegas in ten days. I'd like you to get back to him, cut the nicest deal you can without screwing him financially, but make it work.'

I could see him think. 'How would it be,' he said slowly, 'if we did it for no fee but a sizeable percentage of the gross, say five points? With your name on the marquee, Mr Davis will be guaranteed a distribution deal, so you wouldn't be robbing him.'

'Whatever it takes, make it happen for me, and tell him I want the top suite in the Bellagio.'

He grinned. 'They tell me New York New York is pretty good.'

'I prefer the real version. See you.' I closed the program and he disappeared.

I opened my contacts file and began to scroll down; I stopped at 'K' and dialled a number.

There's this guy I know called Mark Kravitz. I met him a few years ago through Miles Grayson, who hired him as my 'personal assistant' on my first movie project. Actually he was my bodyguard, but that's another story. I don't know exactly where he comes from, or what his background is, but I've made some guesses that I reckon are close to the mark. Whatever he was in the past, he's heavy duty now, and has connections all over the place; I don't use him as a minder any more, I use him to find them. He recruited Jay Yuille for me, then helped Jay find Conrad and Audrey and, in each case, did a damn fine job. He provides other services, though.

He was at home when I called. 'Hi, boss!' (He still calls me that sometimes.) 'What's up? Nothing's gone wrong with Connie and his missus, I hope.'

'No, they're great. But something's happened and it's just a bit outside Conrad's job description. There's an American guy by the name of Paul Wallinger . . .' I spelled it out for him. '. . . who's in my bad books.'

'What's he done?'

I gave him a quick rundown.

'What do you want to know?'

'Anything there is; whether he's got any previous form for openers. I'd like to know whether the FBI might want to speak to him. I'd like to know whether he's still in the Minneapolis area. I'd like to know whether Wallinger's his real name.'

'I'd bet that it is.'

'Why so sure?'

'Work it out: he went to Grosvenor Square to have the child added to his passport; he'd hardly have done that if it was a phoney. That probably tells you that he isn't on anyone's wanted list either. But leave it with me: someone who pulls a con like this is not a beginner, believe me. I'll get something on him.'

'Soonest?'

'Soon as I can. What are you planning to do?'

'I'm planning to help Prim get her money back, and her kid, if I can.'

'By any means necessary?'

'What does that imply?'

'This guy's outside the law, Oz. He's hardly in a position to complain to the police if, let's say, someone used basic methods to persuade him to cough up the child and the cash.'

'Much as I would like to give him a going-over, Mark, I can't go anywhere near there. I've got my reputation to take care of, and my family's well-being.'

He laughed. 'Since when did you get cautious?'

'It comes with age, kids and money.'

'I can't knock that. Wallinger probably wouldn't be too easy to crack, anyway. From what you're saying to me, he's been working on this for three years. He probably targeted your ex; that meeting in Gleneagles wasn't spur-of-the-moment, no chance of that.'

'Wee Tom wasn't in his plans, surely.'

'I don't imagine so, but . . .'

I cut across him. 'That's what I don't understand, Mark. Why did he take the kid?'

'He's his father; maybe he loves him and couldn't stand the thought of never seeing him again.'

'Yeah, and maybe I really did play cricket for England.'

'In that case, there's only one answer: he's going to sell him.'

'Sell him? On fucking e-Bay, you mean?'

'It would probably be legal, in some states at least: he could offer him up for adoption and invite bids. But I wasn't thinking of anything as downmarket as that. Remember who Tom is. He's not just your ex's son, he's Miles Grayson's nephew. Wallinger may have cleaned your wife out, but Miles is one of the richest blokes in Hollywood. Are you going to bet me that at some point, maybe quite soon, he doesn't offer to return the kid to Primavera in return for, let's say, the money he's embezzled already, plus another couple of million sterling?'

'That would be blackmail, man.'

'Bollocks, boss. He's the child's father, and he has *de facto* custody. If Prim agreed to the deal and Miles put up the extra cash, it would all be above board . . . more or less. It strikes me, boss, that friend Paul's been thinking on his feet. Are you sure you don't want him taken out? It would be a hell of a lot cheaper.' He chuckled, but I know Mark: he was being dead serious.

'No, mate,' I told him. 'Potentially it would be a hell of a lot more costly, so let's forget you ever asked me that.'

'The answer's no, then?'

'Absolutely.'

'Fair enough; I like to be totally clear about things like that. I'll get digging straight away and report as soon as I can.'

I hung up, and walked through the house to the leisure wing, as we sometimes called it when we were being flash. Susie was there, feeding wee Jonathan . . . from a bottle: the real stuff had gone with the cutting of the teeth . . . and watching Janet as she played with a toy in the far corner, well away from the pool.

'What do you think?' I asked her.

She bridled at once. 'I think it's bloody disgraceful!' she exclaimed. 'When they get this, this . . . this swine back, I hope they throw the whole bloody set of encyclopaedias at him, never mind the book. Theft, child kidnap, he's got a lot to answer for.'

'Not as much as you might think; for openers, in the absence of a court order against him, a father can't kidnap his own kid. As for the money . . . Prim let him manage it, remember. It might not be as easy as you think to persuade an American court to extradite him.'

I called across to my daughter. 'Hey, Janet, want to come and help me finish making the grown-ups' dinner?' It was a rhetorical question; she came running.

Actually there wasn't much to do; Ethel would have raised hell if I'd let her get fish all over her hands so I gave her the kitchen scales, sat her on a stool and let her weigh out three portions of the gluten-free pasta that Susie and I prefer, a hundred grams each for

67

the women and a hundred and fifty for Daddy, but don't tell them, eh, wee Jan.

She did it very carefully, picking up every piece she dropped on to the work surface and putting it back into the packet. I let her have a Coke for her trouble; when Ethel came to fetch her at bedtime she saw it and treated me to her best nanny glower, but what the hell? My dad let Ellie and me drink the stuff, and he's a bloody dentist.

When Prim came down for dinner, she seemed to be back on an even keel. She saw the fizzy water on the table, and smiled softly. 'Very tactful, Oz,' she said, 'but I don't want any more to drink for a while, so don't let me put you two off having wine.'

'All for one and one for all, d'Artagnan,' I replied.

She shook her head. 'No, I must be Porthos; he was the piss artist among the Musketeers, wasn't he?'

'Don't worry about us,' Susie assured her. 'We give our livers a rest quite often.' That was more tactful than true.

Prim was impressed when she saw the salad, which I'd dressed with balsamic vinegar and chopped herbs. 'Did you teach him to do this, Susie?' she asked.

'No,' I replied. 'My mother did; I made it for you several times. You must have been too blootered to remember.'

'Hey, I didn't drink that much in those days. What you saw this afternoon has only happened recently; since Paul and Tom disappeared, mostly I've hung around the flat, drinking and waiting for the phone to ring.'

'But it hasn't?'

'No.' She paused. 'Well, it has done, a couple of times in the last fortnight. The first time, I nearly jumped out of my skin. I thought it had to be him, but it wasn't, just some bloke looking for him. I told him he didn't live there any more then hung up. When he called again a few days later, I got really stroppy with him, and told him to eff off. Apart from that, for all that I stared at it, for hours on end, the damn thing's been silent.'

Her mouth twisted. 'That's all going to stop; the fight-back begins as of now.'

'As of now?' I quoted back at her. 'Does that mean that you haven't told the police about the theft?'

'Yes,' she admitted. 'Or no; as in no, I haven't.'

'Why the hell not?'

She sighed. 'I don't know, Oz. The attitude of those two idle unsympathetic bastards who turned up when I did call them didn't exactly encourage me to ask for their help again. Plus, I had this vision of Paul being arrested in the States and Tom being taken into care. Or maybe my mind was just fuzzed with the drink. I don't know.'

'It must have been fuzzed. If the police had put you off, why not call Dawn and Miles? Or why not just try my mobile number, without the elaborate charade to make me call you?'

She put down her fork, and looked me in the eye. 'Do you remember the last time I saw you guys, when I came to Edinburgh with Nicky Johnson and Miles laid him out . . . probably for his own relative safety, for God knows what you would have done to him? He and Dawn let me know what they thought of me, and you, you chose that moment to let me find out that you and Susie had a child together.'

'Hey, I didn't choose it on purpose; I honestly thought you must have known.'

'Whatever! After that I could hardly come crawling back to either of you, drunk and tearful, to tell you that I'd made a complete arse of myself. Well, could I?'

'As it happens, the answer to that is "Yes", but all you'd have had to tell either of us was that you were in big trouble and needed help. Dawn and Miles are parents as well, remember.'

She seemed to soften. 'How is Bruce?'

'Nearly as big as his dad, last time I saw him, and he's only just coming up on four. They're talking about having another. You've hurt them, you know, Prim, by cutting them out of your life.'

Her eyes went moist again, my cue to clear away the salad plates.

They were dry when I returned, carrying a big pot filled with

Blackstone's special *pasta pescado*, as I liked to call it, and three bowls, all on a tray. She and Susie were talking quietly, and carried on until I had finished dishing up.

'You never did this for me,' Prim asserted, when she'd tasted the sauce.

'I bloody did, when we had that apartment in St Marti, before . . .' I stopped myself, but I should have known she'd carry on.

'. . . before you left me to go back to Jan.'

'Yeah, okay.'

'No wonder I don't remember it, then.'

'Hey, little Miss Innocent, if we're casting up, what about . . .'

'Enough!' Susie shouted. 'We are not casting up . . .' She grinned. '. . . or the pasta will either get cold or be thrown all around the room, and it's too good for that.'

That was one thing we were all agreed on: it was so good that not only did Prim wolf hers down, by the time she'd had seconds there was hardly any left for me.

Dessert was easy; it was Häagen-Dazs time, vanilla chocolate fudge, with some white-chocolate sauce poured over it. Susie made a disapproving face, but she ate hers all the same; we don't do it often. When she and Prim were finished, they went off to the kitchen with the empties. I moved back to the leisure wing. Being midsummer in Scotland there was still plenty of daylight. I was enjoying it when they returned with two coffees, and what was left in the cafetière. I don't drink much of the stuff these days; my way of keeping consumption under control is not to have it at all at home.

'So,' said Susie, heavily, after she had she folded herself into an armchair, 'what are you going to do, Oz? This bastard Wallinger has got to be brought to book, and Prim has to get Tom back, and her money.'

'I've already done something.' I told them about my call and my instructions to Mark Kravitz.

'I've met him, haven't I?' Prim ventured, tentatively.

I nodded. 'A few years back.'

She gave a quick uncertain look. 'I remember him. He's sort

70

of . . . sinister? No, that's not the word. He's a bit dangerous, isn't he?'

'He can be, but I've told him just to find out whatever he can about the guy and not to have anything nasty done to him.'

'Are you sure he understood you?' Susie asked.

'Certain, love.'

'Could you change that?' Prim muttered, grimly. 'I think I'd like him good and dead.'

I looked at her. 'Let me tell you something: you don't ever say that to me, or anyone else, especially anyone else, ever again. If you come out with something like that in front of the wrong person, and he thinks you mean it . . . you could find yourself in so deep you won't even see the surface.'

'What makes you think I don't mean it?'

'Unless you tell me you don't, I won't lift another finger to help you.'

'You never used to be quite so scrupulous.'

'I'm not playing games, Prim.'

'Okay, I promise, when I find out where Paul is I won't hire a hit man. Is that okay?'

'That'll do.'

'Good, because I want to rip his balls off personally.'

I remembered what Dawn had said about her. 'When we get to that stage, there may be a queue. This man didn't happen upon you by accident, and make it all up as he was going along. There's a fair chance you're not the first rich widow or divorcee he's fleeced. Let me ask you something: when you met him up at Gleneagles, when he was on that golfing holiday, did you ever see his clubs?'

'He told me he hired them from the pro shop.'

'But you never thought to check?'

'Why should I? He was my escape route.'

'Mug. One quick question and you might have saved yourself a lot of grief: a real golfer doesn't hire.'

'Maybe not, but if I had asked that question, I might never have had Tom.' She had me there; I didn't take it any further.

'Oz,' my wife butted in, 'I've been thinking.'

'When are you not, my angel?'

She ignored my idle sally. 'Everett's movie,' she continued. 'If you agreed to do it, you'd be in the US, and maybe you'd have time to ask a few questions.'

'It may have escaped your notice, Sooz, but America is one hell of a big place.'

'I know, but still. If you didn't ask them yourself, you could hire people over there.'

'I'll think about it.' Best to let it be her idea, I reasoned. 'But I've got something else in mind before that. You need some top-class legal advice, Prim, and I know just where you can get it.'

I took my mobile from its hiding place in the breast pocket of my shirt and called my sister. My nephew Jonny's voice sounded in my ear. 'This is the Sinclair residence.'

'And this is your uncle, kid.'

'Hello, Uncle Kid,' he said cheerfully. 'What can I do for you?' I was pleased at his flippancy. Jonny had been through a bad time a few months before; I'd been very worried about him for a while, but he was coming through it okay.

'You can stop being bloody cheeky and put me on to your mother.'

'I'll see if she's available.'

'Why wouldn't she be? Is Perry Mason there?'

'Who?'

'A fictional lawyer; before your time.'

'Ach, you mean Harvey? Yes, he is actually.'

'Well, actually, it's him I want to talk to.'

'Hang on, then.'

I waited for a few seconds, then a few seconds more. Finally, the advocate announced himself. 'Harvey January.' Jonny couldn't have told him who was on the line.

'Hiya, it's Oz here. You and I are having lunch next Tuesday, yes?'

'It's in my diary.'

'Can we do it tomorrow? There's something I want to pick your brain about.'

72

He paused for thought. 'Yes, I suppose so, if it's all right with Ellen.'

'It will be. Where?'

'Where's good for you?'

'How does Gleneagles sound? Bring Ellie and the boys, and their golf clubs, and yours too.'

There was a pause. 'I don't play, Oz.' For a man with prospects of the Bench, that was a surprising admission.

I smiled. 'Let me suggest something to you, then. If you have any plans for my sister that involve impressing our father, her sons, and me, you might give it a try.'

'Wouldn't they like sailing?'

'My dad would drown you if you tried to get him into a boat.'

He sighed, but I could hear a quiet laugh there too. 'Ah, well, if that's what it takes. I'll see you tomorrow.'

'Meet me at midday, for lunch at twelve thirty; we'll get the brain-picking over with first.'

As I put my mobile away the girls were watching me. 'Who was that?' Prim asked.

'That was a man who wants to make a good impression on me. In the process he might do you some good too.'

'But why Gleneagles?'

'One, because it's where this all started, so it's as good a place as any. Two, because it's handy for your parents. The lunch invite doesn't include you. Once we've talked to Harvey, you're going to see your mum and dad, and you're going to do something you should have done a while ago: you're going to tell them about their grandson.'

10

When Ellie came into the lobby of the Gleneagles Hotel and saw Prim waiting with Susie, the kids and me, her mouth dropped open. For a second I thought we were in for a scene: my sister is not the sort to stifle her true feelings. However, I managed to catch her eye and to shake my head very slightly, and succeeded in putting her off.

So instead of coming out with something on the lines of 'What the *&!% is she doing here?', she simply ignored her former sister-in-law altogether, instead rushing up to embrace Susie and make a fuss of Janet and the baby.

The older Jonathan, my nephew, was intrigued, though. I could see his mother's question in his eyes, although without the indignation. He's known Primavera since he was a kid, and wasn't close to any of the aggro that happened between us. As for Colin, the subtleties of inter-personal relationships are lost on him and, I hope, always will be. He just beamed and said, 'Hello, Auntie Prim!'

It all went over Harvey January's head too. The beefy, dark-haired QC stood there, with a vague uncertain smile on his big square face, one of his eyebrows rising a little at Colin's greeting. I guessed that Ellie had filled him in on the family history.

I took charge of events straight away. After I had kissed Ellie hello, whispering, 'Susie'll explain,' in her ear at the same time, I took Harvey by the elbow and ushered him and Primavera through to a small meeting room, which I had reserved for our discussion.

I introduced the two of them. I was right about my sister: I didn't have to explain who Prim was. 'Harvey,' I began, 'I'm proposing to

74

take serious advantage of our brief acquaintance, or of the fact that you're sleeping with our Ellen, however you prefer to look at it. My ex here is in serious trouble, and she needs a guiding hand. I know you can't represent her directly, but you might be able to point her in the right direction, and recommend appropriate people.'

The QC shifted in his chair, frowning. 'Oz, under Faculty of Advocates rules I'm not supposed to do even that without a solicitor's instruction.'

'I know, but that's covered by the phrase "take serious advantage". You're not going to be quoted to anyone, so will you hear us out?'

He gave a diffident smile. 'You mean that this meeting isn't taking place?'

'What meeting? I'm just your girlfriend's brother, filling you in on a wee bit of history, something that began in this very hotel, two years ago.' I carried on and told him Prim's story, as quickly and clearly as I could. A minute into my tale, he produced a hand-held computer from his pocket . . . these days, high-flyers like Harvey and I don't go anywhere without one of those . . . and began making notes on it with a stylus.

When I was finished, he whistled. 'You wouldn't get away with that in court,' I said.

'I might, before some judges I know. In fact they'd probably be whistling themselves after a piece of evidence like that. A carefully planned, long-term, major fraud, with the child as a surprise twist; very little deception on this scale comes before the Scottish Bench, I assure you.'

He glanced at his palm-top, reviewing his notes. 'If this was a consultation,' he murmured, 'I'd ask you a couple of questions, Primavera.'

She leaned forward. 'Such as?'

'The first would be whether Mr Wallinger ever proposed marriage to you, or you to him.'

She shrugged her shoulders. 'Not in the get-down-on-your-knees sense. We discussed it, but we had both come from failure, so we weren't in any rush. I just assumed it was something that would happen eventually.'

'Who initiated these discussions?'

She looked up and over Harvey's head for a few moments, then back at him. 'Now that you ask me to recall it, whenever the subject came up, it was me who raised it.'

'My next questions would be about the fraud, if I were to ask them. Clearly it could only have happened if Mr Wallinger was acting as your financial adviser. Is that the case?'

'Yes. I was pregnant when Paul raised the subject of my financial affairs for the first time. He said that since I was having his child, he supposed that he had a duty as a parent to ensure that its interests were protected properly. He was laughing when he said it, but I saw the sense in it.'

'You took him seriously?'

'Yes.'

'So what did you do?'

'I reconsidered the arrangement I had at the time. My funds were managed in Edinburgh, by a company that Oz had found for me. I remember when I told Paul he gave me one of those kindly looks of his that implied I was an idiot. "It's unusual," he said, "to let your ex have as much continuing influence over your life." I saw the sense in that too, so I asked him if he'd be happier if he was looking after me. He was hesitant, at first.'

'But you persuaded him?'

'Goddamnit, I suppose I did. I thought he was a bloody stock-broker, didn't I?'

'A slight flaw in your case,' said Harvey, 'but not crippling by any means, especially since he presented himself as such. How did you give him the authority to act for you?'

'I wrote to my former manager firing him, and instructing him to send all my papers to me, by registered post, then I signed letters that Paul produced, one for each of the companies in which I was invested, naming him as my new financial adviser and giving him full authority to act on my behalf.'

'How was he described in those letters?'

'As my partner.'

'Excellent. If I was your counsel I'd be able to argue that his appointment was based upon the trust flowing from an established relationship, in which a child was at that time expected.'

'Will you be my counsel, Harvey?' she asked.

'You'll have to instruct me formally, through a solicitor, but if you do that, I will. Do you have a lawyer in Scotland?'

'No, but . . .' She looked at me.

'I have,' I said, diving into my pocket for my phone. 'And when I'm around, he works on Saturdays.'

I rang Greg McPhillips, my personal brief, hoping that he wasn't at his golf club, for mobiles are banned there. As luck had it he had just left; the background noise told me that his Bluetooth connection picked up my call in his car.

'Hi,' he answered cheerily. 'I'm just on my way home, love. I won't be long; we'll be in plenty of time for the wedding, promise.'

'That's good to know, darling,' I replied, 'but I'm having a hell of a fucking job getting my dress to fit, so we might not be going after all.'

'Pillock, Blackstone.'

'I was once told by a homosexual in London that a pillock is a man with a small penis. I ask you to withdraw that remark, or I'll have to instruct you to sue yourself. If you want a list of witnesses against you, there's one sitting right here.' Prim and Harvey both stared at me.

'Withdrawn, withdrawn; I've played squash with you, remember. Now what the bloody hell do you want?'

'I want you, right now this minute, to instruct Mr Harvey January, QC, to act in the case of Miss Primavera Eagle Phillips, against Mr Paul Wallinger.'

'You serious? Harvey January? He's a top silk.'

'Believe it.'

'Have you got his number?'

'Have I ever; her name's Ellen. He's right here; now repeat to him what I just said.'

'Were you serious about the Eagle bit too?'

'I'm afraid so. It's Prim's middle name, so secret that once you know it she has to kill you. Her mother is close to nature;

77

she saw a mountain eagle in Spain on the night Prim was conceived.'

'Thank God it wasn't a vulture!'

'I've often thought that, but never had the courage to say it. Here's Harvey, just repeat the instruction as I gave it to you.' I passed the phone across.

The advocate took it, listened for a few seconds, then said, 'I accept.' They conversed quietly for another minute or so, then Harvey said, 'I'll get back to you as necessary with any specific requirements,' and returned the handset.

'Thanks, Greg,' I told him. 'Enjoy the wedding.'

'I'd rather be cutting my toenails with a chainsaw,' he admitted. 'You keep an eye on that Eagle, d'you hear? She's had her talons in you before; don't let it happen again.'

'It's okay, I'm a protected species too. Cheers.'

I turned back to Harvey. 'Right, that's taken care of. What do we do now?'

'We go on the attack,' he replied at once, 'on two fronts. First thing on Monday morning, we will go to the Sheriff Court to seek, and undoubtedly obtain, an interim interdict prohibiting Mr Wallinger from taking Tom out of the United Kingdom without Primavera's consent. I know that the horse has bolted, but it will also require that he return him here forthwith. We will also initiate proceedings to award her full legal custody.'

He looked at me. 'To do that, we'll need to cite an address in Scotland. Can I use yours, Oz?'

'No, no, a thousand times no. That would make the tabloids in a big way, and neither Susie nor I would like that.'

'Semple House, Auchterarder.' Harvey turned his gaze to his new client. 'That's my parents' address,' she told him. 'Will it do for your purposes?'

'Fine, as long as your parents are upstanding citizens.'

'As up as you'll find,' I assured him.

'We will need, of course, the child's birth certificate. Do you still have it, or did Mr Wallinger take that with him?'

'He took it.'

'In that case we'll need a duplicate. You can apply for one on-line, but that will take a couple of weeks. Do you have a reliable friend in London?'

Prim shook her head. 'No, I was totally wrapped up in Paul. I never had time to make other friendships.'

'I can handle that,' I said. 'What does he have to do?'

'He needs to go to the Family Records Centre in London. It's in Myddelton Street, near King's Cross, and by happy chance it's open on Saturdays, for the convenience of amateur genea-logical researchers. They will issue an official duplicate certificate.'

I called Mark Kravitz there and then; I didn't ask what he was doing, only where he was. He understood the problem at once; better than that, he knew the FRC well, and had a contact there. *Where does he not have a contact?* I asked myself. He undertook to get the replacement certificate that afternoon, and courier it to Greg McPhillips overnight. 'That's done,' I told Harvey. 'What's the other front?'

'At the first opportunity, Miss Phillips must make a formal complaint to the police, alleging theft of her funds by Mr Wallinger.'

'Where?' asked Prim. 'Will I need to go back to London?'

'No, you don't have to do that. If we're asserting your Scottish residence, you can complain to your local force. It's better in some ways; frankly, a two-and-a-half-million-pound fraud is small potatoes for the Metropolitan Police, but it will get attention in Scotland.' He glanced back at me. 'Oz, I don't suppose you have a tame policeman as well?'

'No, but I know someone who has plenty.' I took out the trusty mobile again and called Ricky Ross. He and I were the best of enemies once, but we've turned into pretty good friends. He was a detective superintendent in Edinburgh until he made an arse of himself in an investigation in which I was more than peripherally involved, but he recovered from that débâcle to form a successful security business. He's also kept many of his old CID pals, and that can come in very handy.

79

In his business, he's always contactable. His phone was on auto-answer, but when I left a message, he called me back inside a minute.

'What's up?' he asked. 'It's not my birthday, so I guess something must be.'

'I need to talk to a copper, Rick, someone who's good at chasing embezzled funds.'

I'll swear he started to laugh, then choked it off. 'Who's been daft enough to steal your money?' he exclaimed.

'Not mine, Primavera's.'

'The ex? Where is she?'

'Right now? Auchterarder.'

'That's Tayside. There's a guy in Strathclyde she should speak to; it would be better if she was in their area.'

'That's okay. She's coming back to my place later on today, and that's covered by Strathclyde Police.'

'Fine. I'll speak to him and make an appointment. What evidence does she have, bank statements and the like?'

I asked her. 'Nothing with me,' she replied. 'It's all in my safe at the flat.'

'No worries; you can fly down tomorrow and get it.' I put the phone back to my ear, but Ricky had heard it all.

'I'll fix something up for Monday, then,' he promised, 'assuming the guy's available and not on holiday or anything. His name is Detective Inspector Ian McLaren, and he's a specialist fraud investigator. I'll ask him to go to Loch Lomond; I'll get back to you with a time. By the way,' Ricky paused, 'just so as you know, he was a friend of Mike Dylan.'

'Noted, but he's ancient history. Thanks.' I killed the call. 'Copper taken care of, Harvey,' I said, then glanced at my watch. 'That's enough for now. You go and join the family for a sherry, or whatever you top lawyers drink pre-lunch these days. I'll join you after I've run an errand.'

'What's that?' Prim asked.

'You,' I told her. 'This has been the easy part of your day; in case you've forgotten, I'm now going to take you home, where you will

80

tell your mother and father the whole truth and nothing but the truth.'

She stood and gave me a pale smile. 'Okay, but you may not make it to Semple House. Remember, you've told the world my middle name.'

11

I did, though. Incidentally, on the subject of Phillips forenames: Primavera was christened such because she was conceived in the springtime, in Spain; the Eagle part, you know about. I'll leave you to work out why her sister is called Dawn, but their father once confided to me that she narrowly missed having Kellogg as a middle name, and I don't think old Super-Dave was joking.

I dropped her at Semple House, then watched her walk up the driveway to the front porch and ring the bell: that's how much I trusted her not to do a runner as soon as my back was turned and just spend a couple of hours walking around town or, worse, in the pub. I even waited until I saw the door open before I drove off.

Ellen didn't press me too hard when I got back to the hotel, although we were seated together at the lunch table. 'She's in trouble, is she?' was all she asked.

'Yes. Harvey will tell you all about it later on, I'm sure.'

'Not if he's acting for her, he won't: he's hot on client confidentiality.'

'Tell him I've given you special dispensation.'

'You sound like the Pope. You really do think a lot of yourself these days, wee brother, don't you?'

I crossed myself, surreptitiously. 'Does it show?'

She smiled. 'It's not your public image, don't worry. But you've changed: there's an authority about you that wasn't there before. It used to be that all our lives revolved around Dad, but not any more.' She glanced sideways at me. 'Incidentally, I'm glad you two have made it up, whatever it was that was wrong between you. He mentioned that you'd been to see him.'

82

'What makes you think there was anything wrong?'

'Credit me with sense, and powers of observation, please. Just because I never asked doesn't mean I never knew or didn't care.'

'Okay, I admit it. We had a disagreement, but it's sorted.'

'Well, now that it is, how about you putting in a word with him for Harvey?'

'Hey,' I whispered, 'I'm only just recognising the guy's existence myself.'

'Because it suits you?'

'Of course.' I grinned at her. 'But don't worry, I'm being won over. In fact, if you ask him, I've already advised him that the way to Dad's heart is through a golf swing that's slightly less efficient than his.'

Ellie laughed at that. 'I know; he told me. He's even going to give it a try this afternoon.'

'That's good; I brought a spare set just in case. He can buy himself a pair of golf shoes in the pro shop.'

'You underestimate your future brother-in-law.'

'My what?'

She went a very un-Ellie-like pink at her slip. 'You heard. But shut up about it until he's spoken to Dad and to you, and I've spoken to the boys.'

'That's why Susie set us up to have lunch on Tuesday?'

'Exactly. You see, bro, your women have still got your number . . . even the one who's not here right now. Anyway, as I was saying, you're selling Harvey short. He and Jonny went out this morning, early, and came back with a pair of Footjoy shoes, and a Gore-Tex rain-suit, and last but not least a set of Taylor-made clubs, and a big bag.'

'Balls,' I said.

'It is not! It's true.'

'Did he buy himself any golf balls, Ellen?' I asked her patiently. 'The rest is useless without them.'

I glanced across at my nephew; I had raised my voice so he could hear me. 'Titleist Pro V1, Uncle Oz,' he said, with a grin. 'Two dozen.'

'Let's hope that's enough.' Jonny had done the pro a favour in his advice. The gear Ellie had described must have cost Harvey a right few hundred quid; I found myself hoping for the kid's sake that he didn't turn out to be a no-hoper.

As it turned out, I needn't have worried. I'd booked a four-ball on the Queen's Course, the shortest of the three eighteen-holers, for two thirty. That allowed half an hour after lunch for me to take Harvey into the practice net and show him how to swing, not the full John Daly grip-it-and-rip-it style, but something nice and simple with a short backswing. He seemed to have a natural eye for the ball, for after a few awkward swipes, he was soon able to clip it pretty straight with the four clubs that I advised him to use out of his very expensive full set.

I paired him with Jonny on the course, and I took Colin as my partner. Since he's only a wee lad yet, I told him he could drive off the ladies' tees. Mistake, Uncle Oz: the look he gave me would have done credit to his mother. (To emphasise his point, the tee-shot he hit off the first would have done credit to his grandfather.)

Harvey was nervous, when it came to his turn, but I told him to try to imagine that he was in the High Court, pleading before Lord Emslie. That seemed to settle him down, for he plonked one up the middle, around ten yards short of Colin's ball.

We didn't keep score . . . it wouldn't have been fair . . . but under Jonny's guidance Harvey did okay. I could tell he was concentrating: the Queen's, like all the Gleneagles courses, is one of the most beautiful in the world, but he didn't even notice the scenery. He was surprised when I shook his hand after we had holed our putts on the eighteenth, and even more so when Jonny and Colin did too. Like the rest of the game, that piece of etiquette was new to him.

'Did you enjoy that?' I asked him, as we walked back to the clubhouse.

'I have to admit that I did, very much. Do you think I'm ready to play with your father yet?'

'Have a few more rounds with the boys, and a couple of lessons from a good teaching pro. Then he should be able to take money off you honourably, which is all he'll expect of you.'

'That takes me back to my early years at the Bar.' That was the first piece of humour I ever heard him try. 'Are we still having lunch on Tuesday?' he asked me, as the boys walked on ahead.

'Let's keep our options open on that one,' I replied, 'till we see how Prim's business develops. But for the avoidance of doubt, I wish you and my sister all the best, and I hope you'll be very happy together. I have to say, for the sake of formality, that if you mess her about then, judge or not, I will kill you without hesitation, but I don't think there's a cat's chance in hell of that. Welcome to our crazy family.'

I stopped as we entered the hotel, and made a slight detour into the office area. I'm quite well known there, so just before lunch I'd taken advantage of the fact by asking if they could check something out for me. One of the booking staff knew Prim by sight too, and remembered her meeting up with an American guest.

The woman was waiting for me, looking pleased with herself. 'I've run that check you asked for, Mr Blackstone. The gentleman you mentioned did indeed register under the name Paul Wallinger. He booked a three-night dinner-bed-and-breakfast package . . .'

'Any golf included?'

'No, just accommodation and evening meal; he settled his bill with cash.'

'What, like ordinary folding money, the kind people hardly ever use here?'

'It is unusual, I agree.'

I thanked her and gave her some currency for her trouble, then rejoined the guys.

We found Ellie, Susie and the kids in the coffee lounge. When she saw how sun-flushed and contented her new man looked, my sister smiled with sheer delight, and that pleased me. I ordered three pints of beer shandy, and a Coke for Colin; if the waiter wondered whether or not Jonny was eighteen, he didn't worry enough to ask, so I didn't enlighten him.

I was able to keep an eye on the entrance from my seat. About ten minutes after our drinks had been served, I saw David Phillips's old Rover pull up on the driveway. Politeness, nothing else, made me go to greet them, although I didn't expect him to wait. I saw Prim lean forward from the back seat to kiss his cheek, and say her goodbyes to her mother; then she got out. Elanore turned to look back at her as Dave drove off. I was shocked to see that she was wearing a wig. 'Your mum,' I said. It was a question.

'Her cancer's back, Oz. It's in her lymphatic system. They're giving her chemo down at the Western General in Edinburgh, but the prognosis isn't too good. That's why I didn't say anything about Tom when I was here before.'

'Maybe I was an idiot for making you do it today, then.'

'No, you were right. She was blazing mad that I hadn't told her as soon as he was conceived. Now I feel guilty as hell, for the chances are that she'll never get to see him.'

She looked positively mournful, so I put a hand on her shoulder. 'She will, kid. I promise you that; she will.'

'But how, Oz? Tom's on the other side of the Atlantic, and for all the things that Harvey and Greg are going to do in court, they're not much use if we can't find him.'

'Didn't you hear me, girl? I made you a blood oath there. You came to me for help before anyone else. I'm touched by that, and I'm not going to let you down. Elanore will get to hold her grandson.'

12

On the way home, I told Susie what had happened in the meeting with Harvey, and that Prim was going to have to fly down to London next day to pick up some papers. 'If you fancy chumming her for the trip,' I said, 'I'll stay with the kids, since it's Ethel's weekend off.'

'Nice thought, darling, but I find London unbearably stuffy at this time of year. You're right, though; she should have company. You go with her.'

I wished that I'd kept my mouth shut. I didn't fancy spending my Sunday on the bloody shuttle. 'We could always send Conrad.'

'They've gone to Arran for the weekend, remember. They won't be back till tomorrow night. No, that's settled; you're going.' I waited for Prim to protest that she could handle it on her own, but she just sat there and said nothing.

As Susie said, it was settled. I booked us on to the nine o'clock flight to London next morning, returning late afternoon. I didn't say much on the drive to the airport; I never do, but Prim took it the wrong way.

'Oz, I'm sorry,' she said, as we drove east along the motorway. 'You don't really want to be doing this, do you? I've mucked up your life again with my troubles.'

'Enough of that,' I told her. 'If that was true, I wouldn't be here. You'd be in a taxi with a one-way ticket in your pocket.'

The flight to London was as quiet as I'd expected it to be; there was nobody within three rows of us. I declined British Airways' offer of breakfast, and settled instead for pretending to sleep. It didn't fool Prim, though; we've lived together for a good chunk of the last decade, so she knows the real thing when she sees . . . and hears . . . it.

We were over the Solway Firth when I felt a small sharp elbow in my ribs. 'Why do you think he did it?' she asked me, quietly.

'For money. He's a professional fraudster.'

'You don't think he might have loved me at the start?'

'Did he make you believe that he did?'

'Yes.'

'Did you make yourself believe that you loved him?'

There was a long silence. 'Honestly? No.'

'Not ever?'

'No.'

'Not even when you were carrying his child?'

'Not even then.'

Then I asked a very stupid question. 'How about me?'

'What do you mean?'

'Did you ever make yourself believe you loved me?'

'I didn't have to.'

'I wasn't worth the effort, I suppose.'

'No, you idiot. I didn't have to make myself believe it, because I did love you. From the moment I set eyes on you, in fact.'

For a few seconds I was speechless. Until that moment, I'd managed to persuade myself that our relationship had been based on pure lust and self-interest. Of course we'd said the three words to each other, in the early stages, but I'd said them before and not meant them, and she had too.

I decided against stupid question number two.

Instead I asked, 'So how can you look at Susie and me, far less be with us?'

'Because I'm a realist. I know that you never really loved me, and I know that I was as much to blame for our break-up as you were. Don't worry, I don't harbour any secret dreams of winning you back. I look at you with Susie, and I see how much you've changed. I watched you with your family yesterday. Your dad used to be its bedrock, but now you are.' That made me sit up, since Ellie had said much the same thing the day before. 'You used to be a taker, Oz,' she went on. 'With me, even with Jan, you were a taker. Now you're a giver, not because you're rich and famous, but because you've realised what you were and become a different person.'

'If that pleases you,' I told her, 'you've got Susie to thank for it.'

'Even though she took you from me?'

'Well, maybe "thank" is the wrong word. But it's true: it was Susie who made me look at myself through someone else's eyes, and see what they saw. When I did, I didn't like me very much. I was a very confused guy for a while. For the record, Susie never tried to take me from you. After that happened, even when I knew she was pregnant, I thought that staying with you, trying to make our marriage work, was the right thing to do, and Susie didn't fight against that. But with me filming in Toronto, and you in LA, at the time when we needed to be together, it didn't have a chance; not to mention the fact that you were screwing Nicky Johnson on the side.'

'I was angry with you.'

'I know, and I'm not knocking you for it. What I'm saying is that if I'd done the honest thing as opposed to what I saw as the right thing I'd have told you about the baby and given up the pretence.'

'And maybe I'd have forgiven you, confessed my sins with Nicky, we'd have gone on, me loving you, you doing the right thing. Who knows where it would have ended?'

'In a mess. So why did you run off with Nicky, if you loved me all along?'

'To find out how much you really cared. I knew it wasn't working; I thought . . . inasmuch as I thought about anything . . . that it might shock you into action. I hoped that you would come down to Mexico and we'd have a big scene and that you'd take me back with you. When you didn't, when you only phoned me, I was shocked. When I told you it was over and you didn't argue or try to persuade me, that made it worse.'

'So when you turned up in Edinburgh with Johnson . . .'

'I was still hoping to drag us from the wreckage.'

'Christ, Prim, you got the clown hurt and humiliated in front of a lot of people. His career's gone straight downhill since then, because nobody wants to upset Miles by hiring him. He's gone from being reasonably successful in movies to auditioning for crap parts on television.'

'God, is that true?'

'Yeah, but don't feel too sorry for him. Miles put detectives on him. He was giving one to someone else at the same time he was carrying on with you.'

'That makes me look an even bigger fool.'

I squeezed her hand. Until then, I'd been making a point of not touching her, but I forgot. 'That was then, and this is now. Until everything's sorted we're going to concentrate on two things, Tom and the money, in that order.'

She squeezed back, then raised my hand to her lips and kissed it. 'Thanks, for being a love.' She frowned. 'It's all Mike Dylan's fault in a way. If he hadn't gone bad, he and Susie would be married now, and maybe it would all have turned out differently with us.'

'The flaw in that argument, my dear, is that you and Dylan had a fling when he and Susie were engaged, and you, or so you say, were deeply in love with me.'

'I never said I was perfect.' She chuckled.

There was no answer to that, so I let the conversation lapse as the plane began its descent towards Heathrow.

There are always press photographers there, but happily none of them had thought to meet the Sunday-morning shuttle so we made it unobserved to the taxi rank, where I hailed a black cab and gave the driver Prim's address.

He turned out to be a cricket fan who had been to the movies. 'I saw you in *Red Leather*, Oz,' he began, as we pulled out into the roadway. 'Triffic. I just loved seeing all those Aussies gettin' 'it arahnd the 'ead.' He launched into an anti-Australian diatribe, which lasted all the way to Hammersmith. 'This your missus?' he asked, once his invective had been exhausted.

The words 'cabbies', 'the *Sun*' and 'tip-off' flashed before my eyes. 'My sister,' I lied.

In spite of the monologue, he found the address straight away; I

90

never cease to be impressed by the Knowledge, as the black-cab drivers call their photographic memory of the London street map, even if satellite navigation has overtaken it.

Prim told me that the flat was on the second floor; the block was new, and it looked as if the builder hadn't skimped on materials. There was a lift, but it was going up when we walked into the entrance hall, so we took the stairs instead. I waited while she dug a set of keys from the depths of her bag, then watched her slide a brass key into the mortise lock.

'That's funny,' she muttered. 'It seems to be jammed.' I reached forward and gave the key a twist, but it wouldn't budge.

'Are you sure you locked it?' I asked, getting her 'Do you think I'm daft?' look in return.

'Of course. You know how serious I am about security.'

I turned the key clockwise: there was no resistance and I heard a click. I did it again and heard another. 'Oh, yeah?'

'Damn it!' she said. 'I was sure. I really must have been drinking too much.'

I unlocked it again, then found the Yale key; there was no problem with that. When I stepped inside, though, instantly I was appalled. The door opened straight into a big living room, and the place was a shambles. Most of the sideboard drawers had been left open, newspapers were strewn all over the hardwood floor, a scream-coloured rug . . . No, I don't mean cream: it was so bright and garish that it made me want to scream . . . was crumpled as if somebody had tripped over it, and an empty wine bottle and two glasses stood on a coffee table.

'Bloody hell!' Prim exclaimed behind me.

'As you say, you really must have been boozing.'

'Oz, I didn't leave it like this,' she protested. 'Somebody's been in here. I was right: I did lock up properly.' She rushed off; I followed her into her bedroom. The place had been ransacked. All the drawers and the wardrobe doors were open, and a small wooden filing cabinet lay face down, as if it had overbalanced when both of its drawers were opened at once. I checked the rest of the place. It had been gone over, systematically.

91

I went back to the bedroom and righted the cabinet. Prim was sitting on the bed, both hands to her mouth, looking pale and shocked. I sat down beside her, put an arm round her shoulders, and drew her to me. 'Just what you didn't need, honey,' I murmured, kissing her softly on the forehead. 'I'm really sorry.'

I let her cry for a bit, then picked a box of Kleenex off the floor and wiped her eyes with a couple of tissues. She smiled up at me, wanly. 'I've really got a fucking rainbow on my shoulder, haven't I?' she said.

I smoothed her hair back off her face. 'You're not at your luckiest, I admit. Can you see anything missing?'

She looked around and shook her head, then got up, walked over to the wardrobe, knelt in front of it and threw a shoebox to one side. I looked over her shoulder and saw, where the box had lain, a small safe. I guessed that once it had had a combination lock, but all that was left was a hole, where it had been drilled out. I opened it, reached inside and took out a red jewel box. It was familiar; I had given it to Prim myself. I lifted the lid, and recognised none of what was inside. All that was in it looked like cheap costume stuff.

'Your diamonds?' I asked her. 'The necklace I gave you, those earrings, your engagement ring: were they here?'

'Yes,' she said, looking stunned. 'They're gone, Oz, all gone.'

'Where do you keep your papers, the ones we've come for?'

She jumped to her feet and opened the top drawer of the wooden cabinet. 'In here.' She flicked through a series of folders. 'They look okay,' she announced.

'We phone the police,' I insisted. 'Have you still got their number?'

She found it in a book by the phone in the living room: I let her make the call, listening as she spoke to the switchboard, then someone else. 'Right away?' she concluded. 'Good.'

I looked at the empty bottle on the coffee table: it was Pesquera, a taste Prim had acquired in Spain. 'Looks like that's something else they took,' I remarked. She reached out to pick it up, but I stopped her. 'Fingerprints.'

'Oh, of course.'

The apartment had a balcony overlooking the great grey River Thames; we went out there to wait for the police. As we sat in the two metal-framed armchairs, I noticed that the railings were lined on the inside with sheer plastic, as if to prevent a toddler climbing. 'Tom's toys,' I asked her. 'Did he take them all?'

To my surprise her eyebrows rose and she glared at me. 'I put the rest away in the wardrobe in his room,' she snapped, 'because every time I looked at them, they made me cry.'

She jumped up and ran inside, returning with a handful of framed photographs. She thrust one at me. 'That's him,' she exclaimed, 'with Paul. It's the most recent one I've got; I took it in the park, a week before Paul stole him.'

I looked at the dark-haired, blue-eyed little guy, and fell for him on the spot. He was a sturdy little muppet; he looked like his dad, but I could see a little of Prim about him.

I didn't take to the bloke who was sitting behind him on the grass in the park, though. I didn't take to him one bit. He was smiling, of course, but there was a narrowness to his eyes, and a weakness in them that, knowing what I knew, made me dislike him at first sight. I felt slightly hurt that Prim had thought he looked like me.

I was still gazing at the two of them when the door buzzer sounded: Prim went back into the house to answer its call. When she came back she had forgotten her earlier annoyance with me. 'They're on their way up,' she said. 'Of all people they just had to send the same pair who were here before.'

We went back inside and waited for the ring of the bell. When it came I opened the door; two men in crumpled dark suits walked past me without a look. 'Hello again, Ms Phillips,' said the older of the two. 'What's the panic this time?' He jerked his thumb over his shoulder in my direction. 'Is this the runaway bloke, come back after all?'

Having just seen the runaway bloke for the first time, I was not having that. For a brief period after leaving university, I had been a police officer. Just about the only thing I learned there was that as a public servant it behoved me to speak politely to citizens, at least to the respectable ones. I made that point there and then.

The guy glared at me. If I'd been casting a bad cop for a series I'd have picked him. 'And who the fuck are you, then, Mr Ex-copper? The latest flame?' He peered at me. 'I know you from somewhere, mate. Didn't I nick you a couple of years back?'

'No, you did not. My name's Oz Blackstone; I'm Ms Phillips's former husband. I'm an actor, and it's possible you may have seen me in a movie or on a poster. Now you know who I am, who the fuck are you? Let's see your warrant card, and your mate's.'

He looked at me for a few seconds longer, trying to work out whether or not I was bullshitting, I surmised. When he decided that I was not, he produced his card and nodded to his partner to do the same.

'Detective Sergeant Lacy,' he said, unsmiling but more courteous, 'and this is Detective Constable Garrett. What seems to be the trouble? We were told a robbery.'

'You were told correctly,' I replied. 'The place has been done over, and it must have happened since Primavera left on Friday.'

He looked around. 'I don't see anything obvious missing from here. The telly's there, and that looks like a Bose hi-fi unit.'

'They did nick what used to be inside a very decent bottle of Ribero del Duero,' I said, helpfully, with a nod towards the coffee table.

'You're sure that entry was forced? It looked all right when we came in.'

'The lock was picked, or a skeleton was used.'

'You sure, Mr Blackstone?' asked DC Garrett. He sounded more . . . how should I put it? . . . circumspect than his sergeant. 'Couldn't it have been Mr Wallinger, back for something he might have forgot? Wouldn't he have had a key?'

'No,' Prim told him. 'I had the locks changed a couple of weeks ago. In any event, this is my flat and he has no right being here in my absence.'

'In that case, ma'am,' Lacy countered, 'this is probably just the

94

local talent out to see if you've got anything worth nicking and deciding you ain't.'

'If that was the case, Sergeant,' I said, icily, 'they'd have been even dumber than you. But they weren't for they screwed the safe in the bedroom and took a hundred grand's worth of diamonds.'

'A hundred and fifty grand's worth, if you don't mind,' Prim corrected me. 'I had them revalued last year.'

I looked at the two detectives. 'So, you see, there really has been a break-in and I'd appreciate it if you two took it seriously. Otherwise I'm going to have to call someone else, beginning with your station commander. I promise you, I'll get his attention even if I don't have yours.'

DS Lacy got the message: he moved into full placatory mode. 'Okay, Mr Blackstone, okay; just keep calm. I'll call in our specialists right away.'

'You do that. When they get here, you can tell them that we've disturbed as little as possible; we've just checked on what's missing, that's all.'

'Cheeky bastards,' said Garrett, as his boss dug out a phone from his jacket. 'They turned the place over, drank a bottle of wine and left.'

'Didn't even wash the glasses.'

'It's better than crapping on the carpet. That's the norm.' Prim winced, visibly; the detective caught it. 'Sorry, ma'am.'

I took her out on to the balcony to wait for the forensics people. As we sat there, and as I thought about it, I came to a conclusion as to their likely findings: in a word, fuck all. Prim's visitors had been pros. They had picked the locks, they had searched the place efficiently, they had found the reasonably well-concealed safe, they had opened it expertly, having come equipped to do so if necessary. They had come for something specific, and they had not been about to mess up by stealing anything else, however valuable, that might ultimately have led back to them, or to their employer, had they tried to fence it. Diamonds are easy to move, especially if they're in a necklace, ring and earrings; take them apart and remodel them and they're untraceable.

They'd got what they were after, so would there be fingerprints on those two glasses, or anywhere else? Would there hell, as like.

My musing led my hand into my pocket, and to my mobile. I had patched in Mark Kravitz's number just in case, so I called it. 'Do you have any free time?' I asked him.

'Right now, yes.'

'I need to see you.'

'What? You want me to fly up to Scotland?'

'No need, Mark. I'm in London.'

'Where do you want to meet?'

'You tell me.'

'Okay, the Rockwell Bar in the Trafalgar Square Hilton. You know where that is?'

'If I said Trafalgar Square, would I be far off the mark?'

'Not a lot, but the address is two Spring Gardens, if you take a cab.'

I glanced at my watch: it was twenty past twelve. 'I'll see you at one.'

'What about me?' Prim asked, as I repocketed the Sony.

'You wait here. Starsky and Hutch in there will want to take a statement from you at some point. Plus, you need to get all your papers together, remember, once the scene-of-crime people let you.'

'What if they won't let me take them?'

'They will once they've dusted everywhere. I'd guess they'll find two sets of prints on the cabinet, yours and mine since I put the thing back on its base. Although I suppose they might still find Wallinger's too.'

'I doubt it. My cleaning woman is very thorough.'

'Okay. I'm sorry I have to leave you with these two, but I need to see Kravitz.'

I told the coppers that I was going out for a while. I'd half expected Lacy to ask me to wait till I'd given a formal statement, but he seemed more relieved to be seeing the back of me than anything else.

I left the building like Elvis and copped a taxi straight away, a much easier feat in London than in most cities. For example, in

96

New York, the yellow cabs have a customers' charter entitling passengers to a courteous driver who speaks English and knows his way around the city; finding all three in one man is a challenge, but just finding one who'll stop can be worse.

My second driver recognised me too, but he was much less gabby than the airport guy. He took me across the river and down Whitehall, dropping me at the front door of the Hilton, all done without even the slightest hint of a detour to ramp up the fare.

When I walked inside, I saw that the Rockwell Bar was busy. I was there before Mark and at first I thought I was going to lose out on a booth, but once again, the movie-star thing did the business for me. The blonde who was running things came over, smiling. 'Why Mr Blackstone,' she exclaimed, 'how good to see you again.' I'd never been there before, remember. 'Your table is right here.' She swept me past the other people in the queue . . . some were glaring, some were staring . . . and fixed me up with a view back across the square to old Horatio Nelson on his column. She started to clear away the other place that was set, but I palmed her a twenty . . . miserable Scots bastard, she probably thought . . . and asked her to leave it and to bring me two menus.

Mark arrived ten minutes later, neatly dressed and pressed as always, his stocky frame rendered unremarkable by expensive tailoring. 'Is this okay?' he said, looking around the crowded bistro. 'I meant I'd see you at the bar and we could go on from there, that's all. I wasn't expecting a sit-down lunch.'

He had a point: there was background music and plenty of babble, but when you're in my position you can never be quite sure who might be ear-holing your conversation. 'Tell you what,' he suggested, 'let's order, then go up on the roof terrace for a look around, and tell them. They'll hold it till we get back.'

That seemed sound to me, so we asked our waiter for two large steaks, medium, broccoli with mine and fries with his, plus a bottle of claret, told him to bring them in fifteen minutes then headed for the lift.

Up on the roof we weren't quite eyeball to eyeball with Nelson, but the view was pretty impressive nonetheless. There were plenty of people up there too, but we were able to find a quiet corner. Someone in the crowd spotted me and headed towards us, possibly with autograph in mind, but I've developed a warning-off look that works every time . . . unless I'm in Los Angeles: autograph-hunting is one of its biggest industries.

'What's brought you down here?' Mark asked straight away. 'You never said you were coming.'

I told him, then filled him in on what we had found in Prim's flat. 'Interesting,' he said, when I was finished.

'What do you make of it?'

'I can't say, as yet. Does she know if Wallinger had any friends in London?'

'As it turns out she doesn't know anything about him, nothing that's turned out to be the truth, apart from his real name, and the fact that he has a normal sperm count.'

'Has any mail come for him since he left? Or has anyone been asking after him?'

'The first, I couldn't tell you, but she did mention a couple of phone calls, from a bloke looking for him.'

'Recently?'

'Within the last fortnight. She told him that Wallinger had gone.'

'Then I'd guess he must have watched the place, and when Prim left, sent people in.'

'Could this be the reason why he disappeared so suddenly?'

'Possibly, or at least it could have made him go earlier than planned.'

'With the baby?'

'That's the puzzler.'

'Can you find out who these guys are, or who's behind them? I don't really fancy the boys from Sun Hill to get a result.'

'I can try. Want to hear what I've come up with so far?'

I nodded. 'If you're ready to tell me.'

'Yes, I've got something for you. First of all, our assumption was right: Paul Wallinger is his real name. He's thirty-eight years old, and he was born in St Paul . . . maybe that's where the Christian name came from . . . Minnesota, to John and Martha Wallinger, the oldest of their three children. Pop was a line manager with a firm of mechanical engineers in the city, till he snuffed it five years ago. They seem to have been a respectable middle-class family. Originally, Mr Wallinger was career military. He fought with the Rangers in Vietnam, was decorated several times, and was eventually invalided out with a chest wound that ultimately contributed to his death. Mom worked for a firm of asset managers in Minneapolis, across the river, and had done for over twenty years. While John was in Vietnam, she was a campaign worker for Vice President Hubert Humphrey, when he ran for President for the Democrats against Nixon in 1968. I believe she's still alive, but she'll be sixty-three now, and may be retired.'

'How do you know so much about them?'

'I read John's obituary in the *Minneapolis Star Tribune*. I did a search for Mom's name in the death listings, but I couldn't find it. There are half a dozen Wallingers listed in the twin cities' telephone directories. Three of them have the first initial M; of those two are in St Paul and one's in Minneapolis. I looked for J also, in case she didn't change the listing after her husband died. There's one, but it's in Minneapolis, not St Paul.'

He handed me a sheet of paper; I glanced at it and saw all six Wallingers, with phone numbers and addresses. There was also a business listing, a firm called HHH Asset, in Marquette Avenue. 'That's the company Mother worked for; maybe she still does.'

'Easily checked,' I said. 'What did the obituary say about Paul?'

'Not much, but there were other references to him on the website; he graduated from the University of Minnesota in 1988 with a BA . . .'

'Same year as I did from Edinburgh,' I remarked. 'What was his degree?'

'Theatre Arts, with distinction in vocal production and design and technical. He did an elective in play-writing.'

'Bloody hell, he's a qualified actor.'

'I suppose you could call him that, but when he left university he joined a local theatre as a stage manager rather than a performer. He did become a US Equity and a Screen Actors' Guild member, though, under the professional name of Paul Patrick Walls. Run a trace on that and you'll find him moving around the US through the nineties from theatre company to theatre company as a performer and occasionally as writer-director. He has some film credits too, some bit parts, some as a member of the screen-writing team but none of them in any movies that made serious money, apart from one, a Miles Grayson production called *Kidnapped*.'

'Son-of-a-bitch! Dawn was in that movie. It's where she and Miles met up.'

'I know; I did logistics and security for him on that job.'

'And after that?'

'After that, little or nothing. You might remember that when Miles and Dawn got involved he took some liberties with the storyline and had the script altered to make her role bigger. That led to some changes elsewhere. Wallinger's part was a minor one, and in the shake-up, most of his scenes wound up on the cutting-room floor. Miles never cast him again. He was never unemployed, though; according to the CV I found, he carried on doing theatre work, and had a few television parts. It looks as if his career was going steadily downhill, though, until about three years ago, when it seems to have come to a full stop.'

'The time-frame fits. Come on,' I said. 'Let's get back down-stairs; those steaks must be on the way by now.' I headed for the lift.

'What else do you want me to do?' Mark asked.

'See if you can find out who's behind Prim's visitors; apart from that, nothing. You've done a great job as it is. Send me a bill as soon as you've worked out your time and expenses.'

'I could find you someone in the States to follow up for you.'

'No. I don't want to scare the guy. Who knows how he might behave if he was panicked?'

'So he gets away with it?'

'Shit, no. I've got plans.'

'Such as?'

'Well, for a start, I'm going to pay a call on Granny Wallinger.'

100

13

As I had guessed, the forensics people didn't find a thing. When I got back to the flat they printed me with an electronic reader, but only to confirm that the second prints on the cabinet and the door handles were mine.

They took the two wine glasses, muttering something about DNA comparisons, but I knew that was just a bit of flash nonsense to impress the punters.

In my absence, a senior CID officer had turned up, a woman called DCI Grace. Lacy seemed to have been sent back to his kennel, for she and Garrett took formal statements from us, and promised to get in touch with Prim, should their investigation lead anywhere . . . not that she held out any hope that it would. She was so sympathetic that for a second I thought that maybe we should make the fraud complaint to her, until I remembered what Harvey had said about the Met's scale of priorities, and held my tongue.

I hadn't planned to tell Primavera at that point about my meeting with Kravitz, and what it had turned up, but I should have known better. She let me sit in silence all the way back to Heathrow, through a coffee in the Executive Lounge, and through the buffet service on the plane . . . I gave her my rubber sandwich, since she'd gone without lunch . . . before she began the interrogation.

'So?' she said, as the last crumb was cleared.

It's not what you say, it's the way that you say it. I caved in at once and told her Mark's story, from start to finish. When I'd finished, she looked out of the window, down on the mountains of the Lake District, their craggy peaks standing tall on the cloudless day. 'So it really was all an act,' she murmured.

'Looks like it, only I don't imagine that Tom was in the script. Otherwise, he played the part to perfection. I wish I'd gone to the University of Minnesota if it prepares you that well for a stage career.'

'What happens next?'

'I'm going to find him. I promised you I'd get your kid back.'

She took my arm and leaned against me. 'Oz, love, I'm really grateful for everything you've done already. I can't interfere with your life any more.'

'You try and stop me. I care about you, Prim; this guy's worked you over in the worst possible way. He thinks he's laughing, but he doesn't know the tears that are on the way. He's going to have to answer to me.'

'But how will you trace him?'

'He's left a trail. I'll start with his mother.'

'How are you going to find the time?'

I grinned at her. 'Circumstances make it easy. I've agreed to do Everett Davis's movie in Las Vegas. I've got eight days before I have to be there, maybe more if I can negotiate the shooting schedule with the director.'

'Oz, are you sure?'

'Certain.'

'In that case I'm coming with you.'

I wasn't so sure I liked the sound of that. 'Hey, wait a minute! I'm a big boy, I don't need minding.'

'I'm not thinking about that. I want to be there when you find Tom. You're a stranger; if you turn up out of the blue and confront his daddy, the poor wee thing will be scared out of his wits. Plus, on your own, what could you do? Paul could probably have you arrested for attempted kidnap. But if I'm there . . .'

She had a point. 'Okay,' I conceded, 'but only if Susie's happy with the idea. Otherwise I'll go armed with Harvey's interim interdict and present it to the local district attorney.'

'And by the time he does anything, Paul will have moved on.'

'Let's talk to Susie. Once you explain why you need to go, she probably won't object.'

102

For once, Prim looked doubtful. 'I'm not as sure as you,' she said. 'In her shoes, I don't know if I'd be generous enough to let you go off alone to the US with your ex.'

'Yes, but you're not in her shoes, so you don't know about her generosity. Whether or not she trusts you isn't relevant. The question is whether or not she trusts me.'

'Exactly.'

In spite of myself, I smiled at her. 'The past is just that, Prim. As you said, I'm a different guy now.'

She let it drop.

Glasgow was well in sight when a thought that had been festering all afternoon popped out of the back of my brain. 'You know what's been puzzling me?' I said. 'Since Wallinger's stolen every penny of yours that he could get his hands on, why the hell did he leave you with the diamonds?'

'Pure luck,' she replied. 'The insurance company advised me to change the combination of the safe at least once a month, as an added security precaution. I did it the day before Paul left, and I never told him the number. Not that I needed to; there was nothing of his in there anyway.'

I called Susie from the airport, to let her know that we were wheels down and that we'd be home in half an hour. 'Good,' she said. 'In plenty of time for dinner. Oh, by the way, Greg rang to say that the birth certificate's arrived, and Ricky Ross called too. He said that DI McLaren would be here at nine thirty tomorrow morning.'

'Fine; anything else?'

'Yes, you cunning bastard, Roscoe called.' I was glad that I could hear a laugh in her voice. 'He told me to tell you that the deal with Everett is done on the basis of no fee but five points of the gross. You'd decided to do it all along, hadn't you?'

'I owe Daze, Susie.'

'I know that, and I think you've done the right thing. Roscoe says that you're booked into the Bellagio from next weekend, into a two-bedroom suite so that the kids, Ethel and I can come with you. That's a lovely thought, but I really did mean it. It's too hot there at this time of year. On top of that, I might have some Gantry Group business to take care of in the next couple of weeks. The flotation date's getting closer and Phil Culshaw wants me to go to London with him to make some presentations that our PR company's setting up for us. It's all for the good of the share price, darling.'

'Even so, you might change your mind when you hear what I've got to ask you.'

14

She didn't, though. When I explained to her where we were in the search for Tom, and where we had to go next, she agreed with me one hundred per cent.

When Prim suggested that she hire a detective instead, she almost went ballistic. 'You what?' she exclaimed. 'You think we'd let you go to a place you've never been, with some bloody gumshoe you don't know from Adam, to find a man who's not exactly going to welcome you with open arms? No chance in hell. Oz is going with you, and that's that. I'll have Audrey book your flights first thing in the morning.'

There was one thing that Prim hadn't done the day before and that was to call her sister and tell her the whole story. I made her fill that gap after dinner, leaving her to do it on her own. She was sombre when she came back into the sitting room, where Susie and I were watching the US Open on television.

'Did Dawn give you a hard time?'

She shook her head. 'Far from it; she couldn't have been better. I spoke to Miles too. He was great. He said that any help I needed, to let him know, and that if he wasn't in Australia he'd be on the case himself. When I told him that you were, he was happy.'

When the phone rang a couple of minutes later, I knew who it would be. I picked the hands-free unit from its cradle and was walking out of the room as I pressed the receive button. 'I just spoke to Primavera,' said Miles. The fact that he was using her Sunday name was a sure sign that however 'great' he had sounded, she wasn't his favourite person right then.

'I know.'

'Do you know what you're doing, getting involved in this?'

'I don't see any other option, nor does Susie. Anyway, if I hadn't cut her off, she wouldn't have been drifting around like a lost soul.'

'She'd have worked out a game plan, don't worry.'

'Do you remember this guy, Wallinger?'

'Should I?'

'Ah, Prim didn't tell you his professional name: Paul Patrick Walls.'

'Walls? Walls? Hey, wait a minute, he's a bit player, isn't he? And didn't I use him once?'

'Not much, from the story I heard. You cut all his best scenes out of *Kidnapped* to make way for Dawn.'

Miles fell silent for a few seconds . . . an unusual condition for him. 'Are you trying to tell me that when this guy ripped off Prim he was actually getting even with me?'

'At this stage of the game, pal, I haven't a fucking clue what I'm trying to tell you. But when I have my hands around the bastard's throat, that'll be one of the questions I ask him.'

'If the answer's "yes", then tell him that if mistakes are on a scale from one to ten, that one's a Bo Derek.'

'I'll tell him many things, once he's handed over Prim's kid and her money.'

I wished him a good morning in Sydney, and went back to the golf.

Detective Inspector Ian McLaren arrived spot on time next morning, just five minutes after Greg McPhillips called to say that Harvey had found a sheriff to hear his application for a child-protection interdict at midday, and that there was no way it wouldn't be granted.

The specialist fraud investigator was a tall man in his early forties, with a pencil moustache and wearing a brown suit that looked way too heavy for the weather: I hoped he wouldn't start to sweat. I showed him through to our huge and, happily, air-conditioned office, where Prim was waiting. Susie and Audrey were working together. They looked up when I introduced him to everybody, then carried on with what they were doing.

106

He listened, gravely, as Prim told her story. He examined the documents she gave him, with a suitably earnest frown as he went from page to page, deepening as he reached the statements at the end.

'Did you give Mr Wallinger any specific instructions at any time regarding the sale of your investments?' he asked her, when he had read his way through the lot.

'No, I didn't. I never gave him any instructions at all, other than to make damn sure he took good care of my money.'

'And you don't recall ever telling him to transfer funds elsewhere?'

'Never.'

'How often did you discuss your financial affairs with him?'

'Every few months, I suppose. We were very comfortable financially, and at that time I assumed that he was earning too. I was so focused on my child that I just let him get on with everything. I never asked him for regular reports, like I had from my old fund managers.'

'So you were never told of any crisis, or of any movement of capital?'

'No.'

McLaren arranged the papers in a neat pile on my desk. 'Okay,' he said. 'What do you want the police to do?'

Prim stared at him. 'I want you to find him, I want you to arrest him, and I want you to get me my money back.'

'We can only do the first two of those things, Ms Phillips. The third will be up to the court. A judge in a criminal trial could order him to make full restitution, but there's no certainty of that. You'd be well advised to raise an action in the civil courts to recover your assets.'

'That's under way already,' I told him.

'I'm glad to hear it,' he replied. 'However . . .' There followed a portentous pause.

'What?' Prim demanded.

'. . . in the circumstances,' he continued, 'since you willingly gave Mr Wallinger access to your funds, there's something that will have to happen before anyone gets arrested. We'll have to establish that your money has been deliberately placed beyond your reach.'

'But I don't know where it is!'

'Maybe not, but legally he's your agent, and he does. He's only committed a crime if he's diverted your property to his own use. How long did you say he'd been gone?'

'A bit over two months.'

'Mmm. Not long in a lifetime, is it? Suppose, I'm being devil's advocate here, mind, but suppose he had a legitimate reason for leaving? What if he was in some sort of personal danger, and wanted to shield you from it?'

'By taking my son?' Prim protested.

'Maybe he had other reasons for doing that,' McLaren said quietly.

'Such as?'

'Maybe best not to speculate.'

'Come on!'

She was getting over-excited, rarely a good idea with a police-man; I took her arm as she started to rise from her seat and forced her to stay there. 'I think Mr McLaren may be implying,' I said, switching to my best Larry Hagman voice, 'that Paul might have thought you were a tramp and an unfit mother, Sue Ellen, or at least that he might use that as a reason for taking Tom. Not that he's implying that himself, you understand.'

'He'd better bloody not!' She snorted.

'Be all that as it may,' McLaren continued, clearly grateful for my help and glad to be putting the point behind him, 'what I'm saying is that before I can apply for a warrant for Mr Wallinger's arrest, I have to be able to satisfy the sheriff that I have just cause. For me to do that, in his continuing absence, I'll have to trace your money. That may not be easy, given that it's been a while since it was moved.'

'Is there anything in those documents to tell you where it's gone?' I asked.

'No, nothing at all.' He looked at me. 'There's no indication that it's been converted to another currency. That wouldn't have been

108

such a daft thing to do, by the way, given the strength of the pound in early April. He could even have argued that it was in Ms Phillips's interests.'

'He can argue till he's multi-coloured in the face,' Prim snapped, 'but it won't change the fact that he stole my money.'

'Look, I accept that, and I will pursue this. All I'm telling you is that it's not going to be easy and it will take time.' His posture seemed to change, to relax and become less formal. Suddenly, he looked at me. 'I recognise you, you know,' he said, 'and I don't mean from the movies. I remember seeing you one day . . . oh, it'll be five years ago now . . . when you came into the office to pick up Mike Dylan.'

I saw Susie stiffen; it was a name that wasn't raised in our house very often, and never by strangers.

'I just want to say that, well, I know you were friendly with Mike and, well . . .' He shifted awkwardly. '. . . so was I. I know he went to the bad and all that, but even so, I liked him. So what I'm saying is that I'm not just going through the motions on this. I'm sure that Ms Phillips has been told by her lawyers that she has to make a criminal complaint, if only to back up a civil action. Well, even if that's so, and it looks like a lost cause, I want you to know that you've come to the right man.'

'Thanks,' I said. 'We appreciate that.' I gave him one of my special business cards, with my mobile number on it and the e-mail address that I keep for people close to me. 'You can raise me anytime, anywhere with those.' Another idea occurred as I spoke. I found the list of numbers Kravitz had given me, copied the details of HHH Asset on to a sheet of paper and handed it to him. 'That's the company Wallinger's mother worked for: they're fund managers. It's probably too obvious a place for him to dump the money, but . . .'

'It's worth checking. Quite right; thanks.' He stood, picking up the papers and shoving them into his briefcase. 'I'll get back to you as soon as I have anything new,' he promised.

I walked him back through the house and to his car, which was pulled up at the front door. 'Did you know my wife was once engaged to Mike?' I asked him.

He nodded. 'Mr Ross told me. He also told me that you were in Amsterdam when he got taken down.'

'Not my fondest memory,' I admitted. There were others but, good friend or not, I couldn't let him in on them.

'Nonetheless, take some advice, and look out for yourself and Ms Phillips over this business. When people start playing for the sort of money that's involved here, things can get very serious.'

15

I pulled a grave face and made the right noises at the time, but in truth, I thought that McLaren's warning was over-dramatic, and I didn't take it very seriously. I had done research into Paul Wallinger that he hadn't, and I did not have him marked down as a heavy hitter.

It was good to have him on-side; I had known that Prim's money would be hard to catch up with, maybe impossible for us on our own. The banks would be unlikely to talk to individuals . . . frankly I'd be very pissed off if mine did . . . but with a police officer asking the questions they might be more inclined to co-operate.

When I went back inside, Audrey was waiting for me; she'd found a flight to Minneapolis next day, from Glasgow via Amsterdam, and she wanted me to okay it. I shivered when she told me that; I hadn't been to Schiphol since the day Mike Dylan was shot. Nonetheless I said it was fine, and left her to go firm on the booking. I was taking a hell of a chance: I didn't know for sure that Mother Wallinger was still in either of the twin cities of Minneapolis-St Paul, or that she was anywhere else on Earth for that matter, but we had to begin somewhere.

Conrad took us to the airport next morning; Susie volunteered, of course, but I managed to talk her out of it. It was tough enough saying goodbye to the kids, and I didn't fancy a public emotional farewell at the departure gate, especially as I was flying out with my ex-wife. Instead, we said our serious farewells the night before, and well into the morning.

When we left Prim was carrying a very important document, a notarised copy of the interim interdict that she'd been granted the day before in the Sheriff Court in Edinburgh, ordering Tom's return to the UK pending a full custody hearing. When we found the boy, Harvey's instructions were to engage a local lawyer and have him petition a judge for it to be enforced. By that time, he hoped that we would have grounds for the local police to arrest Paul Wallinger.

I was bleary-eyed when I got to the KLM desk to pick up our travel documents, so when I saw that we were booked as Mr and Mrs Blackstone, I was taken more than a bit by surprise. Then I remembered that Audrey would have had to give them the name on Prim's passport, and that was the one she'd borrowed from me for a while.

Someone else may claim to be the world's favourite airline, but they're not mine. I like flying with KLM or Northwest, and usually I do so out of choice. There were no horrors waiting for me in Schiphol Airport; the place is constantly changing, and so I doubt that I could have found the spot where Dylan went down, even if I'd been trying. We had two and a half hours between flights, which we spent in the comfort of the VIP Lounge. I'd expected to be unnoticed in Amsterdam, but I caught a couple of people looking in our direction. I hoped that none of them were tabloid journalists, although if they had been they'd have had nothing to latch on to. Prim and I barely spoke during the wait, apart from when she asked me if I wanted a drink. I was too busy reading Everett's script, trying to use the time to get into the part that I'd be acting in only a week.

I read it part of the way across the Atlantic too, until the text started to swim before me, and I knew that it was time to rest my eyes. As I stretched out on the club-class seat, I saw that Primavera was watching a movie on her monitor. What the hell was it but *Red Leather*. When it finished, she was smiling. 'You were damn good in that, you know,' she said. The flight attendant must have thought so too: he gave me a special smile as he passed me my meal tray, and filled my wine glass.

Never having been to Minneapolis before, and having been geographically disadvantaged all my life, I was surprised when we were routed over Canada and the Great Lakes. The long overland

112

approach reminded me yet again that North America is a hell of a big place.

They say that MSP International is one of the busiest airports in the world, but it was quiet when we landed. I've been fast-tracked through Immigration before, but not there; still, we were first off the plane and that helped. When we got to the desk and handed over our passports and forms, the officer asked us the standard question: 'Purpose of your visit to the United States?'

I hadn't thought about that one, but I knew that 'searching for a child-snatching con-man' was not an appropriate response. So instead I told her that I was making a movie in Las Vegas and had decided to spend some time in Minneapolis first. 'Mall of America,' Prim added helpfully. That did the trick, for the woman smiled, stamped our passports and clipped a green entry card into each one. She even asked for my autograph. 'We don't get too many movie stars through here,' she confided.

'What's the Mall of America?' I whispered to Prim as we walked away.

'Shops, shops and more shops.'

My body felt like it was after midnight, but the airport clocks and the daylight outside insisted that it was early evening, just before seven when I lifted the last of our luggage off the carousel, and we walked through the gate that led into Minnesota. The only thing I knew about the place at that moment was that they had once elected Jesse 'The Body' Ventura, a wrestler, as governor. The guy didn't do a bad job, sparking a rumour that Everett Davis was going to run for governor of New York. (He might, but not yet.)

The second thing I found out about the state is that they do a very nice line in airport limos; ours was driven by a guy called Charles, and it was a very plush Mercedes, not one of those awful white stretch jobs, which embarrass the hell out of me whenever one turns up to collect me. I asked the chauffeur if he could take us into Minneapolis by the scenic route, but he smiled and said, 'I'm sorry, sir, but we don't have one.'

The posher of the twin cities turned out to be a place with mainly low-rise suburbs, but with a high-rise office and condo community in its heart. We could see the skyscrapers looming up as we approached.

We were cruising along a wide boulevard when Prim grabbed my arm. 'Can we stop there?' she called out to the driver. She was pointing at a wood-fronted building emblazoned with the legends 'Uncle Hugo's Science Fiction Bookstore' and 'Uncle Edgar's Mystery Bookstore', cosily side by side. 'I've got nothing to read,' she explained. Charles nodded, and probably committed a couple of traffic violations by crossing three lanes to park right at the front door.

She jumped out and I followed. Inside, the two shops were actually one; together they occupied quite a big space and it was piled high with stock. Prim headed for the mystery section and started browsing; I picked up a couple of titles myself and looked at them. I was thinking about buying an Elmore Leonard when I was aware of a slim man standing at my side, bespectacled, with a small moustache.

'How do you do, sir?' he greeted me, extending a hand, formally. 'My name's Jeff, and it's a great honour to have you here.'

'Thanks very much,' I told him. 'It's my honour that you recognise me.'

'A lot of people in America will recognise you, Mr Blackstone. We sell a lot of the Skinner books here, and I've admired your work in the movies that have been made of them.'

'That's very kind of you. Has your shop been here long?'

He smiled. 'Thirty years . . . at least, Uncle Hugo has. Uncle Edgar joined him six years later.'

I loved the place. 'You'll be the only specialist in town, I suppose.'

'Oh, no, we have Pat and Gary at Once Upon a Crime, too. Minneapolis is quite a centre for the arts, you know.' He paused. 'What brings you here, Mr Blackstone, if I may ask? Are you making a personal appearance somewhere?'

'Mall of America,' I said.

He laughed. 'You too?'

I shrugged and jerked a thumb in Prim's direction, as if in

explanation. I chose the Elmore Leonard, plus a Sheila O'Flanagan, a Jasper Fforde, and a signed hardback of the most recent Skinner book, and handed Jeff a credit card. 'Whatever she wants, put it on that too; might as well get used to it.'

As we stood there waiting for Prim to make her selection, I scratched my head. 'It's funny, you know. Although I never thought of Minneapolis as a cradle of the arts, I did once run across an actor from here, a guy maybe in the same age ballpark as you.'

'Can you remember his name?'

'Yeah, it was Walls, like the ice cream; Paul Patrick Walls.'

'I don't think I'm familiar with him,' said the shopkeeper.

'That wasn't his real name, though,' I added, as casually as I could. 'It began with Walls, or Wall, but it was longer.'

Jeff's eyes widened in recognition. 'Of course! Paul Wallinger, Martha's son.'

'You know him? Hell, there's a coincidence.'

'Oh, I don't know him, but Martha's a customer of ours. She comes in every so often. She bought a book once and mentioned that her son Paul had been in the television adaptation.'

I chuckled. 'Hey, fancy that. Maybe I should look her up when I'm in town. She does live in Minneapolis, yes?'

'Yes indeed. She used to live in St Paul, but she moved across the Mississippi after her husband died. I might even have an address for her. If you hold on I'll check my mailing list.'

I held on, Jeff checked, and came back a couple of minutes later, with an address, written on the back of one of his business cards. 'There you are,' he said. 'Pleased to have been of help.' I took it from him and slipped it into my wallet, behind my photographic driving licence, just as Prim rejoined us, carrying a Caroline Graham, a Pauline McLynn and a medieval mystery by Michael Jecks. I paid for our picks, signed his visitor's book, and we went back to the limo.

It only took us another ten minutes to reach the Merchant's Hotel; as soon as Charles drew up at the entrance the bellboys were all over us like a rash. Our luggage was commandeered, even the

115

bag with our books in it, and we were ushered into Reception, where the bad news broke.

'Mr and Mrs Blackstone,' the check-in manager gushed, 'how great that you're joining us. If you'll just sign here and let me have a print of your credit card, we'll show you to your room.'

The singular hit me at once. 'Room? My secretary asked for two rooms; I was standing beside her when she made the booking, so I'm in no doubt about that.'

The gush dried up, to be replaced by consternation. 'But . . .' I could see him decide that some blame-shifting was in order. He disappeared into a room behind the desk, and shortly after we could hear raised voices. When he reappeared he was slightly flushed.

'I have to offer our sincerest apologies,' he said. 'There seems to have been a misunderstanding by our booking clerk. She thought that your assistant asked for a premium room with two double beds, and that's what we've allocated. I am terribly sorry, but we don't have another room available.'

'We better find another hotel, in that case: we're travelling together, but we're divorced.'

The manager winced. 'Mr Blackstone, we would be happy to relocate you ourselves, but there's a major event at our convention centre this week. I happen to know that all the quality hotels are full. We could maybe find you a room somewhere, but I doubt if you'd like it.'

I looked at Prim; she looked at me. 'I'm knackered,' she said. I had to admit to myself that I felt much the same.

'Please be assured,' the manager murmured, clearly trying to be as helpful as he could, 'of our absolute discretion.'

I sighed. 'Okay, we'll take it, but please be assured of my total vengeance if word of this leaks out anywhere.' He smiled with obvious relief and showed us to our room himself, even refusing a tip.

The superior room was actually a kind of open-plan suite, with a partitioned dressing room, and a sitting area boasting among other things a narrow couch on which a person smaller than I am might sleep quite comfortably. When I pointed at it, Prim pointed at the two double beds, and said that she would take the one nearer the bathroom.

'Will I have them fix a screen?' I asked.

'It's all right,' she replied. 'I've seen you sleep before. It's not very exciting.'

'I didn't bring any pyjamas with me.'

'It's still not very exciting.' She pointed at the enormous plasma TV screen mounted on the wall of the sitting area. 'Why don't you see if that works, while I take a shower?' She sniffed at her right armpit in a pure Prim way, then pulled the face that had always made me chuckle. 'God, yes!' she exclaimed.

In a supple movement, she slipped the baggy T-shirt in which she had travelled over her head, smiling at my reaction. 'Think of me as a fellow actor you're rooming with on location,' she suggested.

'I don't room with fellow actors.'

'Then think of me as a brother Boy Scout.'

'Difficult,' I murmured.

She frowned. 'In that case, think back to when we were in LA, just before I went off with Nicky. I didn't get you too excited then, even if we did go through the motions a few times.'

I had to admit that she was right: back then we were still playing the parts of husband and wife, but with no sign of enthusiasm. I recalled the last time we'd had sex, three, no, nearer four years earlier. I'd been thinking of Susie all the way through; I didn't want to guess who she'd been thinking of.

'Ah, go on, then; I'll sort us out something to eat. How about a room-service steak?'

'Can we go out somewhere? Nothing dressy-up fancy, though, just somewhere we can see what this city's like.'

'Okay, I'll ask Reception what they recommend. You go and make yourself less smelly.'

When I called down, our new friend at Reception told me that all we had to do was walk across Sixth Street to a bar diner called Gluek's. The place was a hundred years old, he said, although it had

117

been restored after a fire fifteen years earlier. When I said that sounded fine, he undertook to book us a table.

I was honking too, so while Prim sorted out what to wear to a Minneapolis diner, I grabbed a towelling dressing-gown from the wardrobe and had a quick shower myself. Twenty minutes later we were ready to go, looking like a couple of cowboys in blue jeans.

Gluek's turned out to be the sort of American bar I really love. The place wasn't full, so the reservation had been unnecessary, but it was lively and there was a jazz band playing on a stage at the far end of the long room, close enough to our booth for us to appreciate it and far enough away for us to be able to hear each other. The draught beer selection was amazing, and the menu was solid, inviting down-home stuff. We learned that old man Gluek had been a Bavarian brewer who came to the Midwest a hundred and fifty years ago and set up in business there. They still make his original Pilsner, so we started with a couple of tall glasses of the stuff, ice-cold. I hadn't realised I was thirsty until then.

I wasn't worried about Prim's drinking any more. She'd sworn off the hard stuff, and I was used to seeing her with a beer in her hand, so it didn't bother me.

The way I deal with jet-lag is by pretending that it doesn't exist. My watch said nine twenty and so I tried to force my body to agree with it, by ordering Reuben Balls . . . no, I don't know who Reuben is . . . as a starter, followed by Minnesota walleye pike, oven-broiled with white wine butter and almonds and served with French fries and a selection of steamed vegetables. Prim, being smaller, decided to be more conservative. She started with Syd's Artichoke Dip, followed by a Silver Ranch Bison Burger, with Provolone cheese, marinated mushrooms and buffalo sauce.

Once I had packed that lot away . . . Prim had to quit on the last of the marinated mushrooms . . . and had a fresh Gluek Pilsner in my hand, I had moved into a slightly surreal world, in which my normal existence seemed to have been suspended, and I was just another guy in just another city on a night out with someone I liked, no questions asked, no lies told. I don't know if anyone in

118

there recognised me, but if they did, they had the manners not to intrude. The band was good too; a third beer and I was truly mellow. I got so in synch with local time that when next I looked at my watch it was half an hour after midnight, and the place was beginning to empty.

I grinned at Prim. 'Time to retire, honey-pie?' I said, in a light southern accent that I'd learned for a movie a couple of years back.

'Are you pissed?' she asked.

'Not as far as I know. Just call me chilled out.'

She smiled back at me. 'Me too.'

The air was hot and heavy as we crossed Sixth and walked the short distance back to the hotel. The manager had gone, and the night staff were in place. We took the lift up to the twentieth floor and, after a certain amount of fiddling with the key card, managed to open our door. I went to turn on the light then stopped. That high up, you tend not to draw the curtains; Minneapolis isn't that memorable a place, but the view of its downtown skyscrapers, illuminated, their glass walls reflecting each one on to the next, was quite spectacular.

'We've come a long way,' I said, for no reason in particular.

'What do you mean?' asked Prim, as she kicked off her shoes.

'Since we met. Go back to the beginning, what?, eight years ago; ask any bookie to give odds that at this precise moment we'd be standing here, looking at this view, in these circumstances, and he'd have given seven figures to one against.'

'But you know what? I'd have taken the bet.' She smiled up at me. 'The one thing I knew for certain when we met, Oz, was that we were never going to be ordinary. If I'd known the background about you and Jan, I'd probably have crossed the street to get away from you, but I didn't and the die was cast.'

'Do you wish you had?'

'Crossed the street?' She gave me a strange smile. 'No, not for a second. Okay, it didn't work out between us, but we had what we had and we can still stand here as friends, you looking out for me when I need you. I feel very fortunate to be in that position, and I'm grateful to whatever guiding light brought it about.'

119

'You're not going to offer to show me how grateful, are you?' I don't know what made me ask that.

'No more than you're going to ask me. If you wanted me to shag you, I would, even if it meant a hell of a lot less to you than it did to me. But you don't, and that's just as well, for somehow Tom changed everything. We're sexual history, Oz, and I can live with that.' She began to unbutton her shirt. 'Now I'm going to bed. If you want to close your eyes or turn your back, that's up to you.'

I picked up a couple of bottles of water from the mini-bar. When I turned to hand her one, she was stepping out of her jeans. If that was the acid test, I passed it. I wasn't bothered; I'm an actor so I get to see plenty of beautiful women in their underwear or less, but the only one who makes me twitch is my wife.

I handed her the Evian. 'Thanks,' she said, then peeled off the rest and got into bed.

I did the same, but first, I went to my bag, took out the photo of Susie and the kids that I carry with me everywhere I go, and placed it so that when I woke up next morning, it was the first thing I would see.

16

The second thing that I saw when I woke was Primavera, sitting up in her bed with her back against a pillow, reading the Michael Jecks. It was called *The Mad Monk of Gidleigh*. I thought to myself that the man went in for colourful titles, and wondered how much trouble he had getting them past the marketing department.

'What time is it?' I mumbled.

'Twenty past eight. I've been awake for a couple of hours, listening to you snore.'

'I've told you before, I don't snore.'

'Do you ever ask Susie about that?'

'She tells lies as well.'

'Aye, sure.' She saved her page with one of the markers Jeff had given us, and put down the book. 'What are we going to do?' she asked.

'First? You're going to stop being naked, then I will.' Under the duvet I was like a rock, but then I often am when I waken. 'Then we'll have some breakfast; then we'll go and find your boyfriend's mother, and put the thumbscrews on her till she tells us where her fucking son is.'

'As easy as that, eh?' she said, but a little gloomily.

'Let's hope so, till we know otherwise.'

'Will we go straight to the address that man gave you?'

'I thought we should check out HHH Asset first, in case she's still working there. It's not far from here, according to the map.'

'Mmm,' she conceded. 'Good idea.' She jumped out of bed; as she headed for the bathroom, I couldn't help noticing that she'd kept up a healthy tan, and also that whatever had happened to the top deck, her bum was still pretty firm. I turned, looked over my shoulder at Susie's smiling photo and mouthed a quick 'Sorry.'

I shook my head, as if to clear the cobwebs, but also to shake some sense into myself and to make myself bring this quest back under my control. I picked up the bedside phone, pushed the button for an outside line and dialled Susie's mobile number, using that rather than the landline, since I couldn't be sure where she'd be in the middle of the afternoon.

'Hi,' she answered, bright and breezy, 'you up and about yet?'

'Just about. Everything okay?'

'Why shouldn't it be? How was the flight?'

'No problem.'

'And the hotel?'

'Posh. Very high tech, big telly on the wall and all that stuff; there's another one in the bathroom, so you don't have to miss any of *The West Wing* while you're sat on the crapper. I tell you, Janet would love it. I've even managed to sleep off most of the jet-lag.'

'It's good that you were able to. I've been having visions of them buggering up the booking and putting you in the same room.'

I laughed, then swung myself out of bed and walked through to the sitting area, getting as far away from the bathroom as possible, in case the phone was sensitive enough to pick up the sound of the shower.

'Have you made any progress yet,' Susie asked, 'or haven't you had time?'

I told her about our accidental meeting with Jeff, and of his confirmation that Wallinger's mother was still alive and in town. 'We're going to run her to ground this morning.'

'How will you play it?'

'I've still got to work that one out,' I admitted. 'I'll call you later, and tell you how it went.'

'Do that. What's Minneapolis like?'

'Lots of glass. I'll take some photos, once I've had breakfast.'

'Go on, then.'

'Okay. Hey!'

'What?'

'I love you.'

'Don't you forget it either!'

I should have felt better for the call, but I didn't, only more uncomfortable. At some point I'd tell Susie what had happened, but not over the phone, that was for sure.

By the time both Prim and I were groomed to face the day it was gone nine o'clock. We had a buffet breakfast downstairs, then she blagged a street map from the reception desk, to try to work out where we were going. 'Marquette Avenue,' I reminded her, as she peered at the guide.

'We're in luck,' she said. 'It's only two blocks away.' We didn't know how the numbers ran, but when we asked the duty manager, he told us that we were looking for a building on the corner of Marquette and Eighth Street.

The hotel led more or less directly on to the Skyway system. Charles the chauffeur had told us about it, explaining that it links most of the office blocks and malls in downtown Minneapolis by a network of walkways one floor above street level, so that people can get around in comfort all year round, in the heat of the summer and the cold of the winter.

With a couple of weeks in Las Vegas coming up, I wasn't bothered about the heat, but Prim, ever the explorer, insisted that we take it. On the map it looked simple, but it wasn't as easy as all that; we took a couple of wrong turns and found ourselves first in the Wells Fargo Museum, and then in the local version of Saks Fifth Avenue, before finally we reached our destination. There was a big sign over the entrance, which read, 'The IDS Building'. 'Look at that!' I said. 'In Britain they can barely remember his name; here they've named an office block after him.'

We studied the business directory and found HHH Asset, listed alphabetically. As we looked at the board, Prim asked the same question Susie had. 'How are we going to play this?'

I'd been considering that all the way there, which was maybe why we got lost so often. 'I think you should stay out of sight,' I told her, 'at first at any rate. We don't want to spook this woman. Paul might well have warned her that you're likely to show up looking for him, so if you go crashing in there, she might just clam up. Let me go up on my own, and see how I get on.'

'What will you say to her?'

'I'll come up with something, don't worry.'

She was reluctant to miss the moment, but she saw the sense in what I was saying, so I parked her in a Starbucks . . . How did people survive without them and McDonald's? . . . and took the elevator.

HHH Asset seemed to occupy all of one floor; I walked through the glass double doors and into the reception area, where a very well-dressed Chinese girl welcomed me with a dazzling smile. A badge on her jacket said that her name was Mai Lee, and I guessed that she was trained to treat everybody who came through the door as a potential investor.

'Good morning, sir,' she said, in a voice that would have brightened anyone's day, 'and how can HHH be of service?'

'I'm looking for a lady I was told works here.' I have this thing that when I talk to Americans I sort of pick up their inflection. 'Her name is Martha Wallinger.'

'That would be me.'

I turned. An older woman, working at a big desk against a window, had risen and was approaching me. She was stocky, almost square built, heavily made-up and with jet-black hair that looked to be lacquered stiff. If her son looked like me, he must have taken after his father, for she didn't look a bit like my mother.

She didn't look hostile, though; in fact, she looked anything but.

'Mrs Wallinger,' I began, 'I'm . . .'

'I know who you are,' she drawled. 'You're an actor: I saw you in a movie last week. It was called *Red Leather*, wasn't it? If you give me a minute I'll recall your name.'

That was me put in my place, but I extended the hand of friendship nonetheless. 'Oz Blackstone,' I announced.

'Of course, how silly of me not to know straight away. What brings you to Minneapolis, Mr Blackstone?'

'Call me Oz, please. In five words: Mrs Blackstone, Mall of America.'

124

She laughed. That seems to answer everything in the twin cities. Mai Lee smiled too, even more sunnily than before. She really was very pretty; I glanced at her left hand. No jewellery: an unattached movie star might have had a chance there.

'And what,' Mrs Wallinger went on, 'brings you to see me?'

'A promise,' I told her, and then switched back into lying mode. 'I made it to your son Paul, two or three years back, when I met him in Los Angeles. We were working on different projects on the same sound-stage, and someone said that we looked a little alike, so we got talking. I told him a little about me, and he told me about himself, and how he'd got started in the business, through the University of Minnesota and everything. I told him that I'd never been there, and he said that if I ever went, I had to be sure to look up his mom. In my world, a promise is a promise, so here I am.'

She beamed, nearly as wide as Mai. 'How very gallant.' And then she paused. 'The problem is, Oz, that we have a rule at HHH that employees do not have personal visits in working hours, and since I'm the office manager, I can't be seen to break it.'

Oh, bugger, I thought. *That's cut me off short.*

'However,' she continued, 'I only work half the day on Wednesdays.' She smirked. 'I'm older than I look, you see. So I'll be free from lunchtime.'

If she was angling for an invitation that wasn't quite what I'd planned either. I wanted some time alone, no witnesses. 'Damn it,' I exclaimed. 'I'd love to take you to lunch, but I have to meet Mrs Blackstone.' I couldn't make myself say, 'my wife'.

Once again, Mrs W bailed me out. 'In that case,' she said, 'why don't you just call on me? If you have the time, that is. It's not every day that a friend of my rascal son looks me up. In fact, it's not any day. Now my other son, his friends pop in to see me all the time.'

She grabbed a pen and a pad from the reception desk. I watched her scribble down the same address that Jeff in the bookstore had given me, and took it from her. 'That's where I live. It's not far from here, down in the Warehouse District.'

'Okay, that would be fine. Would three o'clock be okay?'

'Three o'clock would be perfect: and you must bring Mrs Blackstone. I insist.'

The two women smiled me out of the door and into the elevator. When I went back to the Starbucks where I'd left Prim, she wasn't there, but that didn't worry me. In all the time I've known her, she's been incapable of sitting on her arse for more than fifteen minutes at a stretch. That's something else that made her holing herself up in that flat of hers all the more out of character.

I allowed myself my one and only coffee of the day and waited for her. In ten minutes she was back, carrying a Saks bag. She showed me what was inside: a pair of pyjamas, men's, XL. 'A present for you,' she announced, 'to preserve your modesty.'

'What did you get for yourself?'

'It's only the bottom half that's the present. The top's for me.'

'Seems fair.'

'How did you get on?' she asked impatiently, as if the distraction had upset her.

I told her about our three o'clock appointment.

'Do you think she knows anything?'

'Prim, I haven't a clue. I told her that I promised Paul in LA that I'd look her up, and she bought it. She didn't say, "Didn't your ex-wife have my son's kid?" or anything else that might have tipped her hand.'

'So will I go with you this afternoon?'

'She's expecting you. If Paul's showed her a photograph of you, she'll twig right away; that'll tell us plenty.'

I ditched what was left of my coffee . . . frothy gunge, mostly . . . we took our joint nightwear back to the hotel, then spent the rest of the morning looking round the very compact city centre, mostly using the Skyway, but coming down to ground level occasionally and out into the relatively modest heat, to look at landmarks like the modest statue of Hubert Humphrey . . . before he was a senator, and then Vice President, he was Mayor of Minneapolis, and if his statue is life-size he wasn't very big . . . the Federal Building, and the remarkable Marquette Plaza, all glass front and angled so that when you stand in front and look at it, all

126

you see is a reflection of the sky, a bit scary when a jumbo out of MSP International flies across it.

By the time we'd done that, grabbed a couple of sandwiches, two root beers, then a coffee for Prim in a diner called Ike's, it was time to head for the Warehouse District.

The map showed us that Mrs Wallinger lived only a few blocks from the Merchant's, but her address was outside the zone of the Skyway, so we took a cab. The experience couldn't have been further from London, in every respect. The driver seemed to be on another plane of existence, and I had to guide him street by street until he found the block we were after.

Residentially, downtown Minneapolis is condominium land, but the Warehouse District is different. It is, as its name suggests, a collection of former storehouses most of them now converted into loft apartments. Martha Wallinger's looked as if it had been done a few years ago, but the refurbished building still looked very smart, as if it was well managed. If I'm ever sentenced to live in Minnesota, I'll want something like it.

It had a concierge, but each apartment had a buzzer out in the street. I pressed the one for F4/3 and waited . . . for about two seconds: she must have been right by the intercom. She was standing by the elevator too, when it opened on to the fourth floor.

'Oz, I can't tell you how good it is of you to call on me,' she exclaimed. She had changed into a lighter, less formal trouser suit than the one she wore to work, but the makeup was still impeccable and the hair immovable.

I watched her as Prim stepped out of the small lift; she'd been standing behind me, so that Mrs Wallinger couldn't see her face until that moment. If she had seen a photograph, it had either been a very bad one, or acting must run in the Wallinger family, for not a flicker of recognition crossed her face.

'This is Mrs Blackstone,' I told her.

Martha took a step towards her, hand outstretched. 'How lovely to meet you, my dear. It must be wonderful being married to a movie star. I always hoped that my Paul would make it big in the business and that I would get to bask in his glory,' she smiled, in a

127

way that could have conveyed sadness or disappointment, or both, 'but it hasn't happened, not yet at any rate.'

She half turned towards her front door. 'Come on in, both of you. There's coffee on the hob.'

She led us into a spacious apartment, a big all-in-one living area with several doors leading off, not unlike Prim's pad in London, except that it was twice the size and the ceilings were a lot higher. I expected it to be hot, since there was a lot of glass, but it was air-conditioned.

'Nice place,' I commented. 'Have you always lived here, Mrs Wallinger?' I knew the answer but I wanted to get her conversational. I learned back in the days when I was a private enquiry agent in Edinburgh that once you start people talking sometimes they can't stop.

'No, I haven't, only for the last few years. John, my husband, and I lived in St Paul and we raised our family there, but it was difficult for me after his death, so I bought this place . . . he was well insured . . . and moved across the river. Oh, and Oz, please call me Martha.' She turned. 'I didn't catch your first name, my dear.'

'It's Primavera,' I told her.

'Primavera! What a lovely name. I've never met anyone called Primavera before.'

'She's called Prim for short.'

'How absolutely charming,' said Martha. 'Well, Prim, will you have some coffee? I've made a fresh pot.'

'That would be nice.'

'Oz, you too?'

'I won't, thank you, but if you have some mineral water, that would be good.'

'Of course I have.'

As she went to the kitchen area to pour, I glanced around the place. It was comfortably, but not expensively furnished, there was a big television in the far corner and much of the available wall space was occupied by bookshelves.

'You're a big reader, Martha,' I called across.

'Sure am, Oz,' she called across. 'Mysteries, mostly; I just love 'em. Can't get enough. You know those Skinner movies you did? I've read all those books, and that other Edinboro' fella too.'

I strolled across to a long sideboard; it looked to be sixties vintage, and I guessed that she might have had it all her domestic life. Several family photographs were displayed on it: a tall, crew-cut man in US military uniform, with a chestful of medals, a graduation photograph starring a young man who looked a bit like me, another showing a second youth, slick, spotless and smiling in a sharp suit, and a fourth of the same man, older and much more casual, with a wholesome all-American blonde and two kids, girl and boy, aged perhaps on either side of ten.

'My little family,' said Martha, as she returned with a tray, which she put on a coffee-table in the middle of the sitting area. She gave Prim a mug of Java and me a glass of something fizzy and slightly tinted, then offered us doughnuts from a big plate. Prim took one; I passed.

She looked back towards the photo display. 'That's John, my late husband; he was in Vietnam, you know. He won two Silver Stars and many other decorations. Then there's Paul, but you know him, of course, and then there's John the Second, my other son, his wife Sheryl, and their children, Lori and John Wallinger the Third.'

I almost said that the kid sounded like a dispossessed Balkan king, but decided that that would not be a good move. Instead I went straight in there. 'Paul doesn't have a family, then?'

'No, I'm afraid he doesn't. I have to rely on Johnny for the supply of little Wallingers.'

'Funny. When I met him he told me that he had a thing going with a British girl, and that she had just got pregnant.'

I'll swear she went pale under the makeup.

'Surely not,' she murmured, her eyes suddenly shifting, as if she had been taken completely off guard.

'That's what he told me, I'm sure. He said that he was based in London when he wasn't working.'

'When was this?'

129

'A couple of years back, in LA, like I said earlier. Actually, maybe it was more recently than that, maybe it was only eighteen months.' I gave her a west-coast laugh. 'Yes, it was winter, but in southern California it's easy to forget, isn't it?'

'He told you that?'

'Yup. You've been to LA, haven't you, Martha?'

She shook her head. 'No, Oz,' she replied, quietly, frowning a little. 'I've never been to California.'

'What? Not even to see where Paul works, much of the time?' I grinned. 'Mind you, who the hell am I to talk? My father's never been there either; he's been too busy pulling teeth in Scotland, just like you've been too busy managing assets in Minneapolis. You should take a trip, Martha, even if it's only to visit Universal Studios; you could take Lori and John the Third. They'd love it, I promise you. It might not be on the same scale as Disney World, but it's pretty spectacular.'

She smiled again, as if she was pleased that I'd gone off on another tangent. 'Maybe I'll do that; too many of us never leave the Midwest, you know. And I do love my grandchildren.' She looked at me, then at Prim. 'You have children, don't you? I'm sure I read somewhere that you do.'

'Two,' I replied. 'Janet and Jonathan; they're at home in Scotland with their nanny.'

Prim put a hand on my arm; for a second I thought she was going to say how wonderful they were, but she didn't. 'Martha,' she said instead, 'do you think I could use your bathroom?' She grinned at me. 'That root beer we had at lunchtime; you know the stuff always does this to me.'

'Me too,' our hostess agreed. 'It's that door straight behind where you're sitting.'

'Thanks. Excuse me.'

I guessed that she might be doing a runner to get out of talking about the kids: but then again, maybe she just needed to pee.

As soon as she was gone, Martha's frown returned. 'I can hardly believe my son said that to you. He was living with a British girl and she was pregnant? The damn fool.'

130

'It happens, Martha; you shouldn't blame the girl.'

'No, I mean it, he's a damn fool. He shouldn't be telling you things like that.'

'Come on, it's a different world we live in, guys like Paul and me.'

'Oz, you're not like Paul. My older son is a fantasist; he sails too close to the wind, he talks too much. I've always feared that one day he'll talk himself right into trouble.'

'Come on, Martha. He's an actor. What sort of trouble could he talk himself into?'

She looked at the floor, as if she was working up the courage to tell me: and then Prim came back from the bathroom.

'That's better,' she said, with evident relief. 'Martha, do you think I could have some more coffee now?'

'Of course, my dear,' her almost-mother-in-law replied, gratefully, picking up her mug and heading back to the kitchen.

'Oz,' Prim whispered, urgently, as soon as she was out of urgent-whisper range, 'go to the bathroom.'

'I don't need to; you're the one had the second root beer.'

'Don't be dense, just do it.'

I followed orders. 'Martha, do you think I might too?' I called across the vault.

'Of course.' She gave a girlish laugh. 'Maybe you could autograph the mirror in lipstick, in case my friends don't believe you were here.'

I got up and went into the bathroom, walking briskly as if I was on an urgent mission. As I closed the door behind me, I looked around. Okay, it was a very nice bathroom, not as nice as the one we had in our hotel room, or any of the five bathrooms I have in my house, but still nice, as American bathrooms, in my experience, tend to be. It was also full of women's things, all carefully arranged. There was nothing unusual about it, though: bath with shower over it, basin set into a marble top, toilet and bidet. (Suddenly I was reminded of a true story. Once, a few years back, before I was famous, my dad and I were in the golf-club bar with some other blokes, and the conversation got round to which of us actually used

131

a bidet and for what. To my surprise my dad owned up. He said that sometimes, rather than have a full bath, he found it handy for washing his bits and bobs. To which our chief inquisitor replied, 'Hey, Mac, washing your bits is one thing, but washing Bob's as well will definitely get you talked about in Anstruther.')

As I tried to work out why Prim had sent me in there, I found that I actually did need to pee; and so I did. I was washing my hands afterwards, looking in the mirror, when it caught my eye, the one item in the place that looked as if it shouldn't have been.

I picked it up. It was a duck, a rubber duck, of the kind one floats in the bath, if one is a child, or a very regressed adult. It was a familiar object to me, for my kids have one each; Janet has lost interest in hers, but wee Jonathan thinks his is great. Theirs are plain ducks, though, the usual yellow. This one was different; it had a slightly superior look about it, and it was dressed, or painted, entirely in the colours of the Union Jack. Martha Wallinger definitely did not strike me as a closet (not even a water-closet) anglophile, and the grandchildren in the photograph were, going by their age and their nationality, more likely to be found shooting ducks than floating them in their baths.

I was musing upon this as I rejoined the ladies. There were two ways I could take things: either I could simply let them drift, or I could start spilling the beans about the fantasist son Paul and putting pressure on his mother to tell us where the hell he was. I had a strong suspicion that if I did the first, as I was inclined to, then sooner rather than later, Prim would launch into the second.

So, as I resumed my seat beside her on the comfortable couch, I slipped an arm around her and gave her right buttock a good, firm squeeze. It was meant to say, 'Yes, I saw it.' It was meant to say also, 'Now keep your mouth shut and leave this up to me.' In days gone by I could express a range of meanings with a squeeze like that, the most common being carnal. I could only hope that she interpreted this one correctly.

'Martha,' I said. 'It's been really nice being with you. Now I have a confession to make. When I looked you up, it wasn't just to keep my promise to Paul. I need to get in touch with him.'

Her eyes narrowed and she peered at me with open suspicion. 'Why would a big star like you want to get in touch with my small-time son?'

'Because I might have a job for him. Miles Grayson and I are looking at a project: it's a little off fulfilment yet, but it'll involve casting an actor who looks reasonably like me in an important supporting role. Paul's worked with Miles in the past and his name came up in conversation. I've undertaken to locate him; my problem is that I can't find him. His agent, or the woman I thought was his agent, told me that they parted company a while back, and the Screen Actors' Guild can't help me either. So I'm keeping my promise and asking you for help at the same time.'

As I spoke to her, I saw her eyes return to their normal size, and the suspicion leave them. *You are good, Blackstone,* I told myself, *seriously fucking good.*

Martha deflated me pretty quickly, though. 'Oz,' she said, 'I wish I could help you, but the fact is that I can't. I haven't heard from Paul in over four years. He came back here when his father died and then a little later to help finalise the estate. I haven't seen or heard from him since. I wouldn't know how to go about contacting him; I'm sorry you've wasted your time.'

She looked at me with sincerity in her eyes. The trouble was, she wasn't as good at faking it as I am: I didn't believe her; or at least I didn't believe the last part of what she'd said.

I kept up my performance, though. 'It hasn't been wasted, Martha.' I rose, drawing Prim to her feet with me. 'I've kept a promise to a fellow actor. Maybe it was conscience that asked me to look you up. Whatever it was, I'll make you a promise. When I find him, I will certainly kick his ass.' I smiled at her as we walked to the door to the hallway, then added, 'And then I'll tell him to get in touch with his mother.'

'That would be appreciated, Oz,' she said, as she closed the door on us.

17

Prim said nothing as the elevator descended to the ground floor and as we walked through the lobby and back out on to Second Street, but I could feel her seething beside me.

The volcano erupted once we had walked far enough along the street to be out of sight of the apartment. 'She was lying, Oz!' Her shout startled me with its violence. 'She was lying in her bloody teeth! She knows where he is: they've been there, him and Tom. That was Tom's duck in the bathroom. I bought it for him myself in Oxford Street.'

I put my hands on her shoulders and turned her to me, to calm her as much as anything else. There weren't many people about, but I didn't want attention drawn to us. 'I know she lied, love, but we're not in a position to beat the truth out of her, are we?'

'Maybe they're still here. Maybe they were in that bloody apartment all the time, in one of the bedrooms.'

'And maybe Tom kept quiet all that time, hearing people in the living room, maybe even hearing your voice. I don't think so.'

'Maybe he was drugged.'

'Prim. Stop and think; Martha invited us to her place, remember. She insisted that you come. She wouldn't have done that if they were still hiding out there. She forgot about the duck in the bathroom, that's all.' I paused. 'No, it isn't. She'd no idea who you were when you stepped out of the lift. When she heard your first name she never even twitched, and she is not that good at pretending, trust me. She may know that Paul is on the run from Britain with his kid, but she doesn't know about you and she probably doesn't know about the money either.'

'So where does that leave us?' she demanded, as I flagged down a cab. It was as old and as battered as any taxi I'd ever seen, but it was there, and that was what mattered.

'The Merchant's,' I told the driver, as we slid into the cramped back seat.

'Where's that, mon?' he asked, in a slightly spaced voice.

'You're on First Avenue,' I told him. 'So is the Merchant's. Just drive straight along it until you get to the intersection with Sixth. Can you do that?'

'I can do dat, mon.'

He did it very slowly and carefully; I had to tell him where to stop.

In the elevator to the twentieth floor I switched my cell-phone back on; it told me that I had two voice messages. I checked them; one was from DI McLaren, the other from Mark Kravitz, and both wanted calls back.

They had to wait, though: I still had Prim to deal with. 'What are we doing here?' she wanted to know. 'We should be back at Paul's mother's place. We could get a car and park across the street, and watch for him.'

'As in a stake-out, you mean?'

'Yes. If he's not there now, he might come back. We could catch him.'

'And what if we hire a car and all the parking bays are full, like they were when we were there? Even if we found one near enough to Martha's place to be worth it, we'd stick out like a sore thumb.'

I sat her down on one of the beds and held her hand. 'Listen to me for a bit.' Her mouth went into one of its stubborn pouts, and her eyes glistened. I touched her chin, to make her look up, and, because it seemed like the best way to get rid of the pout and to get her attention, I kissed her, lightly. She blinked in surprise, but she kept looking at me.

'Listen, now,' I began. 'This is what I honestly believe. Paul was there, yes, and he was there with Tom. But he's been gone for two months, so it could have been weeks ago. He can't have told Martha anything about you . . . or, at least, not the truth about

135

you, for two reasons. One, she genuinely didn't recognise your name. Two, if he had told her, she'd have connected you with me straight away.'

'So maybe he will come back.'

'Is he that daft? He's going to be expecting you to come after him, and he'll assume this will be the first place you'll look. He touched down here with Tom, yes, and he went to see his mother, yes, but he won't have pushed his luck by hanging around. Plus, I'm pretty certain that Martha could contact him if she wanted. Maybe she will get word to him that I'm looking for him to offer him a job. You know what he's going to make of that; he'll figure out that I'm on his trail. I'm hoping that he's going to break cover, and run for it.'

'How will that help us?'

'If he does, what will he do? Sooner or later? He'll go to the money, that's what. Okay, we haven't been able to con Martha into giving us his address, but if we can trace your dough, we'll trace him.'

'But how are we going to do that?'

'We're not, but why in God's name do we employ policemen? McLaren, remember? There's a message on my phone for me to call him back.'

She'd been full of hope since we'd left. It had gone for a while, but now it returned, coloured by obvious relief that we hadn't hit a brick wall. She let out a great sigh. I lay down on my side on the bed, drawing her with me. I smiled at her, and stroked her hair. It was like a couple of times in the old days, when we'd been in trouble.

'It's going to be all right, honey. We'll find him.' I kissed her again, but on the forehead this time.

'What'll happen when we do?'

'Mark reckons that he'll offer to do a deal; he gets to keep the money, all formally agreed, no police, no nothing, and he'll relinquish Tom to you.' I didn't tell her about the extra scenario, where he might try to extort more from Miles.

'He can have the money; I just want my baby.'

'It won't come to that. You'll get Tom back, and Wallinger will get the nick.'

She threw her arms around me as we lay there, and hugged me; I could feel the new, unfamiliar weight of her breasts, I could taste her hair in my mouth, and feel the dampness of her tears on my face. I let her hold on to me, thinking of Susie, not as she'd become, but of how down and despairing she'd been when we'd first got it together, behind Prim's back. 'Funny how life can turn full circle,' I whispered.

'What?' she murmured.

'Nothing.' I rolled her gently on to her back and sat up.

'I wish you loved me,' she said. 'But after you find my son, I'll never ask anything of you again, never: that's a promise.'

'Aye, sure,' I said, with a laugh. 'I'm going to call McLaren.'

'What will I do?' she asked, with some of her old mischief. 'I want to do something for you, and since a blow-job seems out of the question . . . Tell me what I can do to help you.'

I thought about it, but nothing came immediately to mind. 'I dunno,' I admitted.

She frowned for a few seconds, then her face lit up.

'How about this?' she said. 'There's bound to be a hairdresser in this place. What if I find it, and get my hair cut shorter, the practical, nurse's cap way it used to be? To be honest, I've never really liked it this way.'

I looked at her, lying there, and thought of how she'd been in the past, in the good times. 'You're right,' I told her. 'You do that. If you really want to know, I think you look a hell of a lot younger with it shorter.'

'Say no more,' she said. 'You've convinced me.' She jumped up and looked in the mirror, smoothing her hair down, then ruffling it again.

As she launched into the rituals involved in getting ready to go to the hairdresser, I picked up the hands-free hotel phone and went through to our sitting area. I retrieved DI McLaren's number from my pocket PC . . . yes, I'm just like Harvey January in that respect; it goes everywhere with me . . . and called him.

'Mr Blackstone.' There was a bit of echo on the line, but otherwise it was clear. 'I've got some news for you.'

'Good news?'

'Up to a point.'

'You've traced it?'

'Yes.'

'That's a bloody good start, then. It's not in Minneapolis, is it?'

'No, it's nowhere near there. I did make enquiries of the firm whose number you gave me, but I was able to eliminate it right away. HHH doesn't handle funds from outside the USA; in fact, it hardly handles funds from outside Minnesota. It's a specialist local house with an impeccable reputation and, believe me, in these days of money-laundering, American fund managers are very closely scrutinised.'

'So where is it?'

'It's in a sterling account in a private bank called Fairmile and Company in Vancouver, British Columbia.'

'Under what name?'

'Primavera Phillips.'

'It's still in her name? Wasn't that a surprise to you?'

'Not really; I expected that it would be. Wallinger was acting as Ms Phillips's agent, remember, and that's all he was. When he sold up her investments, in the absence of a signed instruction from her to her bank, he'd have had no choice but to transfer the funds into her nominated account, the one into which dividend and interest payments were normally made. And when he went to move the money out, it would have had to go to another account in her name. Unless she told the bank herself, they wouldn't have transferred the money into any other account than one that's in her name.'

'What if he tried to do that?' I asked.

'The transmitting bank would have insisted on a signed authorisation, or on meeting her in person, quite possibly the latter.'

'Did he transfer it straight from the UK to Canada?'

'It wasn't in the UK, it was in the Isle of Man, but the answer is no: he moved it into a Jersey account first, then to Vancouver. He probably thought he was being clever. In other circumstances he might have been, using another off-shore bank as a launching platform, but I have excellent relationships with both of them, and they were prepared to talk to me.'

'How's he going to get the money out?'

'He'll have to go to Vancouver, show them Ms Phillips's letter of instruction and probably evidence of her ownership of the funds. On the basis of that he might be able to arrange some sort of staged transfer to another bank, one that's less scrupulous about setting up accounts.'

'But the money's still there?'

'So far, yes. I'd have expected him to have tried to move it by now, but he hasn't.'

'You've spoken to Fairmile and Company?'

'The local police have. However, there is very little big-scale fraud there; the Vancouver Police Department resources are mainly deployed elsewhere. They've done as much as they can in verifying that the account exists and that Ms Phillips is the owner of record. They can go no further without evidence of a crime.'

I began to realise why he had said that the news was good, up to a point. 'And there isn't any, is there?'

'No, there isn't, not yet; the funds haven't been moved out of Ms Phillips's control, so technically no theft has taken place. Presumption of intent is way short of evidence. That means I can't take this any further, short of taking leave, getting on a plane and going to Canada myself.' He hesitated; for a moment I thought he was going to volunteer to do that, but his loyalty to Mike Dylan didn't stretch that far. 'Where are you, right now?' he asked.

'We're in Minneapolis; we've just seen Wallinger's mother. She says he's her prodigal son and she hasn't a clue where he is. We're not quite so sure, though. We saw some evidence that a fatted calf might have been killed recently.' I told him about Tom's duck.

'Then you've got a choice to make, Oz. Either you stay on the trail of Wallinger, or you go to Vancouver so that Ms Phillips can visit Fairmile and Company in person, identify herself and resume personal control of her funds, cutting Wallinger out of the picture.

Or maybe not; maybe you could do both, with you keeping trying to find him and her going straight to Vancouver; but either way she needs to do that right away.'

'We could always go there and sit tight for a while,' I said. 'She could instruct the bank, then we could just wait for him to turn up, as he's bound to do.' Then I remembered that I had to be in Las Vegas at the weekend.

I was thinking about this when I heard Prim behind me. ' 'Bye,' she called out. 'I'm off to be shorn.'

I could have told her to wait, but I just waved airily in her direction and let her go.

'Okay,' I said to McLaren. 'It's for us to sort out. I really appreciate what you've done so far. At the moment I've got no leads here, so I think we'll both go west. If we get there and find that he's been there since you spoke to VPD, I'll report it to them, and let you know what's happened, if anything has.'

'Yes, do that. The moment he moves money out of that account to his own use he's committed a crime, and I can get a warrant for his arrest.'

I have this habit of coming up with annoying and complicating thoughts just when I don't need them. 'What if he transfers money to Tom?'

'Without her instruction it would still be a crime.'

'Good. Thanks again, Inspector.'

I thought about our discussion for a while longer, and then I returned Mark Kravitz's call.

'What have you got?' I asked him, without preamble.

'Nothing you could hang your hat on, I'm afraid. I haven't traced Prim's break-in merchants, and neither have the police. However, I've been asking around and I've found out that your Mr Wallinger is a bit of a gambler. I wondered whether something like that might be behind it. Turns out that he has an account with a London bookmaker; it's operated through the Internet, but they have a record of his home address. His debts are settled on a direct debit through an American bank, and the arrangement's worked in the past. A couple of months ago, just after Wallinger did his runner, the bookie sent in a debit for ten grand's worth of losers and it rubbered on him.'

'So you're guessing that he sent people to collect.'

'I can't go and ask him, Oz, but it looks like it.'

'So they nicked the diamonds to cover Wallinger's gambling debt?'

Mark grunted. 'That's the way it looks. The insured value of the gems will be way more than the debt, but they'll have to break them up to move them, so overall what they'll get will be pretty close. Meantime, I assume they're insured: yes?'

'I suppose so; she's not daft.'

'Then at least Prim isn't going to lose out of it.'

'There is that to it.'

'Any further instructions?'

'Yes. Do some general asking around. Speak to neighbours, postmen and such; ask if they've seen anyone hanging around, and see if you can find out when Wallinger was seen last. I suppose it's possible that he might have gone back there.'

'What good will that do?'

'Probably none; I want to get a handle on his movements, that's all. It'll keep Prim happy.'

'Will do, boss. What's up where you are? My phone tells me you're in the US.'

When I updated him on McLaren's discovery, he laughed. 'The guy's not as clever as he thought, is he? It leaves you two a bit stretched, though. Do you want Conrad out there as back-up?'

'Conrad's first job is to protect my family. I can manage without him.'

'If you're sure. I'll ask those questions, and contact you again when I've got answers.' I wasn't sure he'd find any, and if he did whether they'd mean anything was just as uncertain.

I thought about Vancouver and made an executive decision, without consulting Prim. Her deductive processes were muddled by the loss of her son, but I reasoned that if she went to Vancouver and secured her money that could only strengthen her hand when it came to negotiating. I don't play cards very often, but when I do, I don't like the other guy to hold all the aces.

141

I called Susie again, although it was damn near midnight at home, told her what was happening, and asked her to have Audrey book us on to a flight to Vancouver next day, find us a hotel there for another couple of nights and to call me back, whatever the time, with the details.

With that behind me, I tried to put in some time with the script, but my concentration was shot. I decided that I needed some hard physical time to clear my mind, so I called Reception to book myself into the hotel's fitness centre and set off down there to punish myself. (For getting so wrapped up in this business? Probably.)

The gym was well equipped, and at that time of day, very quiet; there were a couple of ladies . . . force me to guess and I'd have said they were cabin crew . . . running on treadmills, but that was it. I did some loosening exercises and then set to work on the heavy apparatus, building up until I was pressing some pretty serious weights with both my arms and my legs. I did a bit of circuit training when I was a kid, but it was the guys at the Global Wrestling Association who got me into it seriously. My buddy Liam Matthews showed me how to increase my strength and endurance without bulking up too much, but over the years I have put on quite a bit of muscle, so now I have to keep working at it to make sure that my body shape stays the same throughout the period of filming a project. If you look closely at some celebrated movies you'll see the lead player going from fat to slim then back again.

I had been at it for around three-quarters of an hour when I became aware of a uniformed bellboy standing in the doorway, looking at me, hesitantly. I was in the middle of fifty bench presses, so I finished them and then turned towards him. 'You want me?'

'If you're available, Mr Blackstone: there's a police officer in the foyer, asking if he can see you.'

A cop? What the hell had I done to annoy the local bizzies? I asked myself. 'Tell him to wait in the lounge,' I told the boy. 'I'm just about finished here, but I'll have to warm down properly, then shower. Offer him a drink and put it on my tab.'

I didn't hang about, but it took twenty minutes before I was ready to go down. My hair was still wet, but I slicked it back.

The lounge waiter pointed out my visitor as soon as I appeared. He was sitting with his back to me, facing the door and fidgeting like a nervous gun-fighter. There was a beer on the table in front of him, but it was barely touched. He sprang to his feet when I appeared in front of him, and I knew at once who he was. I'd seen his photograph that very afternoon, on Martha Wallinger's sideboard.

'You'll be John the Second,' I said to him, offering him a handshake. He had a crusher of a grip; he tried it on me, but when I want to, so have I. He was a big guy, though, around six four, and he wasn't smiling.

'Lieutenant John Wallinger, MPD,' he replied, as we sat. 'Narcotics Unit.'

'I don't use them.'

'Glad to hear it: too many public figures do.'

'This one has a wife and a couple of kids. What can I do for you, Lieutenant?' Actually I was wondering what he could do for me, but I thought I'd work up to that.

He went straight to the point, though. 'I'm concerned about your visit to my mother, Mr Blackstone. It's alarmed her, and I don't like that.'

'I'm sorry if that's the case, but presumably she told you why I called.'

'She did, and if it's true that you and Mr Grayson have some significant work for Paul, that'll be excellent for him but, to be honest, that strikes me as a smokescreen.'

'Why should that be?'

'Because I've checked you out since my mother called me, sir, and there's a couple of things that don't sit square.'

'Such as?'

'The lady you had with you today, she wasn't your wife, was she?'

'I never said that she was.'

His eyes hardened, letting me see what Minneapolis drug-dealers

143

were up against. 'Don't play games with me, sir. I checked you up on several websites; your wife's name is Susan, formerly Susan Gantry. Her photograph appears on some of them, and she does not fit the description of the woman you took to meet my mother. So who was that?'

'The websites you saw must have been authorised; they don't discuss my previous marriages. My first wife was killed in a domestic accident; my second wife, Primavera, and I divorced. That's who I took to meet your mother; Mrs Blackstone all right, just not the current model, that's all. They've got a photocopy of her passport at Reception; I'm surprised you didn't check it out.'

He let slip a flash of a smile. 'I did. I wanted you to tell me about it, that's all.'

'Right, so now I have. Where do we go from here?'

'I want you to explain to me just what the hell you really are doing here. The thing that you said to my mother that really upset her was about my brother. You said he told you that he'd got an English girl pregnant.'

'If we're being strictly accurate I said British, not English.'

'What's the difference?'

'Imagine me calling you a Texan. British, but not English; in fact she was Scottish, the same as me, the same as Primavera. In fact, it was Primavera.'

His back straightened in his chair as he stared at me. 'He told you that?'

It was time for a small confession. 'No. The fact is I've never met your brother; it was Prim who told me all about it.'

The big man gasped. 'That's unbelievable . . . Paul?'

I decided to give him the whole story. 'They've been living in London for a couple of years. Prim had a son, called Tom; she thought your brother was a stockbroker. She had so much confidence in him that she gave him control over her investments. A little under three months ago, they vanished. So did Paul. So did Tom. We've come here to find him.'

I could see that he was stunned. 'That's amazing,' he murmured. He looked up at me. 'All the same, Mr Blackstone, you've come to the wrong place. My brother hasn't been here. Didn't my mother tell you that?'

'Yes, she did. But what if I was to tell you that we have evidence that he has?'

The hard look he'd shot me before was a baby beside the one that came into his eyes. 'Then you'd be calling my mom a liar, mister, and that would be a very serious mistake on your part. In fact, it would be liable to make me forget about the badge I carry, and take you for a walk out back.'

In such circumstances, I've always found that the best course of action is to smile; so I did. 'Are you threatening me, Lieutenant?' I asked him.

'Call it a promise,' he growled.

'Well, John,' I said, 'I've had promises like that made to me before in my life; not many, but some. And yet I don't remember one ever being kept. We can go for a walk out back if you like, but big and all as you are, I promise you, I'll walk back in first.'

His eyes didn't alter, and I kept my smile fixed on him; we had a bit of a stand-off going, and I really didn't fancy getting into a brawl with a cop, even if he did look far too straight a guy to stand a chance against some of the tricks I've been taught by my GWA pals. So I decided to offer him a way out.

'I wouldn't dream of calling your mother a liar,' I told him. 'However, I think you should consider the possibility that your brother might have been back here without her knowledge, or yours. How does that hang with you?'

He took a deep breath. 'I'll consider it.'

'Can I ask you something?' I continued, quickly. He nodded. 'Why were you so certain he wouldn't show up here? And why were you so surprised when I told you what he'd been up to?'

'Mr Blackstone,' he replied, 'I'm a police officer, so I'm used to asking questions not answering them. All I'll say is that the Wallinger family does not wash its dirty linen even in private, far less in public. We're Christian people with Christian values, and Paul simply did not live up to them. You misread my reactions: your accusations of deceit and dishonesty don't shock me at all.'

145

I still didn't believe his mother, but him, I did. 'Where should I look for him, John, if not here?'

'I don't know. I'd guess California; if he's still pursuing his dream he'll probably go back there, now that he's got the sort of money that would support a lifestyle there.'

'He doesn't; not yet at any rate. I think he might be setting up a trade: the money for Tom.'

'But . . .'

'But what? Kidnap? He's the kid's father.'

The big man frowned. 'Mr Blackstone,' he murmured, 'I want you to apologise to your ex-wife on behalf of my mother and myself for my brother's behaviour. I want you to give me a number where I can contact you. I've got resources here that you haven't, and access to the means of finding an American citizen in his own country. I'll look for him, and when I find him, wherever he is, I'll put you on his trail. He deserves whatever's coming to him, and you strike me as the man to make sure he gets it.'

I gave him one of my personal cards, and took his in return. 'That'll get me, any time. I'm gone from here tomorrow morning, but I'll be in the States for another two weeks and more.'

'Okay,' he said. 'I'd appreciate it if you didn't approach my mother again. Leave this entirely with me.'

'As you wish. There is one thing you could do for me right now, though.'

'What's that?'

'Suggest somewhere to eat tonight; we did Gluek's yesterday.'

'Try Murray's, twenty-six South Sixth Street; it's our local celebrity restaurant. You better book, though.'

I thanked him and walked with him to the entrance. 'There's one more thing I got to ask you,' he said, as we reached it. 'Since you're travelling with your ex-wife, how come you're in the same room?'

'A clerical error on their part: no kidding. And they promised me discretion, too.'

He grinned. 'My badge overrides that.'

I took his advice about the restaurant. Our discreet friend from the check-in fiasco was back on duty; I considered rattling his cage about spilling the beans to the lieutenant, but simply asked him to make a booking for us.

Prim was back from the hairdresser's when I got back to our room, standing in the dressing area sorting out something for the evening. The tint was gone from her hair, it was blonde again, and the same length as it had been when we met for the first time, if not quite so sun-bleached and a lot less ruffled. I'd forgotten how brown her eyes were. She looked like herself again: it was like stepping back eight years.

I must have been staring; my mouth was maybe even a little open, just a little. 'Will this do?' she asked, coyly. There's nobody does coy like Prim, especially when her shirt's unbuttoned and hanging apart.

'Will it ever,' I heard myself say, then found myself taking a step towards her. I got hold of myself in time and simply put my hands on her shoulders, admiring her makeover. 'Yes,' I told her, 'that does more for me than a blow-job any day.'

'You poor, sad old man.' She laughed.

The restaurant lived up to its billing. Murray's house specialty is a thing called the Silver Butter Knife steak; I'm not sure where it got the name, but the way they pitch it at you, it's more or less compulsory, so we both had it. I was glad I'd earned mine in the gym.

Once we'd finished, and the strolling violinist had done his thing, taken his tip and strolled on, I told her that we were heading for Vancouver next day, together, and why. I'd been worried that she might have seen it as a distraction, but she understood the importance of the move, and the leverage it would give her when it came to getting Tom back.

She misted over again when I mentioned his name. 'I wonder how he is, Oz,' she whispered. 'And how will he be when we find him? He's been gone so long, he'll have grown. Will he even know me?'

'Of course he will. I promise you, he will; I can be away from my kids for weeks at a time, yet whenever I get back they tear me apart.'

147

'But this is such a big chunk of his life.'

'Prim, honey, you could have been separated at birth and I reckon he'd still know you.'

She gave me a strange, quizzical look. 'You're sure of that, are you?'

'I reckon so.'

It was time to give her something positive to think about, so I told her about my visit from Lieutenant John Wallinger the Second. By the time I was finished she was radiating a mixture of excitement and indignation. 'He came to scare you off?' she exclaimed.

'He may have come to try that, but I doubt it. John's just an honest guy, and he'd die for his mom.'

'But she's a liar! We know that.'

I held up a hand. 'Maybe, just maybe, what I suggested was right. Maybe Paul and Tom arrived in Minneapolis while she was away. There's a concierge in that block; maybe he talked him into handing over a key, and spent a night or two there until he was ready to move on. It's not that crazy an idea: the guy's a con-man, remember.'

'Mmm.' She didn't sound convinced.

'Whatever, and whatever the family skeletons might be, the important thing is that we've got his brother . . . his policeman brother . . . playing for our team, and promising to hand him over on a plate. What more can we ask for at this stage? Think of where we were after we'd seen Martha . . . no-bloody-where.'

'I suppose. But if I couldn't trust Paul, are you sure we can trust his brother?'

'I've looked him in the eye. I'm sure.' I hoped that I was right.

She seemed mollified. I paid the bill, and we walked the short distance back to the hotel . . . downtown Minneapolis is so compact that there don't seem to be any long distances. I told the manager we'd be checking out in the morning. There was no message for me about travel details, but it was just a little too early for that. I made sure that whenever a call came in it would be put through, and we took the lift to the twentieth.

There was none of the gauche awkwardness of the night before.

148

We had come to terms with the situation, plus there were no physical secrets between the two of us. We were friends rooming together and, as I saw it, that was that. We sat in the darkness and looked out at the city lights for a while, then Prim went through to the sleeping area and returned, minus the light summer dress she'd been wearing, and unwrapping our joint pyjamas. I didn't turn my eyes away this time.

I gazed at her, almost nostalgically, as she picked at the packaging, taking in the familiar shape of her body. It was unchanged, apart from the bigger bust, and something else I noticed. She caught me looking, and smiled. 'A present from my son,' she murmured. 'Stretch marks; not a damn thing I can do about them.'

I laughed. 'Your Tom's a generous kid.'

She caught my meaning. 'These? I thought they'd go back to normal size after I stopped feeding him, but they never have.' She dropped the pyjamas on to a chair, crumpled the wrapping, and unclipped her bra. 'Gross,' she said.

'I preferred the old models,' I admitted, 'but those have a certain charm to them. Large, my dear, but not gross in any way; you've got the width of shoulders to carry them.'

She raised an eyebrow. 'Take a last look, then, and wish them a fond farewell.' She picked up the pyjama jacket, and pulled it over her head, without unbuttoning it. 'Goodnight,' she said, then leaned over me, kissed me like a sister, on the cheek, and went through to bed.

18

The phone rang. I hoped it would stop, but it didn't, just kept on ringing and ringing until I had swum out of my confused dream about Prim, Spain, and people who were dead. I picked it up, and mumbled a 'Yes?' into the receiver.

'Mr Blackstone, this is the night clerk. I have a call for you.'

I blinked myself awake, and switched on the light. I was aware of Prim in the twin bed, propping herself up on an elbow, looking at me.

I'd been expecting Audrey, but it was Susie. 'Did I waken you?' she asked, solicitously.

'Six-hour time difference, but it doesn't matter.'

'Poor love.' She sounded sorry for me. 'You're booked on a Northwest flight tomorrow morning, direct to Vancouver from Minneapolis, departure nine twenty-seven. You're in the Granville Island Hotel; the travel agent said it's small but very nice.'

'That's good, thanks, love.'

'Is everything going well?'

'Reasonably. We've got help.' I told her about Wallinger's brother.

'That's good,' she said. 'How's Prim bearing up?'

'She won't be happy till she's got Tom back, but she's doing okay.'

'That's good.' She paused. 'I'll tell you what.' Suddenly she was yelling. 'Just you put her on the phone and she can tell me herself!'

Oh, shit!

'Susie,' I started.

'You bastard! And I was stupid enough to insist that she went with you!'

'It's okay!' I exclaimed. 'Honestly, it's okay. There's nothing going on. They made a balls of the booking, that's all.' There are very few occasions on which economy with the truth can be justified, but I felt that I had happened upon one of them. 'It's a bloody great suite,' I protested. 'It's all they had left, but it's about the size of our house. Honest.'

'Are you trying to tell me you're not sleeping with her?'

'No, I'm promising you, okay?'

'Can I believe that?' she asked, with just a little more scorn, scepticism, call it what you like, than I was able to take.

It was the middle of the night. I was tired. I was upset. I was right in the zone for saying something really stupid. 'What?' I barked into the phone. 'On the basis of past performance, do you mean?'

I hit way too close to home. 'You bastard!' she yelled, once, then again in case I hadn't caught it the first couple of times. The line went dead, and I was left staring pointlessly at the handset, until finally I slammed it back into the cradle.

'Are you in trouble?' Prim asked.

'No, my dear. We are in trouble; both of us.'

'Oh, Oz, I'm so sorry. Is there anything I can do to fix it? Should I call her?'

'God, no.' I picked up the phone again and called the night clerk. 'I want you to think very carefully,' I told him. 'When that call came in for me, and the caller asked for me, what were the exact words you used: no approximations, the exact words?'

He sounded unflustered. 'Yes, sir. I said, "Hold on, please, madam, while I put you through to their room." That's exactly what I said, word for word. I hope that was in order.'

I've rarely felt such anger, but I resisted the temptation to roar my response. Instead I spoke slowly and quietly. 'You were given no special instructions?'

'No, sir.'

'Okay, here are some special instructions now. I want you to get in touch with the duty manager who checked us in. I mean get in touch with him at once; waken him, like I was wakened. I want you

151

to tell him exactly what's happened, word for word. Then I want you to give him a message from me. Tell him that I am not a vindictive man, and I have never in my life caused anyone to lose his job. However, he should know this: once I've spoken to the general manager, he will be fucking history here. Did you get that?'

'Yes, sir.'

'Well, do it, please. Once you have, book me . . . us . . . an alarm call for seven, and have a car waiting to take us to MSP International at eight.'

'Very good, Mr Blackstone.'

'One other thing: when I check out, I want the general manager there, in person, so I can make my feelings clear to him.'

I hung up and turned back to Prim. Her brown eyes were wide open. 'It's that bad?' she asked.

'It's that bad.' I held up the duvet on my bed, feeling the Oz Blackstone that used to be take complete control. 'Do you want to come over? If I'm going to be hung for it, we might as well do the crime.'

'You'd hate us both in the morning,' she replied. 'Put out the light, and try to sleep.'

I did. I tried. I couldn't.

19

She was wrong, though: I wouldn't have hated her in the morning, only myself. I knew it as I watched her sleep, as I had many times in the past. The head that had lain on the pillow the night before had belonged to someone else, but the crumpled blonde look was definitely her.

I was smiling when she woke, as the phone rang our alarm bell, and focused on me.

'You've cooled down, then?'

'I reckon.'

'Do you still want me to come over there?'

'No,' I told her, although the part of me without brains wanted just that.

'I'll shower first, then.' She pulled off the pyjama top and climbed out of bed.

'Good morning, ladies,' I said.

The general manager was indeed waiting when I went to check out. His name was Benjamin E. King and he was full of apologies; he promised me a full internal investigation, and he did indeed offer me his assistant's head on a plate. I turned it down, but accepted his offer to waive our bill. Charles's smile was even wider than before as we climbed into the limo. I guessed that word had spread around the staff.

As soon as we had cleared flight security, I found a phone in the executive lounge and called home. Audrey answered, sounding distinctly uncomfortable. 'Oz, it wasn't me,' she said. 'I didn't make the mistake, honestly.'

'I know you didn't. Don't tell me Susie's blaming you.'

153

'She hasn't said anything, but I get this feeling that she might be.'

'I'll sort it, don't worry. Is she around?'

'No, she's gone to the Gantry Group office for a meeting.'

'Okay. When she gets back, please tell her I called, and that I'll call her again from Vancouver.'

It was a long flight, halfway across a continent and a bit more. The weekend was drawing near so I used the time to concentrate on Everett's script, and on my longer scenes. The skies were cloudless, and Prim spent the time staring out of the window at the vastness of the northern states as they unrolled before her. I'd no idea what she was thinking about, but that sight on that sort of day doesn't leave much room in the mind for anything else.

I hoped it was doing her good. As hard as I focused on my lines in the forthcoming movie, Susie's angry voice kept breaking through. I was still kicking myself for the stupid thing I'd said to her in the middle of the night. Effectively I'd told her that when I was married to Prim she hadn't had too many scruples herself, but that was then and this was another world, in which such an argument was irrelevant.

'Fuck it!' I muttered under my breath. 'Who needs to be a nice guy?' But then I thought about Janet and wee Jonathan, and I realised that I did. There was a problem about that, though. The Prim with whom I was travelling was not the shocked, emotionally broken half-drunk who'd tottered off the shuttle a week before, she was a woman who'd recovered her formidable courage and her sense of purpose. More than that she'd transformed her dowdy appearance, and had become a slightly older version of a woman for whom I'd had the serious hots from the very beginning. If she'd taken up my angry proposition in the middle of the night, I could only imagine the trouble I'd be in.

I thought about it and patted her on the shoulder. 'Thanks,' I said.

She looked away from Montana and at me. 'For what?'

'For keeping me honest.'

She smiled, took my hand and squeezed it. 'Someone has to. But to be honest myself, tonight I'll miss sleeping beside you.'

'Yeah, well. If we hadn't messed things up in the past . . .'

'You wouldn't have been as happy as you are now . . . or nearly as successful. Susie's made you, I'd have held you back.'

Suddenly I felt resentful. 'Hey, cool that one,' I told her. 'I've made myself. I've had a lot of help in the planning, but the execution's been down to me.'

I was still thinking about that as we swung out over the strait that divides Vancouver from its island then round for landing.

I'd been to the city before and to Toronto, filming, so I was familiar with the strict formality of Canadian Immigration, but it took Prim by surprise. 'Don't they want people in their country?' she asked, when, eventually, we'd been cleared.

'Sure. They just don't want the wrong people.'

There was another limo waiting for us, sent by the hotel on Audrey's instruction. It wasn't quite as plush as the Minneapolis job, but it was okay, and it was big enough to handle our luggage, which was all I really wanted. When we saw the Granville Island Hotel, I realised that I'd been there already. A couple of autumns before I'd been filming in the city and had been invited to a Scots reception organised as part of Vancouver's annual writers' festival.

It's built on the waterfront, on a sheltered creek that cuts into the city and divides it. Granville Island is really an islet, and you can drive on to it, but it has the feel of a separate community. Once it was all industrial but now it's very arty-crafty, with several theatres and workshops, although there is still a cement factory there, managing to co-exist happily with everything going on around it. The hotel lived up to the rest of the place . . . quirky, modern in design but appealing.

The rooms were fine too, and this time we had one each, one floor up, at the front of the hotel, on either corner, looking down on some quite expensive boats and out across the water. The two corridors were divided by a glass-walled area that contained . . . I could hardly believe my eyes . . . a micro-brewery.

I left Prim to settle in and went to my room, to do an E.T. and phone home. The time change meant that it was still well shy of noon in British Columbia, but evening in Scotland. I had no

155

illusions about the welcome that my wife had in store for me, but I wanted very badly to speak to my daughter.

It wasn't as bad as I'd feared; in the twelve hours since we'd last spoken, or shouted, Susie had cooled down. In fact she'd gone all the way to frosty, but I could put up with that. 'It wasn't Audrey's fault,' I told her at once. 'I heard her make the booking.'

'Yes, I accept that . . . but then you changed it.'

'I didn't, love, honestly. It was the hotel's mistake, they didn't have a second room, and Minneapolis was full of Elks or Shriners, or whatever they call masons there. I'm going to tell you this once and you're going to believe me: we didn't sleep in the same bed. To quote a former president, "I did not have sex with that woman." Or maybe I shouldn't quote him, all things considered.'

'No,' she growled, 'maybe you shouldn't . . . unless you think that blow-jobs don't count as well.' A flutter ran through me at her use of the phrase.

'I had an e-mail, Oz,' she said, making my flutter fly away at once.

'You had a what?'

'An e-mail; it landed in my mailbox at the Gantry Group. It was from pwallinger . . . one word . . . at trickledown dot com.'

'How would he know your e-mail address?' The question was out as I realised its futility: all he'd have to do was look up the Gantry website. All the senior people, including Susie, have addresses listed there. 'What did it say?' I pressed on.

'It said, "Do you really believe him?" That was all. I sent him back a reply, saying "Yes, now fuck off." Then I called you at your hotel, to tell you about it, and to give you your flight information at the same time, and the guy on the switchboard let slip that you and your ex were in the same room. Is the lad still attached to his balls, Oz?'

'By a single hair. Susie, you do believe me, yes? I'll swear to you on anything you like.'

'Since you put it like that, okay. How's your new accommodation?'

'Separate.'

156

'Just as well. How long will you be in Vancouver?'

'Three days, maximum: I have to be in Vegas on Sunday, remember. All we have to do here is secure Prim's money, and see if we can pick up anything at the bank it's in that might lead us to Wallinger. At least that's what I thought; that e-mail changes everything. We're after him, but the bastard's tracking us.'

'How did he know you were in Minneapolis, far less at that hotel?'

Good question, and I could only come up with one answer: dear old Mom had tipped him off. I told Susie about our call on her, and about my visit from brother John the Second. 'What time did you say that e-mail arrived?'

'It was there when I opened my box, less than half an hour before I called you.'

'No, when did it arrive? It should tell you.'

'Hold on, I'm switched on here. I can look.'

I waited for a minute or so.

'It says that it was received at seven minutes past eleven.'

'Well after I'd seen Mamma Wallinger, in that case.'

'Couldn't it have been the brother who tipped him off?' she asked.

'I don't see it. I got the impression that John regards Paul as a non-person. But maybe I was wrong; maybe I'm losing it when it comes to judging people.'

'Maybe I am too,' Susie muttered.

'Hey, don't start that again. Is Janet still up? I want to speak to her.'

I had a conversation with my excited daughter, who updated me on the politics of her nursery school, then spoke to my son, who updated me with the contents of his stomach, judging by the noise he made into the phone, before finally I said goodnight, or good-day, depending on location, to my wife. Her farewell was warmer than her greeting: at least that was something.

I had told Prim that I'd see her at midday; that gave me time to spare. I'm not a computer nerd, but everywhere I go these days I take my laptop. There was direct Internet access in my room, so I

157

dug it out of its flight case and plugged the modem into the wall.

Once it was booted up, I piggy-backed on to my AOL account and hit the 'write' icon. It waved at me and set me up with a blank. I keyed in 'pwallinger@trickledown.com' then wrote in the message box. What I said to him was as follows:

Until you e-mailed my wife, I was only in this for Prim's sake. Now I'm in it for mine, and I'm coming to get you.

I hit the 'send' button, disconnected and switched off the machine without checking the rest of my mail and went off to collect Prim with a feeling of satisfaction.

I didn't tell her about Susie's message: it would only have upset her, and I saw no point in that. Instead I made sure that she had all the papers she would need when we tackled Fairmile and Company, and then we headed downstairs.

Prim had been for calling the bank to make an appointment, but I had talked her out of it. The way I saw it, we didn't know anything about them, and we didn't know what sort of a relationship they had with Wallinger. I preferred to go in with weapons locked and loaded and to take them by surprise, so the game plan was to grab a bite of lunch . . . on Minneapolis time, a very late lunch . . . then head straight there.

We stepped out of the lift and were heading for Reception to find a street map, when someone shouted across the hallway, 'Oz? Oz Blackstone? Is that you?' Surprised, I stared at the source, and saw approaching, with a smile on her face, a small woman with black, grey-flecked hair. She was middle-aged but had an eternally youthful look about her. 'Alma,' she reminded me. 'We met here a couple of years back.'

It clicked into place. She was the director of the Writers' Festival; we'd been introduced at the Scots Night and since she'd originated in Edinburgh we'd hit it off. In fact we'd wound up talking for the rest of the reception and into the evening in the hospitality room that she maintained for visiting authors.

'Hi,' I greeted her. 'How are you doing?'

'Busy as hell,' she told me amiably. 'This is the time of year when much of the work gets done. What brings you to town? Another movie?'

'No. It's a flying visit. This is Primavera; she's my ex-wife.' As the two women shook hands I could read the question Alma was bursting to ask. 'It's a long story,' I said. 'The short version is that Prim has to pay a call on a private bank here in town and she needs a witness.'

'Who are they?'

I told her.

'On Horner Street? I know them. One of my board members was a director until he retired. Have you dealt with them for long?'

'I've never met them,' Prim admitted.

'They're very good, very reputable. If you like, I'll ask Gordon to call them and pave the way for you, make sure they give you the VIP treatment. He still has clout there.' She gave a clear, bell-like laugh. 'Come to think of it, he has clout everywhere, even in my office.'

I thought about her offer, and accepted. A little inside influence couldn't do any harm.

'When were you planning to go there?'

'About two thirty.'

'Gordon will make sure they're expecting you.'

'That's terrific,' said Prim.

'Don't mention it. Anything else I can help with?'

'How about somewhere for lunch?' I suggested.

'The Sandbar, just down there on Johnston Street; make sure you go upstairs. If you're here for breakfast tomorrow, go to Granville Island Market.'

'We'll do all that. Would you like to join us?'

'Love to, but I got to fly.' She waved us goodbye and bustled off towards the door.

I asked the reception manager to book us a car for two fifteen, to take us to Horner Street, then we headed off to find the Sandbar.

It was five minutes' walk away, almost within sight of the hotel. As Alma had advised, we ate on the rooftop deck, from a menu that

159

boasted most of the fish in the Pacific. I ordered a jumbo shrimp starter followed by orange roughy; Prim was in 'bore for Scotland' mode and settled for plain ordinary halibut. Our high table overlooked downtown Vancouver, and the False Creek Ferries that cross the inlet from Granville Island.

We felt more or less normal when we got back to the hotel, although already the day was stretching out in the way it does when you fly across five American states and try to pretend that it's nothing. Prim wanted to do a girlie thing and change into something more formal, but the car was waiting for us, so I told her she looked business-like enough.

In the afternoon traffic ... Vancouver's a busier city than Minneapolis, where most of the cars spend the day in off-street parks ... we got to Fairmile and Company with two minutes to spare, even though it was in a building we could see from the island.

The offices were on the sixth floor of a high-rise: this was not the sort of establishment whose customers walked in off the street to withdraw a couple of hundred loonies ... that's the Canadian equivalent of 'bucks', or 'quid'; they say that the looney is a bird, but I'm not convinced.

Whatever position Alma's pal had held there, it must have been a senior one for, as she said, he still had clout. The uniformed bloke in the lobby who'd directed us to the lift must have been under orders to phone ahead of us, for when I opened the door and stepped into Reception, the chief executive himself was waiting for us. He was a tall, slim, bald bloke, and he looked at least sixty, although if you'd told me he was ten years older than that I wouldn't have argued.

He stepped up to me, hand outstretched. 'Mr Blackstone, I'm Bill Hoover, president. I'm so pleased to welcome you to Fairmile. My former colleague Gordon Barney called to advise me of your visit. Come on through and you can tell me what it's all about.'

I introduced Prim and we followed him into a room that was smaller than mine at the hotel: modest indeed by bank president standards, and deliberately so, I guessed, to make the right

160

impression on clients. In fact, it had the same feel as HHH Asset, for all that I'd seen of it.

'The first thing I should say, Mr Hoover,' I began, 'is that I'm not the principal at this meeting, Prim is. You're holding a substantial deposit here, transferred from an account in Jersey; it's her money and she wants to take full control of it.'

The president frowned. 'I'm aware of the account in question, set up around three months ago by an intermediary.' He ruffled through several files on his desk until he found the right one. 'Mr Paul Wallinger, on behalf of Primavera Phillips.' He looked at Prim. 'That would be your maiden name, yes?'

'That's right,' she replied, then delved into her own papers, and slid two across Hoover's desk. 'These are copies of my birth certificate, and of my passport, to prove that I am who I say I am.'

I smiled. 'And I'm here to verify that she is who she says she is.'

'That isn't in doubt. However, what I'll need to see is proof of ownership of the funds. It's not that I doubt anything that's being said here; we have laws and I have independent supervision, so everything has to be done by the book.'

'Sure,' said Prim. 'I understand that and here is the book.' She took a file from her bag and handed it across. 'Those are papers showing a chain of ownership, from my original investment portfolio put in place by my former advisers, through to its sale by Mr Wallinger and the transfer of the proceeds through Jersey to you. They're all copies, but they've been notarised by a solicitor.' She produced one further document, in a long slim envelope, and gave it to him. 'And that is an original, an instruction by me revoking Mr Wallinger's appointment as my adviser.'

Hoover opened the file and went through it from back to front. When he was finished he looked up and smiled. 'Do I call you Miss Phillips or Mrs Blackstone?' he asked.

'Ms Phillips, but Primavera, or even Prim, will do fine.'

'In that case, Primavera, Fairmile and Company is very pleased to have you as a client for however long you may choose to leave your funds with us.'

'I haven't given that any thought, Mr Hoover. I have other priorities at the moment. How am I invested at the moment?'

'On Mr Wallinger's instructions your funds are in a three-month fixed-term sterling deposit account, earning you around four per cent annual compounded.' He paused and consulted a computer on his desk. 'Your first maturity date is due the week after next.'

'That's fine for now. But if I'm going to stay with you I'll need to do better than that.'

'Prim, we can do better than that. Let me ask you, are you planning to reside in Canada?'

She smiled. 'Much as I like it at first sight, I don't think so.'

'Do you have dependants?'

'I have a son.' She frowned as she replied, but Hoover didn't notice.

'Then I would probably advise you to look at setting up an international trust as a means of protecting your, if I may say so, substantial assets, wherever you decide to go. Within that we would set up an investment portfolio, again internationally based, pretty much like the one you had in Britain, designed to give you a combination of growth and income. As added value to what you had before, we can give you full banking services, cheque books, credit cards, the lot, so that your financial management is concentrated in one place.'

I intervened: 'Bill, I hope you don't mind me asking this, but what's your bank's asset position? To be honest I've never heard of you and I find myself wondering why Wallinger should have chosen to divert Prim's assets here.'

'I don't take exception to your question at all, Oz. I should hope he did it on the basis of high-quality research. We're a wholly owned subsidiary of FedCan, the biggest bank in Canada, set up to provide discreet and very flexible services to high net worth individuals like yourself and Primavera. As far as deposit security goes, we're as safe as the Bank of England.'

'That's comforting to know,' said Prim. She glanced at me. 'Although I would have got round to asking that question myself. How long would it take you to give me a detailed proposal?'

'How long will you be in Vancouver?'

'I don't know for sure.' She looked at me.

'It's up to you,' I told her, 'but I have to go to Vegas this weekend; then there's the other matter.'

'Come back in three hours,' said Hoover. 'I'll put my top team on it and we'll make a presentation then. Normally we close at five thirty, but we'll stay open for as long as it takes.'

'Okay,' said Prim. 'I'll do that.'

The president looked at me. 'Is anything I've said of interest to you, Mr Blackstone?'

I knew he'd have done research on me before I walked through the door. 'It's an area that my wife and I are considering at the moment,' I replied. 'We're taking professional advice, though; I'll have to wait and see what that comes up with.'

'Of course.'

I glanced at Prim, to make sure she was done. 'Can I ask you, Bill,' I said, 'how this account was set up? Did Wallinger come here in person?'

'No, the initial contact was made by telephone. He spoke to one of our relationship managers and told him he had a large sum of money that he wanted to transfer to our bank. He wanted us to set up an international discretionary trust, so that the ownership of the funds would be cloaked, but it was explained to him that we couldn't do anything like that without a personal instruction. It was further explained that we couldn't accept a deposit without evidence of ownership of the funds, and an assurance from the transmitting bank that they were legitimate. It was only at that point Mr Wallinger stated he was an intermediary, not the principal.'

'Did your manager suspect a fraud situation?'

'At first, yes, but when Mr Wallinger accepted what we told him and wanted to proceed, we had no reason not to. He faxed us his authority, and the Jersey bank gave us the assurances we needed, so we went ahead and set up the account. By that time the transaction had been reported to me; I specified that we would only accept the funds if they were put on a minimum three-month deposit. It was my idea of a cooling-off period, just a little safeguard on our part.'

163

'Have you heard from Wallinger since?'

'No, but I didn't expect to, with the funds being locked up for three months and everything. Once the arrangement was made, he said he'd have further instructions for us after the first maturity date about where the interest should go.'

'So he should surface the week after next?'

'That would be right. What do you want me to do if he does?'

'Flush him out. Tell him you will only accept a further instruction if he presents himself at the bank in person, make an appointment, and let us know. Can you do that?'

'Technically, probably not.' His leathery face split into a smile. 'But I will.'

20

We left Mr Hoover to start putting Prim's proposal together, and stepped back out into Horner Street. I wanted to go back to the hotel, but she had other ideas. 'Now I know my money's safe, there are shops in this city and they're calling to me.'

I had not signed up for that, so we agreed that she would occupy herself until it was time for her to go back to Fairmile and Company, and that we would meet up again at the hotel, once her business was done.

We parted, and I started to walk back towards Granville Island. I figured it would be as quick as a taxi and, anyway, I wanted to try the False Creek Ferry. As soon as I was out of Prim's sight, I took my palm-top from my pocket, retrieved Henry Potter's mobile number and called him.

It must have been closing in on midnight in the accountant's world, but he didn't protest. He simply asked what he could do for me, as if it was the middle of his working day. 'What . . . if anything . . . do you know about a bank called Fairmile and Company, in Vancouver?' I asked him.

'It's funny you should mention that name,' he replied. 'The presentation that my team is doing for you and Mrs Blackstone lists them as one of the options. They're a subsidiary of a mega-bank, rock solid, absolutely squeaky clean, and they provide exactly the sort of international services that we believe you and your wife need. What prompted your question?'

'I've just had a meeting with their president, on a matter not related to my own interests.'

'In that case, have I done my firm a favour, against the opposition?'

I came clean with him. 'As of yet you have no opposition. We haven't got round to briefing anyone else, and we won't. You've got a clear field. Mind you, you won't get to play on it for another couple of weeks. I'll be in the States until then. When you're ready, you can contact my office in Scotland and make an appointment.'

I let him go back to sleep and kept on walking until I found the jetty from which the ferry operated. It was a pod-like wee boat, and didn't look all that stable, but it got me across the inlet in five minutes, with a good view of the waterfront thrown in for good measure.

I wandered around the island for a while, looking in the craft shops and galleries, before making my way back to the hotel. I went straight up to my room, switched on my laptop, plugged in the modem and went online. I checked my private e-mailbox first, the one I keep on my own website, with an address that only my family and closest friends know. There was a single message, from Everett, saying that my suite in the Bellagio was available any time I wanted to arrive, but that he expected to see me for lunch on Sunday.

I sent him a quick 'OK' response, then switched to AOL. There were a dozen and more tag-lines displayed there, but there was only one that interested me in the slightest. It was from 'pwallinger@' and the heading was 'Catch me if you can.' I slammed a finger on the enter key to open it, then read,

Well, well, I am honoured. The great Oz Blackstone is out to get me, personally; from what Prim told me about you, that should scare me, but it doesn't. You can't hit what you can't see. You may be coming for me, Oz, but where are you going to start? Right now, I'd guess you're in or near Vancouver, and that Prim's traced her money. That's part of my plan, since I found out I need her to release it. She's tighter than I thought, when it comes to money at any rate. Oh, yes, you can tell her that Tom misses his mom. Ask her, too, what took her so long. That's what Tom keeps asking me.

So, buddy, how are you going to find us in this big country?

Maybe I should give you a clue. Look for us around Manila Bay, at three tomorrow afternoon . . . oh, yes, and be sure to wear some flowers in your hair.

'Fucking nutter,' I snarled. I let a black thought cross my mind. If I called Mark Kravitz and told him that I was rescinding my previous direct instruction, the consequences might well be terminal for Mr Wallinger. The trouble was, there would be a chain, and like all chains it would be as strong as its weakest link. So the phone stayed in its cradle.

I read his message again, and considered not so much what it said, but what it didn't say. So he had a plan, indeed: my guess was that it didn't involve him coming back to Vancouver. The money was gone from Britain and so was he. The bastard had wanted her to follow it because he had no other way of getting his hands on it. He might have been expecting her sooner, but it had all worked out.

I looked at the last paragraph. Manila Bay? How the hell were we going to get to Manila Bay in less than twenty-four hours, far less pin down his location there? And what was this nonsense about bloody flowers in our hair?

I stared at the screen, for one, two, three minutes. I wasn't aware of the tune at first; it started way back in my head, pure background music, the kind that cuts in on your thoughts when you really don't want it to. It got louder; I tried to banish it, but it wouldn't go away, so I gave in and focused on it, trying to recall what it was. Finally it came to me, an old song, from the year after I was born, all about hippies and psychedelia and the summer of love . . . and wearing bloody flowers in your hair. It was one of my mum's favourites; when Ellie and I were kids she was always humming it about the house. San Francisco: the bastard wanted us to go to San Francisco.

'Right, so far so good. Now, what the hell's Manila Bay got to do with it?'

I found a search engine, entered 'San Francisco Manila Bay' and started looking. That got me nowhere, so I focused on the city, and was given a different range of options. I looked at several, before I found myself looking at the city's own website. There was a search window, so I typed in Manila Bay and waited. It gave me a single choice, a two-year-old minute of the San Francisco Arts Organisation, which discussed the refurbishment of a column dedicated to Admiral George Dewey, victor of the battle of Manila Bay, in 1898. It took pride of place in Union Square; I even knew where it was.

When Prim and I were in California in the death throes of our marriage we'd spent a weekend there. I think we'd agreed we were trying to resurrect things; that might not have been really true for either of us, but we gave it a shot, including some fairly passable sex, probably, in truth, the last time we had really got it on. We'd gone walking on the Sunday and had taken a cable car up to the square. I could even picture the statue, a tall white column about one third the height of Nelson's, with an Eros-like figure on top. She was more interested in Saks Fifth Avenue, of course . . . yes, there was a branch there too: she has a thing about that store . . . but I liked the feel of the whole place.

I made another executive decision: I called Reception and asked them to book us two seats on the first available flight to San Francisco next morning, and two of the best rooms that the Campton Place Hotel had available, with a car at the airport as usual. I wasn't sure whether we'd actually be staying overnight, but we needed somewhere to dump the luggage.

By the time Prim came back from Fairmile and Company, everything was done. The bad news was that the flight time was just after seven thirty.

She knocked on my door just before seven. 'I'm back,' she said, as I let her in.

'Self-evident. How did it go?'

'Very well. I've told Bill to get me invested. Do you think I've done the right thing?'

'The guy I checked them out with says you have.' I told her about Henry Potter.

'You really watch out for me, don't you?'

'I do for now; once you get Tom back, you're on your own again.'

168

'Do you think we're on the right track?'

I nodded. 'I told you before. The money's the key.'

'You seem sure of that.'

'Dead certain.'

'Come on down to the bar, then, and I'll buy you a drink for your certainty.' I couldn't see anything wrong with that idea.

The micro-brewery had several products, including something that was pink in colour, probably in honour of the elephants you'd see if you drank too much of it. I wanted no part of any hangovers, so I settled for a sleeve . . . that's Vancouver for pint . . . of their ordinary lager.

'What do you think I should do?' Prim asked. 'Wait here for Paul to show?'

'And then what?'

'I don't know. Confront him, I suppose; do what Harvey said and take the interdict to the court here.'

'The guy's not the best thief in the world, but he's not stupid either. He's not going to show up here, not yet anyway. When you hear from him, he'll be giving you a bank account number for you to transfer the money into. What you'll have to do then is make bloody sure you've got Tom back before it goes anywhere.'

'But how can I do that?'

'You insist that he hands Tom over to Bill Hoover, or his representative, after Hoover gives him a binding assurance that once he has the boy he'll process the transfer.'

She frowned. 'That would mean treating Tom like a commodity.'

'How's Wallinger treating him, then?'

I finished my beer. It was making me morose, but maybe the time shifting and the aggravation with Susie had something to do with that as well. I decided on another, but not there.

'Come on,' I said. 'Let's go back to the Sandbar.'

We walked along Johnston Street to the restaurant. Somewhere along the way Prim linked her arm through mine; I didn't mind, for at the time my mind was on San Francisco.

We reserved a table, then had a drink at the bar, another sleeve for me, and a glass of British Columbia red wine for her. My mind was still going to funny places. 'Do you ever look back?' I asked her.

'Do I ever not?' she answered quietly.

'Do you think there was a time, even at the end, when we might have made it?'

'What makes you ask that?'

'I don't know. I can tell myself, and I do, that what happened to us was your fault as much as mine. But that's not really true. I can tell myself too that Susie didn't really have anything to do with it, but that's not really true either. She did. Maybe I should always have been with Susie, and maybe you should always have been with Mike. I don't know; I don't fucking know.'

Prim squeezed my arm. 'I've got a confession to make,' she said.

'Another one? Who else did you shag? My dad?'

She grinned. 'Your father is a very attractive man ... but I didn't. And the truth is, I never shagged Mike either. There was never anything between us.'

'What about that letter Susie found among his things?'

'It was a joke on my part, a lousy joke as it turned out. Mike did make a pass at me once, at a party we were all at. He was monkeyed at the time, and to pay him back, I sent him a Valentine with a very steamy and suggestive letter in it. But I never signed it. If Susie knew it was from me, she must have recognised the handwriting.' She sighed. 'Poor Mike. He was always just a bit hapless, wasn't he? How awful it was that he should go bad like he did, and die like that.'

'What if he isn't dead?' I asked her. 'What if he was in deep cover and the whole shooting thing was a put-up?'

She raised an eyebrow. 'Then your marriage would have a big cloud hanging over it. Susie really loved that guy, you know.'

'Just like you always loved me?' was on the tip of my tongue, but I let it stay there.

'You are kidding about that, though, aren't you?' she said. 'Mike not being dead and such?'

I made myself laugh. 'Did I get you going there? That's what

170

happens when you're an actor. Everything in life has to have a convoluted plot.'

'Then keep it under control; that one was a bit scary.' She paused. 'Go back to your last real question. Was there a time when I thought we might make it work?'

'Yes. Was there?'

'Yes, once or twice. For example, that weekend we had when we were living in LA and you were back from filming in Canada for a long weekend, the time we went up to San Francisco. That was good. We took a cable car to Fisherman's Wharf for dinner and we had an extra bottle of wine and we went back to the hotel, and it was really terrific. Afterwards I remember lying there, thinking, "We're going to make a go of this after all." And then you went back to Toronto, and the next time you came back, you were as cold as ever you'd been. It just pulled the rug from under me. A few days later I was at a party and I met Nicky Johnson again. When he asked me to go to Mexico with him, I thought, "Why the hell not?" and I did.'

She looked me in the eye. 'So why did you ask me that?'

'Because I've been thinking of that weekend too.'

'Since when?'

The time had come; I couldn't keep it from her any longer. 'Since this afternoon, when I had an e-mail from Paul Wallinger.'

I thought that the shock was going to knock her off her bar stool. She was white-faced as I told her the whole story, about the message in Susie's box, sent after we had met Martha, and around the time that I was speaking to John, and about my challenge to Wallinger and the response it had provoked.

'We've got to go!' she exclaimed, when I had finished.

'Too right we have. Don't worry, the tickets are booked; it's an early start, so don't have too much more to drink.'

She couldn't if she'd wanted to. She spent the rest of the evening fidgeting in her seat, picking at her food and toying with her glass rather than emptying it. I had some more Sandbar fish; I'd have had a dessert too, but Prim was so distracted that she put me off the idea.

The daylight was still lingering on when we got back to the hotel, but we went straight up in the lift, regardless, having booked another six o'clock wake-up. When I walked her to her door, she looked so anxious that I took pity on her. 'Do you want a coffee?' I asked her. She nodded, and I led her across to my room, where I plugged in the machine.

She asked me if she could see Paul's message, so I set up the laptop again, logged on to AOL and displayed it for her. When she reached the part about Tom asking why she was taking so long, she began to cry. She read it over and over again, her hands twisting and kneading together, unconsciously. 'Why's he doing this?' she kept asking. 'Why? Why?'

'We won't know till we get there.'

'Will he have Tom with him, do you think?'

'I don't want to predict anything this guy might do.'

I made her coffee and watched her as she sat in one of the room's two chairs cupping it in her hands, as if she was freezing. 'You should sleep,' I told her. 'Or at least try.'

The big brown eyes looked into mine. 'Oz,' she whispered.

I thought about it: we were occupying two rooms so even if he did mail Susie again to stir her up, there would be no problems. Anyway, when it came to it, I didn't have the heart to send her back to her room. Hell, I'd been married to Prim, and with every step on our journey I was realising more and more how badly I'd used her. Plus, I was still just a wee bit pissed off with my wife for her rush to judgement the night before.

'Okay,' I said. 'Just go and get your half of the pyjamas, will you?'

21

Fortunately, it was a bloody enormous bed; suppose I had fancied any, I'd have had trouble finding her. I don't know whether Prim slept at all, but I know that I did. I sat bolt upright when the alarm rang, picked the phone up and slammed it down again to cancel it.

The light on Prim's side of the bed was on, and she was up; she was showered and sitting in front of the mirror in her bra and pants, blow-drying her hair as I'd watched her do a thousand and more times before. I wondered why she hadn't gone back to her own room to do that, until I remembered that she'd brought all of her stuff across the night before, not just the pyjama jacket.

I got out of bed and made for the bathroom. I looked in the mirror and saw the tension still on her face, so I stopped and stood behind her, putting my hands on her shoulders and kneading the muscles at the base of her neck with my thumbs. They were tight and bunched at first, but soon they relaxed under the gentle pressure. 'How're you doing?' I asked her.

'All the better for that.' She looked up at me in the mirror. 'Will we find him in San Francisco, Oz?'

'We won't know until we get there. The first thing we've got to do is catch this plane.'

We'd cut it fine . . . I hadn't allowed for US Immigration when I'd booked the car . . . but we made the flight. The coach section was busy, but we were in first so we had plenty of room. We had just reached our cruising height when a guy leaned across and tapped my shoulder. 'Hey, aren't you Keanu Reeves?'

I'm good with people, usually, but this one was rude. I looked him in the eye, put on the accent and that deep, sincere voice Keanu's got and said, 'Oh, fuck, I must need a haircut.'

It was not my day for being recognised. When we rolled our luggage through the arrivals gate in San Francisco, we had to search for our chauffeur. Eventually we found a Hispanic woman in uniform, holding a sign that read 'Mr Blackstein'. I had to do some talking to convince her that I was from the Gentile side of the family, but eventually we got under way and headed for the city.

We sat silent on the drive in, and let the driver . . . her name was Carmen . . . do the talking. 'This yo' first time in San Francisco, Mr Blackstein?'

'No.'

'You'll love it.' Clearly she was a woman who worked from a script, regardless of her passengers' answers. 'You got to take the cable car, now, and don' forget go to Fisherman's Wharf. Alcatraz ees good too: don' worry, no prisoners there no more.'

We let her prattle on. She did it to such good effect that she missed a turn and we found ourselves heading across the Bay Bridge on an unscheduled trip into Oakland. 'Sorry, Mr Blackstein,' she said. 'This ees bad. You no wanna go into Oakland.' From what I've heard of the place, I was inclined to agree.

Eventually, she found a turn-off and headed back in the right direction. By this time Prim was agitated. 'What if he's there and we're not?' she muttered.

'The message said afternoon, love, remember.' That quietened her for a while. Eventually Carmen got her bearings and we turned into Stockton Street.

The big brown eyes widened as we stopped in front of the Campton Place Hotel. 'This is where we stayed on that weekend we were talking about last night,' she exclaimed, her earlier panic forgotten. 'What made you choose it?'

'Nothing in particular,' I told her. 'I knew it, so rather than ask the guy on Granville Island to find us something I just told him to book here.'

'Are you sure you weren't remembering that weekend too?'

Maybe I was . . . but I wasn't going to admit it.

I didn't expect our accommodation to be ready at ten thirty-five in the morning, but it was. Their two best bedrooms were contained within a corner suite, with a view over Union Square itself. The Campton Place calls itself one of the world's leading small hotels, and the fittings and furnishings live up to that claim. We settled in, and I was able to have the shave I had forgone in Vancouver. Once I was done, I appraised myself in the mirror. There were a few creases around my eyes that I didn't like; crossing time zones does that to you, and when you're nearer forty than thirty, they don't go away. I really did need a haircut too. But what the hell? There would be people in Vegas to take care of all that stuff.

I surrendered the bathroom to Prim and went to my bedroom to call Susie. At first, she wasn't best pleased when I told her we were in San Francisco . . . it's on her places-to-see list, but we'd never got round to it . . . but she calmed down when I told her why we had gone there. 'Do you think he's ready to hand the kid over?' she asked.

'That's what I'm hoping, but it won't be that easy. Union Square's a public place and it'll be at its busiest at three o'clock. I'm guessing he's picked it for his own security, reckoning that I won't go for him if there are crowds around, but I'll be amazed if he brings Tom with him. Prim would just go berserk and grab him.'

'But where would he leave him, if they're alone?'

'Any number of places. He could be in a hotel with a baby-sitting service. There are big stores around here; there might be a crèche in one where you can leave your baby to be looked after while you shop. Or . . .' I hadn't really considered this before. '. . . he might not be alone. He might have an accomplice.'

'Do you really think so?'

'Sure. His dear old mother, for one; she's had time to jump on a plane and get out here.'

'Whatever it turns out to be, just you be careful. You've got a position to protect, so don't go getting involved in any rough stuff.'

'Who? Me?' I laughed. 'I won't get in any fights, Mummy, I promise. Let me speak to Janet.' I had another earnest conversation

175

with my daughter, in which I promised to take her to California as soon as Jonathan was big enough to come with us, then spoke to Susie again. 'Anything else for me?' I asked.

'Yes. Is there something wrong with your cell-phone? Mark Kravitz has been trying to get through to you, and so has the general manager of the Merchant's Hotel in Minneapolis.'

'What the hell did he want?'

'He didn't say.'

I dug out the Sony Ericsson and tried to switch it on. I'd been so busy using my international adaptor to power my laptop that I'd forgotten to charge it. The thing was as dead as Kelsey's nuts . . . that, incidentally, is a popular American saying, and no, I have no idea who Kelsey was, or what killed them, although I've heard some interesting suggestions.

'I'll get back to him,' I told her, 'when I've got time, once this bloody thing's charged up again.'

'Okay. Let me know how you get on.'

'Will do. Love you.'

Prim was waiting in our sitting room when I went back out. 'What are we going to do?' she asked.

'We're going to relax.' I checked my watch: it was just short of midday. 'We've got three hours to kill, and my stomach's still on Central Standard Time, so I'm going to fancy lunch soon. Let's go to the seaside.'

She saw the sense in that, so we left the hotel and walked a couple of blocks, where we jumped a cable car and rode it down to Fisherman's Wharf. We walked around for a while, breathed in a lungful of the sea air . . . I cherished it, for I knew how dry it would be in Vegas . . . then ate lunch at Ana Mandara, Don Johnson's place on Beach Street: sweet blue crab soup, then wokked beef tenderloin with onions and peppery cress, and a side order of steamed jasmine rice.

The cable car got us back to Union Square at two thirty. I suggested that we go back up to the suite, where we overlooked the square and could see everything and everyone, but Prim vetoed that idea. 'Maybe he won't show himself until he sees us,' she said.

She had a point, so we found ourselves a seat near the Manila Bay monument and waited.

Her eyes were everywhere, scanning every face in the crowds, but recognising nobody. As three o'clock drew closer she became more and more restless, but in the circumstances I forgave her that. Eventually she could sit still no longer. 'Come on,' she said. 'Let's get up and go nearer the monument; maybe he can't see us down here.'

I knew that if he was looking, he could see us well enough; at that moment the square was full of Japanese tourists . . . that nation is full of tremendous, energetic and very well-organised travellers . . . so we were liable to stand out. I went along with it, though, because I didn't want her blaming me for anything that went wrong.

We rose from our bench and walked towards the white stone pillar, mingling with the crowd of Japanese. I realised that some of them actually looked Chinese, and decided that two different tour groups must have converged on the square at the same time. There were a lot of them, but I was quite a bit taller than most of them, so I reckoned we were visible. As I looked around, scanning for Wallinger, my eye was caught by two black guys. I'd seen them in action earlier when we'd got off the cable car, and their pitch had made me laugh. I was near enough to hear as they did it again.

One was carrying a tin with a slot in the top, but there was no doubt that he and his mate were collecting for their personal charity. His companion did the pitching. He fastened on to a Chinese couple and asked them, 'What's the greatest nation on earth?' The Chinese man looked uncertain, so the guy shouted his question again, drawing quite a bit of attention, until finally he laughed and bellowed, 'Do-nation!'

It was worth a buck, and the sucker duly shoved a note into the tin.

I was still looking at them when all hell broke loose behind me. A woman screamed, high-pitched, then Prim grabbed my arm. 'Oz!' she yelled, above the sudden hubbub. I turned and saw a man, as tall as I was, and with the same hair colouring, in the act of turning and taking to his heels, legging it out of the square.

I didn't even think about it; I went after him. He shot off towards the corner, then swung into Stockton Street. *This guy's confident*, I thought to myself. *He's running uphill*. He was too, and running bloody fast at that. I didn't yell after him or anything like that. I saved my breath and dug in.

He ran a full block, with me in pursuit about ten yards back, close enough for him to hear me, not gaining, but not losing ground either. We came to a cross street but the lights were at 'Walk': my quarry and I ignored them and kept on running.

I'm not as fast as I was fifteen years ago, but when I try I can still shift a bit. For all that, the gradient was beginning to hurt, and I reckon he'd have got away from me, if he hadn't done something very stupid. He looked back over his shoulder to see if I was catching him.

When you're running flat out, it's important that you look where you're going, otherwise you won't see the fat bloke who steps out of a doorway and into your way, just like he didn't. He knocked the obstacle flat on his arse, but he lost momentum and I was on him. I hit him in the back with my shoulder, in a spear tackle, knocking him full-length, face down. I landed on top of him, then got to one knee and turned him over.

I didn't expect the gun at all, but there it was in his hand and it was aiming my way. I knocked it sideways just as he fired. I felt a sudden flash of heat on my cheek, and a sudden searing pain near my ear. Before the lunatic could fire again I clamped my left hand around his wrist, and hit him, awkwardly, but seriously hard, with my right. The punch was half hook half uppercut, and not even Iron Mike ever threw one with more lethal intent than I did then. The guy's head snapped back, hitting the concrete of the sidewalk. He went out like a light, but that didn't stop me hitting him again, just for luck.

I tore the gun from his unresisting hand, flicked on the safety and stuck it in my belt. Then I stood up and put a foot on his throat, in case he came round and had any thoughts about going anywhere else in a hurry. Only when I'd done all that did I take a good look at him. He was my size, yes, and had the same colour hair, yes, but no way did he look anything like me or like Paul Wallinger's picture. The big ragged scar on his forehead was a drawback for a start, and so was the fact that he was dark-skinned. I saw something else too, a gent's leather handbag, tucked into his belt.

The fat bloke from the doorway had regained his feet and was looking on. The gunshot had sent everyone in the street diving for cover, but now that the situation was under control they began creeping out to see what had happened.

Porky looked down at the supine figure under my foot. 'Fucking muggers!' he snarled, then spat on the guy.

'You do that again, pal,' I said, 'and when he wakes up I'll give him his gun back and tell him it was you.'

A circle had formed around us, but it parted to let two biker cops through. I thought they might have been inclined to arrest both of us, but they were experienced officers and they knew what had gone down.

'His gun's in my belt,' I told them, lifting an arm so that one of them could withdraw it. Somehow I thought it was better that way. 'The bag that I reckon he stole is still in his.'

The other cop bent over and retrieved it; as he held it up a man in the crowd started shouting excitedly in Japanese. 'It's yours, sir?' the officer asked, while his buddy rolled over the still unconscious thief and cuffed him.

'Jesus,' Cop One exclaimed, 'he's well under.' He looked at me. 'What did you hit him with?'

I held up my right hand. 'This, and the pavement. Since he was trying to shoot me I thought it was the best thing to do.'

He looked at me. 'Buddy, he was more than trying: he scored a homer. You're bleeding.'

I put my hand to my face; it felt sticky, and I realised that the left side of my head was bloody sore. 'Shit!' I swore. 'What does it look like?'

The officer turned my head around and peered at it. 'Looks like he's torn up the top of your ear. It'll clean up, though.'

'How quick, though? I'm due to start shooting a movie next week.'

179

He took another look at me. 'Hey, Keanu Reeves!'

'Don't you start,' I barked at him. 'I agree, we're around the same height, but Keanu's a couple of years older than me. Plus, I'm a harder puncher than he is.'

Cop Two sneered at his mate. 'You fucking dip-shit.' He laughed. 'That's Oz Blackstone, the English guy; he's in Miles Grayson's big-hit sports movie. I caught it last week. Nice job, Oz.'

At last! Fame in America.

'Which?' I asked. 'The movie or nailing him?'

'Both. We got grounds to charge this guy with attempted murder. You wanna proceed?'

'Too fucking right I do. He might not miss the next guy he shoots at.'

'He didn't miss you, remember. One and a half inches to the right and you'd have been minus the back of your head.'

The mugger was starting to come round. 'You want another shot?' asked Cop One, as they hauled him to his feet.

'Certainly.' I hit him again. I was standing and balanced this time so I got some real leverage into the punch. It turned him into two hundred pounds of dead weight all over again. The crowd gave a small cheer.

'Shee-it!' Cop Two whistled. 'You're right. I saw those *Matrix* movies; Keanu don't hit nothing like that hard.'

22

The cops called for a wagon for the mugger and a paramedic crew for me; they were genuinely anxious that I had my ear patched up, so I went along with it.

They followed me on their bikes to the emergency room. The repair work didn't take long; once my ear was stitched back into its customary shape and taped over, the two bikers even flanked the car that took me to the central police station in Vallejo Street. When we got there, I was welcomed by the station commander himself, a captain called Steyenheusen; word had got round.

I made a formal statement, saying that I'd gone in pursuit of the man . . . they told me that his name was Leo Hoorne and he had two previous convictions for assault with a deadly weapon . . . and that when I'd apprehended him he'd fired at me. The fat bloke and three other bystanders had given identical statements. Captain Steyenheusen reckoned that Mr Hoorne would be an old man by the time he got out.

They took me back to the hotel after that; well, not quite after that. They took me back after I'd run the gauntlet of the television and newspaper reporters who were waiting for me outside. The Public Affairs Office had been beating the drum; in fact, they'd made me into a civic have-a-go hero.

I downplayed it, but not too far: you never shun positive publicity in the movie business. On camera, with blood staining the collar of my shirt, I fed them the expected modest 'Shucks, it was nothing' line. I assured them that my wound wasn't serious . . . although I agreed with the woman who said that if I'd been a fraction slower I'd be dead. I told them that I'd been seriously impressed by SFPD.

I told them that I hoped that Mr Hoorne looked upon his years inside as an opportunity for self-improvement . . . that raised a laugh. I told them that I was merely on a visit to San Francisco, before going on to Vegas to start work on Everett Davis's new movie *Serious Impact*. Happily nobody asked me whether I was there on my own.

The story was all over the local TV news by the time the cops dropped me back at the Campton Place, to face the only person in San Francisco who didn't think I was a hero.

'What the hell were you thinking about, chasing off after that guy?' Prim blazed at me, when I let myself back into the suite.

'It happened in an instant,' I told her. 'When I heard you shout I thought that it must have been Wallinger. That's who I thought I was after till I caught up with him.'

'You caught him?'

'Where the hell do you think I've been for the last three hours?'

I picked up the remote and switched on the television, then zapped though the channels till I found the local news station. There I was, on top of the pile, British movie star, Oz Blackstone, accidental tourist, accidental fucking hero. They tailed the piece with a quote from Cop Two, Officer Ronnie Rastrow: 'He sure hits harder than Keanu Reeves.' I liked that one. 'Eat your heart out, Keanu,' I said to the screen.

Prim stared at me. 'You were shot?' she gasped.

I turned my head and showed her my ear.

'Bloody hell! You're an idiot!' Then, in the midst of her anger, she gave me some very good advice. 'You'd better phone Susie right now, regardless of the time in Scotland. If she wakens up and sees that on the news tomorrow . . .'

She was right: I'd have been better off dead. I went into my room and called her right away, even though it was two in the morning back home. Susie had often complained about being unable to sleep properly when I was away; plus, there were wee Jonathan's teeth.

As it turned out she was asleep. I waited till she was properly awake, then told her. 'There's been this thing. I caught a mugger. There was a shot fired.'

'What?'

'It's okay, honest, no damage done. But the telly people here are getting silly, and I didn't want you to hear it from them first.'

'You're sure you're okay?'

'I'm fine; it was just a wee nick.'

'What?'

'It's just a graze, love, really.'

'It's just a what?'

It took me ten minutes but finally I was able to calm her down. 'While all that was going on,' she asked, 'what about this man Wallinger? Did he turn up?'

'Do you know?' I told her. 'I have no idea.'

I left her to a certainly sleepless remainder of the night and went back into the living room of the suite. 'Wallinger,' I said to Prim. 'Did he show?'

'Yes, he did,' she replied, bitterly. 'Just at the very mome̶ turned into Charles Bronson and all hell broke ̶ shouted it was to tell you I'd seen him.'

'And what happened?'

'Nothing. All the commoti̶ just turned on his heel and di̶

You blew it in Union Square, people. Don't mess up in LA tomorrow. Damon and Pythias, Westwood Village, same time.

'Bastard,' I muttered. 'I'm getting heartily sick of dancing to your tune. If you don't show tomorrow, well . . . I'm an all-American hero now. I'll put my friends the cops on your trail.'

Prim frowned at me. 'You won't really do that, will you?'

'Maybe. I just get the feeling we're being fucked about, and I don't like it. This is about extortion, love, plain and simple; you know that. Maybe I should use whatever clout I've got with the police.'

'Yes, and maybe that'll mean I never see my son again. Don't say that, Oz, please.'

'I'll sleep on it. But let's stay positive: he probably will show tomorrow. Better make sure we get to LA on time.'

I shouldn't have uttered the word 'sleep': as soon as I did, the ____ bly the rest of that week, started to catch up with me. ____ called Reception and asked the duty manageress ____ A flight in the morning and into the closest ____ illage. ____ of the nicest parts of LA and

at me. 'And where were you [...]
America?'

'Getting fucking [...]
her; a little.

'What will we d[...]

For the first tim[...]
care quite as much['...]
of guilt at the thou[...]
that, though: to he[...]
me my laptop. Th[...]

She did as I ask[...]
not bothering with[...]
was some Spam, [...]
from media people[...]
of it all, a fresh m[...] AOL. [...]

[...] f messages
[...] he middle

[...]on must have panicked him, for he
[...]sappeared into the crowd.' She glared
[...] when I needed you, Captain Fucking
[...]minded her. That seemed to soften
[...]ked me, quietly.
[...]our quest, I found that I didn't
[...]then had an immediate flash
[...]ot that I told Prim any of
[...]into my room and get
[...] over there.'
[...]oose. When I
[...]nt you

I she...

day, and probab...

I felt dog tired as...

to book us on to an LA fligh...

hotel she could find to Westwood V... ...out taking Prim there. The

We both knew the Village; it's one ...hour, which I had spent

one of the safest. I felt comfortable ...in an attempt to dull a

woman called us back inside ...over the side of my head.

drinking Bud Light from ...pital; they were starting to

growing ache, not just ...n American Airlines flight

They had given me ...the Century, on Wilshire

wear off. She tol... ...rugged, that I'd forgotten to

and that sh... ...used to the way things had

Boulev...

ask... ...time past, but I didn't fancy

...own to the hotel's excellent

...le of room-service salads and

...and spent the evening getting

...can't speak for Prim.

I don't remember who suggested the sleeping arrangements that night. I only know that I woke up slightly feverish in the middle of the night, from a very bad dream involving gunshots, to find that I was in her bed, without a pyjama in sight. For a few moments, I was worried, but I wasn't so drunk that I'd have forgotten that. Still, after I'd relieved myself of the burden of all that beer, I crept back to my own room and flaked out on top of the duvet.

She said nothing about it next day, other than a cheerier 'Good morning' than I had expected. She did ask about my ear, though; the pain wasn't as bad, but it was still there, so I popped a couple of tablets to ease it.

We had room-service breakfast at eight o'clock; they brought a couple of Saturday morning's newspapers with our order. I wasn't the lead story, but I had front-page treatment in both of them. I was glad to be getting out of San Francisco, for all sorts of reasons. As I chucked the last one away, I decided I'd better phone Susie again.

I went to my room to make the call. She was still anxious about me: there had been some footage on the British TV news taken outside the police station and she'd seen the blood on my shirt and the patch on my ear. 'I thought you said it was just a graze,' she said.

'It is, love, honest. They put in a few micro-stitches, that was all. I might have a designer ear for the rest of my life, but there's no lasting damage otherwise. It's all positive: it'll make me look like a war hero and I'll be able to bore dinner parties with the story for years to come.'

'The guy who did it's not going to get out or anything, is he?'

'Not in the full vigour of his youth, that's for sure.'

'That's comforting to know. Just you be sure you don't get into any more trouble. Do you hear me?'

'Yes, my darling, I hear you.'

'Ah, so I'm still your darling, am I?'

'And always will be.'

'That's good to hear, since that carry-on in Minneapolis. The sooner this thing is over with and Prim's far away from you, getting on with her life, the happier I'll be.'

185

'Hopefully that'll be tomorrow.' I told her about Los Angeles. 'He's got to show himself this afternoon. I feel the same way you do; I just want the deal done, whatever it is, and the kid returned.'

'And Prim? How does she feel?'

'What do you mean?'

'Will she give up her fortune for her son?'

'Wouldn't you?'

I heard her sigh. 'Yes, of course. Ignore me, love, I'm super-cynical about people and money, that's all. It's all right talking about sacrifice; actually making it's the acid test. I wonder whether she's hoping that, when the moment comes, you'll be able to muscle the boy away from Wallinger.'

'Hey, if I see a chance to do that, I'll take it . . . as long as it's within the law.'

'You keep that in mind,' she warned me. 'In this world you can be a hero today and a villain tomorrow.'

'I promise.'

'Good.' She paused. 'By the way, I didn't tell you. When I saw you on television, I was prouder of you than I've ever been before. I'll bet your dad and Ellie are too.'

'Oh, Christ, I never warned them!'

'Don't worry, I did.'

'Thanks. Listen, love, I'd better go.'

'Do that. Did you make those calls?'

'What calls?'

'The ones I told you about, remember?'

'Oh, shit. With one thing and another . . . I'll make them now.'

I dug out my pocket PC . . . techno-freak, I know . . . where I keep my contact numbers, for convenience, and found the number of the Merchant's Hotel. As I dialled it, I wondered whether the general manager would be on duty on a Saturday or whether he'd be taking his kids to the lakes, as all good Minnesotans do, but Benjamin E. King was conscientious: he was in his office.

'Mr Blackstone,' he said, as he answered my call. 'I'm so glad you could get back to me. I see from the newspapers that you've been having an exciting time since you left us.'

'One I could have done without,' I confessed. 'Why did you want to speak to me?'

'I wanted to let you in on the results of my investigation into the incident which marred your stay with us. I've spoken to the clerk who dealt with your booking and now I know the whole story.'

'I thought your assistant manager had done that.'

'I'm afraid that gentleman was negligent,' King admitted. 'The story he fed you about your reservation being misunderstood was a fabrication, designed to get him off the hook. The person involved was off duty on Tuesday and only returned to work on Thursday. She tells it completely differently: it's still not a pretty story from our point of view, but it's better than an outright lie.'

'Let's hear it, then.'

'Apparently, your booking was made correctly. You were allocated two of the last three rooms we had available at that point. However, on the morning of the day you were due to check in, the reservations office had a call from a gentleman who said he was your personal assistant. He said that your arrangements had changed, that you were now travelling with your wife and would only require one room. In accordance with our normal practice he was asked to confirm by fax or e-mail. He chose the latter, and a message was received. If the clerk had been super-efficient, it might have occurred to her that the original instruction was confirmed by electronic fax, on your personal letterhead, but she accepted the change at face value. By the time you checked in, your second room had been allocated, and the hotel was indeed full.'

'What was the e-mail address on the message?' I asked.

'Hold on, I have it here.' I waited, but I knew what he was going to say, even before he had started spelling the letters out. 'It reads "p-w-a-l-l-i-n-g-e-r at trickledown dot com". Does that mean anything to you, sir?'

'Oh, yes. It surely does.'

'Then I am afraid that you have been the victim of a practical joke, with our unwitting connivance.'

187

'As a matter of interest, did the person who booked that other room ever turn up?'

'Yes, sir, a Mr Jack Nicholson. He walked in off the street less than half an hour after your booking was changed. He took the room for three nights and paid in cash: unusual these days, I know, but it still happens.'

'Which room was that?'

'Twenty-oh-six; it's across the landing from the room you and the lady occupied.'

'Did he go out a lot, this Mr Nicholson?'

'I have no idea, sir. This is a very large and busy hotel, you understand. But I can tell you that he took all his meals in his room.'

'Did your check-in guy recall anything else about him? For example, did he have a laptop?'

'He may well have done; most of our guests do these days. However, I have no way of knowing for sure.'

I could take a good guess at it, though. I thanked Mr King and hung up, then went back out to the living room, thinking all the way. What he had told me put a new spin on things.

Jack Nicholson, indeed! A name plucked from the flotsam of yet another shattered Hollywood dream? Or just a stupid bastard having a laugh at my expense? If it was, that was yet another mistake: I like to have all the funny lines.

Prim came out of the bathroom as I closed my bedroom door behind me; she had a turban on her head and another towel wrapped around her. 'What's up?' she asked. 'You look worried.'

'It's nothing,' I said. 'Are you finished in there?' She nodded.

In the shower, even though I was concentrating on keeping the spray away from my wound, I thought some more. Wallinger had actually known when we were going to Minneapolis, and what hotel we would be in. The second part of that problem wasn't insurmountable; I'm rich, so he'd assume that I'd be in one of the best hotels. Phoning round them and asking a few questions wouldn't take long. One phone call to his cop brother, if I was wrong in my assessment of Lieutenant John the Second, would have been even quicker, and could have got him all the information he needed. But how the hell did he know when we were going?

He could have been watching Prim all along; he could have tracked her to Scotland, then followed the two of us everywhere we went. It was pretty clear he'd been following our trail across North America, keeping one guess and one step ahead of us. But there was one catch in that theory. If he was cash-flashing Jack Nicholson, as I was certain he was, and he had been snooping on us in the UK, how had he got to Minneapolis ahead of us? No way could he have done that, as we'd been booked on the first available flight.

So that left two possibilities: either he had an accomplice in Britain who'd trailed us all the way up to the KLM desk at Glasgow, worked out the rest from there . . . there are only a couple of ways to get to MSP from Scotland and via Holland is one of them . . . then phoned him, or . . . and this was the one I feared most . . . he had a spy in my camp.

But who knew where I was going and why? Susie did; sure, and it was likely to be her, not. Audrey did, and so did Conrad; they were fairly new in our employ, but they'd been well vetted and neither of them had any obvious link to an obscure American actor. Mark Kravitz knew, but he was my man even more than Connie was. Suppose he could have been bought, who'd have known to buy him? Mark operated in the shadows.

'Miles would have known.' I said it aloud, and was rewarded with pain as I forgot myself and let the shower jet hit my stitched-together ear. And why the hell, I asked myself, would mega-rich Miles Grayson get involved in a conspiracy to extort from his sister-in-law the sort of money that he would regard as small change? Did he and Dawn hate her that much? Rubbish, I told myself.

'But still,' I mused. 'Wallinger: actor; LA connection.'

Roscoe Brown. Roscoe knew my travel plans. Roscoe was an actors' agent and had been for some years. Did Roscoe know Paul Wallinger?

I turned off the jet, grabbed a towel and began drying off, as quickly as I could. As soon as I'd got myself down to merely damp,

I wrapped myself in the hotel's towelling robe to finish the job, went out to the living room and set up the laptop again. I didn't bother with the e-mail this time. I went straight on to Roscoe Brown's website and did what he'd challenged me to do a week or so before: I pulled down his client list.

It was extensive, built up through his years in the business. We were all there, from Adams to Zederbaum, like he'd said, but I was only interested in one letter. I clicked on the Ws and there he was, right at the top of the list . . . Paul Patrick Walls.

Prim had come into the room, behind my back. 'What are you doing?' she asked.

'Just possibly, honey,' I told her, 'I'm pulling someone's world down on his fucking head . . . and maybe if some contracts aren't signed yet, on my own too!'

23

I was seriously pissed off with flying. Whatever happened in Westwood Village, I knew that my next port of call had to be Las Vegas, which was within a drivable distance, so I went on line to Hertz, gave them my gold member number and booked a Jaguar S-type, with satellite navigation, for collection at Los Angeles airport.

That was a positive move after a week of uncertainty, and so I felt a little better as we checked out of the Campton Place. A local television station had found out where I was, and there was a crew outside as we got into our car. They got some footage of Prim, but the reporter wasn't clued up enough to ask who she was, so I wasn't worried about it turning into a story. They were only going through the motions anyway: already I was old news.

I fretted about Roscoe all the way to the terminal and on to the flight. Security there was worse than it had been anywhere else, even for those of us travelling at the front of the plane, so that didn't help. Add all that to my still aching head . . . fuck me, I'd been shot less than twenty-four hours earlier . . . and calling me irritable would have been a major understatement. Prim read this and knew me well enough to keep quiet. When a guy recognised me in the departure lounge and approached me, I froze him with a stare; he actually apologised to me, when all he'd wanted to do was shake my hand and thank me for the day before.

I'd forgotten, and so had Prim, that it would be significantly hotter in LA than it had been in San Francisco, or anywhere else we had stopped that week. We were both in denims, so the transfer to the Hertz pick-up point was a steamy ordeal. As soon as we were in the S-type I switched the air-conditioning on at full blast; and we sat on the tarmac for a few minutes, our shirts unbuttoned, enjoying the refrigerated breeze.

When we were comfortable I programmed our destination into the navigation system and set off, taking every turn it told me to take without question. I felt a strange wave of relief just to be driving again: five days of Charles, Carmen, and assorted taxi-drivers is a lot for anyone, even someone with a less frayed temper than mine was by then.

The city of Los Angeles is an enormous place, but we were lucky in that Westwood Village is relatively close to LAX. The system instructed me to take Century Boulevard, then switch to the Four-Oh-Five freeway, and finally to join Wilshire Boulevard. We arrived at our hotel in under twenty minutes.

The Century was not the poshest hotel we'd been in that week, but it was okay, less than a mile from the meeting place Wallinger had specified, and it had an underground park where I could dump the Jag. It's the oldest building around on that part of Wilshire, but it has a Spanish feel to it that makes up for its age. They gave us what they called a suite, on the first floor with a balcony that overlooked a central courtyard that would have been shaded if the sun hadn't been directly overhead. It was cramped, but it had two enormous beds and a bathroom. When I saw how small it was I asked Prim if she wanted her own room, but she shook her head. 'If you were going to take shameless advantage of me,' she said, 'you'd have done it last night when you crawled drunk into my bed. But you didn't so I reckon we're both safe.'

I was okay with that, not because I wasn't worried about Susie any more but because I had the irrational hope growing within me that somehow the whole business would be sorted that day, I could send Prim on her way, and make my own to Vegas.

I took a long, cool shower in the cramped bathroom, to freshen up and to get my circulation going properly, then dug out my lightest shirt and a pair of Lacoste shorts that I'd packed with Vegas in mind. In those, and a pair of Panama Jack sandals, no socks, I felt dressed for the city. I looked at my suitcase and saw yet another reason for getting to my base camp in the Bellagio: more than half of its contents were destined for the hotel laundry.

By the time Prim had got herself ready . . . her case was smaller than mine; I hated to think what it was like inside . . . it was after two o'clock, but I wasn't worried about the time. I was worried about her, though: she was starting to get twitchy again, impatient, irritable and anxious to get going. We had plenty of time, but I kept her happy; I still had all the headache I needed.

I handed my laptop in to Reception for safe keeping and, while I was there, asked the day manager if he knew where Damon and Pythias was. He didn't, but his young assistant did: she told me that it was a café in either Kinross Avenue or Broxton Avenue . . . she wasn't sure which, but they were adjoining and less than a mile away.

We could have taken the Jag, but that might have caused us a parking problem at the other end so I decided that it was best to walk. Prim was in shorts too, a pair she'd bought at the airport in Minneapolis: her legs had the nice light tan that I remembered, but then so had the rest of her.

We walked down Wilshire as the girl had directed us, then crossed it, turning right into Westwood Boulevard. Kinross Avenue was only a hundred yards along, to the left: we walked along it, but saw no Damons and no Pythiases either, so we carried on until we found Broxton.

The whole area was familiar, and all of a sudden, I knew exactly where I was. When Prim and I had done our brief and ill-fated LA living bit, we'd stayed with Miles and Dawn in Beverly Hills for two or three weeks, until we found a place of our own to rent. The home town of the stars is very close to Westwood Village. It, in turn, is very close to UCLA, and so it has a nice student feel about it. We'd liked it and so we'd hung out there from time to time. I looked up the tree-lined avenue and there it was, on the other side of the street, the place we were looking for, a café with an indoor area and open-air seating under a veranda on the edge of the sidewalk. We'd actually had a drink there a couple of times, although I'd never noticed what the place was called.

'Why the hell did he pick this?' I asked.

193

'I think I know,' said Prim. 'Paul used to ask me about you and me, and what we'd done when we were in California together, before it all went bad.'

'It was bad from the start.'

'No, it wasn't. You may say that now, but it wasn't all bad. That weekend in San Francisco was good for us, and so were the days we spent down here. Maybe you had given up on us even then, but I hadn't. I told Paul about it, and he's remembered. He's been taking me to places I know, places I'm familiar with.'

She had a point: it certainly looked that way. 'He's also keen on meeting you in the open. First Union Square, now here.'

'He's cautious, that's all. If he's been planning this for a couple of years, he's not going to take any chances, and he's certainly not going to be stupid enough to go anywhere near you, other than in the middle of a crowd.'

'Would it help if I wasn't here?'

'It's too late for that. If he doesn't see you now, he'll wonder where you are.' Again, I had to agree with her. 'Let's go across there,' she said.

I wasn't so keen on that; I guess that getting shot the day before had made me a little more cautious. I didn't want to repeat the experience, and while there was no evidence that Wallinger had anything against me personally, I was paranoid enough not to fancy the idea of being a sitting target.

'No,' I told her. 'It's only twenty to three. We stay out of sight until then.' I looked around and spotted a bookshop, another crime specialist . . . Americans are very big on mysteries . . . more or less directly opposite Damon and Pythias. 'Let's go in there.' I didn't give her the chance to object; I took her hand and marched towards it.

The store was wonderfully cool; its air-conditioning was helped by Venetian blinds, but they were angled so that we could see out and across the street.

There was a man behind the counter, but nobody else in the place. 'Hi there,' he greeted us. 'Welcome to the Mystery Bookstore. My name's Shelley; can I help you?'

194

He wasn't a tall guy, and he'd eaten a few lunches in his time, but the thing that would have made him stand out in any crowd was his remarkable taste in shirts. The one he had on would have made Duffy Waldorf, American golf's sartorial legend, look like an Amish elder: its sleeves were ablaze with delicate colours, and its centrepiece seemed to be a map of all of the islands that make up Japan. (For geographic simpletons like me, it had 'Japan' emblazoned across it.) The rest of the available space on his ample chest was filled by images that I took to denote the country's varied culture, including a depiction of Mount Fuji and, for some reason, two baseball players. I thought about asking him where the sumo wrestlers were, but decided against it, in case he thought I was getting personal.

'Just browsing,' I told him, and turned to a stand of books, although in truth I could have browsed Shelley's shirt for the rest of the afternoon. I picked up a few volumes and looked through them, glancing across the street every so often to observe the café action. There wasn't much. It was gone lunch-time so the place was reasonably quiet, although a few Saturday-afternoon shoppers . . . or browsers . . . had stopped off there. A couple of kids vacated a table, a couple of ladies took another, and a slim, bearded guy in shades and a light jacket came out of the indoor area, but that was all. Prim saw nothing: she had been trapped in conversation with Shelley, who was trying to sell her a collectable publisher's proof of *The Day of the Jackal*.

He failed with that pitch, but I bought a signed copy of the new Michael Connelly, to thank him for the use of his premises. He blinked at the name on my credit card, then placed me. I asked him if he had any of the Skinner books in stock, but he told me they usually sold out fast.

At two minutes to three we crossed Broxton Avenue and took a table in Damon and Pythias. Our backsides were hardly on the chairs before a girl came to ask what we'd like to drink and to explain that we were in a vegetarian restaurant. She looked like a cheerleader; the place was cheap and cheerful so I guessed that its staff . . . and maybe most of its customers . . . were students. I told her we'd like a chilled bottle of Pinot Grigio, some still water, and that we'd already eaten.

Having been distracted by the bookstore, Prim was back on edge, big-time. Her eyes were all over the avenue; as she picked up her wine-glass I saw that her hand was trembling slightly. I covered it with mine, to still it, and as I did so I was aware of a young man standing behind me.

He was wearing a waiter's apron and he was shifting from one foot to the other. 'Sir,' he ventured, 'would you be Mr Oz Blackstone?'

I nodded. The kid wanted an autograph, he could have an autograph, and then get the hell out of the way; I waited for him to hand me a book and pen.

Instead, from behind his back, he produced a brown envelope, and handed it to me. 'I was told to give you this, sir.' He reached into a pocket and took out a Nokia cell-phone. 'I was also asked if I could let you use this.' He gave it to me. 'It's mine,' he explained quickly, in case I thought it was a gift. He was okay on that score: I know the mobile phone industry is pushy but it doesn't yet hire students to give them away free on the streets . . . or does it?

As I stared at it, the thing began to sing; I think it might have been Beyoncé Knowles, but all those divas sound the same to me. Prim had been watching the whole performance, incredulous, but the musical ring-tone sparked her into life. 'Answer it!' she snapped at me, as if there was a chance I wouldn't.

I pressed a green button and put it to my ear. 'Hello, you thieving, kidnapping bastard,' I said.

'Nice to speak to you at last, Oz.' The accent was smooth, bland, professional and American. 'You told my mom we'd met before, but I'm afraid I can't remember it.'

It was as if his voice was a trip-wire inside my head and I'd stumbled over it. I felt myself explode. 'The next time we speak, you'll remember it, Wallinger. Thanks to you I've been taken away from my family, compromised, embarrassed and nearly fucking killed. When I catch up with you, you will be picking teeth out of your arsehole.'

'That's exactly why I don't intend to go face to face with you.

After your escapade in San Francisco, I'm seeing you in a different light. I had you taped as just another effete actor like me, but it seems that you might really be as dangerous a son-of-a-bitch as Primavera said you were. So I've changed the plan. In that envelope my young waiter friend just gave you . . . kids will do just about anything for a hundred bucks, you know . . . you'll find a document. I've had it drawn up by a lawyer. It sets out the terms under which I will be prepared to yield custody of Tom to his mother.'

'Give me that phone!' Prim demanded, beside me.

'Don't do that, Oz,' said Wallinger. 'She'd only yell at me, and I don't need that. Just listen to me carefully. This is not a negotiating thing; what you have there is how it has to be. I've signed the agreement, and I expect Primavera to sign it also. Since you've come this far, you can be her witness. I think you'll find it's legal and that it can't be construed as extortion. You can take it to the Nevada State Attorney if you don't believe me.'

'Nevada? Why Nevada?' I asked. Prim stared at me.

'That's your next stop, isn't it, Oz? That's where you have to be? So, you take Primavera along for the trip. You'll be contacted there. The signed document will be handed over and arrangements for the trade will be made.'

'The trade?' I shot back at him. 'This is a child you're talking about.'

'This is two and one half million British pounds I'm talking about . . . or however many US dollars that buys.'

I stood, looking up and down Broxton Avenue, but I couldn't see anyone talking into a phone. 'Where are you, you bastard?' I growled.

'I'm near, but far enough away.'

I took a shot. 'You're not in Roscoe's office, are you?'

'Hey,' he whistled, 'you really are a detective, but no, that's not where I am.'

'Is Tom with you?'

'Tom is safe; Primavera needn't worry about that.'

'God, he better be.'

'Oz,' said Wallinger, patiently, 'ask yourself this. Suppose you and the third Mrs Blackstone came to this, and you were forced to take your kids to negotiate a fair share of your joint property, would they be in the remotest danger from you?'

'Is that how you really see this? As a palimony thing? You're fucking crazy, man.'

'If that's so, in a few days from now I'll be rich and crazy. Go to Vegas. I'll find you there.'

There was a click and the line went dead; I was on the point of chucking the Nokia as far as I could down the street, when I remembered that it was the kid's. Instead I scrolled through the menu till I found the number from which the call had been made. It was LA local, and I had no doubt that it was a public telephone. Wherever it was, he'd had us in sight when he'd called, because he'd known exactly when to ring. I looked along Broxton and saw any number of shops and restaurants, each with its own payphone, I was sure.

I handed the phone back to the waiter. 'Describe the guy.'

'He was around your height,' he replied, 'but not as solid. I can't tell you much about him. He wore Ray-Bans, and he had a beard. He had on a tan-coloured jacket and a light blue hat, like you see golfers wear sometimes.'

I had seen him from the Mystery Bookstore; I had actually seen Paul Wallinger, and I had let him get away from me.

'What happened?' I asked the waiter, tersely.

'He came into the restaurant about a quarter before three. I offered to seat him, but he didn't want to eat. He said that you'd be coming in here to meet with him but he couldn't wait. He said he'd give me a hundred dollars to deliver that envelope. That's more than I'm going to make this afternoon, so I said okay. Then he asked me for our payphone number; he said he wanted to call you to make sure it was okay. I told him it was bust, but I said that he could call you on my cell, if it was that important. He took the number, gave me the envelope and a hundred bucks, and that was it.'

I returned the boy's phone and gave him another hundred for the aggravation. He'd given us the envelope, unopened. Another kid

the money. Still, I took the package into the bathroom. I undid the bow carefully; it was tied tight and the wrapping was pretty crude, a sure sign that it had been done by a man. (There's an old Scots saying, 'Let on you're daft and you'll get a hurl for nothing,' which means, loosely translated and put into context, that if one makes a real bollocks of wrapping a present, one will never have to do it again. It's a principle I've followed all my life, but I've never had to feign incompetence.)

Eventually I just tore the ribbon loose and ripped off the paper, feeling that involuntary pang of regret that is part of my Scots heritage at the knowledge that it couldn't be reused. It had enclosed a small, square yellow box, around six inches by six by six. I lifted the lid off, cautiously, and saw that it was packed with tissue paper. I removed the top layers, until I came to a red plastic circle with regular upraised dots all the way around: a baby's teething ring.

I took it out and saw a small square of paper folded below it. I unfolded it: written in a scrawled hand was, *Tom doesn't need this any more, Mommy. It's been such a long time.*

I took them through to the bedroom and showed them to Prim. She grabbed the ring with both hands, her eyes moistening. Her mouth twisted into a scowl as she read the note; when she was finished she crumpled it and threw it away. 'What's he doing?' she exclaimed.

'He only does it to annoy, because he knows it teases,' I murmured.

'What?'

'Alice in Wonderland. It's the duchess talking about the sneezing boy.'

'And what did she recommend be done about him?'

I smiled. 'She recommended that the crap be beaten out of him, actually.'

'She knew what she was talking about,' Prim muttered.

24

We thought about checking out of the Century Wilshire and driving straight to Vegas, where Everett had said my suite was waiting. Prim was all for it, but she wasn't driving: it would have taken us until midnight and I did not fancy arriving that late.

Instead we walked back down to the Village and ate in a place called the Napa Valley Grille . . . no, I don't know where the 'e' came from. It was glass-walled so we were pretty visible, but I didn't care. In fact, I found that I didn't care about anything much, other than getting to the Bellagio, meeting up with my friends and starting work on their movie.

I hadn't forgotten about Susie's message, or her advice to check my e-mail, but there was a practical difficulty with that. Our hotel had no in-room access, and the one terminal they did possess seemed to have been commandeered permanently by a Japanese salesman.

Prim was pretty subdued over dinner. I could see that she was wrestling with the decision she had to make. When I considered it again, the teething-ring trick had been quite cute, a piece of psychological pressure applied just at the key moment.

In fact we hardly spoke to each other, we seemed consumed with our own thoughts, chose automatically from the menu . . . I can't even remember what we ate, and that's unusual for me . . . and then just picked at our food.

We were back at the hotel and in our suite when the dam burst. I had just closed the door when I saw her shoulders start to shake; she buried her face in her hands and sat on the edge of the bed closest to her. I let her sob for a while, and then, when it had started to subside, I drew her to her feet and held her to me.

'Oz, I'm so sorry,' she mumbled into my chest. 'I should never have got you involved in this. It's taken you away from home, it's cost you a packet, and it's made all sorts of trouble for you. I can, can . . .' She broke off as a big sob racked her. '. . . can tell that you've had enough, and that you'd rather be out of it.'

I'd been thinking just that, in spite of myself, but I could hardly admit it, could I? Besides, we had travelled a long way together, and not just in that week. And there was this too; in the course of our latest journey I had come to feel completely isolated from what I knew as home, and from the person around whom it all revolved. Susie had more or less ordered us both on this mission, and now she was giving me grief.

So I whispered into Prim's ear the traditional Scottish words of comfort, 'Don't be fuckin' daft,' and pressed her even tighter to me. We stayed that way for the rest of the night.

When I woke next morning, at seven, my right arm was numb, trapped under her head. I eased it out without disturbing her, then peeled off the clothes in which I had fallen asleep, and headed for the shower. When I returned, still trying to dry myself adequately with a towel that was moist from the previous day, she was sitting on the bed we had slept on, with her knees pulled up to her chest, and her newly discarded clothes at her feet. Her face was puffed and blotchy, but she managed a small smile.

'How can you do that?' she asked. 'You sleep all night in your clothes, yet ten minutes later you're looking like a movie star.'

'I am a bloody movie star,' I reminded her.

'Yes, now, but you've always been able to do that.'

I grinned at her. 'Well, now's your chance to do the same . . . although you've got a bit of work to do.'

'I'd better get to it then.' She jumped from the bed, only to pause on her way to the bathroom. 'Do you know what's sad, though?' she said. 'Now you are a movie star, you don't fancy me a bit.'

I looked down at her figure; it had been trim before, but now it qualified as voluptuous. 'Don't you believe it,' I told her. 'I may be a happily married man, but I'm still a man. So, please, get all that out of my sight.'

She seemed cheered up by that dismissal; she spent about half an hour in the bathroom, but after she was done and dressed for the journey, everything was restored to normal. We ate a very light breakfast in the hotel courtyard, then checked out and set off on our journey.

I'd never driven from LA to Las Vegas before, but technology's a wonderful thing. I switched on the GSP and did what I was told. All I had to do was steer the thing. It took us out of Westwood on Interstate 405, then on to I-10, through the mass of Los Angeles itself and out to San Bernadino, where it took the I-15 and headed for Nevada, across mostly open country, much of it desert. I put the Jaguar into cruise control and leaned back with not much more than a finger on the wheel, to enjoy the view from the almost empty highway.

Eventually, in the distance, Las Vegas loomed up before us; it's one of the most amazing things I have ever seen, that fantastic skyline rising from the flat, arid landscape. The effect was as if we were standing still and it was coming up from the very ground itself to engulf us. It reminded me of the great scene in Spielberg's *Close Encounters*, when the mother ship appears for the first time, and you're stunned by the sheer size of the thing.

And engulf us it did, although the navigation system did its job to the end. It guided us along the Strip, past the steel and concrete wonderlands, until it told me to turn off and into the driveway of the Bellagio Hotel and Casino.

I left the valet to park the Jaguar, and to tell Hertz they could come and collect it, then I allowed a porter to wheel our luggage inside. The Bellagio's reception area turned out to be around the same size as the whole of the Century Wilshire, if not slightly larger; at least, that was how it seemed.

There wasn't just one clerk at Reception, there was a team, and they all knew who I was. They gave us the royal treatment, and within a minute we were being escorted to the lift. The suite that awaited us was bloody enormous. It was on the top floor with a view up and down the Strip. There were two bedrooms, each with his and hers bathrooms, and a living area the size of a driving range. I looked at Prim. She looked at me. I was used to luxury accommodation when I was working, but this left me as gob-smacked as she was.

There was a bottle of champagne in an ice-bucket on the dining-table with a note attached. It was from Everett and it read, *Welcome to the City of Dreams, Daze. I'm in suite eleven.* I called him straight away to tell him I'd arrived, but Reception had already done that.

'Hi, buddy,' he greeted me. 'When did your flight get in?'

'I drove.'

He gave a great booming laugh. 'From San Francisco?' He had seen the telly news as well.

'From the City of the Angels.'

'Why the hell were you there? Are your wife and kids with you?'

'One of my wives is, no kids; the extra room will be used, don't worry. It's a long story; I'll explain when I see you.'

'I can't wait. Get yourselves settled in, then come along to my suite for lunch. Say around two.'

'Okay,' I said, 'but I'll be on my own. Primavera's expecting a phone call.'

'Primavera? The lady we met in Barcelona? I thought you got divorced a few years back.'

'We did, and we still are. That's part of the long story.'

I left him wondering and picked up Prim's case from the foyer . . . the suite actually had a foyer . . . where the bellboy had left it. I carried it through to the bedroom to the left of the living area. 'This is yours,' I told her. 'I'll be away over there.'

She grinned at me. 'We might as well be in separate hotels,' she said.

'Maybe we should have been all along,' I muttered. I took my suitcase to the other bedroom and unpacked it. I found a laundry bag and crammed all my used stuff into it, then called Housekeeping and asked them to pick it up straight way. I went to tell Prim she should do the same, to find her opening the champagne.

She shrugged her shoulders. 'The ice is melting.'

'Can't let that happen,' I agreed. 'I'll do that; you go and bag up your noxious knickers and all your other stuff. The Seventh Cavalry laundry service is on its way to the rescue.'

'Thank Christ for that.'

When she returned I handed her a glass; we walked across to the window and looked out, taking in the amazing view. They say that all great cities are a collection of villages that have gradually evolved into a single mass, while retaining some of their own distinctive colour and characteristics. Las Vegas isn't like that, not one bit, although for my money it's a great city too. It's a collection of extraordinary visions and follies, all of which have swum together to create a fairyland nobody could ever have imagined had they looked out across what was then desert, sixty years ago. It's said that the place in which we stood cost a billion dollars, and it's just one among many, and not even the biggest. God knows how much dough's been sunk into the Strip, all of it dedicated to separating Mr and Mrs America from theirs.

Susie doesn't know what she's missed, I thought to myself.

That thought extended to the message left on my cell-phone, and to my e-mail. Whatever was on it, I knew it would be grief of some sort; I really didn't need any more at that point, but I knew that I had to get it over with. So I fetched my laptop, booted it up and plugged the modem lead into the dedicated jack-point in the suite's office area.

I went straight to my AOL box; it had been a couple of days since I checked it, so there were quite a few messages waiting, including one from Ellie and one from Jonny. They were in touch all the time, and I was pretty sure they would be routine, so I left them unopened and concentrated on the two that were of interest, new mails from Paul Wallinger and from Susie, hers despatched more recently, judging by its place in the queue.

I went to Wallinger's first; as soon as it appeared on screen I saw that it was addressed to both Susie and me. There was no heading and no message, just an attachment labelled 'Untitled 2.1 zip'. I hit the download button and watched as a series of images was displayed in a strip at the foot of the screen. After the week I'd just had, nothing should have shocked me, but these did.

'Come here and see this,' I called out to Prim, with an edge to my voice that brought her running to stand behind me, her hands on my shoulders, as she looked at the laptop. I hit the command that says 'view as a slideshow', and watched as each picture was displayed, full screen size.

There were five of them and they had all been taken in our hotel in Minneapolis, from a point high on one wall, on our first night there, when we'd got back to our room after dinner and a few beers in Gluek's. They showed the living area and a part of one of the beds, beside the screen. All but one of the images featured Prim, almost facing the hidden camera. In the first, she was unbuttoning her shirt, in the second she was stepping out of her jeans, in the third she was letting her bra fall on to the floor, and in the fourth she was naked, back to the camera and heading towards the bedroom. The last of the images showed me; I was in my boxers, thank God, and I'd been going from the bathroom to my bed, but anyone looking at the shot would have thought I was about to get into the one in which Prim could be seen lying.

We stared at the incriminating photographs, as they ran over and over again before us. Prim's fingers were digging into my shoulder, harder and harder with each frame. 'He bugged our room, Oz,' she gasped. 'The dirty bastard bugged our room. How could he have done that?'

'Probably quite easily if he was in the room next door,' I told her.

'But why's he sent these to you now?'

'For information, you might say. He's also sent them to Susie.'

'Oh, no!' Her hands left my shoulders; as I killed the slideshow and turned round to face her, I saw that they were pressed to her cheeks. 'God,' she gasped, 'what's she going to think?'

'What she was meant to think, when he cancelled our second room and set this up.'

'Paul did that?'

'The very boy.'

'But why?'

'I have no idea.' I looked up at her. 'Leave me alone for a bit, will you? There's a message from Susie; I'd better read it.'

She went back to the window, and I opened Susie's mail. I winced as I read it.

So this is the bloody great suite you told me you had. It looks like an ordinary hotel room to me. You lied to me, Oz, and I don't think I'll ever believe you again. If you want her, fucking stay with her, but don't think you're getting anywhere near the kids.

I tried to make myself angry with her, but I couldn't. If that had been her in those photos, with someone else, someone would have had to scrape me off the ceiling. I thought about picking up the phone there and then, but could see only a yelling contest in prospect, so instead I replied to her mail.

My darling [I wrote], *you must believe me when I tell you that nothing's happened between Prim and me, in Minneapolis or anywhere else. We were set up there by Paul Wallinger; he cancelled our second room by pretending to be on my staff, and he occupied it himself. He bugged our room and took those pictures. We had had a couple of drinks and maybe we were not as decorous as we should have been, but I promise you that it was no more than that. I don't know why the guy did it, but I expect to catch up with him pretty soon, and when I do, and when Prim has got Tom back, I promise you I will get the truth out of him.*

He's playing a game with Prim. He's showed part of his hand, in that he's given her a draft agreement to sign, swapping Tom for the money she has in Vancouver. He wants to make the trade here in Las Vegas. Whether she does it or not is her call. I've still got her with me in the hope that when he contacts her again, I'll be able to locate the kid while they negotiate, and enforce Harvey's court order. We need to be close if this is going to work, or she could lose her money and her son. I don't like this any more than you do, but you sent me, remember. If your trust in me has evaporated, get on a

210

plane and come straight out here. Believe this or not as you will, but I've missed you from the moment I stepped out of our front door.
Love
Oz.

I re-read it, hit the 'send' button, then went back over to the window, and Prim. I picked up my abandoned glass and stared out at the city for quite a long time, seeing none of it.

'Is she as steamed up as I'd be in her shoes?' she asked, at last.

I shook my head. 'Compared to Susie, your temper is a breeze beside a hurricane. You have been in her shoes, remember. She's much more steamed up than you ever were.'

'Can you fix it?'

'I hope so. I love her, Prim, don't be in any doubt about that,' I felt grimmer than at any time before in my life as I picked up the bottle and refilled my glass. 'If I lose her, and Wallinger's to blame, you can forget anything I've said up to now. I'll make a phone call and he'll be dead.'

She looked at me anxiously. 'Then you'd better not lose her, and drag yourself down in the process.'

As she spoke I heard a click from the laptop, telling me that I had more mail. I went back across and reopened my box. Susie must have been sitting beside her computer; my message had been answered.

It was not good news.

All well and good [she'd written], *but if I put detectives on your trail what would they find, in Vancouver, and in San Francisco or in Los Angeles? Give me a straight answer, Yes or No, to this question. Did you and Prim sleep together in the Century Wilshire last night?*

I took a deep breath; I hadn't told her we were booked into the Century Wilshire. I began hammering on the keyboard.

*I'm not playing, Susie. This is my straight choice for you. You
either believe Wallinger's lies and insinuations or you believe
my truth. I am not having an affair with Prim or anyone else.*

I sent the message and stayed by the laptop. The reply came
through inside three minutes.

*When the chambermaid in the Campton Place made the beds
in your discreet two-bedroom suite on Friday morning, yours
hadn't been slept in. Shove it, Oz.*

I sighed. She had indeed put detectives on my trail, or Wallinger
had spoken to the chambermaid himself. Either way, I'd stitched
myself up, well and truly.

I sent her one last message.

It's all smoke and mirrors, Susie. I love you.

Then I switched the damned machine off.

'What can I do?' I asked myself aloud. *What have you always
done when you were in deep shit?* I heard myself reply, inside my
head.

I picked up the phone and I called my dad. In the few times in
my life when all else has failed, he's always been there. As soon as
he heard my voice, he knew that it wasn't just a 'hello' call.

'What's up, son?' he asked me.

'Dad, I want you to do something for me. My life might depend
on it. I want you to call Susie and tell her I've promised you that I
haven't betrayed her. You don't need to know the details; just tell
her I've sworn that to you on a stack of Bibles and asked you to
pass it on word for word.'

'I take it that you've already told her this but she's having trouble
believing you.'

'You take it right.'

'Then what makes you think she'll believe me?'

I thought about that one for a bit. 'Dad,' I told him, when I'd worked out the answer, 'I might know that you're not perfect, but nobody else does. As far as Susie's concerned, when Moses came down from the mountain with the Ten Commandments, he looked just like Mac the Dentist.'

He chuckled. 'I never did tell you about that burning bush I saw on the way home from the pub one night, did I? Okay, son, I'll do it; I won't promise that it'll do any good, but I'll do it. Oh, aye, and by the way, your sister's got engaged. The guy even came and asked me if it was all right. He's not so bad after all; a crap golfer, but not so bad. Goodnight.'

Hey, I thought, *a piece of good news.*

I went back into the laptop and read Ellie's message. It confirmed formally what my father had just told me, and what she'd let slip a week before. I sent her a quick

Congratulations, I couldn't be more pleased for you.

then looked at Jonny's. He told me the same story, then asked,

What do you think of the law as a career, Uncle Oz? Harvey seems to be pretty well fixed.

I replied,

I know two sorts of lawyers, the boring ones and those who overcome the turgidity of their profession and remain interesting, amusing human beings. If you believe you can be the latter, go for it.

I think Jonny sees me as a Moses substitute as well. I hoped that after I'd climbed out from under the ruins I found myself buried in he'd feel the same way.

I looked at the box again, in case there was another message from Susie. There wasn't. I clicked a button and deleted everything, then switched off once more.

I checked my watch; it was coming up for two. I left Prim with

213

the rest of the champagne, told her to order whatever lunch she wanted from Room Service, then went in search of the big man's suite.

As he'd said, it was just along the corridor. I knocked on the door and, as always, when it opened everything went dark. Everett Davis is so big he blocks the light from nearly every doorway he approaches. I still laugh when I remember the first time he came to see me in Glasgow; I thought there had been an unscheduled eclipse.

Since those days Daze, to give him his ring name, had gone on to become one of the biggest names in sports entertainment, as professional wrestling is called now for very good US tax reasons. He was everything in the game, performer, talent spotter, promoter and president of a company that he had founded and built to the point at which it was quoted on the New York Stock Exchange.

As I stepped into his suite I had entered the presence of a genuine dollar billionaire.

'It's great to see you, Oz,' he began. 'I want you to know how much I appreciate your being here. It could be the difference between success and failure for this movie.'

I looked up at him; way up. 'Come on, man, failure's never an option for you. I might make you a few more dollars; that's what you mean, isn't it?'

'Let's just say I'll appreciate having your name on the marquee when we première.'

'Is Diane here?' I asked.

'No, she's in Jersey with the family.' Everett's kids are around the same age as mine. 'Before we go in there,' he said quietly, 'gimme a rundown on your ex's problems.' I gave him the quick, five-minute version, leaving out all the aggravation between me and Susie.

'This guy's in Vegas, you reckon?' he asked, when I was finished.

'So we believe.'

His eyes grew hard; you wouldn't want to be the cause of him looking like that. 'If you need any help to round him up, I've got a small army here.'

'Man, you're a large army in your own right. Thanks for the offer; I'll bear it in mind if I need help, but I'm looking forward to crucifying this guy myself.'

He led me into the suite; it wasn't as big as mine. The table was set for lunch, four places, and the other two were occupied by my friend Liam Matthews, who had the lead role in *Serious Impact* . . . although he'd be billed below me . . . and the director, Santiago Temple. I'd never met him but I recognised him from the pages of *Empire* magazine. A couple of waiters were hovering in the background, ready to go to work.

'Hi, slugger,' said Liam, in his light Irish accent. He looked at my patched-up ear. 'What the hell did that?'

'A soft-nosed point three eight bullet, according to what was in the rest of the chamber. That's what you get when you're an all-action movie star, sunshine.'

'On this movie, when I shoot you, I'll be using blanks, I promise.'

'I may not take you on trust.' Liam and I weren't always pals. In fact, the first time we met I took a punch at him for chatting up my wife; I was married to Jan then.

'I will check every round personally,' said Temple.

I shook my head. 'I've never met you before,' I told him. 'You may not know the difference between a dummy and the real thing. I think I'd rather the armourer did it.' I was grinning when I said it, but I wasn't kidding. There have been accidents in the past: take a look at the end of the short career of Brandon Lee.

He glanced at the plaster. 'What's under that?' he asked me.

'Some very neat stitching; makeup should be able to hide it, if you're worried.'

'As it happens, I'm not. The rescheduling will give you time to recover.'

I looked at Everett as we took our seats and the waiters moved in. 'Come again?'

He smiled. 'Something I've been holding out on you. You'll have noted that the majority of your scenes involve Jerry.' I had; I was to play the smooth bad guy, and Jerry Gradi was to play my muscle. 'Well, we've had a little problem.' Jerry's nearly as big as

215

Everett; I couldn't imagine any of his problems being little, but I was wrong. 'He's caught chickenpox from his little boy,' said Daze with a huge smile, 'and he's been quarantined.'

I had to grin too, at the thought of the mighty Behemoth being flattened by a few spots.

'He'll be out of action for another week,' Everett went on. 'However, Santiago's managed to move things around. If it's okay with you, we'll switch your scenes with Liam to this week and compress your action with Jerry into the week following, but with the best will in the world, we can't get you into action before Wednesday, at the earliest, and maybe even Thursday.'

I found myself wondering whether that would give me time to fly home to see Susie, but I realised pretty quickly that if I did I'd be lucky to be able to spend more than half an hour with her, and that wouldn't be nearly enough. Still, hopefully it would give me a window to get Prim's thing done.

'It's okay with me,' I said.

That was the only piece of business we had to do, and it was over in a couple of seconds. The main purpose of the get-together was to give me a chance to get to know Santiago, or Santi, as he insisted I call him. He was an earnest young guy, still in his twenties; he'd done fewer movies than I had, and he'd only directed two of them. However, I knew that Everett wouldn't have hired him if he'd had any doubts about his ability to deliver a good product, so I felt comfortable with him from the start.

We spent the next couple of hours just catching up. Liam and Everett spent a good chunk of the time pulling my chain about the San Francisco incident. After all, they were the professional athletes, and I was supposed to be the dilettante, the pretender; they thought the whole thing was a great laugh.

Eventually, though, the joke was played out and so were the black grapes and Stilton. Santi gave me a copy of the revised shooting schedule, and I promised to look in on the set before Wednesday to get to know the rest of the cast and the key crew members. I'd enjoyed the break, but the overriding problems hadn't gone away. For all I knew, Susie might have called me while I was away, or sent me another e-mail, or Prim might have had a call from Wallinger about the completion of their business.

I put the two together and came up with the scenario of Susie calling and Prim answering. That sent a shiver through me, so I said, 'So long,' to the guys and headed back to my, our, suite.

I was halfway along the corridor when my mobile sounded. I tore it from my pocket, in the hope that it might be my wife wanting to kiss and make up, but the incoming number read-out showed me at once that it wasn't. My caller was American, but it wasn't anyone in my phone book. I pressed the receive button and muttered a noncommittal, 'Yes,' in case it was a wrong number.

'Mr Blackstone?' a man's voice rumbled; a voice I thought I knew.

'It is.'

'This is John Wallinger.' I'd been right. 'Can you speak? Are you alone?'

'Yes to both. What is it?'

'Mr Blackstone, I want you to meet with me.'

I joined up a number of mental dots, to form an ugly picture. 'Has this become a family enterprise all of a sudden?' I asked him. 'Or was it all along?'

'I don't know what you mean by that. I repeat, I'd like you to meet with me. It's of vital importance to me that you do, and I believe it will be to you also.'

'Lieutenant, I'm in Las Vegas, and I'm here to work. I can't just hop on a plane and go to Minneapolis.'

'I'm not in Minneapolis. I'm in Santa Fe, New Mexico. There's someone here I'd like you to meet.'

'John, I can trust you, can I? If I go there I will be coming back, yes?'

'I promise you, Mr Blackstone, I wish you no harm; the opposite in fact.'

'Okay, I'll be there. But tell me, man, what the hell's it about?'

'I don't want to talk about it over the phone. It's best that you see for yourself. And one other thing, sir: don't tell anyone about this, anyone at all.'

'However you want it. What's another mystery to me? Where do I meet you, and when?'

'Midday tomorrow, at a restaurant called the Cowgirl Hall of Fame. I'll be waiting in the bar.'

I must be crazy, I thought. By that stage in the enterprise, I probably was, so without a second thought I headed down to the lobby and to the concierge. 'You do travel bookings?' I asked.

'We do, sir,' said yet another of the stunning women who seemed to populate the place.

'Can you get me a flight to Santa Fe? I have to be there, in the city, by midday tomorrow, returning later in the day.'

She shook her perfectly coiffured head. 'By schedule, sir, that's impossible. All the flights from McCarron go via Denver.'

'Could I drive?'

'Sir, it's seven hundred miles. You'd need to leave now.'

'What do I do, then?'

'Private charter is your only option. I can probably find you a Lear jet for tomorrow. How many passengers will there be?'

'Just me. Do it.'

I waited while she called someone. Whoever it was they were on first-name terms; she was Anita, and he was Troy. When the conversation was over . . . it involved a lot of nodding, as if they could see each other . . . she came back to me. 'That's a reservation, sir. Your pilot's name is Troy Hawkins, and he asks that you be at the Hawkins Air reception desk at McCarron airport by eight thirty tomorrow. It'll be a two-hour flight, departing at around nine. That will give you time to make your meeting in the city. I've taken the liberty of asking Troy to have a car and driver at your disposal at Santa Fe.'

'No liberty at all, Anita, that's fine.'

I paid for the charter there and then. Her smile grew even toothier when she saw the name on the credit card. Mine almost disappeared when I saw the cost, but I kept it fixed on, and signed on the dotted line.

25

I said nothing to Prim about my trip. John Wallinger had made me promise to tell no one, and I sensed that he hadn't envisaged any exceptions. Besides, I feared that she wouldn't like being left alone, and the idea of having two women pissed off at me at the same time didn't attract me.

There had been no call from Susie, or from Wallinger, and when I checked AOL I found no new e-mails either.

Prim wasn't keen on leaving the suite but I wasn't keen on staying there either, so I persuaded her that we should see some of the sights. We waited until some of the heat had gone from the day, and then set out.

We stopped on the bridge that crosses the road from the Bellagio to watch the fountains, the hotel's main public attraction . . . apart from the slot machines, roulette and black-jack tables inside. They kicked off every half-hour or so, in a fantastic choreographed display, with Andreas Bocelli and Sarah Brightman singing their wee hearts out in the background.

When that was done, we headed across the bridge and past Bally's until we came to Paris, an enormous casino complex with streets lined with shops and restaurants and its own Eiffel Tower rising up out of it all, not quite as tall as the real thing, but going on for five hundred feet high, with an observation platform on top and a restaurant on the eleventh level. When we'd done that, we moved on to Venice, which has its own Grand Canal, singing gondoliers, the works. The people who are building Las Vegas . . . oh, yes, it's still growing . . . don't think small: they want Americans to keep their money in America, so they've brought Europe to them.

We knew the real thing, though, so we crossed the Strip and explored New York, New York, which is a sort of Medium-sized Apple, with its version of the Statue of Liberty. I didn't look for an inscription on its base, but if there is one I'll bet it doesn't say, *Give me your tired, your poor, your huddled masses* . . . like the real one does. There's a fair chance you'll leave tired and poor, but the casino owners want you to arrive rich and wide awake.

We grabbed a couple of chimichangas in a Mexican restaurant in a reproduction of SoHo village, then lost a few bucks in the slot machines . . . you feel you have to; maybe their constant tinkling din is addictive . . . before walking back to the Bellagio just before eleven, soaking up the spectacle of the Strip, all lit up in its night clothing.

Before going up top, we looked in at the Fontana Bar; Liam was in there, with Erin, his wife, so we stopped to have a drink with them. If Erin was puzzled to see Prim with me, rather than Susie, she didn't show it; but she was an air steward, so she'd probably seen all sorts of celebrity situations in her time. Liam, of course, knew Prim from Barcelona; there had been an incident there once, involving Jerry Gradi, and her nursing skills had come in very handy indeed.

There were no messages showing on the phones upstairs, and nothing new on e-mail when I checked. I had to be downstairs for the car at eight, so I turned in. I looked at Prim. 'How are you feeling?' I asked her.

'Okay. I know what I'm going to do: I just have to wait for Paul to contact us again, that's all.'

'Good. In that case, since there don't look like being any floods of tears tonight, that's your room and that's mine. Sleep tight.'

She smiled at me. 'You too. I really am sorry I've caused you all this bother, Oz.'

Still I hadn't said anything about my trip to Santa Fe. My intention was to be out of there before Prim surfaced in the morning, leaving her a note to say I'd be back later and to call me on the mobile if anything happened. But it didn't work out that way: when

I stepped out of my room, there she was in the living area, in T-shirt and shorts, and drinking coffee.

'Where are you going?' she asked, when she saw how I was dressed.

I improvised. 'I told Santi Temple I'd look in on the filming, to get to know the boys and girls.' You see? It wasn't a direct lie. I'd have told her the truth, whatever John Wallinger had said; I didn't, only because I thought that if I had, she might have been afraid that I was walking into a trap, designed to take me out of the picture. Actually, I hadn't discounted that possibility entirely: the private plane and car were a kind of insurance. If I didn't show up for the return journey, the alarm would be raised right away.

'I'm not sure how long I'll be,' I went on. 'You know how to get in touch with me if you need to.' I was out of the door before she had a chance to ask me anything else.

Troy Hawkins's Lear jet turned out to be a Hawker Siddeley; I was pleased by that, because it's slightly wider than the Lear. Captain Hawkins was a very sharp dude indeed, as was his co-pilot, Matthew, and the steward Rafaela, for all that her English was largely incomprehensible to my ear . . . even the unmangled one.

We took off two minutes early from McCarron airport; when Matthew gave me our flight plan to New Mexico I wondered how we'd manage to get that high in that little bird, but the journey was as smooth as silk. I'd brought my script with me, and spent much of the time learning my lines for the scenes I'd be shooting with Liam through the week. I wasn't worried about the part at all; there was nothing taxing in it. All the viewer needed to know was that my character, Oscar, was a thoroughly bad dude; they didn't have to be given a window into his soul.

Our touch-down at Santa Fe airport was as smooth as our take-off had been; we taxied into the general aviation terminal, and the door was opened in no time at all. I told Troy that I expected to be back in three hours, and that if there was to be any change in that I'd let him know.

The car they had waiting for me was a Buick; my first

impression was that New Mexico does not go big on European imports. When I told Jesus, my driver, where I wanted to go, he grinned; I could read the words '*gringo* tourist' clearly from his expression.

He took it steady on the way into the city. I had plenty of time and I didn't want to be early; since Wallinger had summoned me there, he could get the bloody drinks in. We drove in through the suburbs on Highway 85, but since the airport is around twenty miles give or take a few, from the centre, we didn't have that much time to kill.

I read somewhere that the late Will Rogers . . . he's an American institution, but I'm not certain why . . . said, when he was still running to time, that the person who designed Santa Fe did so while riding on a jackass, backwards and drunk. I didn't see any jackasses, going in either direction, drunk or sober, on the way, but by the time we'd reached the meandering heart of the place and Jesus began to pick his way though a maze of one-way streets, I began to get old Will's drift.

Many of the street names in Santa Fe are more redolent of Old Mexico than New. The Cowgirl Hall of Fame is on South Guadalupe Street, where it meets Aztec Street. I told Jesus to find the car park and wait for me somewhere visible. I didn't quite tell him to keep the motor running, but he got my drift. His expression had changed as he looked at me; now it was switching between 'drug courier' and 'hit man'.

I stepped inside. My first thought as I looked around was that I'd never realised there were so many cowgirls; Calamity Jane and Annie Oakley are the extent of my knowledge of the breed. The bar was called La Cantina, and it could have been a wild west movie set, apart from the television mounted high on the wall.

John Wallinger was sitting at a table, waiting. I was pleased to see that he was by himself, with only a Coke and a dish of peanuts for company. He rose as I came in, and extended his hand; this time he didn't try the crusher grip.

'I'm glad you could make it, Mr Blackstone. Did you drive?'

'No danger, I hired a plane . . . and call me Oz.' I looked across in the direction of the Mustang Grill. 'Would you like to eat?' I asked.

'If you would,' he said, 'but we don't have long.'

The lieutenant ordered a buffalo burger; I settled for a catfish po' boy and a pint of Breckenridge. We had them served on the outdoor patio area; it was set up for music, but happily there was none. I knew what it would have been and I wasn't in Merle Haggard mode.

I quizzed him as we ate on the purpose of the expedition, but he wouldn't tell me a thing. 'I want you to see for yourself,' was all he said. He asked me a few things, about Prim and about her problem. I repeated the story, but this time I added the bit about how they'd met at Gleneagles, when he'd been playing the part of the jilted broker finding consolation on the golf course.

That amused him. 'My brother and golf have never been compatible,' he said. 'If you'd asked him about Tiger Woods, he'd have thought it was a jungle full of fierce creatures.'

We skipped the coffee; I waved to the waitress for the tab but John insisted on picking it up. 'Come on,' he said. 'Where we're going isn't far from here. We have to be there for one o'clock. That's when the rest hour begins; they don't like visitors after that.'

'Yes, but you're a cop.'

'Not here.'

'Okay, then: I'm a movie star.'

'That won't cut any ice either, not with these people.'

'I've got a driver waiting,' I told him. 'We can go by car.'

'Trust me, we're quicker walking.' He set off at a brisk pace along South Guadalupe. I had no option; I caught him up.

In no time at all we'd reached the Santa Fe River, which is actually more of a stream in the summer. We crossed the bridge, then turned right into West Almeda Street, and took a left turn a few hundred yards along. Almost immediately John stopped in front of a three-storey stucco building that covered half a block. There was a sign over the dark brown entrance door, reading 'The Blessed Sisters'.

'What the hell is this?'

'You'll see.' The big detective turned the heavy metal handle and led the way into a cool shaded hallway. In a corner, there was what looked like a reception desk, only there was nobody receiving. He stepped up to it and rang a hand bell. It made hardly a sound, but it did the job: in seconds a blue-habited nun appeared through a door.

'Lieutenant,' she said softly, then looked at me. 'Is this your friend?' Her Irish accent sounded wildly incongruous in the state capital of New Mexico, except . . . a convent's a convent wherever it is. 'You're just in time. If you go on through, he's been made ready for you.'

For the first time, I realised what was happening.

The big guy led the way out of the foyer and into a long corridor. All the doors off had opaque glass panels, which helped to light it. He stopped at the third on the right, opened it and went in.

There was a bed in the room, but it was empty; the man who, I assumed, was its usual occupant was sitting in a wheelchair by the window, wearing pyjamas and with a light rug over his knees. It had a view over the trickling river; he was looking out, but I could tell at once that he wasn't seeing anything. He was stick thin, with lank dark hair, and he had the pallor of a man who hadn't been in the sun for a while. His eyes were unblinking and his mouth hung open slightly, a trickle of saliva coming from one corner.

John took the handles of the chair and turned it towards me. 'Oz,' he said. 'I'd like you to meet my older brother, Paul Wallinger.'

26

The man I'd been hunting had a permanent smile on his face; whatever was going on inside his head, it looked as if it was happy. I found myself smiling back at him.

'He can't see you,' John told me. 'His vision went with the stroke, along with just about everything else.'

'How long have you known he was here?'

'For a couple of days, that's all. There's one thing you can't run away from in America, Oz, and that's your social-security number, if you have one. After we had our talk on Wednesday, I contacted the SSA and told them I had a missing-person enquiry. They came back to me on Friday, and told me he was here. I flew down as soon as I could, and got here yesterday.'

'What is this place?'

'It's a charity nursing home, run by the Blessed Sisters of Our Lord. It's ironic that he should wind up here, since he spent half his life laughing at my beliefs and at those of our parents.'

'What happened to him?'

'As I said, he had a stroke, a cerebral haemorrhage.'

'Here in Santa Fe?'

'No. He was in Albuquerque at the time; he was appearing in a play in a local theatre, and rooming in a boarding house with the rest of the cast. As near as I can piece together he collapsed during a performance, on stage. They rushed him to hospital, where his condition was stabilised, but there was no hope of recovery. The hospital kept him for as long as they had to, then found this place. The sisters agreed to accept him, and he's been here ever since.'

'Ever since when?'

John looked at me; his sombre expression was in contrast to his brother's permanent goofy grin. 'He's been here for over two years,' he replied.

Two years? I couldn't believe what I was hearing, but the evidence was in the chair before me. The man's body looked completely wasted.

'So how come this is the first you've heard of it? Didn't they try to trace his family?'

'His social-security card was in the name of Paul Patrick Walls. The listed address was somewhere in Palo Alto, but that was long out of date.'

'What about the theatre company? Couldn't they have helped?'

'The play was almost at the end of its run when Paul took ill. At first all the hospital staff cared about was saving his life: when it came time to ask who he was, the company had all left town.'

'What about Roscoe?'

'Who?'

'Roscoe Brown; he was your brother's agent.'

'I think they tried that, but there was nothing in his records that led back to us.'

'Hell, man, my detective was able to trace him on the Internet in ten minutes.'

'Sure, starting with the name Wallinger. Not so easy if you don't have that.'

I wasn't sure that was true; I guessed that someone hadn't tried that hard.

'What you have to realise, Oz,' John continued, 'is that when he was transferred here, Paul brought nothing with him. He had no papers, only his social-security card. He must have had some effects at the boarding house, but either they stayed there or another cast member took them. What you have to realise also is that nobody at our end was looking for him. Paul was an outcast from our family. His lack of respect for our values, his, forgive me, but his choice of profession, they drove a wedge between him and my father and me. When you add in his gayness . . .'

'He's gay?'

'Since high school. My father was a career soldier, Oz, until he was invalided out. He had pretty inflexible views on that sort of thing; I have to admit that he passed them on to me.'

'What about your mother?'

'Paul never had anything but contempt for our mother. That's why the idea of him going to her for help was preposterous to me.'

He was hitting me with a lot of information: the way it was coming across, Prim had been conned even more spectacularly than she'd realised. She'd had a child by someone, had lived with someone without knowing not just what he was but who he was.

John must have keyed into my thoughts. 'This guy,' he asked. 'What do you know about him?'

'I know that he fixed it for Prim and me to be sharing a room in Minneapolis, then bugged it and took some candid photographs of her in her skin. I know that he sent them by e-mail to my wife, which does not make me her favourite husband at the moment. I know that he did fly from London to Minneapolis with Prim's kid, and that he was there at the same time as us. I know that he diverted her money to a Canadian bank, to this side of the Atlantic, set up so that she can use it to buy Tom back from him. There's only one thing I don't know about him.'

'What's that?'

'I don't know who the bloody hell he is.' I paused. 'No, there's one thing more. He flew as Paul Wallinger, and before that he took Paul Wallinger's passport to the US Embassy in London and had Tom Wallinger's name added to it.'

I could feel the fire in my eyes as I looked at him. 'John, can you use your badge to ask question in the passport office? This guy's got himself a passport in your brother's name. I know that Paul must have had one of his own, at some time, because he had a part in a movie in Scotland a few years back. The phoney may be using that one; it may have come from the stuff at the boarding house. But if he is, he's had to change the photograph, and I don't see him taking a doctored passport to the embassy. Can you find out when, and even where the last application was made for a passport in the name of Paul Wallinger? If he does have a new one, the passport office will have a copy of the photo that's in it. Get hold of that, and at least we'll know what he looks like. We might even know who he is.'

'Get hold of that, buddy,' the detective rumbled, 'and I can loose the full might of the FBI on him: I do not believe that applying for a passport in someone else's name is in accordance with federal law. More than that, since the child is travelling on a false passport also, he can be taken into custody.'

The day seemed brighter somehow, and then it dimmed.

'That leaves one problem,' I said. 'We still have to flush him out. Even now, he might be setting up the trade with Prim in Las Vegas, with me out of the way. John, if you can bring in the Feds that will be great; but meantime, I have to get back there.'

'You do that. I'll make some calls from here.'

I nodded, then smiled at the chair again. 'What are you going to do about Paul?'

'I think I'm going to leave him here. If I take him back to Minneapolis will he even know? Not a chance. The Mother Superior told me that the medical staff don't expect him to live more than another year or two, at most. She's anxious that he should stay, so he will. I'll come and visit him when I can; I may even bring Mom. Blood's blood, after all.'

I was with him on that; I remembered how much my brief estrangement from my father had hurt us both. 'Good for you,' I told him.

I was ready to leave. He saw it and waved me towards the door; I was almost through it when another piece of the obvious forced its way into my addled brain. 'There is just one last thing,' I said. 'Whoever we're looking for knows Paul. He knew that he'd been ill, and that he wasn't getting better. We could well be looking for someone who was in that touring company, or who knew about it and was a close associate of his at the time. I know it's a long time since you saw him, but if you or your mother can recall anyone he might have mentioned in the past . . . you never know.'

'I'll try, but don't die waiting. Now get on your way.'

I left him there and walked back the way we'd come, across the river and down to the Cowgirl. Jesus was there, waiting for me; when I arrived I thought he looked relieved that I wasn't carrying a briefcase I hadn't had before. 'Back to the airport,' I ordered. 'I have to leave town in a hurry.' I suppressed a smile as I saw the 'hit man' scenario reappear on his face.

Leaving Santa Fe seemed to be easier than arriving; soon we were on cruise, heading down Highway 85, towards the airport. I leaned back against the leather upholstery and thought about the family skeletons I'd stirred up for John Wallinger the Second. When we'd parted I'd decided that he was glad of my intervention; now he'd be able to give them a decent burial. I thought about him, his mother and the attitudes that had torn their family apart. I thought about Martha, about our time in Minneapolis and about the things that had happened there.

And as I did, slowly but surely the realisation came to me that in all of my going-on-for-forty years on the Planet Earth, I'd never been so unbelievably fucking stupid.

27

The jet was fuelled and ready when we arrived back at the airport, but I held it on the ground for a few minutes while I made a few phone calls.

When we did take off, the return flight was as smooth as the outward journey had been. At first we were headed east; Troy flew a little further than was strictly necessary before banking and turning towards Nevada, so that I could enjoy the pampered tourist view of the mountains that make Santa Fe a ski resort in winter.

I was grinning to myself for much of the way, barely looking at my script. Rafaela must have wondered what a man can get in Santa Fe that isn't on offer in Las Vegas, but the only thing she asked me was whether I wanted my white wine topped up. I knew that I'd been drinking too much over the previous week, but that would change soon enough. Lots of things would change.

The Strip was just starting to cool down, and heat up, when the courtesy car brought me back to the Bellagio. I wondered whether Prim would be waiting for me in the suite, but she was, curled up on one of the big couches in the living area, wearing a sarong that I hadn't seen before. It looked as if it had come from one of the shops downstairs. There was an ice-bucket on the coffee table, with a bottle of Chablis Premier Cru and two glasses. As I came in she smiled at me, got up, and poured me a glass.

'How did your day go?' I asked her, as she handed it to me. 'Any contact?'

She nodded solemnly. 'He called. He wants to do it tomorrow.'

'Who called?'

She looked at me as if I was an idiot; which, of course, I was. 'Paul.'

'Can't have been Paul,' I told her. 'I've just seen Paul, or what's left of the poor bastard. His brother found him, in a sanctuary for the nearly dead in Santa Fe.'

Prim's mouth dropped open and her knees sagged; for a moment I thought she was going to faint, but she sat back down on the couch. 'You're mad,' she gasped. 'What story did he feed you?'

I loosened my shirt, kicked off my loafers . . . no socks in Vegas . . . and slid down beside her. 'The only thing he fed me was a catfish po' boy,' I told her. 'The guy who's been dogging our footsteps for a week is not, never was and never will be Paul Wallinger. I have seen the real Paul, not an imitation.' I was thirsty; I insulted the Chablis by draining half the glass in a swallow, but made up for it by reaching out to top it up again.

'Are you certain?'

'Absolutely. Your Paul couldn't have been Paul. You want to know why? Two reasons. One, when your guy was making love to you in Gleneagles Hotel, Paul was having a stroke on stage in Albuquerque. Two, the real Paul wouldn't have fancied you at all, for he's gay.'

I found that I was laughing. I shouldn't have, for she looked so bewildered. 'So if he isn't Paul, who is he?'

'Ah, fuck it. Let's just call him Jack. That's the name he used in Minneapolis; Jack Nicholson.' I looked at her, in a way I hadn't for a while. 'I just can't believe that you were taken that badly, love. Hook, line and fucking sinker.'

My eyes locked on hers. I went to sip the Chablis, but stone me, it had evaporated again. This time she poured my refill. I chuckled as I sipped it; at least, I thought I was sipping it; the stuff really was very drinkable. 'What's the deal, then?' I asked her.

'What do you mean, the deal?'

'You know. The deal, trade, kiddie barter.' Suddenly I felt hot, very hot; I unbuttoned my shirt all the way down, and tugged it from my waistband. Or at least I thought at the time that I had done it; maybe it was Prim.

'Well, here's the deal,' she whispered. She leaned into me and kissed me. And then it all got confused. I gave the sarong a tug; it just seemed to come away in my hand. I tried to focus on her; I couldn't, but it didn't matter. I knew her body well enough; the extra bits were just a bonus. All at once I felt euphoric, exultant, calm and enormously, extravagantly horny. As she undid my belt and slid off my pants, I wasn't thinking of anything but her and how funny, outrageous and amazingly stupid the whole thing had turned out to be.

As we rolled off the couch and she went down on me on the carpet, all I could do was giggle like a clown. As she straddled me all I could think of was that she was a fucking lunatic, but right at that moment I didn't care because I was loving what I was getting. It was so good that a little light kept flashing before my eyes, every few seconds or so.

'It was the duck, you know,' I chuckled into her ear. 'Now, it's so fucking obvious that you put that duck in Martha's bathroom, then made sure I went for a slash.' I laughed louder. 'You even drank all that fucking root beer so I wouldn't think anything of it. I fell for it too. I bought it all,' I giggled, 'right up till this afternoon.'

She arched her back, with me deep inside her, rolled her eyes, and then laughed back at me. 'None of us are quite as clever as we think we are, Oz, especially you. Now shut your eyes, shut your mouth and enjoy, because this is the most expensive shag you will ever have in your life. *Indecent Proposal* was cheap stuff compared to this.'

Even that obvious clue would not have begun to untangle the slithering mass of snakes that had engulfed my brain. I hadn't a bloody clue what she was talking about. As I looked up at her I felt that I didn't even care what she was talking about. Okay, it had been a set-up all along, an ingenious outrageous set-up, with me as the set-ee . . . I laughed even more manically at that . . . but so fucking what? This was great, Prim and me the way it used to be, the way it might have been, the way it could be again, and all I wanted to do was sleep off this one then have another, whatever the price-tag. All of it, the real meaning of it, would have passed me by, but for one thing.

232

It was just then, with the last small piece of my brain that was still functioning, that I realised that we were not alone. There was someone else in the room, a faint hazy figure, and either he was a waiter come in to clear away the ice-bucket . . . no way, José, that's good stuff and it's not finished . . . or he was someone else, doing something else. As I peered at him over Prim's shoulder, another of those funny lights went off in a flash. This was no waiter.

Under any condition, if there's one thing I hate it's a fucking sneaking peeping Tom . . . an ironic label in the circumstances.

There is a dangerous moment in intoxication: it comes when a happy drunk becomes an unhappy drunk, and if one is in the wrong place at the wrong time, it can have serious consequences.

For Prim, these manifested themselves in me heaving her off me, and tossing her clean over the back of the couch, in a single action. For the guy with the camera, they took the form of me surging to my feet, instantly detumescent, and lurching, snarling, after him. Fortunately for him, my legs weren't working too well. He had a further lucky break when Prim rose like a dragon from behind the upholstery and went for me, in an entirely different way from before. She didn't delay me for long, only for the amount of time it took me to clip her on the chin and knock her on her arse again . . . You're shocked that Oz hit a woman? You can't believe that Oz hit Primavera? Well, get over it! . . . but it was crucial.

By the time I reached the door it was open, and he was through it, and heading for the nearest escape route, in this case an open lift door. Nothing was holding me back, though: I was going to catch the bastard, I was going to tear him into the smallest pieces I could manage, and then I was going to eat them. I set off after him; I thought I was sprinting, but I think I was really doing a slow-motion jog through candyfloss.

Life's small coincidences can make so much difference. By sheer chance, as I passed the nearest elevator, it opened and Liam Matthews stepped out, with Erin behind him. He took one look, and grabbed hold of me. 'What the hell are you doing?' he asked, not unreasonably.

233

I struggled against him, pointing along the hallway: 'I'm going to kill that bastard,' I shouted. 'The fucker with the camera.' Liam glanced over his shoulder, just in time to see the man . . . He was wearing shades and a tan jacket, but he was clean-shaven. Isn't it funny how tiny details stick in your mind? . . . disappear into the lift.

'Not in that state you're not, Oz,' he said, then he slapped a half-nelson on me, wrestled me back to my room, and forced me inside. Someone else might have had trouble doing that, but not him. 'Liam,' I pleaded, almost coherently, 'you've got to get him. Don't let him leave the hotel.'

'I won't,' he promised. 'At least I'll try. Now you get control of yourself, and cover that monster up.' He slammed the door in my face.

Prim was still on the floor when I went back into the living area. She was groggy, but I picked her up, slung her over my shoulder and staggered off towards her room, grabbing the discarded sarong as I went. The door was open; even in my confused state I remembered that it had been closed earlier, and guessed that she had hidden her partner there.

As I threw her on to the bed I was still dazed from whatever it was that had happened to me. It must still have been working on me, for part of me . . . the part with a forked tail and horns . . . wanted her again.

Thankfully, the side of me with the white gown, the wings and the halo won the internal battle. It was pretty close, but he just nicked it on a split points decision.

I dragged her across to the big wardrobe, slung open the door and used her slinky garment to lash her wrists to the hanging rail. She didn't like it, but she had the sense not to resist. Okay, it might not have been a very angelic thing to do, but I hope you'll agree that, all things considered, it was understandable.

28

I wove my way back to my own room. My vision was still a bit fuzzy and my mind was all over the place. I tried to pull all the strands of what had happened together, but couldn't hold them in place for more than a couple of seconds at a time. I stared around me for a while, at nothing at all, until I caught sight of a large naked figure looking at me. I focused on him, and that was when I realised that the mirrored doors of the wardrobe were closed. I realised also that I looked totally out of my skull.

I went into 'His' bathroom and stood under the shower. After a couple of minutes, it occurred to me to switch it on, full blast.

I put my palms flat against the wall and let the needle-sharp spray pound into my head for quite a while . . . for more than five minutes, to be a little more accurate. (I wasn't completely naked; I still had on my Rolex.) My ear stung, but I didn't care as I felt my other senses return along with the pain.

I towelled myself more or less dry as quickly as I could, slipped on a pair of jeans and a seriously loud Paul Smith shirt that I'd bought on the Strip the night before, and went back out to the scene of the crime. I was picking up my discarded clothes when I heard Prim yell my name.

I went through to her room. Even in my bamboozled state I'd made a good job of tying her up. The knots were tight and the rail was strong; she was just where I'd left her, as I'd left her. There must have been some of the goofy juice left in my bloodstream, for I grinned at her, licked my lips and started to unzip my fly. She looked at me in something like horror, until I winked at her, zipped it up again and untied her.

Just then there was a thump on the door. I went through to open it, to find Liam there, with Daze, blocking out the light as usual. 'Did you catch him?' I asked, but I could read the answer in their eyes, even before the big man shook his head.

'We looked all over the place,' said Liam. 'Eventually I found a bellboy who said that he saw a man in a tan jacket running out of the door and across the bridge.'

I took them into the living area. 'If you want a drink, use the bar,' I told them. 'Don't touch the Chablis or those glasses.' They were both still on the table; mine was empty, but the other was untouched. 'I'll be back in a minute.'

When I walked in on Prim she was trying to smooth the wrinkles from her sarong. 'I need to shower,' she muttered, glaring at me.

'Go ahead,' I told her.

'Well, get out, then.'

I laughed. 'I'm not taking my eyes off you, honey. You shower, I watch, to make sure you don't do anything else stupid.'

She took a lot less time than I had: she was in and out of there in under two minutes. I found a Bellagio robe hanging behind the door and handed it to her. 'You'll dry in that,' I said. Then I took her back to the wardrobe and tied her up again.

'What are you doing?' she protested.

'Call it a citizen's arrest,' I told her. 'You and I are going to have a long talk, but only when I'm good and ready. Until then you're staying here. Oh, yes, and don't think about yelling again. There's nobody out there who'll come to help you.'

I looked at her. 'You did it so well, you know. You did meet a guy at Gleneagles two years ago, and he was registered as Wallinger, but it was after the real Paul had his stroke. You've really been setting me up for that long?'

She nodded; there was an air of triumph about her. 'I really have.'

'What did you use on me? Rohypnol?'

'Hell, no, that turns everything blue these days. I used stuff called GHB; it's known on the street as Fantasy, or sometimes Georgia Home Boy, or even GBH. Colourless, odourless and virtually tasteless; you'd never notice it in a bottle of Chablis . . .

236

and, Oz, my love, I've never seen you turn down a glass of Chablis in my life. Its effects, mixed with alcohol . . . well, big boy, you know about them now.' She paused. 'So do I, come to think of it. Expansive, you might say; I must try it on someone again sometime.'

She frowned. 'I wasn't sure about the dose, though. If we'd overdone it you'd have gone comatose on me, but as it turned out we didn't give you quite enough.'

I hated to think what any more would have done to me. 'That's just one small detail, though; you were so bloody meticulous with everything else, but what about the break-in at your flat? Why did you fake that?'

'To back up the Paul identity, of course. We set up a fake account for him with a bookie, then built up some debts just before it was time to make our move, to give everyone who might investigate yet another reason for him to have done a bunk. I knew that you and your spy Kravitz would go looking for him. We had to give you something to find.'

'What did you do with the diamonds?'

'They're in a safe deposit box in Los Angeles.'

'And the money? It never was out of your control, was it?'

She laughed at me. 'Oh, come on, Oz, of course it wasn't. You don't think I'd be that bloody stupid, do you?'

'So what's in it for your partner?'

'One third.'

'One third of what?'

'You'll find out.' I was sure that I would, and even in my still slightly dazed condition, I could guess how.

'Why not an even split?'

She gazed at me as if I was simple. 'Because it was all my idea, my brainchild. I even put up the expenses. One third's quite generous, all things considered.'

'And all of it done just to get even with me? That's what it was all about?'

'You and that bitch Susie. You don't think I ever forgave her either, do you?'

237

'But why wait so long?'

'I wanted you to be really big-time, so that when I did get even it would hurt all the more . . . as it's going to. When I saw how well *Red Leather* had done, I knew it was time. You're a big star now.'

'Kind of you to say so, but that's not what I meant. Why drag me all across America?'

'To be truthful . . .'

'That'll be a novelty for you.'

'Very funny . . . We were going to do it that first night in Minneapolis, but when you signed up for Las Vegas, I decided to spin it out for a while. I was hoping I wouldn't need the drug to set you up. I gave you all the inducements I could, but no, Oz, you really have gone straight, haven't you?'

'So what made you pick today?'

'I asked the concierge if she knew where you'd gone, and she told me. I knew it wasn't to any film set, because I followed you downstairs this morning and saw you get into a car with Hawkins Air on the side.'

'So you knew where the real Paul was?'

'Oh, yes.'

Until then, I'd been fascinated; for the first time I was repelled. 'In that case, setting his mother up like that was pretty cruel.' I was tired of her, and I'd heard almost enough. 'What makes you think we haven't caught your partner, the phoney Paul?' I asked.

'If you had, you wouldn't be in here talking to me like this, would you?'

'In that case, are you going to save me some time by telling me who he is?'

'Why the hell should I?' she retorted, her eyes spitting fire at me now, not lust. 'This isn't going to make any difference, you know. You're done, Oz. You just don't know how badly yet.'

My wicked side smiled. 'Don't underrate yourself, baby. I thought I was pretty spectacularly done, actually.' I closed the wardrobe door on her and went back to the boys.

'What's happened?' Everett asked. He was worried, and although he's a good friend, I knew it wasn't just my welfare that was on his mind. He had a lot of money sunk in the *Serious Impact* project, and I was an integral part of it.

'Remember all that stuff I told you, about Prim's problem?' I told him. 'It's all a front; she fooled me every step of the way. I shouldn't be in your movie, she should. What a fucking actress she is! I've known her for a good chunk of my life now, I've been married to her, and yet she fooled me. What a performance!'

I took my palm-top pocket PC from the pocket of my gaudy new Paul Smith shirt. It's top-of-the-range, an amazing piece of kit; it'll play you music, it'll show you pictures, it'll let you go online and it'll even record sound. I switched it to playback and let them hear everything that Prim had said.

'Jaysus,' Liam gasped, when it was done, reverting to his Irish accent. 'I hope nobody ever gets as mad with me as she is with you.'

'What happens now?' asked Everett.

'In a very short time, I'm going to get a message. Going by past performance it'll be an e-mail.'

I went over to the laptop and booted it up, then logged on to AOL; my mailbox was empty, but I left it open. For safety's sake, I linked up the pocket machine and put a copy of Prim's voice file on the laptop's hard drive. For even greater insurance, I opened it and edited out my last two sentences.

I'd only just finished when the AOL lady told me I had mail. 'That was bloody quick,' I exclaimed. Everett and Liam both looked up. I clicked the box open and verified that the new message was from Paul Wallinger Mark Two. 'It's him,' I told them. 'He's got to be close by.'

'He could have had a car in the hotel park,' Liam suggested. 'He could be miles away.'

'Then why did he run away from it?'

'He could have grabbed a cab on the Strip.'

'That shows how often you've been outside. Las Vegas taxis aren't allowed to pick up passengers on the street, only from hotels. With you on his tail he wouldn't have gone and stood in the queue across at Bally's. He's got a bolt-hole, and it's not far from here.'

I turned back to the laptop and clicked open the message. It went straight to the point:

You take an excellent picture, Mr Blackstone, but then we've always known that. These should go down well with certain newspapers in every part of the English speaking world, and in Europe too. They'll take you from Class A status to Class Z in an instant; you may get work as a porn star but that will be it.

If you want to avoid this, and keep your career into the bargain, it will cost you five million pounds sterling. I realise that it may take a couple of days to raise that sort of cash, so that's what you've got: two days. During that time, you will transfer that amount into P. Phillips account Number 2 in Fairmile and Company, Vancouver, British Columbia. If the money isn't there next Thursday morning, you will be as notorious world-wide as you were famous in San Francisco last week, only much more so.

Don't be naïve enough to believe that by paying this money you'll get the photographs back. We'll retain them in order to protect our interests, and ourselves. Arrangements will be made so that, should anything happen to Prim or me in the future, they will automatically go global.

Mrs Blackstone, you may not want to go along with this for your husband's sake, but for that of your children we recommend that you do.

I looked at the address strip again. Yup, he'd sent it to Susie too.

I took a deep breath and opened the attachments; they took a while to download, but they were what I had expected, and feared. Under the influence of the drug, I looked as if I was on Planet Ecstasy, putting on the performance of a lifetime. You couldn't see Prim's face, of course: the pixels had been scrambled. Mine, however, was all too clear, and not just my face. The tabloids would go mental . . . but not nearly as crazy as Susie.

I closed the images and deleted them, then went back to the message and sent a reply.

240

Okay. Sit tight.

When that was done, I sent Susie a mail; no text, just an attachment. Then I turned back to my friends. Liam had his impish look about him, but Everett was stone-faced: he could see his movie, his investment, and much of his business reputation heading up in smoke.

'Give me a minute,' I asked them. 'I have to speak to my wife.'

I left them there, went into my bedroom and phoned Susie. I reckoned it was about four in the morning, even she would be asleep. *Let her be anywhere,* I thought, *except sitting staring at her computer.*

My small prayer was answered. She was awake, but she'd been in the toilet. 'What is it?' she asked, abruptly. 'Wouldn't your dad call me this time?'

'Love,' I told her. 'After "Will you marry me?", this is the second most important thing I'll ever ask you. Do you love me, with all your heart, as I love you?'

I waited, until finally she said, very quietly, 'Yes, you silly bugger, of course I do.'

'Then I want to ask you to do something for both of us. When you open your e-mail you'll find another message from Wallinger. I want you to delete it, unread; all of it. You'll also find one from me; it's an audio file. I want you to play it. Will you do that, love, please?' I was aware that I sounded desperate, but I didn't care.

'If you say so, of course I will.' I heard a great sigh explode out of me; no doubt she heard it too. 'Just tell me what's up.'

'I'm the new Loch Lomondside village idiot,' I replied, 'and we're being blackmailed.'

'Who's blackmailing us?'

'Primavera, and her partner in crime.'

'You mean all that was a lie?'

'Yup, designed to sucker me in and knock me down. She took me, every step of the way.'

'Then move over, idiot, because I bought it too. Have you caught them?'

'One down, one to go: I still have to find the guy, though, and I'm not sure how to go about it.'

'Don't let her go, Oz,' Susie warned me. 'I want to see that cow again.'

'Then get over here. I know you don't like to, but leave the kids with Ethel and come out here.'

'Bet on it,' she said. 'I'm on my way.'

29

I was grinning when I rejoined Liam and Everett, but by that time nothing was going to surprise them. 'I need a doctor up here,' I announced. 'I want blood and urine samples taken before all of that drug leaves my system.'

The giant nodded. 'Sound idea. I'll make that happen.'

'Then I want the rest of the contents of that bottle analysed, and fingerprints taken from it, and the two glasses; their contents should be tested as well. I want to prove that her in there handled it as well as me and, if possible, I want to prove that she added the dope after she'd poured her own.'

'Sounds to me that you want the cops,' Liam suggested.

'That's the last thing any of us want, until it's absolutely necessary. But I need to be ready if it comes to that. I need sworn affidavits taken from us all. If this does blow up on me and those photographs hit the press, I want to be able to fight back as hard as I can. Maybe it won't get that far. Prim doesn't scare easily, but if she sees herself winding up in jail, that might make her back off.'

'Oz, you're not going to throw her in the slammer.'

'Liam, my son, for five million quid . . .'

He grinned. 'Okay, I take your point.'

Everett picked up the nearest phone and started giving orders. Within half an hour, the house physician had taken samples of my blood and piss. Half an hour after that detectives acting for the GWA's lawyers had taken formal statements from the three of us, and had taken a computer disk with Prim's confession on it.

'Hey,' said Liam, just as they left. 'Shouldn't the doc have taken a sample from her as well?'

'He'd have got it all over his shoes if he'd tried. Anyway, she's been tied up in that wardrobe for so long she's probably given one by now.'

I was on my way to release her when the phone rang. It was Susie: she'd listened to the audio file, and she was firing off fifty rounds a second. 'She drugged you! The bitch drugged you! Get the police, Oz.'

'We don't need the limelight, if it can be avoided.'

'How much do they want?'

I told her.

'Five mi . . .' She gasped. 'Five fucking million! Get the police, Oz, no arguments!'

'I will, if I have to. But, Susie, you're forgetting something. There's a kid involved.'

'Come on, she invented the kid.'

'No, Tom exists.'

'What makes you so certain?'

'Because he was on that plane to Minneapolis; we checked, remember. I've had Mark re-interview the private investigator she said she hired, and verify the passenger list.'

'Maybe he was someone else's: the man she's working with, he could have a child.'

'Susie, Prim's had a child.'

'How do you know for sure?'

I told her as discreetly as I could: 'The same way I can look at you and know you have.' She understood.

'If you're not going to call the police, how will you handle it?'

'I've got two days to find the guy and get those images off him. Either I scare Prim enough to call him and tell him to quit, or I have to locate him.'

'Shouldn't we pay them, to be on the safe side?'

'No chance in hell. She thinks she knows me so well; maybe she does, up to a point, but she's wrong about that.'

'To protect the kids, then?'

'From what? Janet's not four yet and Jonathan's a baby. Ultimately it's their fortune I'd be giving her. She can dream on.'

'But how will you find the man, if she doesn't help you?'

'There's one lead I can follow, one link I might be able to run down. Let me get on with it; it's getting late here.'

'And early here. Go on, then. Love you; see you soon.'

I hung up, went to Prim's room and released her. She swore at me, then headed straight for the bathroom. When she returned, I took her through to the living area, where the guys were still waiting.

'Hello again,' said Everett, ponderously. She glared at him as if he was a five foot bellboy, rather than a seven foot plus ebony giant.

'Here's the deal,' I began, as she sat. 'Tell me who and where he is, and we'll all be nice to you.'

'Five million,' she retorted.

'Not a chance.'

'Fuck off, then.'

'Do you know how long you could get in this state for feeding me that drug? Everett's lawyer says thirty years to life.'

'You're not going to do that.'

'It'll cause me pain, but I'll get over it.'

'You're bluffing.'

'Try me.'

'I will.'

'Okay,' I said. 'You want me to play it the hard way, fair enough, but how about a wee clue?'

She looked at me scornfully. 'You certainly don't have one right now.'

'Help me, then. What's the link between you and Paul Wallinger? Not your pal, the real one.'

'Why should there have been a link? He was just a name we picked.'

'No, he wasn't. You knew who he was and you knew where he was. You told me so yourself, remember. You said that when you found out I was going to Santa Fe, you decided that you had to make your move right now. Know what I think?'

'Tell me.'

245

'I think your buddy needed to adopt an identity, because I know his real one. You chose Wallinger's because you knew that he wasn't suddenly going to appear on the scene, other than as an extra in a zombie movie. So, you know what I'm going to do?'

'Thrill me.'

'I'm going to speak to his agent, the guy who put him in the Albuquerque gig.'

'He didn't have one by then,' she shot back, then tried to choke off her words, as if she could.

'Thanks. So you are beginning to co-operate. That might get you a couple of years less, if your attorney plays his cards right.'

'Attorney, is it? You're turning into a Californian, Oz.'

'I may buy a house there; my accountant says I should.'

'You won't be able to afford to, minus your five million.'

'Actually, honey, you're wrong, but that's academic, because you're not having it.'

'If you fancy the consequences, so be it. I'm out of here.' She rose from the couch, but Everett reached out a huge paw and shoved her back down.

'News for you, honey,' he boomed. 'You're not just messing with him, you're tangling with me.'

'You can't keep me here.'

I shrugged my shoulders and lied a little. 'I don't have to. I can hand you over to the FBI as a material witness.'

'In what?'

'Their investigation of your accomplice for fraudulently obtaining a US passport; John Wallinger called them in this afternoon.' I wasn't one hundred per cent sure that he had, but I took a chance. 'These days, with international terrorism and everything, they take that as a helluva serious offence. So here's the way it is: you either stay here, incommunicado, under our guard all the time, or you go in the bin.'

She smiled; I knew she was going to hardball to the end. 'Oz, you can't guard me. You're going to be busy finding my friend, remember.'

'Who said I was going to be your jailer? We've got just the man

246

for the job. You know big Jerry Gradi, the Behemoth, our co-star who's in chickenpox quarantine? Well, he and his family are in suites five and six, one floor down. Sally, his wife, was a wrestler too.'

Her smile faded and her eyes narrowed. 'I remember Jerry; I also remember saving his life in Barcelona. He owes me; he won't keep me prisoner.'

'He will,' said Everett, ad-libbing like the true pro he is. 'He'll do it to keep you from going to jail, and he'll do it because, as much as he does owe you, he owns a part of the company and he stands to lose out if what you do shafts our project.'

Prim glared at him and held out her wrists. 'Slap on the cuffs then,' she snapped, then glared at me. 'But I'm still not telling you a bloody thing.'

30

Liam and I searched her room before we put her back in it. We found a cell-phone, which I confiscated; I checked it, but after she had used it, as I was certain she had, constantly, to keep her partner in touch with what was happening, she'd deleted all the numbers she'd dialled. We also found a small clear glass bottle, which I was fairly sure had held the GHB. I pocketed that to send to the lab.

But we found nothing else, no hint of the identity of the mystery man, only her passport, some papers from Fairmile and Company, the books I'd bought her and some boarding stubs from our flights.

When she was safely tucked up in bed or at least lying on it in a monumental huff I went back out to play my only card.

I retrieved Roscoe Brown's home number from my list and called it, feeling so grateful that when I'd suspected him of being the spy in my camp, I hadn't gone blazing into him.

'My hero!' he exclaimed, as he answered. 'What the hell was that action in San Francisco? Did you bribe the guy? Your price has gone up another three million after that, and nobody's arguing.'

'It may go down to zero very soon, if I drop a ball I'm carrying.' I explained the problem to him and heard him deflate.

'I need to ask you about one of your clients, Roscoe. I know you keep us all confidential, but this is important to both of us. It's a guy by the name of Paul Patrick Walls, in reality Paul Wallinger.'

'Who?' Roscoe asked; not a good sign. I repeated both names.

'Ah, him. Oz, he's been gone for years. He got silly with Miles Grayson a few years back, and he paid the price, as does everyone who bad-mouths Miles. I only kept his name on my list to fatten it out. I don't know where he is, and I don't know what he's doing.'

'I do. He's in a permanent vegetative state in a clinic in New Mexico. But that's beside the point. When he was on your list, can you recall any particular buddy he had, anyone he was close to?'

I'll swear the sound I could hear on the phone was Roscoe scratching his shiny black head. 'PP Walls,' he muttered. 'PP Walls.' He lapsed into silence. 'Yes, there was one client he was close with. They looked alike so that led to their bonding in a way. PP did some doubling for this guy, when he was reasonably big. The Nickster, Nicky Johnson.'

Nicky Fucking Johnson. Prim's old lover. Why wasn't I surprised?

'Where is he now, Roscoe?'

'Dramatically speaking, my friend, he is in the shitter, for the same reason PP was. But, hell, you know all about that. However, the Nickster has a second string he falls back on. He's a pretty talented singer and pianist, and since his movie career went bad, he's been doing those gigs. Not as Nicky Johnson, though; he still has vain hopes of a movie comeback. When he plays the clubs he uses his real name.'

'What's that?'

'Didn't it appear on your divorce papers?' Roscoe really does know everything.

'No, that was a quickie job; no names, no fuss. So what's he called?'

'Nichols, Johnny Nichols.'

I laughed out loud. Johnny Nichols. Jack Nicholson. So he hadn't been taking the piss in Minneapolis after all, just playing around with his own name.

'Do you know where he is, Roscoe?' I asked, a little urgently.

'Sure I do. I got him a club gig last week, starting yesterday. He's playing Le Bistro Theatre, in the Riviera, Las Vegas. Does that help you?'

I felt a huge smile engulf my face. 'Oh, it helps. Does it ever help! Tonight Mr Nichols is going to get the biggest ovation of his life.'

31

Liam called the Riviera, putting on a wonderful star-struck Irish tourist act, and told the reservations desk that his aunt in Dublin had seen a great cabaret singer called Johnny Nichols the last time she was in the USA, and had told him not to come home without his autograph.

The hostess told him that it was his aunt's lucky night: Le Bistro Theatre did four shows every evening, and Johnny Nichols was scheduled for eleven thirty. There were vacancies, and he'd be able to buy a ticket at the box office before the show.

We delivered Prim into the tender hands of Jerry and Sally Gradi . . . I saw the Behemoth through the door of their family suite: he was still covered in spots and looked a likely non-runner for even the following week . . . and headed along the Strip in one of the Bellagio's courtesy limos. (I'd have been happy with a taxi, but Everett doesn't fit into one too easily.)

We passed Caesar's, Treasure Island, the Fashion Show Mall . . . too bad Prim was locked up, I thought, she'd have loved that . . . and the Stardust, before we came to the relatively modest frontage of the Riviera. Clearly it was one of the oldest casinos on the Strip, dating back before the days of the imitation cities, but there was plenty of buzz about it when we stepped inside.

The ten o'clock show was only halfway through when we arrived: we could hear the laughter from inside Le Bistro as we went past, following the directions to the box office. When we got there I asked the woman who was on duty if she could find the theatres manager for us.

'Can't I help?' she asked.

'No.'

'Well, if you're sure?'

'The theatres manager, please.'

She picked up a phone and pressed a button. 'Mr Ricci,' I heard her say. 'There are three gentlemen here to see you.' There was a pause and she looked at us. 'Who are you?'

'My name's Oz Blackstone, the gentleman on my left is Mr Liam Matthews and our acromegalic friend is Mr Everett Davis.' (Actually Daze doesn't suffer from acromegaly at all. He's just naturally enormous, but I'm chuffed that I know the word and, being an actor, I like to show off from time to time, to time, to time, et cetera.)

Mr Ricci must have recognised at least one of the names, because he came without any further argument. As soon as he saw the big man, he placed us. As the song goes, or would if he was a footballer and not a wrestler, 'One Everett Davis, there's only one Everett Davis . . .'.

The manager was a tubby guy in his fifties, and keen to be helpful from the off. He might have figured that he didn't have enough security on the premises to handle us, but we didn't care whether he was being genuinely friendly or just discreet. 'How can I help?'

'We'd like to see Johnny Nichols,' I told him. 'He's an old acquaintance of mine. He called on me earlier today at the Bellagio, but I wasn't able to talk to him. I'd like to catch up with him now, before he goes on.'

Ricci shrugged his shoulders. If he wondered why Daze and Liam had come along with me, he didn't ask. 'I don't see why not,' he said, with an expansive grin. He checked a book behind the desk. 'Yes, he's in six ten, North Tower. I'll call him and let him know you're here.'

'I'd rather you didn't,' I told him. 'I'd like to surprise him.'

The manager chuckled. 'Okay, you do that.' He winked at me. 'I am going to have an eleven thirty show, yes?'

I chuckled back. 'Don't you worry about it; he'll be singing his fucking heart out after I've talked to him.'

251

The lift to the North Tower was a fair distance away, tucked in behind a twenty-four-hour bar with gaming consoles set in its counter, but we found it. We rode the lift up to the sixth . . . it was tight with Everett in it . . . and followed the signs to room ten. The place looked older, somehow, than the rest of the complex and there were ice machines and Coke dispensers every thirty yards or so, making an incredible racket. I was pleased by that: it would lessen the chances of anyone hearing the boy Johnny squeal.

We found his room and I thumped on the door. Liam put his thumb over the spy-hole as we waited, to make it a real surprise for him when he opened the door. Only he didn't. I banged again, but that didn't produce a response either.

'Excuse me,' said Daze, quietly. We stood back, and he kicked the heavy-duty door open, with just one shot. Liam led the way into the room.

There was no sign of Johnson, but the bathroom door was closed. Everett kicked that in too . . . it wasn't locked so he didn't need to, but he had switched to full action-man mode by that time. Our man wasn't there either, nor would he be back. The wardrobe doors were open, and there was nothing hanging inside. All he had left behind were some empties and a pile of tangled bedclothes . . . at least, that was what we thought, until they stirred slightly.

I grabbed a corner of the sheet and yanked it off: there was a red-head lying beneath. Her hair was a mess, she had a butterfly tattooed round her navel and she wasn't a real red-head; those were the first three things I noticed about her. The fourth was that she was out of it. The new A Team had just battered its way in on her and she hadn't flickered an eyelid.

Everett put the covers back on her, while I took a look at the room's coffee table. There were two highball glasses on it, one of them still almost full, but the other drained. Beside them there stood a three-parts-empty bottle of bourbon and a few ginger-ale mixer discards. I looked around on the floor under the table; I almost stood on the small clear phial before I spotted it.

I turned round to see Liam sitting on the side of the bed, shaking the girl gently. I watched as she came to; I saw the look of dazed

252

panic spread across her face, and I saw her mouth open as if to scream. Everett put a hand on her shoulder; when he wants to, he can be one of the gentlest people in the world. 'It's okay, honey,' he said, quietly. 'We're the good guys.'

I pointed at the bottle on the floor. 'She's been on the same trip I took,' I told the two of them. I picked up the phone, identified myself and asked the operator to connect me with Mr Ricci.

'Yes, Mr Blackstone,' he murmured. 'Did you find Johnny?'

'No. I'm sorry, I was wrong earlier; your eleven thirty show's off. I think you should tell your general manager to come to six ten, and send a doctor and a couple of cops up here too. You'd better make sure that at least one of them's a woman.'

32

Eventually a lieutenant and a sergeant from the Metro Police Department domestic crimes unit turned up, both of them women. By that time we were in the corridor, waiting as a police medical examiner took blood and other samples from the girl.

Her name was Lola, and she was a dancer in one of the shows in La Cage, another Riviera theatre. She was still too stunned to give any detailed account of what had happened, but by the time we'd told the detectives what we'd found when we burst into the room, they were in no more doubt than we were. It didn't occur to either of them to ask us why we'd kicked our way in, but none of us was about to jog their elbow on that.

Within ten minutes of their arrival there was an all-state alert out for John Nichols, on suspicion of date rape.

I took the lieutenant aside; her name was Oakley, and I wondered if she'd ever been a cowgirl. 'If you catch this guy,' I said to her, 'he'll have something on him that's important to me. It'll be a digital camera, and I expect you'll also find a laptop computer in his possession. There will be material stored on them that relates to me, and that was obtained without my knowledge or consent. However, it does not relate to this crime, so I want it to be seen only by officers who need to see it, and then destroyed immediately they have.'

She looked at me shrewdly. 'Mr Blackstone, do you want to make a complaint against this man?'

'Lieutenant Oakley, I want you to lock this man up for this crime alone. I just want to make sure that what I ask you to do is done.'

She was sharp, this woman. 'Sir, would I be correct if I guessed that Nichols is trying to extort money from you with this material?'

'At this stage, I'm not prepared to make such a complaint. Is that a good enough answer for you?'

'It'll do.'

'In that case, you should know that if necessary I'm prepared to take legal action to protect myself.'

She smiled at me and made a decision. 'That won't be necessary. When Nichols is apprehended he'll be brought to me. I and I alone will view any material he may have. Unless you're wrong and I decide that it does relate to this case, or unless it shows you committing a crime, I'll erase it.'

'Thanks, Lieutenant Oakley,' I told her, sincerely. 'This is not a financial inducement, you understand, but I'd be grateful if you'd let me know the address of your department's benevolent fund.'

She grinned. 'The Sheriff's Office will do just fine, Mr Blackstone.'

They didn't find Johnson, of course . . . I still couldn't get used to calling him Nichols . . . not that night or next morning. Eventually the police worked out that he'd had an hour and a half start on them, time enough to get well clear of Vegas, across the state border and west into California, or east into either Arizona or Utah. But they'd tried, so I made a note in my pocket PC to send them a cheque as soon as I could.

I had Prim brought back to my suite for breakfast, and told her what he'd done, but she didn't bat an eyelid. 'You don't surprise me,' she replied. 'Nicky sourced the GHB. It's just like him to keep some for himself and use it. He can be such a sleaze-bag.'

'You didn't think that when you were screwing him.'

She gave me the most withering look I've ever experienced, even worse than the one I got from an English teacher when I asked if I could use a comic-book version of *Treasure Island* for exam revision.

'You are such a self-obsessed idiot, Oz,' she said. 'I never was screwing Nicky Johnson. I went to Mexico with him to provoke you into coming after me. I brought him to Scotland for exactly the same reason. Obviously it didn't work either time. You were so obsessed by Susie and your kid that you jumped at the chance to get rid of me.' She raised an eyebrow. 'What would you have done if I'd come back to you?'

'Good question. I'd probably still have left.'

'But only probably. So you agree that the times weren't all bad then?'

I looked at her. Most of the anger had left me now; what was left was focused on Johnson. 'That's why you took me to San Francisco and Westwood, isn't it?' I asked.

'Of course it is. And,' she added, heavily, 'I didn't even have to suggest the Campton Place. You did that all by yourself, which told me a hell of a lot.'

When I thought about it, I had to admit that it told me the same. I'd been lying to myself back then: it had been good at times.

'Prim,' I asked her. 'Please tell me where I can find this guy. I'm not giving you any money; you have to know that by now.'

'I know,' she conceded. 'But that's not important any more. Fucking your career and your marriage good and proper will be more than enough for me.'

'You can forget wrecking my marriage. That's secure.'

'What makes you so sure?'

I grinned and played her my pocket PC recording. 'Susie's heard that. She's on her way here, right now.'

She glared at me, in the purest frustration. 'And what about your career?' she shot back.

'If I have to defend it by having you thrown in jail and obtaining world-wide court injunctions to suppress those shots I'll do it.'

'Well, you're going to have to,' she hissed, 'for Nicky's out of my control.'

'And what about Tom?' I asked her. 'Who's controlling him?'

She took me completely by surprise, as she'd done a week and more before, by flushing and starting to cry. 'You leave Tom out of this,' she said. 'He's being well looked after, and he's safe.'

'Until when? Until he becomes a bargaining chip?'

'That won't happen!'

256

'Are you so sure? Your sleaze-ball friend Nicky's on the run from the police now. All he's got to look forward to is spending the next thirty years having his arsehole cored in some maximum-security jail. You think he won't use your kid as a free ride out of the country? Are you really sure of that, in what passes for your heart of hearts?' Suddenly I was angry with her again, even angrier than I'd been before, and I couldn't quite work out why.

'Are you sure?' I yelled at her. I grabbed her by the arms, picked her off the couch and shook her like a doll. 'Are you sure?'

Her face twisted, contorted into something that looked like real pain. 'No,' she whispered. 'No, I'm not.'

'Right, to hell with Nicky. I'll deal with him when I've got the time. Tell me where I can find Tom.'

She fought for composure, then looked up at me, fearfully, 'I can't,' she whispered. 'I don't know.' I thought she was lying to me until she said, 'You'll have to ask John Wallinger.'

In my surprise, I loosened my grip. She twisted free of me and ran sobbing into the bedroom.

33

'Oz, I truly do not understand what you're saying to me.'

I hadn't gone in swinging when I'd phoned the lieutenant, but I was ready to if it came to it. I repeated Prim's words, exactly. 'That's what she said,' I insisted, 'and for once in her life I don't think she was lying.'

'Then I can't think what she means.'

The certainty in his voice was as great as hers had been; I was puzzled. I scratched around for anything else to tell him, and then I came up with something to ask. 'Does the name Nicky Johnson mean anything to you?'

There was a pregnant silence, which eventually gave birth to one softly uttered word. 'Fuck.' It wasn't what I'd expected from an upright God-fearing Midwesterner.

'It has to be Marcie,' he murmured.

'Who's Marcie?'

'My sister.'

It's funny how you can overlook little things at first, then see how they fall perfectly into place. In mystery novels, they call them clues. When Mark Kravitz had told me about the obituary of John the First, he had said that Paul was the oldest of three children.

'Her name's Marcela,' he went on. 'If Paul was the black sheep of our family, I suppose you could call her the black ewe. She was just as much of a nonconformist as him, so they always bonded. She didn't have any talent of her own, so she basked in his. When he left, she went with him, and she's drifted around California ever since.'

'So you've kept in touch with her?'

'I've made it my business always to know where she is.'

'What do you talk about?'

'Her life, what she's doing, anything but Paul . . . I've always made it clear that he was a forbidden subject. Given what I know now, she really did take me at my word.'

'Where does Johnson come in?'

'She's been living with him, on and off, for years. They met through Paul, and they developed this thing; half the time she hates him, but she can't let him go.'

'Have you ever met him?'

'Hell, no. I haven't seen Marcie since Dad died, far less got to know her lovers. What's he done, this guy?'

'He's the man who's been impersonating Paul. When the passport agency runs down his application, they'll find his photograph on file.'

'I should have worked that out for myself,' he muttered into the phone. 'Some detective, huh? Where is he now?'

'On the run from Las Vegas Metro Police, on a date-rape charge, and from me, for other things. I think he's gone to your sister. I think that's where Tom is too, with her. I need you to help me find her.'

'I should give any information I have to Metro. You know that, don't you, Oz?'

'Yes. All I'm asking is that we run him to ground before you do that.'

I expected him to hesitate, but he didn't. 'Date rape?' he murmured. 'Get a flight to San Francisco, and hire a car. Meet me at the information desk in the main terminal, five o'clock tonight.'

I delivered Prim back into the care of the Gradis, then booked myself on to an afternoon America West flight to San Francisco . . . I thought about using Troy Hawkins again but that would have been pushing it . . . and another S-type from Hertz, with a navigation system, of course. I'd no idea where I was being taken, so I expected it to come in handy.

I went down to the arcade and bought myself a light bag. I packed enough for a one-night stay, told Everett where I was going and set off for McCarron. The flight was delayed by almost an hour, but that still left me enough time to pick up the car, park it and be at the information desk in the domestic terminal for five.

John Wallinger the Second was flustered when he arrived, towing a medium-sized case behind him. I'd no idea how he'd travelled from Santa Fe, but it must have been tortuous.

As we retrieved the Jag from the park and drove out of the airport, John gave me an address. 'Fourteen-ten Cabrillo Highway South, Half Moon Bay.'

I entered it into the system's data bank and let it take over; I had no idea where I was going, or even in which direction. I just did as I was told, taking Interstate 280 until it was time to turn on to Highway 92 West, a twisty road that reminded me of Scotland in parts. We weren't on it for long, though, only about eight miles, before I was ordered to take a left turn on to Cabrillo Highway.

We almost drove past the place we were after; I'll swear the system shouted at me to stop. I pulled up at the side of the road and looked at it. There was a big sign outside that read 'Cameron's Pub and Inn', and had a Union Jack emblazoned across it. Just in case anyone didn't get the message, there was a red telephone box in the front, and a couple of genuine old-fashioned London double-decker buses parked outside.

'You sure?' I asked John.

'This is what Marcie said last time I spoke to her. If she'd moved on she'd have told me.'

I cruised into the car park and we jumped out. If Johnson was looking for us we'd be easy to spot out there, so we got ourselves under cover, sharpish. There was a shop just inside the door; even at a glance I noticed that it sold mainly British products. The pub itself had God knew how many beers on tap, around twenty I reckoned.

There were a few early-evening customers in and a couple of people behind the bar but one of them was the boss, for sure. He was a massive bloke and had that air about him. He clocked us as from out of town straight away; not too difficult since John still

260

wore his Minneapolis suit and I had on another Paul Smith shirt that was definitely not from around those parts.

'Gentlemen,' he greeted us. 'I'm Cameron Palmer; welcome to our pub. What can I get you?'

'Probably a pint, eventually, but first we're looking for someone.'

He didn't back off at all. 'Yes?' he said. 'Who would that be?'

'My sister,' John told him. 'I believe she's staying here. Her name's . . .'

'Marcie?'

'That's right, Marcie Wallinger.' He dug out his detective badge and showed it to Cameron.

'Sure, Marcie's a guest. She and little Tom are in one of our B and B rooms . . . that's bed and beverage.' He laughed. 'We don't do breakfast, I'm afraid. Let me take you along there.'

'Thanks,' I said, 'but before you do, can you tell us, is there a guy with her?'

He frowned. 'Not as far as I know, but I can't be sure. My wife and I have been away for a few days. We only got back last night.' He called along to the barman. 'You happen to know if Marcie's got a fella with her?' The guy gave him a 'don't ask me' shrug.

We let Cameron lead the way to a small wing at the side of the pub and restaurant. I walked behind him up to a door with '3' printed on it. 'This one has a private shower and bathroom,' he announced. 'It's best for Marcie with the little boy.'

'I'm sure.'

'I'll leave you to say hello then,' he said, rapping the door with a ham-sized hand, before turning and walking away.

As I waited, I heard a sound from inside; this wasn't the sort of place that needed spyholes, so there wasn't one. The door opened with a slight creak.

I looked past the woman who held it ajar. He was there inside: Nicky Johnson, né John Nichols, standing in front of the bed, as if frozen. I'd only met the guy once, but my mind's eye put a beard, Ray-Bans and a wee blue hat on him, and I knew I'd seen him a couple of times after that.

261

My residual paranoia from San Francisco made it occur to me afterwards that if he'd had a gun I would have been in trouble; I think the odds against being shot twice in a week and surviving are quite long.

He didn't have a gun, though. He stared back at me, he saw the look in my eyes and he knew that he was a dead man. So he did what the Nicky Johnsons of this world are always liable to do: he weighed up the fight-or-flight options for a micro-second, then dived through the open window...

... and landed in the arms of big John Wallinger, who'd positioned himself there to guard against precisely that circumstance. I smiled as the sound of a fugitive being vigorously restrained floated back into the pleasant room.

'Hi, Marcie,' I said, gently. 'I'm Oz.'

She nodded. 'I know who you are.'

'That's your brother John outside,' I told her, 'beating the crap out of your boyfriend. I'm afraid he's wanted in Las Vegas for a fairly nasty rape, involving narcotics. He's going back there too; there's extradition between here and Nevada, as I'm sure you'll know. I'm sorry we're not meeting under happier circumstances.'

'Me too,' she replied, sadly. 'I could guess there was trouble, the way he turned up in the middle of the night.'

I looked around the room. I could see a kid's bed but no kid. 'Where's Tom?' I asked.

She was about to answer, but at that moment, a door on the right swung open and a child ran in from a sunny porch to the side of the main room. But this boy wasn't a year old: he was big and sturdy and looked to be at least three.

'Hello,' he greeted me, looking up at me with the uncomplicated innocence of childhood, through blue eyes, set in a fresh face, beneath a mop of dark hair. 'Who're you?'

I looked down at him, and as I did, I experienced what I swear to you was, still is, and always will be, the most unexpected and, somehow, terrifying moment of my life.

I looked down at him: in that little figure, I saw someone I recognised from photographs taken way back in my past, around thirty-five years back, in fact. In an instant, I knew everything: there was no thought process involved, I just knew everything. I waited until I had mastered my shock, and until my heart rate had returned to something like normal, then I knelt down beside him.

'Tom,' I answered, trying to keep my voice steady, 'my name's Oz. Has your mother ever told you about me, and who I am?'

He beamed. 'Sure,' he replied, in an accent that had much of Marcie's Midwest twang about it. 'You're my dad.'

34

John called the California Highway Patrol to advise them that he'd apprehended and detained a felon on the run from Las Vegas, and I called Lieutenant Oakley to give her the good news.

Then I called Dawn; I'd expected her to be in Australia with Miles, but they had arrived back in America that morning. She was stunned when I told her about her nephew; Prim had given her no hint of his existence, and neither, as it turned out, had her parents. Apparently, when I'd dropped Prim at Semple House ten days earlier, she'd said, 'Hello', 'Thanks for lunch', 'Lovely to see you, must go now,' and not much more. They'd been totally puzzled by the visit.

Dawn told me something else too. On the previous Wednesday, Elanore's condition had begun to deteriorate more rapidly. 'The consultant's told Dad that it's a matter of weeks now. He's been trying to get in touch with Prim, but he couldn't.'

'Tell him that he has now.'

'You know where she is?'

'Yes, and I'll make sure that she gets in touch with David.'

'Thanks, Oz,' she said, relief in her voice. 'You know, you're the only person who's ever really been able to control my sister. If only she hadn't been such a God-damned idiot, you two might still be together, and that little boy might have had conventional parents, like everyone else.'

I almost laughed at her. For all her fame Dawn's retained a gentle view of life; she thinks her world's conventional, and on top of that, she thought I could control Prim. If she only knew; the truth is that the two of us have never really been fully in control of ourselves.

By the time the state troopers arrived to take possession of Johnson and his effects, I had found his camera, wiped clean the chip with my candid-camera shots, and erased beyond recovery the entire contents of his computer's hard drive. I had also found a pen drive on which he'd made a back-up. I got rid of that by a less technical method: I smashed it into tiny pieces under the heel of my Panama Jack sandal. My son watched me, fascinated. Eventually I let him help, which he did enthusiastically. When I judged that the fragments were small enough, I swept them up and tossed them out of the window, after their former owner.

Marcie had in her possession Tom's passport, and the substantial majority of fifteen thousand dollars in cash given her by Johnson, from Prim, when he had flown the boy across the Atlantic. She also had his birth certificate: he had been registered in Lewes, Sussex, three years, three months and five days before, by his mother, Primavera Eagle Phillips. The father's name on the certificate was given as Osbert Blackstone.

After the police had taken Johnson and his effects away, the four of us, three adults and Tom, stood in the bright, dusty, yet suddenly fresher car park. I had explained the happenings to a slightly alarmed Cameron and had booked rooms one and two for the night, for John and me.

'What do I do now?' Marcie asked her brother. 'Nicky may have turned out to be a shit-heel, but he's all I had.'

'We all have our weaknesses,' he replied, dismissing him. 'But, sis, you should have told me about Paul.'

'He wouldn't have wanted me to,' she countered, 'even if he'd been capable of making a decision. And you said you never wanted to hear of him again.'

'You want to know what I think you should do?' I asked her, then told her, whether she wanted to hear it or not. 'I think you should take what's left of that fifteen grand, go back to Minneapolis, and hang out with your mother for a while. She's a very nice lady, and she deserves better of you.'

As it turned out, that was exactly what she did want to hear. And so it was agreed. We stayed over in Cameron's, had a few beers in his pub . . . Its most spectacular attraction was a wall of beer cans. They turned out to be Cameron's hobby: he'd been collecting them since he was a kid . . . then ate in his restaurant, where I introduced John to bangers and mash, English style, but only after some serious Boston clam chowder. We even had a pot of PG Tips. Tom seemed to know the menu well: he went straight for a burger and fries.

It turned out that the two buses weren't there for show. One's for smokers, to give them a place to indulge their habit . . . it's a no-no in public places in California . . . and the other's full of video games for the kids. Tom took me in there and showed me a couple.

Next morning I . . . or rather the navigation system . . . drove both Wallingers to San Francisco Airport, and dropped them off for a flight eastwards.

Tom and I, we headed on south, down Interstate 5, bound for Los Angeles . . . Marcie's old jeep, which she sold to Cameron, who reckoned his brother could use it, had a child seat in it.

The drive's pretty scenic and I enjoyed it, but even more I enjoyed my son's constant chatter from the back. He'd been attached to Aunt Marcie; she'd done a great job of mothering him since he'd been in America, and I understood from what I'd learned the night before, and from what he said to me, that she'd been a fixture in his life for as long as he could remember. He'd been upset when the time had come to part, but I'd promised him he'd see her again one day.

He asked about his mother . . . Mommy . . . too, of course; he seemed to be used to her going in and out of his life, but still there was adoration in his voice when he spoke about her. I had to tell him that she'd be gone for a little longer, but that most of the time he'd have me around. That seemed to satisfy him.

I tried to explain to him why I hadn't been around for him, but he was too young to take any of it in. The important thing was that he was glad I was there now, and bursting with pride that we were off on an adventure together. On the way down, I told him about his aunt Dawn, his uncle Miles and his cousin Bruce. As far as I could tell from his reaction, he'd never heard of any of them, apart from Miles . . . Aunt Marcie had shown him a picture in a magazine, and had told him that he was very famous, more famous than me, or even Bugs Bunny. I came to understand that Bugs is Tom's benchmark for fame.

With cruise control engaged, and the navigation system silent for three hours, I made good time, and reached Beverly Hills in the early afternoon. Dawn was expecting us, but Miles had been forced to go to his office for a meeting with the casting director on his next project.

Bruce was there, though. It was interesting to watch the cousins meet for the first time, sizing each other up like a pair of young cats, before deciding to get on. It made me realise that Tom had no experience of interaction with other children; that was going to change before he was much older.

We had lunch under an awning on the Grayson sun-deck watching the boys as they splashed in the pool. I made Tom wear armbands, but soon I could see that he didn't need them. He's like a fish; so was I at his age.

I told Dawn the whole story, from start to finish; some I'd had from Primavera, and I'd filled in a few blanks for myself. Prim's nursing job in England, after our split, and after the confrontation in Edinburgh with her and Johnson had backfired on her, had been a sham. She'd lived in Sussex for a while, getting her affairs in order, carrying Tom, and then giving birth to him, alone all the time, with nothing to do but plot my humiliation and downfall.

When the baby was almost a year old, she'd taken him to Los Angeles, to meet up with Nicky Johnson. That was when she'd met Marcie Wallinger, and her brother: that was when the photograph of Tom and Paul together had been taken. Originally she'd planned to recruit Paul, to hire him like an actor, to play the part, but out of the blue, he'd had his stroke, during the run of a play in which Nicky was also appearing. So Prim had made a mid-course correction: instead of using him, they'd stolen his identity, knowing that he would be in Santa Fe for the rest of his inevitably short life.

'It was like a legend in a spy novel,' I explained. 'Prim planned everything, then Johnson helped her make it happen, so that when the time came it would look real, and wouldn't be questioned. They went through the ritual of the meeting at Gleneagles, so they'd be remembered. While they were doing that, Marcie looked after Tom. He's spent half his life with her, you know. She's a good woman; she didn't deserve Nicky.'

'Maybe we can find a way of looking after her,' Dawn mused. 'But about Tom?' she asked. 'If he was supposed to be Prim's child with Wallinger, then he'd only have been a year old now. So how did they . . .'

'Easy. She registered a birth that never happened; she said it was a home confinement, to get round the hospital problem. Then Nicky, who had Wallinger's passport by this time . . . they looked alike, so with a moustache and some makeup it wasn't difficult to get one . . . added Tom's name to it in London, using the fake birth certificate.'

'But isn't all that illegal?'

I laughed. 'Too bloody right it is. As well as his date-rape charge in Vegas, Nicky's committed a couple of federal offences as well. The boy's cooked, I'll tell you, completely bloody cooked. As for Prim, that's where it all really got out of control for her. False registration's a crime in itself, but when she did feed me the bait and get me involved, I brought in a lawyer, and that made it worse. He got her a court order requiring Tom's return to Britain. It was based on a false statement and a fake birth certificate. At the very least that's contempt of court, maybe even perjury, and perverting the course of justice.'

'So she's in big trouble back home?'

'I'm afraid so. My future brother-in-law's been acting for her, so he's been embarrassed. I told him about it last night. He's going to have to petition to withdraw the interdict, but more than that. He's an officer of the court, so he's going to have to report everything that happened. When . . . I don't think it's an if . . . she's prosecuted, he won't even be able to appear for the defence, as he'll be a Crown witness. So, if it comes to it, will I.'

'Can't you do something?'

I couldn't keep the frown off my face. 'Pull some strings, you mean? Keep her out of court? Have you any idea what your sister tried to do to me, Dawn? She tried to end my marriage, she tried to ruin my career, and she tried to extort five million quid out of me. Why? Because she wanted to get back at me, and at Susie, for the way our marriage ended.'

'More than that, I think,' said Dawn, softly. 'Not just get back at you; she wanted to get you back.'

'By ruining me?'

'Yes. It's happened before, remember. You left her before, for Jan, and when she died, you came back to her. The whole thing hasn't just been about revenge. She'll have calculated that when you came crawling out of the rubble of your life, you'd come crawling back to her. I'm sure of it, Oz.'

'Why would she do that?'

'Because she loves you, like Juliet loved Romeo, Darby did Joan, Ronnie did Nancy. She loves you like crazy . . . maybe literally so, I don't know.'

'She loves me so much she hid my son from me?'

'Maybe she thought he'd be the final lure to bring you back. Or maybe she knew that when she started you on the false trail she'd mapped out you'd wind up finding him.' Her mouth seemed to tighten for a second. 'The sad thing for me is that she'd use a little boy like that. Does she feel anything for him, anything at all?'

I thought about that, and about the way Prim had been the night before. 'She does, I'm pretty sure. Look at him, he's as healthy and happy a wee chap as you've ever seen.'

'Are you going to take him from her?' she asked.

'I'm going to apply for legal custody. I've told my solicitor to get on to that straight away; the process will be under way by now. But I can't cut his mother out of his life, can I? She might wind up in jail in Scotland for a while, but when she comes out, of course she'll have access.'

'Miles and I will supervise that if you like . . . to make sure she doesn't disappear with him again.'

I appreciated her offer and I told her so. 'That's long-term, though. There's something I'd like you to do before that.'

'What?'

269

'When all this started, I gave my word on something to Prim, but really it was to your mother, and I'd like you to help me keep it. I promised that Elanore will see her grandson before she dies. I'd like you to take him there.'

35

It took me a little while to explain to Tom that I was going to have to leave him again. But I promised that he'd have a great time with his auntie Dawn, his uncle Miles, and Bruce, and that there would be other people for him to meet as well, not least his grandpa, a great big man who'd tell him funny stories about pulling teeth.

When he was ready to let me go, I promised that I'd see him soon in Scotland, kissed him farewell, not goodbye, and drove back to Vegas, almost picking up a speeding ticket on the way, courtesy of the Californian Highway Patrol. (The officer settled for an autograph and a handshake.)

It was getting dark when I reached the Bellagio. I arranged the return of the car to Hertz, with a mental note to put a Jag in the garage of the house in Beverly Hills when we bought it. (My non-stop tour of North America had changed me: I'd decided that the next time the accountants recommended we go offshore, I was going to agree with them.)

I took the lift up to my suite, walked into my room and dumped my bag on the floor. There was someone in my bed: her red hair was all over the pillow, like it always is, and she was sound asleep. There had been no skin and feathers in the living area, so I guessed that when Liam had picked her up from McCarron, as I'd asked him to do, he'd made damn sure she didn't get anywhere near Prim.

She was still in the Gradis' suite when I went along there . . . I was pleased to see that the Behemoth's spots were fading, finally; maybe he was going to make next week. I told her nothing, only that she was moving out, to a suite in the Mandalay Bay, at the end of the Strip, then waited as she packed and took her along there.

She was tense all the way; once or twice she started, as if she was going to ask me something, but I told her to shut up, that I would talk to her when I was good and ready.

Once she was checked in, I took her to the China Grill. She looked as if she hadn't been eating properly since I left, and I was getting peckish again.

I told her what had happened over a couple of Shanghai lobsters. She wept a bit when I told her Tom was safe and with his astonished aunt Dawn, a little more when I savaged her for keeping his existence from me, and a lot more when I told her that she probably wouldn't see him again for quite a while.

It might have been a bit embarrassing for the waiters but, frankly, by that time I didn't give a flying fuck at a rolling doughnut.

When I had softened a little, I told her about her mother; I expected her to cry about that too, but she didn't. It seemed as if her tears were reserved for Tom. She was upset, don't get me wrong, but what I was telling her wasn't news. She was a nurse by profession, after all, and she'd known what was coming.

Finally I told her that I wanted her to make me some promises.

'One, you don't fight me over Tom's custody. You'll find it difficult from a jail cell, but if you do I'll win, and it'll be harder for you in the long run. Go along with it, and he'll spend as much time with you as he does with me.

'Two, you phone your father tomorrow, and this time you really do tell him the truth, so that he can prepare Elanore before Dawn turns up on the doorstep with our son.

'Three, as long as you're in Vegas . . . you're paying for this lot, by the way, now I know you're not really skint, so how long that is, is up to you . . . you don't come anywhere near Susie and me, especially Susie. You go near her, and she'll tear your head off.

'Four, tomorrow morning, first thing, you will phone Harvey January and apologise to him, until the profuseness is leaking from your ears.

'Five, once you've had time to think about things, you'll come back to Scotland and give yourself up. You're not facing any criminal charges here, but there are things over there that won't go

272

away till you've dealt with them. I'd rather my son's mother has a prison record than she's a constant fugitive.

'All of those things: do you promise them, now?'

She dabbed her eyes. 'Yes,' she said, quietly. And I believed her. So far, I have to say, she's kept her word.

36

That's not where it finished, of course. I went back to the Bellagio, woke Susie, and told her everything she hadn't known up until then, especially the fact that I had a son neither of us had known about till the day before. (Maybe it was two days before in Susie's case: I'm really crap when it comes to time differences.)

She took it all pretty well, although when I told her that Prim wouldn't be liable to arrest in the US, and that I'd turned her loose, she huffed for a bit.

She stayed in Vegas with me for the rest of my commitment to *Serious Impact*. That's just been released, by the way. It's doing a bundle at the box office, and Liam, the spotless Jerry, Santi Temple, the new girl in GWA, whose name is Gamma Raye, and I are getting some very nice reviews.

When it was finished we went back to Scotland, with things to do. Some of them involved the flotation of the Gantry Group, making us even more stupidly rich. Some of them involved receiving Henry Potter's proposal and accepting it, to the extent of going shopping for homes in LA and Monaco. Some of them involved my sister's wedding to Harvey January, who, for some reason, asked me to be his best man. (Jonny was excellent as an usher, but Colin was a complete disaster. My dad held up well; it's not right that a man should fork out for two weddings for one daughter, so I picked up the tab.)

However, above and before all that, there was another more important item on my agenda. As soon as I had dumped my luggage, I drove up to Auchterarder to pay my respects to Elanore, and to collect my overjoyed, exuberant son.

He chatted all the way back to Loch Lomond, where I introduced him to his tearful . . . I'd seen so many of those that I feared I was beginning to dissolve . . . stepmother, and to his half-sister and half-brother.

I'd explained to Janet who he was; she simply accepted him, welcoming him to the team more or less as her deputy, more or less as her mother would have welcomed a new member of staff. Wee Jonathan looked at Tom, then bit him, his own form of acceptance. In time, my application for custody was granted, uncontested, and, fortunately, unreported.

Primavera returned to Scotland a week later, and gave herself up to the police in Edinburgh. She was charged and released on bail, then went straight to Auchterarder. She and Dawn were by Elanore's side when she died, a few days afterwards.

I took Tom to the funeral . . . she was his granny, after all . . . and he rode in the car to the church and the cemetery with his mother and me. There wasn't a lot said between them, indeed among the three of us; Tom watched us, curiously. No wonder: it was the first time he'd seen his parents together. I don't know what was going on in his head, for he hasn't told me yet.

A week after that, Prim pleaded guilty to charges of perverting the course of justice and contempt of court. The judge took pity on her downcast expression and was impressed by her well-expressed remorse and gave her only six months. With a good behaviour discount she'll be out soon, although it might be another couple of months before they give her back her passport. It'll be interesting to see what she does then.

I won't be in Scotland to welcome her out of the nick, though. I'll still be in Toronto, finishing off the rock-star movie that Roscoe fixed for me. We changed our minds about taking the whole family there. Instead, Susie and the three kids, plus Ethel, Conrad and Audrey, are in our new place in Beverly Hills, sometimes being neighbourly with Miles and Dawn at theirs. When they do that, all four youngsters are looked after by their new carer, Marcie Wallinger. (Nice touch, that, Dawn.)

Nicky Johnson? Thirty years.

And that's just about it, save for one thing.

On our last night in the Bellagio, after I'd done my big closing scene, been shot again, and been given the clapperboard that they used on it . . . Hollywood tradition . . . Susie and I had dined with the team and were getting ready for bed, when she turned to me and gave me one of those looks that always fill me with anticipation.

'Hey, Oz,' she murmured, in the voice that goes with them, 'do you know where you can buy that GHB stuff?'

'Not a clue. Why do you ask?'

She winked at me. 'You don't really think I wiped those pictures, do you?'